NEBULA AWARDS 30

NEBULA AWARDS

SFWA's Choices

for the Best

Science Fiction

and Fantasy

of the Year

EDITED BY

WITHDRAWN

PAMELA SARGENT

A HARVEST ORIGINAL

Harcourt Brace & Company

San Diego   New York   London

The Library of Congress has cataloged this serial as follows:
The Nebula awards.—No. 18—New York [N.Y.]: Arbor House, c1983–
v.; 22cm.
Annual.
Published: San Diego, Calif.: Harcourt Brace & Company, 1984–
Published for: Science-fiction and Fantasy Writers of America, 1983–
Continues: Nebula award stories (New York, N.Y.: 1982)
ISSN 0741-5567 = The Nebula awards
1. Science fiction, American—Periodicals.
1. Science-fiction and Fantasy Writers of America.
PS648.S3N38   83-647399
813'.0876'08—dc19
AACR 2 MARC-S
Library of Congress [8709r84]rev

ISBN 0-15-100113-8
ISBN 0-15-600097-0 (pbk.)

Designed by G. B. D. Smith
Printed in the United States of America
First edition
A B C D E

Permissions acknowledgments appear on pages 349–50, which constitute a continuation
of the copyright page.

In memory of:
Robert Bloch
Raymond Z. Gallun
Karl Edward Wagner

Contents

In Memoriam: Robert Bloch
FRANK M. ROBINSON

The Martian Child
DAVID GERROLD

Rhysling Award Winners
W. GREGORY STEWART and ROBERT FRAZIER
JEFF VANDERMEER
BRUCE BOSTON

Understanding Entropy
BARRY N. MALZBERG

I Know What You're Thinking
KATE WILHELM

A Defense of the Social Contracts
MARTHA SOUKUP

From a Park Bench to the Great Beyond: The Science Fiction and Fantasy Films of 1994
KATHI MAIO

The Matter of Seggri
URSULA K. LE GUIN

An excerpt from
Moving Mars
GREG BEAR

Appendixes

Introduction

PAMELA SARGENT

T he Science-fiction and Fantasy Writers of America, formerly
the Science Fiction Writers of America, has been in existence for thirty years. Damon Knight, the founder of SFWA (and
this year's recipient of the Grand Master Nebula Award), remembers
the organization's beginnings this way:

> One day in 1964 I opened the mail and found a request to reprint
> a short story in exchange for a flat fee; it was the third one that week,
> and that did it. I sent out one-page flyers denouncing flat-fee anthologists, and ended, "If you would like to receive more information like
> this, send your $3."
>
> Next week the responses began rolling in. When I had seventy-
> eight writers, I declared them the charter members of SFWA, wrote a
> set of by-laws, and announced elections.

Knight was duly elected SFWA's first president, Harlan Ellison
was pressed into service as vice president, and Lloyd Biggle Jr. volunteered to be secretary-treasurer. Biggle's idea of raising money for
the fledgling guild by publishing an annual anthology of works by
members soon grew into the Nebula Awards.

The first Nebulas were given for works published in 1965, and
the winners were Best Novel: *Dune* by Frank Herbert; Best Novella:
"The Saliva Tree" by Brian W. Aldiss and "He Who Shapes" by
Roger Zelazny (tie); Best Novelette: "The Doors of His Face, the
Lamps of His Mouth" by Roger Zelazny; Best Short Story: " 'Repent,
Harlequin!' Said the Ticktockman" by Harlan Ellison.

Dune, widely acknowledged now as a classic, took time to find
its audience but became one of the first science fiction best-sellers
during the 1970s. Brian W. Aldiss is now the dean of British science
fiction, a brilliant and literate writer who is also one of the genre's
most interesting critics. Roger Zelazny was a pioneer among the
young "New Wave" writers of the 1960s and became one of science

fiction's most popular authors. (As I was writing this introduction, word came of Zelazny's death at the much too early age of fifty-eight. He will be remembered in next year's Nebula Awards anthology.) Harlan Ellison has become a master of science fiction and fantasy in the shorter lengths, and his prose remains as vigorous as it was thirty years ago. Both Roger Zelazny and Harlan Ellison appeared as finalists on this year's Nebula ballot, Zelazny with his delightful novel *A Night in the Lonesome October* and Ellison with his stunning and compelling novella "Mefisto in Onyx."

The runners-up for the first Nebula Awards included stories by J. G. Ballard, Gordon R. Dickson, Larry Niven, and James H. Schmitz, all writers who have enriched the field. The first Nebula Awards set a very high standard for all the Nebula Award winners and nominees who were to follow; to measure up to that standard remains a great challenge.

The 1994 Nebula Awards Final Ballot

For Novel

*mark *Moving Mars* by Greg Bear (Tor)
Parable of the Sower by Octavia E. Butler
    (Four Walls Eight Windows)
Gun, With Occasional Music by Jonathan Lethem
    (Harcourt Brace & Company)
Towing Jehovah by James Morrow
    (Harcourt Brace & Company)
Temporary Agency by Rachel Pollack
    (St. Martin's Press)
Green Mars by Kim Stanley Robinson
    (Bantam Spectra)
A Night in the Lonesome October by Roger Zelazny
    (William Morrow/AvoNova)

For Novella

"Mefisto in Onyx" by Harlan Ellison
    (Mark V. Ziesing; *Omni,* October 1993)

*Indicates winner

"Haunted Humans" by Nina Kiriki Hoffman
    (*The Magazine of Fantasy & Science Fiction*, July 1994)
"Forgiveness Day" by Ursula K. Le Guin
    (*Asimov's Science Fiction*, November 1994)
°"Seven Views of Olduvai Gorge" by Mike Resnick
    (*The Magazine of Fantasy & Science Fiction*,
    October/November 1994)
"Fan" by Geoff Ryman
    (*Unconquered Countries*, St. Martin's Press;
    Interzone, March 1994)
"Cold Iron" by Michael Swanwick
    (*Asimov's Science Fiction*, November 1993)

For Novelette

"Necronauts" by Terry Bisson (*Playboy*, July 1993)
°"The Martian Child" by David Gerrold
    (*The Magazine of Fantasy & Science Fiction*, September 1994)
"The Skeleton Key" by Nina Kiriki Hoffman
    (*The Magazine of Fantasy & Science Fiction*, August 1993)
"The Singular Habits of Wasps" by Geoffrey A. Landis
    (*Analog*, April 1994)
"The Matter of Seggri" by Ursula K. Le Guin
    (*Crank!* #3, spring 1994)
"Nekropolis" by Maureen F. McHugh
    (*Asimov's Science Fiction*, April 1994)

For Short Story

"Inspiration" by Ben Bova
    (*The Magazine of Fantasy & Science Fiction*, April 1994)
"None So Blind" by Joe Haldeman
    (*Asimov's Science Fiction*, November 1994)
"Understanding Entropy" by Barry N. Malzberg
    (*Science Fiction Age*, July 1994)
"Virtual Love" by Maureen F. McHugh
    (*The Magazine of Fantasy & Science Fiction*, January 1994)
°"A Defense of the Social Contracts" by Martha Soukup
    (*Science Fiction Age*, September 1993)

"I Know What You're Thinking" by Kate Wilhelm
    (*Asimov's Science Fiction*, November 1994)

Grand Master Nebula Award

Damon Knight

The list of novels on this year's final ballot seemed especially fine to me. Kim Stanley Robinson's *Green Mars* and Greg Bear's *Moving Mars* are both, in their different ways, fascinating and realistically detailed depictions of the future colonization of Mars. Octavia E. Butler, recently awarded a MacArthur Fellowship, is gaining recognition as an important American writer; her *Parable of the Sower* is an apocalypse seen through the eyes of a young African-American woman. Jonathan Lethem does a skillful and entertaining riff on old genre themes in *Gun, With Occasional Music,* while Rachel Pollack's *Temporary Agency* is a genuinely original and quirky vision. James Morrow, in his theological tour de force *Towing Jehovah,* again proves that he is becoming one of our most important fantasists.

Writers excelled in the short fiction categories as well, and I urge readers to seek out all of the finalists on this year's ballot. Among stories I would have liked to include in this volume, Michael Swanwick's "Cold Iron" combines hard science fiction and fantasy in its own rigorous and original way, while Geoff Ryman's "Fan" is a compulsively readable study of obsession. Ursula K. Le Guin's "Forgiveness Day" is a love story set on a world eerily similar and yet quite different from our own, while Geoffrey A. Landis offers a science-fictional Sherlock Holmes pastiche in "The Singular Habits of Wasps." Maureen F. McHugh's "Nekropolis" combines an exotic setting with a carefully extrapolated future, and Terry Bisson, in "Necronauts," offers a technologically based view of the afterlife. Nina Kiriki Hoffman presents two tales of modern horror in her stories "The Skeleton Key" and "Haunted Humans."

I also wish to direct the attention of readers to works on this year's preliminary Nebula ballot, listed in an appendix in the back. Among the works on that list that measure up to or even exceed the standards set by the first Nebula Awards are novels by Peter S. Beagle, Michael Bishop, Lisa Goldstein, Nicola Griffith, Gwyneth

Jones, James Patrick Kelly, Robert J. Sawyer, Delia Sherman, and Gene Wolfe. In the list of short fiction, I particularly recommend the works by A. A. Attanasio, Neal Barrett Jr., Michael Bishop, Kathleen Ann Goonan, Kij Johnson, James Patrick Kelly, Brian Stableford, and George Zebrowski.

There is a wealth of good reading on these lists, as well as in this volume. With such a variety of gifted voices, one can hope that the next thirty years of Nebula Award winners and nominees will be even more rewarding than the first three decades have been.

NEBULA AWARDS 30

The Year in Science Fiction and Fantasy: A Symposium

JOHN KESSEL

NICOLA GRIFFITH

PAUL DI FILIPPO

JACK DANN

SHEILA FINCH

PAT MURPHY

JAMES GUNN

So much science fiction and fantasy is published each year, by such a varied and diverse number of writers, that it is nearly impossible for one person to have a coherent view of the field or to assess the relative importance of various works and trends. Therefore, I have asked several eloquent and knowledgeable writers to discuss the state of the genre.

John Kessel is a past Nebula Award winner who has also won the Theodore Sturgeon Memorial Award and the Locus Award. His novels include *Freedom Beach* (written with James Patrick Kelly) and *Good News from Outer Space*. He is also the author of a short story collection, *Meeting in Infinity*. He teaches American literature and fiction writing at North Carolina State University.

Nicola Griffith's first novel, *Ammonite*, won the James Tiptree Jr. Memorial Award for gender-bending science fiction and the Lambda Literary Award, which is given to outstanding science fiction on gay and lesbian themes. Her short fiction has appeared in *Asimov's Science Fiction* and other publications, and her second novel, *Slow River*, was recently published. A native of England, she now lives in Seattle, Washington.

Paul Di Filippo is the author of *The Steampunk Trilogy*, a collection of three novellas of alternative history; his short stories have appeared in *Amazing Stories, The Magazine of Fantasy & Science Fiction*, and several past Nebula Awards anthologies. He writes reviews and essays for *Asimov's Science Fiction, Science Fiction Age,* and *F&SF,* and lives in Providence, Rhode Island.

Jack Dann is a writer and anthologist with many Nebula Award finalists among his works. He is the author of a short story collection, *Timetipping,* and the novels *Starhiker, Junction,* and *The Man Who Melted.* He has edited over twenty anthologies and is also a consulting editor for Tor Books. His most recent book is *The Memory Cathedral,* a novel about Leonardo da Vinci. He divides his time between upstate New York and Melbourne, Australia.

Sheila Finch was born in England but has lived in the United States since the 1960s; she now lives in Long Beach, California. Her novels include *Infinity's Web, Triad, The Garden of the Shaped, Shaper's Legacy,* and *Shaping the Dawn;* her short fiction has appeared in *The Magazine of Fantasy & Science Fiction, Amazing Stories,* and other magazines and anthologies.

Pat Murphy won Nebula Awards for her novel *The Falling Woman* and her novelette "Rachel in Love." Her other honors include a Locus Award, a Theodore Sturgeon Memorial Award, a World Fantasy Award, and a Philip K. Dick Award. Among her books are *The Shadow Hunter, Points of Departure,* and *The City, Not Long After.* She lives in San Francisco, where she works as an editor at the Exploratorium, a museum of science.

James Gunn, Director of the Center for the Study of Science Fiction at the University of Kansas, began publishing science fiction in 1949. He has contributed to the genre both as writer and critic; he is the editor of *The Road to Science Fiction* anthologies and the author of *Station in Space, The Joy Makers, The Listeners, Some Dreams Are Nightmares, The Magicians, Kampus, The Dreamers,* and *The Immortals,* on which the television series *The Immortal* was based. He has been honored with a Hugo Award and a Pilgrim Award and is a past president of the SFWA.

Genre Collapses! Thousands Crushed!
JOHN KESSEL

The strictures of a genre like science fiction can be a black hole sucking in any work that falls within its influence, through its history, its publishing practices, its audience expectations, its habitual plot devices and language and characters. When Jane Techno sits down before her word processor to write a story about a generation starship, over her shoulder loom the shadows of van Vogt, Heinlein, and Aldiss; when Joe Frodo writes his fantasy novel, his conception of his hero must contend with J. R. R. Tolkien, *The Sword of Shannara,* the marketing departments of a dozen publishers, and a hundred covers on the books in the fantasy section of his local bookstore. A paranoid critic could convince himself that not a single aspect of an SF or fantasy story today is free of the distorting effects of genre.

The nonparanoid critic might reply that genre also supplies a story with a structure against which the writer can play his individual variations, the way a jazz musician uses the chord progression of "The Sunny Side of the Street" to ground his improvisational flights. In some way every SF work we read fights a battle between form and formula, between the artistic structure a genre gives and the deadening effect of genre expectation.

But SF writers like to imagine alternatives, so let's do it. Suppose the infrastructure of SF collapses tomorrow (an earthquake, a tsunami, a tornado, a plague). The SF section of your bookstore disappears. The publishers turn to romances and books about UFO abductions. The TV shows are zapped. No movies are made. *Locus, SF Chronicle, SF Eye, The New York Review of SF, Foundation,* and *SF Studies* cease publication. *Asimov's, Analog, F&SF,* and *Omni* die. Conventions are not held. Fans switch from SF to baseball, or quilting, or wine tasting. Would SF no longer exist?

Certainly a lot of what we see now on the bookstore racks would disappear without a trace, and that which persisted would have more trouble reaching print. But something like SF would arise to satisfy the needs SF satisfies. Imagine this new fiction. In some ways it is less sophisticated, more clumsy than what we have today. In others it is freed up. How might the books of 1994 look in this alternate universe?

Some books would remain fundamentally the same. *Brittle Innings,* by Michael Bishop, for instance. In it, Bishop tells the tale of Frankenstein's monster as minor league first baseman Jumbo Clerval during World War II. But this is really a novel about the coming of age of Danny Boles, a young man in the South in a lost time. Bishop uses the science fiction conceit—more a literary borrowing than an

SF speculation—to show how hard it is to be a (good) man. Both Danny and Jumbo—one a teenaged shortstop with a speech impediment, the other an immortal creature sewn together from parts of corpses—are outsiders looking to become men.

Within this conceit, Bishop develops some real moral complexity. His characters are fully human, capable of evil and good acts, done for all sorts of reasons. Both Jumbo and Danny discover that to fall into humanity is to fall into the world of mixed motives. *Brittle Innings* may seem like a literary game, but it's not just baseball we're playing here. Because it is not close to SF at all, this novel might not be a word different if SF as we know it had never existed.

Parable of the Sower, by Octavia E. Butler, is a heartfelt and harrowing description of the breakdown of American society in the twenty-first century. Lauren Olamina leads a band of refugees across the California countryside in an attempt to found a new society based on her religion of "Earthseed," whose two founding propositions are that God is change and humans are earthseed, destined to colonize space. The part of this novel detailing the social ills that eventually destroy Lauren's home feels authentic, almost too contemporary. It arises from and speaks to the real world and would do so without genre moves. It's Earthseed's "seed the stars" preachments that feel like the tug of the genre. Given the predicaments of these characters, unless you are familiar with SF's tradition of space travel as human destiny, outer space is not the first solution that comes to mind.

Much of *Wildlife*, by James Patrick Kelly, seems to arise directly from the main currents of the genre: its techniques of exposition, plotting, and description have long traditions, and its specific futuristic developments in genetic manipulation, computer technology, and space exploration owe much to cyberpunk. Without the cover of genre Kelly would have had to set forth his future quite differently, or risk losing his audience. Yet he uses techniques from outside the genre, notably a mosaic narrative structure, to give a Citizen Kane view of his protagonist, Wynne Cage. Beneath its trappings this is a novel of identity, parenting, self-discovery, growing up. It does about as much as can be done to become a novel of character while staying within the orbit of SF.

On the evidence of *Gun, With Occasional Music*, Jonathan Lethem has carefully studied the black hole of genre SF (as well as the neighboring gravity well of the hard-boiled detective novel). But for the work of Philip K. Dick and Raymond Chandler, this book would not exist. For the novel's first third, Lethem seems merely to be playing with these genres, mixing and matching game pieces, pushing them into different configurations to see what effects he can generate: film noir lowlifes who are animals, hard-boiled private eye in a future where asking questions is illegal. Then at some point in the middle it finally catches fire, and one starts to care about his characters. Only in the dark world limned in its background, getting darker, does *Gun* pull away from genre, but the novel reminds us how an intelligent writer can use the conventions as a backbone and not a straitjacket.

Maureen F. McHugh's second novel, *Half the Day Is Night,* is really her first, and shows some of the problems of a writer not wedded to SF trying to find a story to tell within the genre. On the plus side are vivid characters and setting. But I had the feeling in reading this that McHugh was coming to science fiction from some other place, trying to force herself closer to the black hole; the novel doesn't want to stay there and at every opportunity slips away from its genre plot and futuristic setting into characterization or examination of the politics of the Third World. In *China Mountain Zhang* she avoided the traps of genre by refusing to provide a genre plot or characters.

Slow Funeral by Rebecca Ore tries to imagine a sort of fantasy independent of thirty years of increasingly rigid genre tropes. Instead of Middle-earth, we are in backwoods Virginia; instead of a barbarian princess or apprentice sorcerer, our heroine is a Berkeley dropout called back home by a family struggle that turns out to be as much about class as wizardry. Ore shows us the real rural Virginia culture and uses magic as a kind of metaphor for social structures that control people. But gravity is strong, and the novel still ends up with a battle of witches—albeit an unconventional one.

On the face of it, one cannot imagine Kim Stanley Robinson's *Green Mars* without the dozens of books about the colonization of Mars that the genre has produced over the decades. But though Robinson will acknowledge SF's past by naming a Martian town "Bradbury" and describing it like a place from *The Martian Chronicles,* it is possible to imagine *Green Mars* as existing independent of

SF's history. Robinson's attention to political process, to the Martian landscape, and to the development of character are all so overwhelmingly detailed that it's as if nobody had ever written this story before. His Dorsa Brevia manifesto (really about Earth's political problems today as much as about Mars in the twenty-second century), the world as seen through the eyes of the unworldly scientist Sax Russell, and Maya Toitovna's manic-depressive assaults on her own history and that of her two dead lovers carry *Green Mars* past the black hole by driving right through it.

Strangely, like Robinson, with whom he has in the past expressed little in common, Bruce Sterling in *Heavy Weather* also seems to be trying to imagine an SF without SF. Not as intense as earlier Sterling, not as jam-packed with nifty ideas, this novel gives perhaps his best-developed characters. From contemporary technology, from his sympathy with the slacker/counterculture/bohemian worldview, Sterling tells of a tribe of Storm Troupers who pursue the apocalyptic F-6, a hurricane-size tornado predicted by their atmospheric modeling to result from global warming. Sterling lovingly shows us the culture of this nomadic techy-bohemia, feels confident enough about his characters' essential likability to criticize them, even to bring most of them in the end into the mainstream of society. The climactic scenes of the novel are perhaps not as impressive as the advance billing has led us to believe, but in moments like his description of Alex Unger flying an ultralight over the midnight Texas plains, Sterling comes closer to a human poetry than he has ever done.

Each of these novels, in the degree to which it advertises or evades its connection to the genre, points forward to a new fiction as well as back to the old. Would a new SF-without-SF be better than what we have now? Would it gain more than it lost by the collapse of seventy years of development as a distinct genre?

It's an academic question. Back in the real world, the publishers aren't out of business. In fact, more money than ever is being made—with a little anxiety about the whole enterprise visible around the edges. As the Dow Jones average creeps over 4000, the fundamentals look a little shaky, the speculators cast nervous glances at the exits and try not to contemplate the prospect of the bubble bursting. But that's another essay.

The New Aliens of Science Fiction

NICOLA GRIFFITH

Science fiction is largely concerned with an exploration of the Other, the Not-Self, the Alien. Nothing new about that. What is new is the *kind* of alien science fiction concerns itself with today. Let me take you on a quick tour.

The first aliens of pulp SF were green slimy bug-eyed monsters from the nether regions of the solar system. Nothing like us, except they were recognizably (and rather adolescently) male: they were war leaders, they had no kids hanging around to spoil the fun, and they often abducted good-looking and scantily clad human women for nefarious purposes.

In the thirties and forties, the green slime monsters turned into androids and robots: metal men. (Some of these robots had female names, but we weren't fooled . . .) Then came the McCarthy era. In keeping with the paranoia of the time, the aliens became those who *pretended* to be us: vegetable beings grown in pods in the back garden who took the place of Mom and Dad; amoeboid extraterrestrials who rode invisibly on the backs of their unsuspecting hosts—Roy Rogers with a two-legged Trigger.

And then came the sixties. This era of pot and peace left us feeling more kindly disposed toward the alien. In John Wyndham's *The Chrysalids,* postholocaust radiation led to minor mutations such as six toes, or telepathy. Those who deviated from the norm, even those who looked normal (perhaps especially those who looked normal), were hunted down and killed. A sort of deadly "Don't ask, don't tell" policy. For the first time, the story was told from the viewpoint of a mutant. Suddenly—as far as the reader's sympathies were concerned—there was no longer that clear dividing line between *Us*—humanity—and *Them*—the monstrous enemy.

And then, of course, there were the aliens who were human, biologically speaking, but who were raised by aliens and therefore suspect. A prime example comes from Heinlein: Valentine Smith, the *Stranger in a Strange Land.* (In Hollywood, a similar process was occurring. Example: films about pregnant white woman abducted by Apache. Mother dies in childbirth. White boy-child grows up behaving as and believing himself to be Apache. Until the cavalry come along and tell him, hell no, he's a *real* man, not a savage.)

So, by the sixties we had progressed from green slimy *Non-Mankind*, to robotic *Fake* Mankind, to the muties and pod people of *Twisted* Mankind.

Where were the women?

In early SF, female characters served as the scientist's ignorant girlfriend or the hero's reward for a job well done. By the fifties and sixties, women were allowed to be heroic as long as they did it in their own sphere—courageous mothers defending their children, or human housewives who set up coffee klatches with alien housewives and thereby achieved world peace. Shining fictional examples of socialization. But in the 1960s, in the real world, women began to protest this socialization. We stood up and said: "That's not who we are!" And so male SF writers turned to an examination of who women might be.

This examination manifested itself largely through writings about women-only societies: the so-called sex-battle texts. The women in these books were not fully human. We were portrayed as being bereft of sexual feeling; or we had plenty of sexual feeling but were frustrated and embittered by having no men to express those feelings with; we did not understand Art; we did not understand science and were technologically backward. We were often portrayed as insectlike (for example the hive mentality displayed in Wyndham's *Consider Her Ways*). This type of work operated very much out of traditional cultural assumptions—often nothing more than a reversal of male/female roles. The female characters were alien because they weren't "proper" women.

In the late sixties, women writers took over the job of talking about the alien. Writers like James Tiptree Jr., Joanna Russ, Vonda N. McIntyre, and Suzy McKee Charnas examined not the "woman as alien" but the alienation of being a woman in Western society. And throughout the seventies and early eighties, a few writers turned away from the sex-battle text, the idea of "men" versus "women," and more toward the entire concept of gender. The best of these include the work of Russ, Tiptree, Theodore Sturgeon, Octavia E. Butler, and—perhaps the most well known—Ursula K. Le Guin's *Left Hand of Darkness*. But even the Le Guin book posits a "genderless" society in which all characters are referred to as "he" unless they become specifically female for the purposes of sex with another character, who has become specifically male. It could be argued that *The Left Hand of Darkness* is really about men and gender, and that the potential (and willingness) to assume "nonmale" gender is what makes the characters so alien.

At this point, the early seventies, a lot of male writers began pumping out dreadful, reactionary stuff: Edmund Cooper was guilty of this, as was Heinlein. (There are always exceptions to any rule, and in this case they were John Varley and Samuel R. Delany.)

Then, it seems to me, SF writers looked up, saw the next inevitable step in the examination of the alien—*sexuality* and gender—and panicked. All of a sudden there was a renewed interest in high-concept SF: hard science, action-adventure, the reemergence of famous Golden Age work (and the attendant phenomenon of "sharecropping"). There was also, of course, cyberpunk: a revisiting of film noir ideas and, at its worst, a regression to the Nerd Triumphant school of literature. Cyberpunk does discuss ideas of alienation, particularly in the relationship between people and machines, but generally this occurs within the context of those same old traditional cultural tropes about men and women. (Some of the worst cyberpunk is nothing but a hybrid of nihilism—all those gray, raining mean streets where no one cares and nothing makes a difference—and the shop-and-fuck novel—brand names, the lust for consumer durables, descriptions of women's clothes . . . usually tight, black, spike-heeled, and shiny.)

As this backlash eased off, sex, sexuality, and gender again became hot topics. Many women writers—mainstream as well as SF—emerged for the first time, or reemerged. Writers like Margaret Atwood and Marge Piercy, Gwyneth Jones and Joan Slonczewski were all writing novels looking at how women have become or remain Other. Many of their fictional characters were lesbians. Men were reading these books, too, and then—rather startlingly—began to write them. Geoff Ryman's *The Child Garden* has a lesbian protagonist. And twenty- and thirty-something straight white boys—particularly in England, I'm not sure why—started writing novels and short stories with lesbian or bisexual women protagonists: Simon Ings, Colin Greenland, and Eric Brown come to mind. And now American men seem to be doing the same thing: Allen Steele's latest novel has a dyke protagonist; one of Mark Tiedemann's short stories, "Rust Castles," mentions two lesbians. In fantasy, too, men are happily writing about women who love women: Charles de Lint's *Memory and Dream* is one example, Cole and Bunch's *The Warrior's Tale* is another. There are many more, in both genres. So why are straight men writing about dykes? Some are exploring the alien, trying to understand. Some are simply exploiting what they perceive of as being the political climate: macho heroes who pilot anything that flies, drink anything that pours, and fuck anything that moves are politically incorrect, so—lacking the imagination to reenvision what a non-macho man would do, but still seeking approval—these writers turn John into Joan and zoom off into the ether, guilt-free. (This may well be happening the other way around, too. Straight women writing about gay men—though more in fantasy than SF.)

But as well as the enlightened humanists, there are the fundamentalists of the radical Christian Right. The year 1994 marked the publication of a nasty little book called *Colorado 1998*. Written by Mark Olsen, the communications director for Colorado for Family Values—the nice people who tried to enshrine in law discrimination against lesbians and gay men—this book purports to describe how America would really look if queers ruled the world. It's a classic role-reversal tale where the writer gives away his prejudices: in attempting to show how awful lesbians are, Olsen simply holds up a mirror to the kind of persecution and hatred happening today *against* queers. Like most tourists, Olsen is about thirty years behind the rest of the genre. This book is not essentially different from the sex-battle texts of the fifties, sixties, and seventies.

Nineteen ninety-four has seen a resurgence of women writing about women. Melissa Scott in *Trouble and Her Friends* is explicit about the alienness of being queer, and female, in the future. Carrie Richerson's short fiction is chilling and exciting and different: not only are her women dykes, but they're dead, too. A double whammy. Suzy McKee Charnas's *The Furies* takes a brave and unflinching look at how women and men can be utterly alien to each other, the difference in their violence, and the ways in which they might try (or not, as the case may be) to find common ground.

In an indication that these issues—sex, sexuality, gender—are here to stay in SF, there is now even a prize, the James Tiptree Jr. Memorial Award, handed out every year to the novel or short story that best examines and expands gender roles. The award has sparked some controversy mainly—in my opinion—due to a misreading of the jury's brief: to look for the fiction that examines *and expands* gender roles. Any number of writers, from old SF hands like David Brin to those such as P. D. James who dabble in the slums, have postulated futures in which women are the dominant sex. While such fiction may be role reversing, it is not necessarily role expanding.

In the midnineties, writers of SF and fantasy have this vast history of the examination of the alien on which to draw: slimy bug-eyed monsters, robots, muties and pod people, women, lesbians, and gays. It's interesting that we seem to be playing more with the *Us* end of the Us-Them spectrum. The alien is getting closer every day.

Embers

PAUL DI FILIPPO

What keeps a writer writing?

In the first few years of a career, common motives might span a wide gamut. Perhaps a high-minded desire to improve the world or to stamp one's personal vision and imprint on a certain branch of literature. Maybe a burning need for sheer Whitmanesque self-expression. Fame and money are always potent attractors. The Gassian notion of liberated words frolicking on the page rules some, as does the Tolkien-Joyce-Cabell aesthetic of writer as subcreator. A sense of love or playfulness is valuable. The lure of pure Story is a siren call. Enlisting with peers in a doctrinal jihad where the weapons are manifestos and books offers a lot of kicks. To be sure, there are probably as many goads and pulls to produce a first book as there are individual writers.

But whatever motivates the composition of a first novel (or even a second, or a fourth, or a tenth) has got to be a hell of a lot different from the mysterious and as yet barely charted feelings that drive a writer once more to pick up the frayed thread of narrative after a career of fifty, sixty, or even *seventy* years, setting out to trace his or her way one more weary time through the labyrinth of Story.

Seasoned and stripped down by struggle, bent like a seaside tree from enduring decades of the gales blowing between literature and commerce, possibly gravely ill, certainly feebler in body, if not in mind, approaching the statistically determinate end of all ambition, emptied already of hundreds of thousands, if not millions, of previous words, these rare survivors continue to write.

But why? Probably enjoying at least a modest fiscal stability (if only a monthly government check), sated with honors and awards, their place in the history books assured, enemies and friends and original sponsors all fallen away along the long road, the charms of simple invention paling—what can move these elders to the production of yet another book?

It is my contention that at the end of a long and illustrious career, two factors compel an artist to continue.

The first, and more superficial one, is sheer habit.

Years and years of self-discipline, of ritual and routine, Skinner-esque conditioning, have turned writing into something akin to a reflexive pleasure like smoking; or, to put a nobler cast on it, a sought-after meditative state of mind. The writer is literally hooked—self-induced motor patterns and neural states conspiring to produce a high as necessary and addictive as drugs.

Sometimes, for one-dimensional writers, this is a necessary and sufficient impulse. Writers like this could yet kick their addiction, and retirement would become an option.

But for more complex individuals who keep at the craft, there is another force at work, not felt by all. And as best as I can name it, it is the gnawing, growing stimulus produced by the accumulated weight of a simple, yet irritatingly unsolvable mystery, a quarry chased through countless pages, yet still elusive: The whys and wherefores of our shared state of being (as opposed to nonbeing), and the organic accretion of each unique self, of arrival on this earth, growth and dissolution. An eternal question or set of linked enigmas whose signifiers in fiction are birth, death, transfiguration, struggle, defeat, and transcendence.

No longer greatly or primarily concerned with making him- or herself completely understood by readers, the writer at this stage is to a lesser or greater extent elaborating Jungian psychodramas that revolve around deep-seated, long-felt riddles, dramas that seek to explicate and palliate his core unease and deliver whatever distillate of bittersweet wisdom he has found.

Though a relatively thick or thin patina of craftsmanly narration might remain, the subtext is very often a personal quest on the part of the author for elusive truths relating to his whole being.

The most obvious example of this in the SF field is, of course, Robert Heinlein, whose solipsistic concerns at the tail end of his career fully emerged and diverged sharply from what his audience demanded, causing widespread dissatisfaction among readers and critics alike.

The year 1994 brought at least four new examples of this affecting and intriguing phenomenon: Jack Williamson (born 1908, first publication 1928) released *Demon Moon* (Tor Books); Andre Norton (born 1912, first publication 1934) released *The Hands of Lyr* (AvoNova); Frederik Pohl (born 1919, first publication circa 1939) released *The Voices of Heaven* (Tor); and Poul Anderson, the youngster among this crew (born 1926, first publication 1947) released *The Stars Are Also Fire* (Tor).

It is no coincidence that the jacket of Williamson's book bears endorsements from all these other three. Like calls to like, and the comradeship of other seekers on the path is some small comfort.

Williamson began his career as an emulator of the exotic and preposterously captivating fantasies of A. Merritt. This book is a return to those roots. Its voice contains echoes of Leigh Brackett and Edmond Hamilton, of Fritz Leiber and *Planet Stories,* a whole era of writers shaped by a simpler world, albeit a time whose harshness included a worldwide Depression bookended by cataclysmic global wars.

On an unnamed planet, on a small island whose limited borders afford the classic bounded venue of fantasy, humans transplanted long ago from Earth struggle to survive—with the help of friendly, intelligent flying unicorns—amid "dragons," wyverns, banshees, and the "demons" who return with the millennial approach of a sister planet. That the "dragons" turn out to be cybernetic mining devices and the "demons" plasma life-forms is testament to Williamson's eclectic palette. Magic vies with computers, and intriguing clear-eyed speculations abound. For instance, Williamson's unicorns have only two limbs (their forehooves are on the "elbows" of their wings) and they need long "flight decks" for takeoffs.

But beneath all this bejeweled scenery lies Williamson's real meat. Our protagonist is Zorn, heir to an exiled nobleman. His childhood on a "prison farm" (meant to evoke Williamson's own childhood, as he admits up front in a note) is lovingly detailed. Zorn grows up unsure of his identity. Then, amidst crisis, one is thrust on him: he is to play Nuradoon, mythic hero who rescued the world during the last demon attack. In passages that are positively Ballardian in their perverse insistence that "saying the absurd will make it so," the other characters thrust this role on Zorn.

Mixed in with this is the patented Williamson contest between Good Girl Kye and Bad Girl Lyrane for Zorn's body and soul. Lyrane "wins" and Kye "loses." But since neither is wholly good or bad, the result is ambiguous.

The climax of the book is Zorn's attainment of self-knowledge, at which point the dangers evaporate and heretofore implacable foes are integrated into a new society.

The large-scale adventures and trials of *Demon Moon* are plainly a recapitulation of the arc of individual human maturation: innocence and bewilderment transformed to inner peace, thanks to insight into the self. No surprise from a writer who was undergoing professional psychoanalysis before most of his readers were born. . . .

It is a common cliché that writers who evolved in the pulps learned to be loquacious, thanks to the penny-per-word constraints on their income. Yet Williamson's prose is compact and spare, showing a kind of Clint Eastwood terseness that bespeaks America's West. As can be seen in the work of many elderly visual artists, his lines have lost their clutter, only essentials remaining.

Andre Norton's prose in her *Hands of Lyr,* however, evinces no such economy of verbiage. Beneath a somewhat prolix undergrowth is a simple narrative that conceals an even simpler archetype. In another nameless land where an old evil, the vampiric immortal, Razkan, is stirring, two lowly teenagers, a girl named Alnosha and a boy named Kryn, must recover fragments of the goddess Lyr's power, reuniting the scattered Fingers of her statue to defeat Razkan and his human minions.

The world Norton portrays, rife with torture and blasted landscapes, is only a remnant of a shattered golden age, positively Gnostic in its sense of laboring under a malevolent demiurge. The only pure ones in it—and the ones most susceptible to persecution—are its children. Only they can speak with animals and reliably feel goddess magic. Although nubile, Alnosha rouses no sexual feelings in Kryn when they are forced to bundle together for warmth, and she sees him as trapped prematurely in a "man-shell."

How strange that a woman in her eighties continues to choose such viewpoint characters. But perhaps it isn't so strange, when we recall a poet such as Wordsworth and his *Prelude* (1850), with its glorification of childhood as the mortal state closest to those lost heavenly clouds of glory.

This is the heart matter of the book: the struggle to retain and reconcile the soul of childhood with the passage into the inexplicable and dark world of adulthood.

Further proof of Norton's core concern is how abruptly the book trails off once the pair of questers attain their goal, plot threads snipped left and right. The *uber* adult and authority figure Razkan disintegrates into a pile of bones—Death simultaneously triumphant and put in its proper place. Alnosha and Kryn kiss for the first time, embarking on their own inevitable maturity, which draws a curtain between them and their supernal memories, also foreclosing the author's own interest in the story.

Pohl's *The Voices of Heaven* conceals its ontological burden beneath a more deftly controlled story surface. The clues to its unraveling lie in three areas: its mode of narration, its setting, and its threatened catastrophe.

Ostensibly, *Voices* is the simple story of one man's misadventures on the colony planet of Pava. Barry di Hoa, one of Pohl's patented psychologically flawed Everymen, is shanghaied from his comfortable job and life on a settled Luna and shipped as a corpsicle to one of humanity's four faltering star colonies. There he learns to adjust to his new fate, becomes friends with the resident aliens, and incidentally rescues faraway Earth from a long-range threat by a faction of religious extremists among the colonists.

So far so simple. Yet consider.

The novel is cast in the form of a flashback inspired by the interrogation of di Hoa by one or more initially unrevealed Others, much like John Crowley's *Engine Summer* (1979). And just as in Crowley's book, these Others are revealed to be "angels." In Pohl's case, the interrogators are the alien race, known as "leps." They are explicitly cast as angelic beings living on a world that has never known original sin (shades of James Blish and C. S. Lewis). Grilling di Hoa, the leps demand an explanation and justification for his life and the actions of his fellows, chief among which is the attempted destruction of Earth by the aborted launch of a ship filled with antimatter pods.

Curiously and revealingly, this is the almost exactly the same threat to the planet Pohl posed in his earlier *Mining the Oort* (1992). Obviously, it has great psychological resonance for him, a talisman for the maximum personal guilt one being can assume. The fact that in *Voices* a single man standing for all humanity must craft an apologia to the angels for both his good and bad deeds—culminating in the possible life or death of an entire planet—is testament to Pohl's vision of individual existence as an example of the Butterfly Effect: small efforts wreaking big results. (That the leps end their metamorphic lives as literal butterflies is perhaps no mere coincidence.)

As di Hoa says of a boring meeting, "Everything ends, if you just wait long enough." And in Pohl's version, the end of any individual life demands examination, justification, expiation.

Fully a generation younger than Jack Williamson, Poul Anderson at first glance seems too young to be included here. It's hard for me personally not to think of him as the bright newish voice he seemed when encountered even a mere thirty years ago. Yet his latest work, *The Stars Are Also Fire*, shares the end-of-the-road ambience of the work of his older peers.

The Stars Are Also Fire cannot be considered alone, but must be yoked with its immediate predecessor, *Harvest of Stars* (1993), to which it is a strange and lesser prequel/sequel/codicil.

The initial two-thirds of the first book, *Harvest*, was basically an elaborate chase and showdown between two warring forces in an Earth-Luna setting some dozen or so decades hence. Anson Guthrie, ex-mortal, now downloaded cyberintelligence and head of the libertarian Fireball corporation, played cat-and-mouse with various authoritarian types over the course of a few days, eventually winning a partial victory that allowed him and his followers to emigrate to another star system. The final third of the book outlined their subsequent nine hundred years of development there, culminating in the evolution of a planetwide Gaia figure.

The lopsided proportions here testify to a struggle with hard questions embodied in recalcitrant material. Plainly Anderson was reluctant to leave his beloved familiar playground of bold human sagas. The bravura joy evident when his feylike, elven Lunarians and the knightlike, robot-bodied Guthrie are on stage hark back to his *Broken Sword* (1971) and *Midsummer Tempest* (1974). Yet Anderson simultaneously wants to move beyond the sphere of hearth and castle, to confront titanic issues of human evolution, immortality, and the responsibility of godhood. His prose is consistently elevated, wringing poesy from sociotechnics. That he achieves by book's end any partial depiction of the human consequences of transfiguration is testament to his skills.

Yet despite an ostensible offstage continuation of the human adventure at the end of *Harvest,* the overall tone is autumnal and brooding, a Viking pyre. Consider just the note sounded by the decision to launch the novel with the drear "Epilogue."

The newer book fills in both the back story as to how the Lunarian race was born (picking up an attractive, yet already discarded toy) and follows the human action on an Earth ruled by omnipotent artificial intelligences known as sophotects, some three hundred years after Guthrie's departure. Backing down from any real investigation of superhuman intelligence, Anderson keeps the sophotects behind a curtain for almost the entire book. Only their wired human agent, Venator, gets to experience their reality, in an unsatisfyingly numinous way.

Too many powerful events from the first book are mere echoes here. As a single example, the climactic cat-and-mouse space chase run by protagonists Kenmuir and Aleka parallels that of Guthrie and Kyra Davis in *Harvest.* The jumpy narrative is a distraction too. The reader must deal with both "realtime" and this realtime's flashbacks. Yet the whole novel is an immense flashback from the perspective of its predecessor.

The language in the sequel is nothing like that of *Harvest,* less florid and mystical; and its quest and action not half so bold—yet both are too similar to their sire. Important retrofitted characters never mentioned in *Harvest* disturb a sense of continuity. That the solution to the book's MacGuffin comes from a half-insane ghost intelligence is symbolic of a sense of desolation that comes when the best answer has been tried and found wanting. And looming over the text is another potent symbol: abortion, both literal and metaphorical. Yet bundled together, these two books stand as an assault on the highest pinnacle, with a brave, if dispirited, retreat.

What makes SF amenable to such long careers, so productive of these philosophical twilight musings masquerading as straight entertainments? Mainstream careers do indeed seem to be plays without any second acts, as Fitzgerald characterized them. One is hard-pressed to find in the larger ocean writers similar to these four, capable of such extensive and relentless labors. Perhaps it is the luxury of loyal audiences, or a little less flavor-of-the-month mentality among editors. But almost certainly a field that encourages flinty-eyed speculation in all matters will tend to produce more work that does not shy away from the hard, ultimate realities of life and death.

After a lot of froth has bubbled away, the year 1994 may very well be recalled as the year these four books that glow with varying shades of the four authors' original fires were published.

And even embers can flare and hurl back the darkness for a time.

Double Vision

JACK DANN

Living on the other side of the world, in a culture that's analogous to the U.S. but not coextensive with it, I sometimes feel that I'm suffering from double vision. I've been "commuting" between Melbourne, Australia, and upstate New York, where I keep an office; but I'm really based here in Australia. Thanks to fax machines, phone, and E-mail, I can do business from here almost as easily as from New York. I don't feel left out of the publishing loop, yet I find that many Australian writers have a sense of isolation and frustration. They feel that although they can break into the short-fiction magazine and anthology markets, the book-publishing market is "riddled with unwritten rules that seem designed to exclude people who do not have prior inside knowledge and friends." Australian writers can tell you publishing horror stories, which are, in fact, not unlike what most American authors usually experience early in their careers. The problems of dealing with agents and editors and publishers are certainly exacerbated by distance and cultural differences. There just isn't a sense here of how American publishers work. (Admittedly, this is also true for many American writers, but it usually applies to novices, not veterans.)

It's also difficult to support oneself as a writer here, for although Australia is a reading culture with the highest per capita consumption of books in the world, there simply isn't the population to support a vigorous science fiction publishing industry on the scale of the U.S. or England. Unless Australian SF writers are selling regularly to British or American publishers (or writing in the very successful young adult category), most have to supplement their incomes; a few can hope for government writing fellowships. (Damien Broderick received a $30,000 fellowship this year from the Literature Board of the Australian Council.) Granted, most writers can't live on their income from writing alone, no matter where they live; but American and British SF writers with reputations can expect to sell their books for advances larger than $5,000.

Nevertheless, about thirty-five genre titles were published in Australia in 1994, which include adult novels, young adult novels, anthologies, and single-author collections. Notable books published by Australian writers in 1994 were *Permutation City* by Greg Egan (published by the British publisher Millennium), *Genetic Soldier* by George Turner (published in the U.S. by William Morrow), and *Voices in the Light* by Sean McMullen (Aphelion). Young adult novels included *Foxspell* by Gillian Rubenstein (Hyland), *Turn Right for Zyrgon* by Robin Klein, and *Deersnake* by Lucy Sussex (Hodder). There were several anthologies: *Metaworlds,* edited by Paul Collins (Penguin); *The Oxford Book of Australian Ghost Stories,* edited by Dr. Ken Gelder (Oxford University Press); *Alien Shores,* edited by Peter McNamara and Margaret Winch (Aphelion), which published original work by Frank Bryning, Stephen Dedman, Shane Dix, Amos Fairchild, Leanne Frahm, Ian McAuley Halls, Sue Isle, Jeff Harris, Sean McMullen, Carole Nomarhas, Yvonne Rousseau, Edith Speers, E. W. Story, Dirk Strasser, Lucy Sussex, Kurt von Trojan, George Turner, and Sean Williams; and the horror anthology *Deeds of Doom,* edited by A. Markidis (Galley Press), which published original work by Marilyn Arnold, Marja Baume, Don Boyd, Tony Van Dyke, Ann Steward Galwey, Dianne Gardner, Laurie James, Ned Mccann, Tosh Mackay, Paul Merrick, Felicity Pulman, Pauline Scarf, Paul Statham, Tom Stewart, and Stephen Wescombe. Lucy Sussex also edited two young adult SF anthologies, *The Lottery* and *The Patternmaker*, which published original work by Isolbelle Carmody, Brian Caswell, Gary Crew, Leanne Frahm, Alison M. Goodman, Dave Luckett, Sean McMullen, Sophie Massen, Michael Pryor, Gillian Rubenstein, Sam Sejavka, Dirk Strasser, Lucy Sussex, Paul Voermans, and Mustafa Zahirovic. Three short story collections were published by small presses: *Radical Takeoffs* by Glyn Parry (Little Ark), *The Prisoner Gains a Blurred Skin* by Nicholas Playford (Black Pepper), and *Doorway to Eternity* by Sean Williams (MirrorDanse).

Although genre young adult books do very well in Australia and are a staple of commercial publishing, commercial publishers are showing signs of becoming more involved in genre publishing. Pan Macmillan began a very successful series of fantasy novels in 1990 that launched the careers of Martin Middleton, Tony Shillitoe, Shannah Jay, and others. Pan published six fantasy titles in 1994 by David Sale, John Marsden, Beverly MacDonald, Shanna Jay, and G. M. Hague. Tor Books is interested in the Australian market and is actively looking to publish Australian authors in Australia and the U.S. But the heroes of SF publishing are small presses such as Aphelion Publications of Adelaide and MirrorDanse Press of Sydney. They are at the center of the science fiction publishing scene. Although they can't pay a lot of money, they have maintained personal, supportive relationships with their authors and continue to publish them, thus giving them a presence among the overwhelming amount of science fiction for sale on the stands here from the U.S. and Great Britain. Because of various Commonwealth agreements, it's actually cheaper to buy books from Great Britain and the U.S. And books are expensive here: a hardcover costs about $40.00A, a trade paperback about $20.00A, and a mass market paperback about $15.00A.

Australian, American, or British science fiction magazines can really only be found in specialty SF stores such as the Galaxy Bookshop in Sydney, Ellison Hawker in Hobart, and Slow Glass Books and Minotaur in Melbourne, but not on newsstands. The major Australian science fiction magazines are *Eidolon*, run by an editorial committee, and *Aurealis,* edited by Dirk Strasser and Stephen Higgens. *Eidolon* published short fiction by Simon Brown, Terry Dowling, Duncan Evans, Robert Hood, Trent Jamieson, Rick Kennett, Margaret Laurence, and Sean Williams. *Aurealis* published short fiction by Bill Congreve, Hoa Pham, Helen Sargeant, Jain Scott, and Paul Voermans. The major horror magazine is *Bloodsongs,* edited by Melbourne writers Chris Masters and Steve Proposch. *Bloodsongs* published short fiction by Bill Congreve, Richard Harland, Robert Hood, Kate Humphrey, Rick Kennett, Misha Kumashov, Christopher Sequeira, B. J. Stevens, Barbara Welton, Sean Williams, and Maurice Xanthos.

Damien Broderick's critical work *The Architecture of Babel: Discourses of Literature and Science* was published by Melbourne University Press in 1994. Broderick is the science reviewer for *The Australian,* Australia's national newspaper. Although he is an award-winning fiction writer, he has lately been concentrating on nonfiction. His latest book is *Reading by Starlight: Postmodern Science Fiction,* published by Routledge in London and New York in 1995; it is a rigorous, semiotic analysis of science fiction that concentrates on cyberpunk and postmodern SF.

Although Rosaleen Love did not publish any fiction (that I could find) in 1994, she deserves mention here. She is perhaps Australia's premier short story writer. Her short stories remind me of the best work of Elizabeth Bowen and Carol Emshwiller. Her short story collections include *The Total Devotion Machine and Other Stories* (1989) and *Evolution Annie and Other Stories* (1993). Both collections were published by The Women's Press in Great Britain.

It should also be noted that Greg Egan won the 1995 Ditmar Award in the novel and short fiction category for *Permutation City* and "Cocoon," which was published by *Asimov's Science Fiction.* (Greg Egan and George Turner are probably the best-known Australian science fiction writers and are widely published internationally. Turner, who is seventy-nine and still writing after suffering a stroke in 1993, has a critical reputation that ranks with Stanislaw Lem's.) Peter Nicholls was given a special William Atheling Jr. Award for his contribution to science fiction scholarship. Nicholls coedited *The Encyclopedia of Science Fiction* with John Clute in 1993; it is perhaps the single most important reference work in the field. *Thyme* won in the Best Fan Magazine category.

One writer put it very well, I think, when he compared Australian science fiction with a corner store selling good quality merchandise.

> Down the road, however, is the U.S. science fiction market in the form of a supermarket that is immensely visible and convenient. It has nothing against the corner store, it merely swamps it by being so big. Australian authors walk into their own bookshops to see the shelves groaning with books by U.S. and British authors. They know that the best Australian SF is often as good as (and sometimes better than) the books that come flooding in from overseas, and they know that the problem is mostly marketing and visibility. They go home and think dark thoughts about marketing, visibility, and the peculiarities of the U.S. market . . . and some of them even manage to snap out of it, turn on the PC, and keep on writing.

(The author acknowledges his debt to Sean McMullen, Peter Nicholls, Janeen Webb, Alan Stewart's Thyme, *and the staff of Slow Glass Books for information and insight. Any mistakes, omissions, and misinterpretations are, of course, the author's own.)*

Doctor, Will the Patient Survive?

SHEILA FINCH

How healthy is science fiction? As a longtime reader of the genre, I seem increasingly to have the experience of finishing a story in an SF magazine and wondering what on Earth it was doing there. The fantasy stories seem to thrive (although a lot of them begin to sound alike, a side effect of the genre's popularity, I suppose), but I think something more disturbing has been occurring in science fiction.

Gary Wolfe once referred to this trend as "creeping mainstreamism": a trend that produces stories that embrace all the aspects of literary fiction, style, character development, and so on, but lose the element of speculativeness that marks science fiction. What we're all too likely to find in the magazines these days (with *Analog* a notable exception) is the story that might just as well have appeared in *The New Yorker* or any of the literary journals. What's happened here?

If we imagine genre fiction—westerns, romance, SF, and so on—as an archipelago in the literary sea, then on our island of science fiction we find the mountains are healthy but the coastline is eroding rapidly. Traditional hard-core, high-tech science fiction is alive and well at the novel length: witness the recent Mars novels by Greg Bear, Kim Stanley Robinson, and Kevin J. Anderson, the grand-scale meteorology disasters of John Barnes. No problems here. And there seem to be endless new entries in the *Star Trek* and *Star Wars* universes and their like, which are genuinely SF even if many of them tend toward the space opera end of the spectrum.

What worries me is that especially in short fiction it's getting harder and harder to find the middle-ground story of the kind James Blish and Clifford D. Simak used to write, or A. E. van Vogt and James Tiptree Jr., and Judith Merril, the story that doesn't require the reader's familiarity with advanced scientific concepts or terminology, but which turns on a genuine scientific point. Such stories satisfy the reader's hunger for experience of a life and times different from her own, events that compel page turning, and ideas that linger in the mind long after the story is done. "Ask the next question," Theodore Sturgeon advised. Unfortunately, I think too many stories today don't begin to answer the first.

The rule I learned said, "If you can take the scientific gadgetry out and still have a story, then take it out and write mainstream." But the stories I'm concerned about don't even pay that much lip service to science or technology; they simply have no speculative core. (I'm not talking about alternate history stories here, an interesting use of the traditional SF story-generating question, *what if. . . .*) Often, the only element of the tale that makes a nod toward a territory not mapped out by the mainstream is a vague reference to something along the lines of the telepathic abilities of a character—they hear voices or are given sudden flashes of insight into people or events. Yet it often seems the mere introduction of such ideas has satisfied the author's sense of obligation to the readers; the implications and consequences of these abilities mostly go unexplored, and I'm left daydreaming about what Alfred Bester or Sturgeon would have done with such stories. What we have instead, to change our metaphors, is prose by authors who've lost their nerve for the high-wire act of science fiction. I suspect there are several reasons for the rise of this type of story.

The first cause is rather obviously the rising number of nonscientist writers. We're witnessing the growing community of writers who are humanities and liberal arts majors, bringing with them a greater familiarity with the classics of the literary canon and the pronouncements of literary critics rather than the papers in *Science*. This is a trend that began decades ago with the New Wave. I'm not denying the good things such writers have done for the field: deeper attention to characterization, a finer sensitivity to language and style, an opening up of the traditional SF plot and theme to ambiguity and complexity. When such refinements are brought to bear on an extrapolation of scientific ideas, the result is the best kind of literature in or out of the genre.

But literary stories often promote these stylistic values over the exploration of idea or concept, with the result that too often the stories read as if the author were writing with her graduate thesis professor frowning over her shoulder (a rather grim individual for whom scientific advance began and ended with Newton). The science in these stories is either unexceptional, unimaginative, or nonexistent.

A related cause of the problem is that in a fair world many of these writers would find their true homes in mainstream magazines, which would pay them in something other than copies and distribute their work to the appropriate audience. Alas, such paying markets for short story writers have shrunk disastrously in the last few years, leaving the genre magazines as the only real alternative for writers who also like to eat once in a while. Since, as we've noted, the quality of the writing in these stories tends to be high, I'm not surprised editors are attracted to them. But they leave many SF readers feeling hungry.

I believe another culprit is the current admiration for South American magic realism. Fiction from south of the border has become fashionable, and as a result we're seeing too much emulation of Gabriel García Márquez and too much adulation of Isabel Allende. In magic realism, we're drawn into settings (the Revolution, colonial days) where complex characters with believable goals and problems are explored realistically, and whimsical or supernatural events (floating above the ground, green hair) are described casually. Yet the fantastic elements aren't the whole cloth of these stories; they're an enrichment of the plot, a subtle embroidery of theme.

But a lot of short science fiction these days is built around a thin thread of a fantastic detail that *is* the whole story. Nothing other than this slender magical or genteelly bizarre element is offered to the reader. When George Scithers was editor of *Amazing*, he cautioned would-be authors against committing the "tomato surprise" story that revolved around one vital point, usually withheld until the end. I'm seeing a lot of surprising tomatoes these days, stories where once such a fantastic or magical point is removed, the story not only isn't science fiction, it isn't even much of a story.

Luckily for us, there are still short story writers in the genre like Jack McDevitt, Martha Soukup, Maureen F. McHugh, Mike Resnick, Joe Haldeman, Bradley Denton, Ray Aldridge, and many others, who can tell a gripping SF tale, peopled with complex, well-drawn characters, and pull it all off with elegance and subtlety. Their stories are the ones we stay up late to finish reading, then wake in the night to think about again. They are the vitamin pills worth looking for in a gaudy jar full of word candy.

If the genre is going to survive and attract new readers, these are the writers who'll make it happen. Some of them, I'm happy to say, are represented in this volume.

Biker Nuns and Social Revolution:
An Optimistic Assessment of 1994
PAT MURPHY

As a judge for the 1994 James Tiptree Jr. Memorial Award, my reading focused on a particular subcategory of science fiction and fantasy. The James Tiptree Jr. Memorial Award is presented annually to the short story or novel that best explores and expands gender roles in science fiction and fantasy. The award's aim is not to look for work that falls into some narrow definition of political correctness, but rather to seek out work that is thought provoking, imaginative, and perhaps even infuriating. I agreed to be one of the 1994 judges as an excuse to read a type of science fiction that I love—works that explore different models for society and human relationships, works that challenge our cultural assumptions about the way the world and human societies function.

All in all, I thought 1994 was an exceptional year for science fiction and fantasy that pushes the envelope of gender roles. This year's two Tiptree Award winners are indicative of the wide range of approaches and attitudes taken in the works considered for the award, and they reflect the variety of subgenres included in the broader category of science fiction and fantasy.

Nancy Springer's novel *Larque on the Wing,* one of the two winners, considers the startling adventures of Larque, a middle-aged woman whose midlife crisis takes on concrete form. A ten-year-old version of Larque (blinked into existence by Larque's own uncanny abilities) leads Larque into an exploration of her life and the compromises that she made while growing up. While searching for the part of herself that she has lost, Larque finds the other side of things—the magical other side of a street on the wrong side of town, the other side of her family, and the many other sides of herself. In the course of her unlikely adventures, she is transformed into a handsome young man and deals with the unpleasant truth—she doesn't want to return to her original form. Though the novel touches on serious concerns, it remains light and playful, belching and farting as it strives to tell the truth. This is a rollicking, offbeat, thoughtful fantasy for our time.

The other 1994 Tiptree winner was "The Matter of Seggri," by Ursula K. Le Guin, a novelette published in *Crank!* magazine. "The Matter of Seggri" deals with gender issues in a way that only science fiction can—by creating a society that differs from our own in certain significant ways, thus forcing us to examine our own cultural assumptions. Fascinating for its anthropological detail, "The Matter of Seggri" makes stunning use of different viewpoints to give us an understanding of the society that we couldn't obtain any other way, demonstrating the emotional and societal consequences of a different social organization, and the consequences of changing or disrupting that organization.

To anyone who has interest in exploring cultural assumptions, there are a number of other 1994 publications that I'd recommend very highly. *The Furies,* the third volume in the epic work that Suzy McKee Charnas began with *Motherlines* and *Walk to the End of the World,* challenges the assumption that all women are warm and nurturing. This is a relentlessly fierce book that tells a powerful tale of revenge. The Free Fems who fled the Holdfast in the earlier books return to tear it down. It's a dark and violent story, but one that's extremely compelling.

And 1994 also included works that challenge some basic assumptions about sexuality and how it's portrayed in science fiction. In past years, most lesbian relationships that appeared in science fiction were either on the fringes of the main story or occurred in works that were set in all-women societies. In 1994, two notable novels presented lesbian relationships as a natural part of a society of men and women. In both *Temporary Agency* by Rachel Pollack and *Trouble and Her Friends* by Melissa Scott, the sexual orientation of the protagonist is simply part of the fabric of the novel—and part of the fabric of the society in which the novel is set. In *Temporary Agency*, a novel that is delightful for its matter-of-fact use of demons and magic in an otherwise contemporary world, Ellen Pierson and her lover—using limited resources and their wits—save the world. In *Trouble and her Friends*, Melissa Scott makes a place for lesbians among the cyberpunks and the high-tech outlaws.

Reading short fiction for the Tiptree Award made me aware once again of the continuing strength of the science fiction and fantasy short story market. From *Xanadu 2*, an original fantasy anthology edited by Jane Yolen, I'd particularly recommend Delia Sherman's haunting "Young Woman in a Garden," which delicately exposes underlying assumptions about gender and art. In *Asimov's Science Fiction* Eleanor Arnason continues her exploration of an alien society with "The Lovers," a story about heterosexual love in a society in which such a thing is unthinkable. Two collections—Ursula K. Le Guin's *Fisherman of the Inland Sea* and Geoff Ryman's *Unconquered Countries*—offer both originals and great stories from earlier years that are otherwise unavailable.

The last book I'll mention here, *Little Sisters of the Apocalypse* by Kit Reed, has a premise that I couldn't resist. The "Little Sisters" of the title are sixteen biker nuns. They are, Reed writes, "brilliant hackers, who market technology to support their mission to the homeless." These futuristic nuns "pray for the dead and, when they have to, ride out on their bikes to defend the living."

Reed's tale takes place on Schell Isle, a protected enclave inhabited by a community of women. Five years before, all the men went off to war, leaving the women to "keep the homefires burning" and wait for the men to return. In spare and evocative language, Reed describes how the women live in fear and anticipation of the return of their men and tells of other forces that are converging on the isle. The Outlaw family, led by Queenie, a ferocious woman described as "huge, hairy, and malodorous," are returning to reclaim the land. Sister Trinitas, responding to a call she does not fully understand, is leading the motorcycle-riding Little Sisters to the isle. And of course, there are the men—out of the picture, but always in the characters' minds—coming home and expecting to be welcomed. Taken as a whole, *Little Sisters of the Apocalypse* is a strange—and strangely successful—mixture of disparate elements.

All in all, reading for the Tiptree Award in 1994 made me extremely optimistic about science fiction and fantasy writers' continued efforts to consider social revolution and its consequences. It's wonderful to be working in a genre that has room for biker nuns and transgender hackers, stories of haunting delicacy, and novels of rage and revenge.

The Year in Science Fiction

JAMES GUNN

At one time, science fiction was a reader-driven category; so little money was to be made from it that editors often chose the books to publish that they themselves liked or respected. And the audience for science fiction was such that almost every worthwhile novel sold two thousand to five thousand copies in hardcover and fifty thousand to one hundred thousand copies in paperback. Of course, the top of the SF range became a ceiling; SF publishers printed no more copies than they anticipated would sell, and Doubleday would rather publish a new novel than reprint one, since they had an arrangement with libraries that meant an automatic sale for new titles. Only when books such as *A Canticle for Leibowitz, The Martian Chronicles,* and particularly *Dune* and *Stranger in a Strange Land* began to sell hundreds of thousands of copies in paperback did it become apparent to publishers that SF had the capacity to produce best-sellers and to make money. That, and the film and television audience for SF, has resulted in a boom even bigger than the one that was anticipated after

World War II, which happened only in the imagination of publishers.

Today science fiction is a market-driven category, in which the expectations of retailers anticipate, and in some measure control, the responses of book buyers and shape the expectations of publishers. The sky is the ceiling for those books that can capture the fancy of an inexperienced public, and so many books are published that the field no longer has a floor. Readers can't buy all SF books anymore; they must be guided by name recognition, special-interest appeals, or the same kinds of nonspecific audience stimuli that move books in other categories.

A recognition of this fact of life has led over the past couple of decades to the dependence of the editorial process on the reports and then on the projections of the sales division. The sales personnel, who are in close contact with the book buyers for chains and sometimes with individual book dealers, estimate the sales of any title even though they have not read the book and wouldn't have the time to do so even if they had the desire. Of course, sales projections are a self-fulfilling prophecy; the books in which the sales force has no confidence often do not get published, and those that are published may not be pushed with enthusiasm, tend not to be ordered by the local buyer, and are not available or are not displayed in a way that will encourage widespread purchasing. As a consequence, even those editors who still make publishing decisions independent of input by sales personnel must spend considerable amounts of time preparing to promote their titles with the sales force at special meetings, often held in expensive resort areas. So deeply ingrained is the mythology of the sales-oriented system that no amount of evidence to the contrary is going to shake it, and critics of the process who want to improve it must learn to work within the system.

In the annual *Locus* "The Year in Science Fiction" issue, evidence continues of SF's slow contraction from its peak of nearly two thousand books in 1991, but the field is still too large for anyone to comprehend it all: 1,736 books were published in 1994, 1,109 of them new titles.

The contraction comes about in spite of Tor's expansion of the past few years (although it has not yet climbed back to its 1988 peak) and the creation of the new line called HarperPrism at HarperCollins. The decline in the number of titles at Bantam/

Doubleday/Dell has been halted, but Putnam/Berkley/Ace continues to shrink, as well as Morrow/Avon, while Baen and DAW remain about the same. In early 1995, however, some comics-related and games-related publishers began to enter the field of general publishing, led by White Wolf.

Perhaps more significant than mere numbers is the growing preponderance of fantasy titles over SF. By 1991 the traditional advantage of SF had almost evened out: SF was still ahead by seven books. By 1994 fantasy led by thirty volumes, and horror novels were fewer than thirty titles behind SF. Media-related books were only seventy behind. What the market picture looks like—if, indeed, SF, fantasy, and horror are competing for the same readership—is not a two-category SF-dominant field but a four-category field in which SF occupies little more than a fourth.

The magazine field continued to expand in number of titles while contracting in total circulation. *Amazing* and *Aboriginal* were looking for buyers; *Amazing* dropped its monthly issues and started a quarterly digest-size publication, which may become only an anthology, and *Omni* recently announced that it would publish quarterly while putting most of its efforts into electronic publication. *Science Fiction Age* remained successful in terms of appearance and circulation, and was joined by *Realms of Fantasy* at nearly the same circulation, but *Analog, Asimov's Science Fiction,* and *Fantasy and Science Fiction* continued to decline, ranging in sales from seventy-five thousand down to about fifty thousand. *Tomorrow, Galaxy, Pulphouse, Offworld, Pirate Writings,* and a few other hopefuls illustrated the inexpensiveness of printing (in some cases desktop publishing) and the difficulties of distribution.

The proliferation of science fiction on television and in films may help explain the rise in media-related books and perhaps the continuing decline in book and magazine publishing. I am reminded of the situation in the mid-1950s when the SF boom collapsed during a period of growing interest in science and technology. John W. Campbell Jr. suggested that the desire for science and speculation was being satisfied by the daily newspaper, and Robert Bloch suggested that people were being turned off by the misrepresentation of SF in film in the same way that, in an earlier era, they were turned off by the covers on the cheaper SF pulps. Today when people are surrounded by more science news than ever before, scientific ignorance and retreats into mysticism seem to be more prevalent than ever, from UFOlogy to New Age to the rise of fantasy and horror. Now the SF urge may be satisfied by the half-dozen SF weekly TV series, and viewers who go looking for something like what they enjoy watching may settle for graphic novels and comic books or their memory books in media-related publications.

All of this, of course, has little to do with the quality of the writing within the field. With more authors having an opportunity to be published, more of them educated in literary craft as well as science, and more of them able to write full time, good fiction may be more prevalent in SF books and magazines than ever before in its history. The fact that the best writing is more difficult to find in the welter of publication is only the contemporary condition that authors, readers, publishers, and critics must take into account.

Science fiction may be in the same condition I ascribed last year to SF scholarship: it may be a mature art. That is, most of the important things may have been written, and now all that remains is to write them better or to fill in the gaps. Looking around at the state of science fiction, one sees occasional examples of excellent art surrounded by substantial clusters of good art and all that hidden, like buried treasure, in a vast area of what some publishers call "product." But what one does not see is innovation.

Although the lack of innovation would not be a matter of concern in many fields, SF is a genre of difference, and part of the general mood of melancholy that now seems prevalent may be due to the fact that nothing truly exciting or revolutionary is going on or can be seen approaching. Looking back at the history of the genre, one notes the towering figures of Jules Verne and H. G. Wells, who single-handedly changed the way their readers looked at the world. In the twentieth century, revolution became the task of publishers such as Hugo Gernsback and editors such as John W. Campbell Jr. What they did not only excited their readers but changed their worldviews through the stories of authors such as E. E. "Doc" Smith, Isaac Asimov, Robert Heinlein, and A. E. van Vogt, none of them, perhaps, altering their readers' perceptions as radically as Verne and Wells, but collectively providing insights that transformed individual readers in individual ways.

Other editors created revolutions: Horace Gold with *Galaxy* and its social revelations led by Frederik Pohl and C. M. Kornbluth and Alfred Bester; and Tony Boucher and J. Francis McComas with *Fantasy and Science Fiction* and their group of more literary writers. Gold's *Galaxy* was more transforming than *F&SF*, because the latter's goal was to demonstrate that SF had always been part of the literary spectrum. The last revolutionary editor of SF was Michael Moorcock, who harnessed the anti–science fiction of J. G. Ballard and the other entropists, as well as the less classifiable talents of Brian W. Aldiss, to the service of the New Wave.

Since then the revolutions have been smaller and more tied to such social developments as feminism, with authors such as Pamela Sargent and Sheri S. Tepper, and occasionally Ursula K. Le Guin, and gay and lesbian fiction; and to scientific breakthroughs: physics and cosmology beginning in the 1960s, with authors such as Larry Niven; biology in the 1970s, with authors such as John Varley; and computers in the 1980s, with authors such as William Gibson and Bruce Sterling. Although some, like feminism and cyberpunk, seemed briefly transforming, none of them, perhaps because of the breadth of the field, seemed to affect everybody and everything as had previous revolutions.

To sum up: the state of affairs in SF seems to have settled into the condition of literature in general—more and more about less and less. One might note a couple of straws in the wind: the interaction of SF and fantasy in works such as those by Michael Swanwick, Jack Williamson, and Robert Silverberg; and a greater realism, or skepticism, about such traditional SF goals as planetary colonization and alien contact, in such works as the Mars novels of Kim Stanley Robinson, Greg Bear, and many others, and the deadly aliens (revisiting Wells's envious Martians) of such novelists as Gregory Benford, Greg Bear, Vernor Vinge, and Charles Pellegrino and George Zebrowski. Both of these trends, though producing exciting individual works, seem a bit less than the revolutionary developments necessary for the continuing evolution of SF.

But I cannot conclude without a caveat or two. My perception may be conditioned by the Golden Age syndrome. That is, the golden age of science fiction is twelve. Readers who did not live through the transcendental experiences of the 1920s, the 1930s, the 1940s, the

1950s, or even the 1960s may find contemporary SF just as exciting, just as mind expanding, as the older generations found their SF. Certainly the appreciation of SF is much broader than it was in earlier decades, though it may not be as deep. That acceptance may be part of the problem, however—it isn't simply a matter of putting SF back in the gutter where it belongs so much as the fact that SF is a revolutionary literature. At its most commonplace it questions the status quo ("the way things are is not the way things will be"), and at its most extreme it raises alternatives to contemporary ways of organizing, behaving, or even thinking ("the way things are isn't the way things should be"), and sometimes it questions the nature of reality itself ("the way things are isn't even the way things are"). So, widespread acceptance of a revolutionary literature may mean that it is no longer revolutionary; the revolution is over—it has either succeeded or it has been infiltrated and defused.

The other caveat is that even now revolutionaries may be gathering in attics and cellars, organizing their takeovers and plotting their strategies. Someone, somewhere, may be carving into tablets new and mind-altering revelations. They will find me waiting at the foot of the mountain, ready to applaud.

Seven Views of Olduvai Gorge

MIKE RESNICK

Mike Resnick is a frequent traveler to Africa and has set some of his most memorable stories there, among them the Hugo Award–winners "Kirinyaga" and "The Manamouoki." His many novels include *Santiago, The Dark Lady, Stalking the Unicorn, Ivory, Paradise, Second Contact*, and two tetralogies, *Tales of the Galactic Midway* and *Tales of the Velvet Comet*. He is also the editor of several anthologies, among them *Alternate Presidents, Whatdunits*, and *Alternate Warriors*. Forthcoming novels are *A Hunger in the Soul* and the *Widowmaker Trilogy*.

"Seven Views of Olduvai Gorge" is another Resnick work inspired by Africa. This striking novella also won a Hugo Award and tied for first place for an award and cash prize given annually by the Polytechnic University of Catalunya in Barcelona for the best science fiction novella of the year. Mike Resnick has this to say about his Nebula Award–winning novella:

"The seed for 'Seven Views of Olduvai Gorge' was sown one hot September day in Botswana, when my wife Carol and I were on safari. She and our driver happened to see a spring hare—an African rabbit—and we pulled to a stop so the two of them could observe and discuss it. There were a hundred elephants just over the next hill; I could hear them, and even smell them—but I couldn't interest Carol or the driver in leaving the spring hare just yet. And I muttered something like, 'Who comes to Africa just to look at a goddamned rabbit?'—and it suddenly occurred to me that, between poaching and habitat destruction, the day was perhaps not long off when that was precisely what people came to Africa to see, and I decided to write the story when I got home.

"Well, it was a long safari and it took a long time to get home, and by the time we arrived I had another future safari story to tell. And Carol suggested a third riff on the theme, and we spent a few months discussing it while I wrote other things, and suddenly I had an eons-long Stapledonian story that could be set in one location in Africa."

T he creatures came again last night.

The moon had just slipped behind the clouds when we heard the first rustlings in the grass. Then there was a moment of utter silence, as if they knew we were listening for them, and finally there were the familiar hoots and shrieks as they raced to within fifty meters of us and, still screeching, struck postures of aggression.

They fascinate me, for they never show themselves in the daylight, and yet they manifest none of the features of the true nocturnal animal. Their eyes are not oversized, their ears cannot move independently, they tread very heavily on their feet. They frighten most of the other members of my party, and while I am curious about them, I have yet to absorb one of them and study it.

To tell the truth, I think my use of absorption terrifies my companions more than the creatures do, though there is no reason why it should. Although I am relatively young by my race's standards, I am nevertheless many millennia older than any other member of my party. You would think, given their backgrounds, that they would know that any trait someone of my age possesses must by definition be a survival trait.

Still, it bothers them. Indeed, it *mystifies* them, much as my memory does. Of course, theirs seem very inefficient to me. Imagine having to learn everything one knows in a single lifetime, to be totally ignorant at the moment of birth! Far better to split off from your parent with his knowledge intact in your brain, just as *my* parent's knowledge came to him, and ultimately to me.

But then, that is why we are here: not to compare similarities, but to study differences. And never was there a race so different from all his fellows as Man. He was extinct barely seventeen millennia after he strode boldly out into the galaxy from this, the planet of his birth—but during that brief interval he wrote a chapter in galactic history that will last forever. He claimed the stars for his own, colonized a million worlds, ruled his empire with an iron will. He gave no quarter during his primacy, and he asked for none during his decline and fall. Even now, some forty-eight centuries after his extinction, his accomplishments and his failures still excite the imagination.

Which is why we are on Earth, at the very spot that was said to be Man's true birthplace, the rocky gorge where he first crossed over the evolutionary barrier, saw the stars with fresh eyes, and vowed that they would someday be his.

Our leader is Bellidore, an Elder of the Kragan people, orange-skinned, golden fleeced, with wise, patient ways. Bellidore is well-versed in the behavior of sentient beings, and settles our disputes before we even know that we are engaged in them.

Then there are the Stardust Twins, glittering silver beings who answer to each other's names and finish each other's thoughts. They have worked on seventeen archaeological digs, but even *they* were surprised when Bellidore chose them for this most prestigious of all missions. They behave like life mates, though they display no sexual characteristics—but like all the others, they refuse to have physical contact with me, so I cannot assuage my curiosity.

Also in our party is the Moriteu, who eats the dirt as if it were a delicacy, speaks to no one, and sleeps upside down while hanging from a branch of a nearby tree. For some reason, the creatures always leave it alone. Perhaps they think it is dead, possibly they know it is asleep and that only the rays of the sun can awaken it. Whatever the reason, we would be lost without it, for only the delicate tendrils that extend from its mouth can excavate the ancient artifacts we have discovered with the proper care.

We have four other species with us: one is an Historian, one an Exobiologist, one an Appraiser of human artifacts, and one a Mystic. (At least, I *assume* she is a Mystic, for I can find no pattern to her approach, but this may be due to my own shortsightedness. After all, what I do seems like magic to my companions and yet it is a rigorously applied science.)

And, finally, there is me. I have no name, for my people do not use names, but for the convenience of the party I have taken the name of He Who Views for the duration of the expedition. This is a double misnomer: I am not a *he*, for my race is not divided by gender; and I am not a viewer, but a Fourth Level Feeler. Still, I could intuit very early in the voyage that "feel" means something very different to my companions than to myself, and out of respect for their sensitivities, I chose a less accurate name.

Every day finds us back at work, examining the various strata. There are many signs that the area once teemed with living things, that early on there was a veritable explosion of life forms in this place, but very little remains today. There are a few species of insects and birds, some small rodents, and of course the creatures who visit our camp nightly.

Our collection has been growing slowly. It is fascinating to watch my companions perform their tasks, for in many ways they are as much of a mystery to me as my methods are to them. For example, our Exobiologist needs only to glide her tentacle across an object to tell us whether it was once living matter; the Historian, surrounded by its complex equipment, can date any object, carbon-based or otherwise, to within a decade of its origin, regardless of its state of preservation; and even the Moriteu is a thing of beauty and fascination as it gently separates the artifacts from the strata where they have rested for so long.

I am very glad I was chosen to come on this mission.

We have been here for two lunar cycles now, and the work goes slowly. The lower strata were thoroughly excavated eons ago (I have such a personal interest in learning about Man that I almost used the word *plundered* rather than *excavated,* so resentful am I at not finding more artifacts), and for reasons as yet unknown there is almost nothing in the more recent strata.

Most of us are pleased with our results, and Bellidore is particularly elated. He says that finding five nearly intact artifacts makes the expedition an unqualified success.

All the others have worked tirelessly since our arrival. Now it is almost time for me to perform my special function, and I am very excited. I know that my findings will be no more important that the others', but perhaps, when we put them all together, we can finally begin to understand what it was that made Man what he was.

"Are you . . . ," asked the first Stardust Twin.

". . . ready?" said the second.

I answered that I was ready, that indeed I had been anxious for this moment.

"May we . . ."

". . . observe?" they asked.

"If you do not find it distasteful," I replied.

"We are . . ."

". . scientists," they said. "There is . . ."

" . . . very little . . ."

". . . that we cannot view . . ."

" . . . objectively."

I ambulated to the table upon which the artifact rested. It was a stone, or at least that is what it appeared to be to my exterior sensory organs. It was triangular, and the edges showed signs of work.

"How old is this?" I asked.

"Three million . . ."

". . . five hundred and sixty-one thousand . . ."

". . . eight hundred and twelve years," answered the Stardust Twins.

"I see," I said.

"It is much . . ."

". . . the oldest . . ."

". . . of our finds."

I stared at it for a long time, preparing myself. Then I slowly, carefully, altered my structure and allowed my body to flow over and around the stone, engulfing it, and assimilating its history. I began to feel a delicious warmth as it became one with me, and while all my exterior senses had shut down, I knew that I was undulating and glowing with the thrill of discovery. I became one with the stone, and in that corner of my mind that is set aside for Feeling, I seemed to sense the Earth's moon looming low and ominous just above the horizon . . .

Enkatai awoke with a start just after dawn and looked up at the moon, which was still high in the sky. After all these weeks it still seemed far too large to hang suspended in the sky, and must surely crash down onto the planet any moment. The nightmare was still strong in her mind, and she tried to imagine the comforting sight of five small, unthreatening moons leapfrogging across the silver sky of her own world. She was able to hold the vision in her mind's eye for only a moment, and then it was lost, replaced by the reality of the huge satellite above her.

Her companion approached her.

"Another dream?" he asked.

"Exactly like the last one," she said uncomfortably. "The moon is visible in the daylight, and then we begin walking down the path . . ."

He stared at her with sympathy and offered her nourishment. She accepted it gratefully, and looked off across the veldt.

"Just two more days," she sighed, "and then we can leave this awful place."

"It is not such a terrible world," replied Bokatu. "It has many good qualities."

"We have wasted our time here," she said. "It is not fit for colonization."

"No, it is not," he agreed. "Our crops cannot thrive in this soil, and we have problems with the water. But we have learned many things, things that will eventually help us choose the proper world."

"We learned most of them the first week we were here," said Enkatai. "The rest of the time was wasted."

"The ship had other worlds to explore. They could not know we would be able to eliminate this one in such a short time."

She shivered in the cool morning air. "I hate this place."

"It will someday be a fine world," said Bokatu. "It awaits only the evolution of the brown monkeys."

Even as he spoke, an enormous baboon, some 350 pounds in weight, heavily muscled, with a shaggy chest and bold, curious eyes, appeared in the distance. Even walking on all fours it was a formidable figure, fully twice as large as the great spotted cats.

"*We* cannot use this world," continued Bokatu, "but someday *his* descendants will spread across it."

"They seem so placid," commented Enkatai.

"They *are* placid," agreed Bokatu, hurling a piece of food at the baboon, which raced forward and picked it up off the ground. It sniffed at it, seemed to consider whether or not to taste it, and finally, after a moment of indecision, put it in its mouth. "But they will dominate this planet. The huge grass-eaters spend too much time feeding, and the predators sleep all the time. No, my choice is the brown monkey. They are fine, strong, intelligent animals. They have already developed thumbs, they possess a strong sense of community, and even the great cats think twice about attacking them. They are virtually without natural predators." He nodded his head, agreeing with himself. "Yes, it is they who will dominate this world in the eons to come."

"No predators?" said Enkatai.

"Oh, I suppose one falls prey to the great cats now and then, but even the cats do not attack when they are with their troop." He looked at the baboon. "That fellow has the strength to tear all but the biggest cat to pieces."

"Then how do you account for what we found at the bottom of the gorge?" she persisted.

"Their size has cost them some degree of agility. It is only natural that one occasionally falls down the slopes to its death."

"Occasionally?" she repeated. "I found seven skulls, each shattered as if from a blow."

"The force of the fall," said Bokatu with a shrug. "Surely you don't think the great cats brained them before killing them?"

"I wasn't thinking of the cats," she replied.

"What, then?"

"The small, tailless monkeys that live in the gorge."

Bokatu allowed himself the luxury of a superior smile. "Have you *looked* at them?" he said. "They are scarcely a quarter the size of the brown monkeys."

"I *have* looked at them," answered Enkatai. "And they, too, have thumbs."

"Thumbs alone are not enough," said Bokatu.

"They live in the shadow of the brown monkeys, and they are still here," she said. "*That* is enough."

"The brown monkeys are eaters of fruits and leaves. Why should they bother the tailless monkeys?"

"They do more than not bother them," said Enkatai. "They avoid them. That hardly seems like a species that will someday spread across the world."

Bokatu shook his head. "The tailless monkeys seem to be at an evolutionary dead end. Too small to hunt game, too large to feed themselves on what they can find in the gorge, too weak to compete with the brown monkeys for better territory. My guess is that they're an earlier, more primitive species, destined for extinction."

"Perhaps," said Enkatai.

"You disagree?"

"There is something about them . . ."

"What?"

Enkatai shrugged. "I do not know. They make me uneasy. It is something in their eyes, I think—a hint of malevolence."

"You are imagining things," said Bokatu.

"Perhaps," replied Enkatai again.

"I have reports to write today," said Bokatu. "But tomorrow I will prove it to you."

The next morning Bokatu was up with the sun. He prepared their first meal of the day while Enkatai completed her prayers, then performed his own while she ate.

"Now," he announced, "we will go down into the gorge and capture one of the tailless monkeys."

"Why?"

"To show you how easy it is. I may take it back with me as a pet. Or perhaps we shall sacrifice it in the lab and learn more about its life processes."

"I do not *want* a pet, and we are not authorized to kill any animals."

"As you wish," said Bokatu. "We will let it go."

"Then why capture one to begin with?"

"To show you that they are not intelligent, for if they are as bright as you think, I will not be able to capture one." He pulled her to an upright position. "Let us begin."

"This is foolish," she protested. "The ship arrives in midafternoon. Why don't we just wait for it?"

"We will be back in time," he replied confidently. "How long can it take?"

She looked at the clear blue sky, as if trying to urge the ship to appear. The moon was hanging, huge and white, just above the horizon. Finally she turned to him.

"All right, I will come with you—but only if you promise merely to observe them, and not to try to capture one."

"Then you admit I'm right?"

"Saying that you are right or wrong has nothing to do with the truth of the situation. I *hope* you are right, for the tailless monkeys frighten me. But I do not know you are right, and neither do you."

Bokatu stared at her for a long moment.

"I agree," he said at last.

"You agree that you cannot know?"

"I agree not to capture one," he said. "Let us proceed."

They walked to the edge of the gorge and then began climbing down the steep embankments, steadying themselves by wrapping their limbs around trees and other outgrowths. Suddenly they heard a loud screeching.

"What is that?" asked Bokatu.

"They have seen us," replied Enkatai.

"What makes you think so?"

"I have heard that scream in my dream—and always the moon was just as it appears now."

"Strange," mused Bokatu. "I have heard them many times before, but somehow they seem louder this time."

"Perhaps more of them are here."

"Or perhaps they are more frightened," he said. He glanced above him. "Here is the reason," he said, pointing. "We have company."

She looked up and saw a huge baboon, quite the largest she had yet seen, following them at a distance of perhaps fifty feet. When its eyes met hers it growled and looked away, but made no attempt to move any closer or farther away.

They kept climbing, and whenever they stopped to rest, there was the baboon, its accustomed fifty feet away from them.

"Does *he* look afraid to you?" asked Bokatu. "If these puny little creatures could harm him, would he be following us down into the gorge?"

"There is a thin line between courage and foolishness, and an even thinner line between confidence and overconfidence," replied Enkatai.

"If he is to die here, it will be like all the others," said Bokatu. "He will lose his footing and fall to his death."

"You do not find it unusual that every one of them fell on its head?" she asked mildly.

"They broke every bone in their bodies," he replied. "I don't know why you consider only the heads."

"Because you do not get identical head wounds from different incidents."

"You have an overactive imagination," said Bokatu. He pointed to a small hairy figure that was staring up at them. "Does *that* look like something that could kill our friend here?"

The baboon glared down into the gorge and snarled. The tailless monkey looked up with no show of fear or even interest. Finally it shuffled off into the thick bush.

"You see?" said Bokatu smugly. "One look at the brown monkey and it retreats out of sight."

"It didn't seem frightened to me," noted Enkatai.

"All the more reason to doubt its intelligence."

In another few minutes they reached the spot where the tailless monkey had been. They paused to regain their strength, and then continued to the floor of the gorge.

"Nothing," announced Bokatu, looking around. "My guess is that the one we saw was a sentry, and by now the whole tribe is miles away."

"Observe our companion."

The baboon had reached the floor of the gorge and was tensely testing the wind.

"He hasn't crossed over the evolutionary barrier yet," said Bokatu, amused. "Do you expect him to search for predators with a sensor?"

"No," said Enkatai, watching the baboon. "But if there is no danger, I expect him to relax, and he hasn't done that yet."

"That's probably how he lived long enough to grow this large," said Bokatu, dismissing her remarks. He looked around. "What could they possibly find to eat here?"

"I don't know."

"Perhaps we should capture one and dissect it. The contents of its stomach might tell us a lot about it."

"You promised."

"It would be so simple, though," he persisted. "All we'd have to do would be bait a trap with fruits or nuts."

Suddenly the baboon snarled, and Bokatu and Enkatai turned to locate the source of his anger. There was nothing there, but the baboon became more and more frenzied. Finally it raced back up the gorge.

"What was that all about, I wonder?" mused Bokatu.

"I think we should leave."

"We have half a day before the ship returns."

"I am uneasy here. I walked down a path exactly like this in my dream."

"You are not used to the sunlight," he said. "We will rest inside a cave."

She reluctantly allowed him to lead her to a small cave in the wall of the gorge. Suddenly she stopped and would go no further.

"What is the matter?"

"This cave was in my dream," she said. "Do not go into it."

"You must learn not to let dreams rule your life," said Bokatu. He sniffed the air. "Something smells strange."

"Let us go back. We want nothing to do with this place."

He stuck his head into the cave. "New world, new odors."

"Please, Bokatu!"

"Let me just see what causes that odor," he said, shining his light into the cave. It illuminated a huge pile of bodies, many of them half-eaten, most in various states of decomposition.

"What are they?" he asked, stepping closer.

"Brown monkeys," she replied without looking. "Each with its head staved in."

"This was part of your dream, too?" he asked, suddenly nervous.

She nodded her head. "We must leave this place *now!*"

He walked to the mouth of the cave.

"It seems safe," he announced.

"It is never safe in my dream," she said uneasily. They left the cave and walked about fifty yards when they came to a bend in the floor of the gorge. As they followed it, they found themselves facing a tailless monkey.

"One of them seems to have stayed behind," said Bokatu. "I'll frighten him away." He picked up a rock and threw it at the monkey, which ducked but held its ground.

Enkatai touched him urgently on the shoulder. "More than one," she said.

He looked up. Two more tailless monkeys were in a tree almost directly overhead. As he stepped aside, he saw four more lumbering toward them out of the bush. Another emerged from a cave, and three more dropped out of nearby trees.

"What have they got in their hands?" he asked nervously.

"You would call them the femur bones of grass-eaters," said Enkatai, with a sick feeling in her thorax. "*They* would call them weapons."

The hairless monkeys spread out in a semicircle, then began approaching them slowly.

"But they're so *puny!*" said Bokatu, backing up until he came to a wall of rock and could go no farther.

"You are a fool," said Enkatai, helplessly trapped in the reality of her dream. "*This* is the race that will dominate this planet. Look into their eyes!"

Bokatu looked, and he saw things, terrifying things, that he had never seen in any being or any animal before. He barely had time to offer a brief prayer for some disaster to befall this race before it could reach the stars, and then a tailless monkey hurled a smooth, polished, triangular stone at his head. It dazed him, and as he fell to the ground the clubs began pounding down rhythmically on him and Enkatai.

At the top of the gorge, the baboon watched the carnage until it was over, and then raced off toward the vast savannah, where he would be safe, at least temporarily, from the tailless monkeys.

"A weapon," I mused. "It was a *weapon!*"

I was all alone. Sometime during the Feeling, the Stardust Twins had decided that I was one of the few things they could not be objective about, and had returned to their quarters.

I waited until the excitement of discovery had diminished enough for me to control my physical structure. Then I once again took the shape that I presented to my companions, and reported my findings to Bellidore.

"So even then they were aggressors," he said. "Well, it is not surprising. The will to dominate the stars had to have come from somewhere."

"It is surprising that there is no record of any race having landed here in their prehistory," said the Historian.

"It was a survey team, and Earth was of no use to them," I answered. "They doubtless touched down on any number of planets. If there is a record anywhere, it is probably in their archives, stating that Earth showed no promise as a colony world."

"But didn't they wonder what had happened to their team?" asked Bellidore.

"There were many large carnivores in the vicinity," I said. "They probably assumed the team had fallen prey to them. Especially if they searched the area and found nothing."

"Interesting," said Bellidore. "That the weaker of the species should have risen to dominance."

"I think it is easily explained," said the Historian. "*As* the smaller species, they were neither as fast as their prey nor as strong as their predators, so the creation of weapons was perhaps the only way to avoid extinction . . . or at least the best way."

"Certainly they displayed the cunning of the predator during their millennia abroad in the galaxy," said Bellidore.

"One does not *stop* being aggressive simply because one invents a weapon," said the Historian. "In fact, it may *add* to one's aggression."

"I shall have to consider that," said Bellidore, looking somewhat unconvinced.

"I have perhaps oversimplified my train of thought for the sake of this discussion," replied the Historian. "Rest assured that I will build a lengthy and rigorous argument when I present my findings to the Academy."

"And what of you, He Who Views?" asked Bellidore. "Have you any observations to add to what you have told us?"

"It is difficult to think of a rock as being the precursor of the sonic rifle and the molecular imploder," I said thoughtfully, "but I believe it to be the case."

"A most interesting species," said Bellidore.

It took almost four hours for my strength to return, for Feeling saps the energy like no other function, drawing equally from the body, the emotions, the mind, and the empathic powers.

The Moriteu, its work done for the day, was hanging upside down from a tree limb, lost in its evening trance, and the Stardust Twins had not made an appearance since I had Felt the stone.

The other party members were busy with their own pursuits, and it seemed an ideal time for me to Feel the next object, which the Historian told me was approximately 23,300 years old.

It was the metal blade of a spear, rusted and pitted, and before I assimilated it, I thought I could see a slight discoloration, perhaps caused by blood . . .

H is name was Mtepwa, and it seemed to him that he had been wearing a metal collar around his neck since the day he had been born. He knew that couldn't be true, for he had fleeting memories of playing with his brothers and sisters, and of stalking the kudu and the bongo on the tree-covered mountain where he grew up.

But the more he concentrated on those memories, the more vague and imprecise they became, and he knew they must have occurred a very long time ago. Sometimes he tried to remember the name of his tribe, but it was lost in the mists of time, as were the names of his parents and siblings.

It was at times like this that Mtepwa felt sorry for himself, but then he would consider his companions' situation, and he felt better, for while they were to be taken in ships and sent to the edge of the world to spend the remainder of their lives as slaves of the Arabs and the Europeans, he himself was the favored servant of his master, Sharif Abdullah, and as such his position was assured.

This was his eighth caravan—or was it his ninth?—from the Interior. They would trade salt and cartridges to the tribal chiefs, who would in turn sell them their least productive warriors and women as slaves, and then they would march them out, around the huge lake and across the dry flat savannah. They would circle the mountain that was so old that it had turned white on the top, just like a white-haired old man, and finally out to the coast, where dhows filled the harbor. There they would sell their human booty to the highest bidders, and Sharif Abdullah would purchase another wife and turn half the money over to his aged, feeble father, and they would be off to the Interior again on another quest for black gold.

Abdullah was a good master. He rarely drank—and when he did, he always apologized to Allah at the next opportunity—and he did not beat Mtepwa overly much, and they always had enough to eat, even when the cargo went hungry. He even went so far as to teach Mtepwa how to read, although the only reading matter he carried with him was the Koran.

Mtepwa spent long hours honing his reading skills with the Koran, and somewhere along the way he made a most interesting discovery: the Koran forbade a practitioner of the True Faith to keep another member in bondage.

It was at that moment that Mtepwa made up his mind to convert to Islam. He began questioning Sharif Abdullah incessantly on the finer points of his religion, and made sure that the old man saw him sitting by the fire, hour after hour, reading the Koran.

So enthused was Sharif Abdullah at this development that he frequently invited Mtepwa into his tent at suppertime, and lectured him on the subtleties of the Koran far into the night. Mtepwa was a motivated student, and Sharif Abdullah marveled at his enthusiasm.

Night after night, as lions prowled around their camp in the Serengeti, master and pupil studied the Koran together. And finally the day came when Sharif Abdullah could no longer deny that Mtepwa was indeed a true believer of Islam. It happened as they camped at the Olduvai Gorge, and that very day Sharif Abdullah had his smith remove the collar from Mtepwa's neck, and Mtepwa himself destroyed the chains link by link, hurling them deep into the gorge when he was finished.

Mtepwa was now a free man, but knowledgeable in only two areas: the Koran, and slave-trading. So it was only natural that when he looked around for some means to support himself, he settled upon following in Sharif Abdullah's footsteps. He became a junior partner to the old man, and after two more trips to the Interior, he decided that he was ready to go out on his own.

To do that, he required a trained staff—warriors, smiths, cooks, trackers—and the prospect of assembling one from scratch was daunting, so, since his faith was less strong than his mentor's, he simply sneaked into Sharif Abdullah's quarters on the coast one night and slit the old man's throat.

The next day, he marched inland at the head of his own caravan.

He had learned much about the business of slaving, both as a practitioner and a victim, and he put his knowledge to full use. He knew that healthy slaves would bring a better price at market, and so he fed and treated his captives far better than Sharif Abdullah and most other slavers did. On the other hand, he knew which ones were fomenting trouble, and knew it was better to kill them on the spot as an example to the others, than to let any hopes of insurrection spread among the captives.

Because he was thorough, he was equally successful, and soon expanded into ivory trading as well. Within six years he had the biggest slaving and poaching operation in East Africa.

From time to time he ran across European explorers. It was said that he even spent a week with Dr. David Livingstone and left without the missionary ever knowing that he had been playing host to the slaver he most wanted to put out of business.

After America's War Between the States killed his primary market, he took a year off from his operation to go to Asia and the Arabian Peninsula and open up new ones. Upon returning he found that Abdullah's son, Sharif Ibn Jad Mahir, had appropriated all his men and headed inland, intent on carrying on his father's business. Mtepwa, who had become quite wealthy, hired some 500 *askari,* placed them under the command of the notorious ivory poacher Alfred Henry Pym, and sat back to await the results.

Three months later Pym marched some 438 men back to the Tanganyika coast. Two hundred and seventy-six were slaves that Sharif Ibn Jad Mahir had captured; the remainder were the remnants of Mtepwa's organization, who had gone to work for Sharif Ibn Jad Mahir. Mtepwa sold all 438 of them into bondage and built a new organization, composed of the warriors who had fought for him under Pym's leadership.

Most of the colonial powers were inclined to turn a blind eye to his practices, but the British, who were determined to put an end to slavery, issued a warrant for Mtepwa's arrest. Eventually he tired of continually looking over his shoulder, and moved his headquarters to Mozambique, where the Portuguese were happy to let him set up shop as long as he remembered that colonial palms needed constant greasing.

He was never happy there—he didn't speak Portuguese or any of the local languages—and after nine years he returned to Tanganyika, now the wealthiest black man on the continent.

One day he found among his latest batch of captives a young Acholi boy named Haradi, no more than ten years old, and decided to keep him as a personal servant rather than ship him across the ocean.

Mtepwa had never married. Most of his associates assumed that he had simply never had the time, but as the almost-nightly demands for Haradi to visit him in his tent became common knowledge, they soon revised their opinions. Mtepwa seemed besotted with his servant boy, though—doubtless remembering his own experience—he never taught Haradi to read, and promised a slow and painful death to anyone who spoke of Islam to the boy.

Then one night, after some three years had passed, Mtepwa sent for Haradi. The boy was nowhere to be found. Mtepwa awoke all his warriors and demanded that they search for him, for a leopard had been seen in the vicinity of the camp, and the slaver feared the worst.

They found Haradi an hour later, not in the jaws of a leopard, but in the arms of a young female slave they had taken from the Zaneke tribe. Mtepwa was beside himself with rage, and had the poor girl's arms and legs torn from her body.

Haradi never offered a word of protest, and never tried to defend the girl—not that it would have done any good—but the next morning he was gone, and though Mtepwa and his warriors spent almost a month searching for him, they found no trace of him.

By the end of the month Mtepwa was quite insane with rage and grief. Deciding that life was no longer worth living, he walked up to a pride of lions that were gorging themselves on a topi carcass and, striding into their midst, began cursing them and hitting them with his bare hands. Almost unbelievably, the lions backed away from him, snarling and growling, and disappeared into the thick bush.

The next day he picked up a large stick and began beating a baby elephant with it. That should have precipitated a brutal attack by its mother—but the mother, standing only a few feet away, trumpeted in terror and raced off, the baby following her as best it could.

It was then that Mtepwa decided that he could not die, that somehow the act of dismembering the poor Zaneke girl had made him immortal. Since both incidents had occurred within sight of his superstitious followers, they fervently believed him.

Now that he was immortal, he decided that it was time to stop trying to accommodate the Europeans who had invaded his land and kept issuing warrants for his arrest. He sent a runner to the Kenya border and invited the British to meet him in battle. When the appointed day came, and the British did not show up to fight him, he confidently told his warriors that word of his immortality had reached the Europeans and that from that day forth no white men would ever be willing to oppose him. The fact that he was still in German territory, and the British had no legal right to go there, somehow managed to elude him.

He began marching his warriors inland, openly in search of slaves, and he found his share of them in the Congo. He looted villages of their men, their women, and their ivory, and finally, with almost 600 captives and half that many tusks, he turned east and began the months-long trek to the coast.

This time the British were waiting for him at the Uganda border, and they had so many armed men there that Mtepwa turned south, not for fear for his own life, but because he could not afford to lose his slaves and his ivory, and he knew that his warriors lacked his invulnerability.

He marched his army down to Lake Tanganyika, then headed east. It took him two weeks to reach the western corridor of the Serengeti, and another ten days to cross it.

One night he made camp at the lip of the Olduvai Gorge, the very place where he had gained his freedom. The fires were lit, a wildebeest was slaughtered and cooked, and as he relaxed after the meal he became aware of a buzzing among his men. Then, from out of the shadows, stepped a strangely familiar figure. It was Haradi, now fifteen years old, and as tall as Mtepwa himself.

Mtepwa stared at him for a long moment, and suddenly all the anger seemed to drain from his face.

"I am very glad to see you again, Haradi," he said.

"I have heard that you cannot be killed," answered the boy, brandishing a spear. "I have come to see if that is true."

"We have no need to fight, you and I," said Mtepwa. "Join me in my tent, and all will be as it was."

"Once I tear your limbs from your body, *then* we will have no reason to fight," responded Haradi. "And even then, you will seem no less repulsive to me than you do now, or than you did all those many years ago."

Mtepwa jumped up, his face a mask of fury. "Do your worst, then!" he cried. "And when you realize that I cannot be harmed, I will do to you as I did to the Zaneke girl!"

Haradi made no reply, but hurled his spear at Mtepwa. It went into the slaver's body, and was thrown with such force that the point emerged a good six inches on the other side. Mtepwa stared at Haradi with disbelief, moaned once, and tumbled down the rocky slopes of the gorge.

Haradi looked around at the warriors. "Is there any among you who dispute my right to take Mtepwa's place?" he asked confidently.

A burly Makonde stood up to challenge him, and within thirty seconds Haradi, too, was dead.

The British were waiting for them when they reached Zanzibar. The slaves were freed, the ivory confiscated, the warriors arrested and forced to serve as laborers on the Mombasa/Uganda Railway. Two of them were later killed and eaten by lions in the Tsavo District.

By the time Lieutenant Colonel J. H. Patterson shot the notorious Man-Eaters of Tsavo, the railway had almost reached the shanty town of Nairobi, and Mtepwa's name was so thoroughly forgotten that it was misspelled in the only history book in which it appeared.

"Amazing!" said the Appraiser. "I knew they enslaved many races throughout the galaxy—but to enslave *themselves!* It is almost beyond belief!"

I had rested from my efforts, and then related the story of Mtepwa.

"All ideas must begin somewhere," said Bellidore placidly. "This one obviously began on Earth."

"It is barbaric!" muttered the Appraiser.

Bellidore turned to me. "Man never attempted to subjugate *your* race, He Who Views. Why was that?"

"We had nothing that he wanted."

"Can you remember the galaxy when Man dominated it?" asked the Appraiser.

"I can remember the galaxy when Man's progenitors killed Bokatu and Enkatai," I replied truthfully.

"Did you ever have any dealings with Man?"

"None. Man had no use for us."

"But did he not destroy profligately things for which he had no use?"

"No," I said. "He took what he wanted, and he destroyed that which threatened him. The rest he ignored."

"Such arrogance!"

"Such practicality," said Bellidore.

"You call genocide on a galactic scale *practical?*" demanded the Appraiser.

"From Man's point of view, it was," answered Bellidore. "It got him what he wanted with a minimum of risk and effort. Consider that one single race, born not five hundred yards from us, at one time ruled an empire of more than a million worlds. Almost every civilized race in the galaxy spoke Terran."

"Upon pain of death."

"That is true," agreed Bellidore. "I did not say Man was an angel. Only that, if he was indeed a devil, he was an efficient one."

It was time for me to assimilate the third artifact, which the Historian and the Appraiser seemed to think was the handle of a knife, but even as I moved off to perform my function, I could not help but listen to the speculation that was taking place.

"Given his bloodlust and his efficiency," said the Appraiser, "I'm surprised that he lived long enough to reach the stars."

"It *is* surprising in a way," agreed Bellidore. "The Historian tells me that Man was not always homogeneous, that early in his history there were several variations of the species. He was divided by color, by belief, by territory." He sighed. "Still, he must have learned to live in peace with his fellow man. That much, at least, accrues to his credit."

I reached the artifact with Bellidore's words still in my ears, and began to engulf it . . .

Mary Leakey pressed against the horn of the Land Rover. Inside the museum, her husband turned to the young uniformed officer.

"I can't think of any instructions to give you," he said. "The museum's not open to the public yet, and we're a good 300 kilometers from Kikuyuland."

"I'm just following my orders, Dr. Leakey," replied the officer.

"Well, I suppose it doesn't hurt to be safe," acknowledged Leakey. "There are a lot of Kikuyu who want me dead even though I spoke up for Kenyatta at his trial." He walked to the door. "If the discoveries at Lake Turkana prove interesting, we could be gone as long as a month. Otherwise, we should be back within ten to twelve days."

"No problem, sir. The museum will still be here when you get back."

"I never doubted it," said Leakey, walking out and joining his wife in the vehicle.

Lieutenant Ian Chelmswood stood in the doorway and watched the Leakeys, accompanied by two military vehicles, start down the red dirt road. Within seconds the car was obscured by dust, and he stepped back into the building and closed the door to avoid being covered by it. The heat was oppressive, and he removed his jacket and holster and laid them neatly across one of the small display cases.

It was strange. All the images he had seen of African wildlife, from the German Schillings' old still photographs to the American Johnson's motion pictures, had led him to believe that East Africa was a wonderland of green grass and clear water. No one had ever mentioned the dust, but that was the one memory of it that he would take home with him.

Well, not quite the only one. He would never forget the morning the alarm had sounded back when he was stationed in Nanyuki. He arrived at the settlers' farm and found the entire family cut to ribbons and all their cattle mutilated, most with their genitals cut off, many missing ears and eyes. But as horrible as that was, the picture he would carry to his grave was the kitten impaled on a dagger and pinned to the mailbox. It was the Mau Mau's signature, just in case anyone thought some madman had run berserk among the cattle and the humans.

Chelmswood didn't understand the politics of it. He didn't know who had started it, who had precipitated the war. It made no difference to him. He was just a soldier, following orders, and if those orders would take him back to Nanyuki so that he could kill the men who had committed those atrocities, so much the better.

But in the meantime, he had pulled what he considered Idiot Duty. There had been a very mild outburst of violence in Arusha, not really Mau Mau but rather a show of support for Kenya's Kikuyu, and his unit had been transferred there. Then the government found out that Professor Leakey, whose scientific finds had made Olduvai Gorge almost a household word among East Africans, had been getting death threats. Over his objections, they had insisted on providing him with bodyguards. Most of the men from Chelmswood's unit would accompany Leakey on his trip to Lake Turkana, but someone had to stay behind to guard the museum, and it was just his bad luck that his name had been atop the duty roster.

It wasn't even a museum, really, not the kind of museum his parents had taken him to see in London. *Those* were museums; this was just a two-room mud-walled structure with perhaps a hundred of Leakey's finds. Ancient arrowheads, some oddly shaped stones that had functioned as prehistoric tools, a couple of bones that obviously weren't from monkeys but that Chelmswood was certain were not from any creature *he* was related to.

Leakey had hung some crudely drawn charts on the wall, charts that showed what he believed to be the evolution of some small, grotesque, apelike beasts into *Homo sapiens.* There were photographs, too, showing some of the finds that had been sent on to Nairobi. It seemed that even if this gorge was the birthplace of the race, nobody really wanted to visit it. All the best finds were shipped back to Nairobi and then to the British Museum. In fact, this wasn't a museum at all, decided Chelmswood, but rather a holding area for the better specimens until they could be sent elsewhere.

It was strange to think of life starting here in this gorge. If there was an uglier spot in Africa, he had yet to come across it. And while he didn't accept Genesis or any of that religious nonsense, it bothered him to think that the first human beings to walk the Earth might have been black. He'd hardly had any exposure to blacks when he was growing up in the Cotswolds, but he'd seen enough of what they could do since coming to British East, and he was appalled by their savagery and barbarism.

And what about those crazy Americans, wringing their hands and saying that colonialism had to end? If they had seen what *he'd* seen on that farm in Nanyuki, they'd know that the only thing that was keeping all of East Africa from exploding into an unholy conflagration of blood and butchery was the British presence. Certainly, there were parallels between the Mau Mau and America: both had been colonized by the British and both wanted their independence . . . but there all similarity ended. The Americans wrote a Declaration outlining their grievances, and then they fielded an army and fought the British *soldiers*. What did chopping up innocent children and pinning cats to mailboxes have in common with that? If he had his way, he'd march in half a million British troops, wipe out every last Kikuyu—except for the good ones, the loyal ones—and solve the problem once and for all.

He wandered over to the cabinet where Leakey kept his beer and pulled out a warm bottle. Safari brand. He opened it and took a long swallow, then made a face. If that's what people drank on safari, he'd have to remember never to go on one.

And yet he knew that someday he *would* go on safari, hopefully before he was mustered out and sent home. Parts of the country were so damned beautiful, dust or no dust, and he liked the thought of sitting beneath a shade tree, cold drink in hand, while his body servant cooled him with a fan made of ostrich feathers and he and his white hunter discussed the day's kills and what they would go out after tomorrow. It wasn't the shooting that was important, they'd both reassure themselves, but rather the thrill of the hunt. Then he'd have a couple of his black boys draw his bath, and he'd bathe and prepare for dinner. Funny how he had fallen into the habit of calling them boys; most of them were far older than he.

But while they weren't boys, they *were* children in need of guidance and civilizing. Take those Maasai, for example; proud, arrogant bastards. They looked great on postcards, but try *dealing* with them. They acted as if they had a direct line to God, that He had told them they were His chosen people. The more Chelmswood thought about it, the more surprised he was that it was the Kikuyu that had begun Mau Mau rather than the Maasai. And come to think of it, he'd noticed four or five Maasai *elmorani* hanging around the museum. He'd have to keep an eye on them . . .

"Excuse, please?" said a high-pitched voice, and Chelmswood turned to see a small skinny black boy, no more than ten years old, standing in the doorway.

"What do you want?" he asked.

"Doctor Mister Leakey, he promise me candy," said the boy, stepping inside the building.

"Go away," said Chelmswood irritably. "We don't have any candy here."

"Yes yes," said the boy, stepping forward. "Every day."

"He gives you candy every day?"

The boy nodded his head and smiled.

"Where does he keep it?"

The boy shrugged. "Maybe in there?" he said, pointing to a cabinet.

Chelmswood walked to the cabinet and opened it. There was nothing in it but four jars containing primitive teeth.

"I don't see any," he said. "You'll have to wait until Dr. Leakey comes back."

Two tears trickled down the boy's cheek. "But Doctor Mister Leakey, he *promise!*"

Chelmswood looked around. "I don't know where it is."

The boy began crying in earnest.

"Be quiet!" snapped Chelmswood. "I'll look for it."

"Maybe next room," suggested the boy.

"Come along," said Chelmswood, walking through the doorway to the adjoining room. He looked around, hands on hips, trying to imagine where Leakey had hidden the candy.

"This place maybe," said the boy, pointing to a closet.

Chelmswood opened the closet. It contained two spades, three picks, and an assortment of small brushes, all of which he assumed were used by the Leakeys for their work.

"Nothing here," he said, closing the door.

He turned to face the boy, but found the room empty.

"Little bugger was lying all along," he muttered. "Probably ran away to save himself a beating."

He walked back into the main room—and found himself facing a well-built black man holding a machete-like *panga* in his right hand.

"What's going on here?" snapped Chelmswood.

"Freedom is going on here, Lieutenant," said the black man in near-perfect English. "I was sent to kill Dr. Leakey, but you will have to do."

"Why are you killing anyone?" demanded Chelmswood. "What did we ever do to the Maasai?"

"I will let the Maasai answer that. Any one of them could take one look at me and tell you that I am Kikuyu—but we are all the same to you British, aren't we?"

Chelmswood reached for his gun and suddenly realized he had left it on a display case.

"You all look like cowardly savages to me!"

"Why? Because we do not meet you in battle?" The black man's face filled with fury. "You take our land away, you forbid us to own weapons, you even make it a crime for us to carry spears—and then you call us savages when we don't march in formation against your guns!" He spat contemptuously on the floor. "We fight you in the only way that is left to us."

"It's a big country, big enough for both races," said Chelmswood.

"If we came to England and took away your best farmland and forced you to work for us, would you think England was big enough for both races?"

"I'm not political," said Chelmswood, edging another step closer to his weapon. "I'm just doing my job."

"And your job is to keep two hundred whites on land that once held a million Kikuyu," said the black man, his face reflecting his hatred.

"There'll be a lot less than a million when *we* get through with you!" hissed Chelmswood, diving for his gun.

Quick as he was, the black man was faster, and with a single swipe of his *panga* he almost severed the Englishman's right hand from his wrist. Chelmswood bellowed in pain, and spun around, presenting his back to the Kikuyu as he reached for the pistol with his other hand.

The *panga* came down again, practically splitting him open, but as he fell he managed to get his fingers around the handle of his pistol and pull the trigger. The bullet struck the black man in the chest, and he, too, collapsed to the floor.

"You've killed me!" moaned Chelmswood. "Why would anyone want to kill me?"

"You have so much and we have so little," whispered the black man. "Why must you have what is ours, too?"

"What did I ever do to you?" asked Chelmswood.

"You came here. That was enough," said the black man. "Filthy English!" He closed his eyes and lay still.

"Bloody nigger!" slurred Chelmswood, and died.

Outside, the four Maasai paid no attention to the tumult within.

They let the small Kikuyu boy leave without giving him so much as a glance. The business of inferior races was none of their concern.

"These notions of superiority among members of the same race are very difficult to comprehend," said Bellidore. "Are you *sure* you read the artifact properly, He Who Views?"

"I do not *read* artifacts," I replied. "I *assimilate* them. I become one with them. Everything *they* have experienced, *I* experience." I paused. "There can be no mistake."

"Well, it is difficult to fathom, especially in a species that would one day control most of the galaxy. Did they think *every* race they met was inferior to them?"

"They certainly behaved as if they did," said the Historian. "They seemed to respect only those races that stood up to them—and even then they felt that militarily defeating them was proof of their superiority."

"And yet we know from ancient records that primitive man worshipped nonsentient animals," put in the Exobiologist.

"They must not have survived for any great length of time," suggested the Historian. "If Man treated the races of the galaxy with contempt, how much worse must he have treated the poor creatures with whom he shared his home world?"

"Perhaps he viewed them much the same as he viewed my own race," I offered. "If they had nothing he wanted, if they presented no threat . . ."

"They would have had something he wanted," said the Exobiologist. "He was a predator. They would have had meat."

"And land," added the Historian. "If even the galaxy was not enough to quench Man's thirst for territory, think how unwilling he would have been to share his own world."

"It is a question I suspect will never be answered," said Bellidore.

"Unless the answer lies in one of the remaining artifacts," agreed the Exobiologist.

I'm sure the remark was not meant to jar me from my lethargy, but it occurred to me that it had been half a day since I had assimilated the knife handle, and I had regained enough of my strength to examine the next artifact.

It was a metal stylus . . .

February 15, 2103:

Well, we finally got here! The Supermole got us through the tunnel from New York to London in just over four hours. Even so we were twenty minutes late, missed our connection, and had to wait another five hours for the next flight to Khartoum. From there our means of transport got increasingly more primitive—jet planes to Nairobi and Arusha—and then a quick shuttle to our campsite, but we've finally put civilization behind us. I've never seen open spaces like this before; you're barely aware of the skyscrapers of Nyerere, the closest town.

After an orientation speech telling us what to expect and how to behave on safari, we got the afternoon off to meet our traveling companions. I'm the youngest member of the group: a trip like this just costs too much for most people my age to afford. Of course, most people my age don't have an Uncle Reuben who dies and leaves them a ton of money. (Well, it's probably about eight ounces of money, now that the safari is paid for. Ha ha.)

The lodge is quite rustic. They have quaint microwaves for warming our food, although most of us will be eating at the restaurants. I understand the Japanese and Brazilian ones are the most popular, the former for the food—real fish—and the latter for the entertainment. My roommate is Mr. Shiboni, an elderly Japanese gentleman who tells me he has been saving his money for fifteen years to come on this safari. He seems pleasant and good-natured; I hope he can survive the rigors of the trip.

I had really wanted a shower, just to get in the spirit of things, but water is scarce here, and it looks like I'll have to settle for the same old chemical dryshower. I know, I know, it disinfects as well as cleanses, but if I wanted all the comforts of home, I'd have stayed home and saved $150,000.

February 16:

We met our guide today. I don't know why, but he doesn't quite fit my preconception of an African safari guide. I was expecting some grizzled old veteran who had a wealth of stories to tell, who had maybe even seen a civet cat or a duiker before they became extinct. What we got was Kevin Ole Tambake, a young Maasai who can't be twenty-five years old and dresses in a suit while we all wear our khakis. Still, he's lived here all his life, so I suppose he knows his way around.

And I'll give him this: he's a wonderful storyteller. He spent half an hour telling us myths about how his people used to live in huts called manyattas, *and how their rite of passage to manhood was to kill a lion with a spear. As if the government anyone kill an animal!*

We spent the morning driving down into the Ngorongoro Crater. It's a collapsed caldera, *or volcano, that was once taller than Kilimanjaro itself. Kevin says it used to teem with game, though I can't see how, since any game standing atop it when it collapsed would have been instantly killed.*

I think the real reason we went there was just to get the kinks out of our safari vehicle and learn the proper protocol. Probably just as well. The air-conditioning wasn't working right in two of the compartments, the service mechanism couldn't get the temperature right on the iced drinks, and once, when we thought we saw a bird, three of us buzzed Kevin at the same time and jammed his communication line.

In the afternoon we went out to Serengeti. Kevin says it used to extend all the way to the Kenya border, but now it's just a twenty-square-mile park adjacent to the Crater. About an hour into the game run we saw a ground squirrel, but he disappeared into a hole before I could adjust my holo camera. Still, he was very impressive. Varying shades of brown, with dark eyes and a fluffy tail. Kevin estimated that he went almost three pounds, and says he hasn't seen one that big since he was a boy.

Just before we returned to camp, Kevin got word on the radio from another driver that they had spotted two starlings nesting in a tree about eight miles north and east of us. The vehicle's computer told us we wouldn't be able to reach it before dark, so Kevin had it lock the spot in its memory and promised us that we'd go there first thing in the morning.

I opted for the Brazilian restaurant, and spent a few pleasant hours listening to the live band. A very nice end to the first full day of safari.

February 17:
We left at dawn in search of the starlings, and though we found the tree where they had been spotted, we never did see them. One of

the passengers—I think it was the little man from Burma, though I'm not sure—must have complained, because Kevin soon announced to the entire party that this was a safari, that there was no guarantee of seeing any particular bird or animal, and that while he would do his best for us, one could never be certain where the game might be.

And then, just as he was talking, a banded mongoose almost a foot long appeared out of nowhere. It seemed to pay no attention to us, and Kevin announced that we were killing the motor and going into hover mode so the noise wouldn't scare it away.

After a minute or two everyone on the right side of the vehicle had gotten their holographs, and we slowly spun on our axis so that the left side could see him—but the movement must have scared him off, because though the maneuver took less than thirty seconds, he was nowhere to be seen when we came to rest again.

Kevin announced that the vehicle had captured the mongoose on its automated holos, and copies would be made available to anyone who had missed their holo opportunity.

We were feeling great—the right side of the vehicle, anyway— when we stopped for lunch, and during our afternoon game run we saw three yellow weaver birds building their spherical nests in a tree. Kevin let us out, warning us not to approach closer than thirty yards, and we spent almost an hour watching and holographing them.

All in all, a very satisfying day.

February 18:
Today we left camp about an hour after sunrise, and went to a new location: Olduvai Gorge.

Kevin announced that we would spend our last two days here, that with the encroachment of the cities and farms on all the flat land, the remaining big game was pretty much confined to the gullies and slopes of the gorge.

No vehicle, not even our specially equipped one, was capable of navigating its way through the gorge, so we all got out and began walking in single file behind Kevin.

Most of us found it very difficult to keep up with Kevin. He clambered up and down the rocks as if he'd been doing it all his life, whereas I can't remember the last time I saw a stair that didn't move when I stood on it. We had trekked for perhaps half an hour when I heard one of the men at the back of our strung-out party give a *cry and point to a spot at the bottom of the gorge, and we all looked and saw something racing away at phenomenal speed.*

"Another squirrel?" I asked.

Kevin just smiled.

The man behind me said he thought it was a mongoose.

"What you saw," said Kevin, "was a dik-dik, the last surviving African antelope."

"How big was it?" asked a woman.

"About average size," said Kevin. "Perhaps ten inches at the shoulder."

Imagine anything ten inches high being called average!

Kevin explained that dik-diks were very territorial, and that this one wouldn't stray far from his home area. Which meant that if we were patient and quiet—and lucky—we'd be able to spot him again.

I asked Kevin how many dik-diks lived in the gorge, and he scratched his head and considered it for a moment and then guessed that there might be as many as ten. (And Yellowstone has only nineteen rabbits left! Is it any wonder that all the serious animal buffs come to Africa?)

We kept walking for another hour, and then broke for lunch, while Kevin gave us the history of the place, telling us all about Dr. Leakey's finds. There were probably still more skeletons to be dug up, he guessed, but the government didn't want to frighten any animals away from what had become their last refuge, so the bones would have to wait for some future generation to unearth them. Roughly translated, that meant that Tanzania wasn't going to give up the revenues from three hundred tourists a week and turn over the crown jewel in their park system to a bunch of anthropologists. I can't say that I blame them.

Other parties had begun pouring into the gorge, and I think the entire safari population must have totaled almost seventy by the time lunch was over. The guides each seemed to have "their" areas marked out, and I noticed that rarely did we get within a quarter mile of any other parties.

Kevin asked us if we wanted to sit in the shade until the heat of the day had passed, but since this was our next-to-last day on safari we voted overwhelmingly to proceed as soon as we were through eating.

It couldn't have been ten minutes later that the disaster occurred.

We were clambering down a steep slope in single file, Kevin in the lead as usual, and me right behind him, when I heard a grunt and then a surprised yell, and I looked back to see Mr. Shiboni tumbling down the path. Evidently he'd lost his footing, and we could hear the bones in his leg snap as he hurtled toward us.

Kevin positioned himself to stop him, and almost got knocked down the gorge himself before he finally stopped poor Mr. Shiboni. Then he knelt down next to the old gentleman to tend to his broken leg—but as he did so his keen eyes spotted something we all had missed, and suddenly he was bounding up the slopes like a monkey. He stopped where Mr. Shiboni had initially stumbled, squatted down, and examined something. Then, looking like Death itself, he picked up the object and brought it back down the path.

It was a dead lizard, fully grown, almost eight inches long, and smashed flat by Mr. Shiboni. It was impossible to say whether his fall was caused by stepping on it, or whether it simply couldn't get out of the way once he began tumbling . . . but it made no difference: he was responsible for the death of an animal in a National Park.

I tried to remember the release we had signed, giving the Park System permission to instantly withdraw money from our accounts should we destroy an animal for any reason, even self-protection. I knew that the absolute minimum penalty was $50,000, but I think that was for two of the more common birds, and that ugaama and gecko lizards were in the $70,000 range.

Kevin held the lizard up for all of us to see, and told us that should legal action ensue, we were all witnesses to what had happened.

Mr. Shiboni groaned in pain, and Kevin said that there was no sense wasting the lizard, so he gave it to me to hold while he splinted Mr. Shiboni's leg and summoned the paramedics on the radio.

I began examining the little lizard. Its feet were finely shaped, its tail long and elegant, but it was the colors that made the most lasting impression on me: a reddish head, a blue body, and gray legs, the color growing lighter as it reached the claws. A beautiful, beautiful thing, even in death.

After the paramedics had taken Mr. Shiboni back to the lodge, Kevin spent the next hour showing us how the ugaama lizard functioned: how its eyes could see in two directions at once, how its claws *allowed it to hang upside down from any uneven surface, and how efficiently its jaws could crack the carapaces of the insects it caught. Finally, in view of the tragedy, and also because he wanted to check on Mr. Shiboni's condition, Kevin suggested that we call it a day.*

None of us objected—we knew Kevin would have hours of extra work, writing up the incident and convincing the Park Department that his safari company was not responsible for it—but still we felt cheated, since there was only one day left. I think Kevin knew it, because just before we reached the lodge he promised us a special treat tomorrow.

I've been awake half the night wondering what it could be. Can he possibly know where the other dik-diks are? Or could the legends of a last flamingo possibly be true?

February 19:
We were all excited when we climbed aboard the vehicle this morning. Everyone kept asking Kevin what his "special treat" was, but he merely smiled and kept changing the subject. Finally we reached Olduvai Gorge and began walking, only this time we seemed to be going to a specific location, and Kevin hardly stopped to try to spot the dik-dik.

We climbed down twisting, winding paths, tripping over tree roots, cutting our arms and legs on thorn bushes, but nobody objected, for Kevin seemed so confident of his surprise that all these hardships were forgotten.

Finally we reached the bottom of the gorge and began walking along a flat winding path. Still, by the time we were ready to stop for lunch, we hadn't seen a thing. As we sat beneath the shade of an acacia tree, eating, Kevin pulled out his radio and conversed with the other guides. One group had seen three dik-diks, and another had found a lilac-breasted roller's nest with two hatchlings in it. Kevin is very competitive, and ordinarily news like that would have had him urging everyone to finish eating quickly so that we would not return to the lodge having seen less than everyone else, but this time he just smiled and told the other guides that we had seen nothing on the floor of the gorge and that the game seemed to have moved out, perhaps in search of water.

Then, when lunch was over, Kevin walked about fifty yards away, disappeared into a cave, and emerged a moment later with a small wooden cage. There was a little brown bird in it, and while I was thrilled to be able to see it close up, I felt somehow disappointed that this was to be the special treat.

"Have you ever seen a honey guide?" he asked.

We all admitted that we hadn't, and he explained that that was the name of the small brown bird.

I asked why it was called that, since it obviously didn't produce honey, and seemed incapable of replacing Kevin as our guide, and he smiled again.

"Do you see that tree?" he asked, pointing to a tree perhaps seventy-five yards away. There was a huge beehive on a low-hanging branch.

"Yes," I said.

"Then watch," he said, opening the cage and releasing the bird. It stood still for a moment, then fluttered its wings and took off in the direction of the tree.

"He is making sure there is honey there," explained Kevin, pointing to the bird as it circled the hive.

"Where is he going now?" I asked, as the bird suddenly flew down the riverbed.

"To find his partner."

"Partner?" I asked, confused.

"Wait and see," said Kevin, sitting down with his back propped against a large rock.

We all followed suit and sat in the shade, our binoculars and holo cameras trained on the tree. After almost an hour nothing had happened, and some of us were getting restless, when Kevin tensed and pointed up the riverbed.

"There!" he whispered. I looked in the direction he was pointing, and there, following the bird, which was flying just ahead of him and chirping frantically, was an enormous black-and-white animal, the largest I have ever seen.

"What is it?" I whispered.

"A honey badger," answered Kevin softly. "They were thought to be extinct twenty years ago, but a mated pair took sanctuary in Olduvai. This is the fourth generation to be born here."

"Is he going to eat the bird?" asked one of the party.

"No," whispered Kevin. "The bird will lead him to the honey,

*and after he has pulled down the nest and eaten his fill, he will leave
some for the bird."*

*And it was just as Kevin said. The honey badger climbed the bole
of the tree and knocked off the beehive with a forepaw, then climbed
back down and broke it apart, oblivious to the stings of the bees.
We caught the whole fantastic scene on our holos, and when he was
done he did indeed leave some honey for the honey guide.*

*Later, while Kevin was recapturing the bird and putting it back
in its cage, the rest of us discussed what we had seen. I thought the
honey badger must have weighed forty-five pounds, though less excitable members of the party put its weight at closer to thirty-six or
thirty-seven. Whichever it was, the creature was enormous. The discussion then shifted to how big a tip to leave for Kevin, for he had
certainly earned one.*

*As I write this final entry in my safari diary, I am still trembling
with the excitement that can only come from encountering big game
in the wild. Prior to this afternoon, I had some doubts about the
safari—I felt it was overpriced, or that perhaps my expectations had
been too high—but now I know that it was worth every penny, and
I have a feeling that I am leaving some part of me behind here, and
that I will never be truly content until I return to this last bastion of
the wilderness.*

The camp was abuzz with excitement. Just when we were
sure that there were no more treasures to unearth, the Stardust Twins had found three small pieces of bone, attached together
with a wire—obviously a human artifact.

"But the dates are wrong," said the Historian, after examining
the bones thoroughly with its equipment. "This is a primitive piece
of jewelry—for the adornment of savages, one might say—and yet
the bones and wire both date from centuries after Man discovered
space travel."

"Do you . . ."

". . . deny that we . . ."

". . . found it in the . . ."

". . . gorge?" demanded the Twins.

"I believe you," said the Historian. "I simply state that it seems
to be an anachronism."

"It is our find, and . . ."

". . . it will bear our name."

"No one is denying your right of discovery," said Bellidore. "It is simply that you have presented us with a mystery."

"Give it to . . ."

". . . He Who Views, and he . . ."

". . . will solve the mystery."

"I will do my best," I said. "But it has not been long enough since I assimilated the stylus. I must rest and regain my strength."

"That is . . ."

". . . acceptable."

We let the Moriteu go about brushing and cleaning the artifact, while we speculated on why a primitive fetish should exist in the starfaring age. Finally the Exobiologist got to her feet.

"I am going back into the gorge," she announced. "If the Stardust Twins could find this, perhaps there are other things we have overlooked. After all, it is an enormous area." She paused and looked at the rest of us. "Would anyone care to come with me?"

It was nearing the end of the day, and no one volunteered, and finally the Exobiologist turned and began walking toward the path that led down into the depths of Olduvai Gorge.

It was dark when I finally felt strong enough to assimilate the jewelry. I spread my essence about the bones and the wire and soon became one with them . . .

His name was Joseph Meromo, and he could live with the money but not the guilt.

It had begun with the communication from Brussels, and the veiled suggestion from the head of the multinational conglomerate headquartered there. They had a certain commodity to get rid of. They had no place to get rid of it. Could Tanzania help?

Meromo had told them he would look into it, but he doubted that his government could be of use.

Just *try*, came the reply.

In fact, more than the reply came. The next day a private courier delivered a huge wad of large-denomination bills, with a polite note thanking Meromo for his efforts on their behalf.

Meromo knew a bribe when he saw one—he'd certainly taken

enough in his career—but he'd never seen one remotely the size of this one. And not even for helping them, but merely for being willing to explore possibilities.

Well, he had thought, why not? What could they conceivably have? A couple of containers of toxic waste? A few plutonium rods? You bury them deep enough in the earth and no one would ever know or care. Wasn't that what the Western countries did?

Of course, there was the Denver Disaster, and that little accident that made the Thames undrinkable for almost a century, but the only reason they popped so quickly to mind is because they were the *exceptions*, not the rule. There were thousands of dumping sites around the world, and ninety-nine percent of them caused no problems at all.

Meromo had his computer cast a holographic map of Tanzania above his desk. He looked at it, frowned, added topographical features, then began studying it in earnest.

If he decided to help them dump the stuff, whatever it was— and he told himself that he was still uncommitted—where would be the best place to dispose of it?

Off the coast? No, the fishermen would pull it up two minutes later, take it to the press, raise enough hell to get him fired, and possibly even cause the rest of the government to resign. The party really couldn't handle any more scandals this year.

The Selous Province? Maybe five centuries ago, when it was the last wilderness on the continent, but not now, not with a thriving, semi-autonomous city-state of fifty-two million people where once there had been nothing but elephants and almost-impenetrable thorn bush.

Lake Victoria? No. Same problem with the fishermen. Dar es Salaam? It was a possibility. Close enough to the coast to make transport easy, practically deserted since Dodoma had become the new capital of the country.

But Dar es Salaam had been hit by an earthquake twenty years ago, when Meromo was still a boy, and he couldn't take the chance of another one exposing or breaking open whatever it was that he planned to hide.

He continued going over the map: Gombe, Ruaha, Iringa, Mbeya, Mtwara, Tarengire, Olduvai . . .

He stopped and stared at Olduvai, then called up all available data.

Almost a mile deep. That was in its favor. No animals left. Better still. No settlements on its steep slopes. Only a handful of Maasai still living in the area, no more than two dozen families, and they were too arrogant to pay any attention to what the government was doing. Of that Meromo was sure: he himself was a Maasai.

So he strung it out for as long as he could, collected cash gifts for almost two years, and finally gave them a delivery date.

Meromo stared out the window of his thirty-fourth floor office, past the bustling city of Dodoma, off to the east, to where he imagined Olduvai Gorge was.

It had seemed so simple. Yes, he was paid a lot of money, a disproportionate amount—but these multinationals had money to burn. It was just supposed to be a few dozen plutonium rods, or so he had thought. How was he to know that they were speaking of forty-two *tons* of nuclear waste?

There was no returning the money. Even if he wanted to, he could hardly expect them to come back and pull all that deadly material back out of the ground. Probably it was safe, probably no one would ever know . . .

But it haunted his days, and even worse, it began haunting his nights as well, appearing in various guises in his dreams. Sometimes it was as carefully sealed containers, sometimes it was as ticking bombs, sometimes a disaster had already occurred and all he could see were the charred bodies of Maasai children spread across the lip of the gorge.

For almost eight months he fought his devils alone, but eventually he realized that he must have help. The dreams not only haunted him at night, but invaded the day as well. He would be sitting at a staff meeting, and suddenly he would imagine he was sitting among the emaciated, sore-covered bodies of the Olduvai Maasai. He would be reading a book, and the words seemed to change and he would be reading that Joseph Meromo had been sentenced to death for his greed. He would watch a holo of the Titanic disaster, and suddenly he was viewing some variation of the Olduvai disaster.

Finally he went to a psychiatrist, and because he was a Maasai, he choose a Maasai psychiatrist. Fearing the doctor's contempt, Meromo would not state explicitly what was causing the nightmares and intrusions, and after almost half a year's worth of futile attempts to cure him, the psychiatrist announced that he could do no more.

"Then am I to be cursed with these dreams forever?" asked Meromo.

"Perhaps not," said the psychiatrist. "*I* cannot help you, but just possibly there is one man who can."

He rummaged through his desk and came up with a small white card. On it was written a single word: MULEWO.

"This is his business card," said the psychiatrist. "Take it."

"There is no address on it, no means of communicating with him," said Meromo. "How will I contact him?"

"He will contact you."

"You will give him my name?"

The psychiatrist shook his head. "I will not have to. Just keep the card on your person. He will know you require his services."

Meromo felt like he was being made the butt of some joke he didn't understand, but he dutifully put the card in his pocket and soon forgot about it.

Two weeks later, as he was drinking at a bar, putting off going home to sleep as long as he could, a small woman approached him.

"Are you Joseph Meromo?" she asked.

"Yes."

"Please follow me."

"Why?" he asked suspiciously.

"You have business with Mulewo, do you not?" she said.

Meromo fell into step behind her, at least as much to avoid going home as from any belief that this mysterious man with no first name could help him. They went out to the street, turned left, walked in silence for three blocks, and turned right, coming to a halt at the front door to a steel-and-glass skyscraper.

"The sixty-third floor," she said. "He is expecting you."

"You're not coming with me?" asked Meromo.

She shook her head. "My job is done." She turned and walked off into the night.

Meromo looked up at the top of the building. It seemed residential. He considered his options, finally shrugged, and walked into the lobby.

"You're here for Mulewo," said the doorman. It was not a question. "Go to the elevator on the left."

Meromo did as he was told. The elevator was paneled with an oiled wood, and smelled fresh and sweet. It operated on voice command and quickly took him to the sixty-third floor. When he emerged he found himself in an elegantly decorated corridor, with ebony wainscotting and discreetly placed mirrors. He walked past three unmarked doors, wondering how he was supposed to know which apartment belonged to Mulewo, and finally came to one that was partially open.

"Come in, Joseph Meromo," said a hoarse voice from within.

Meromo opened the door the rest of the way, stepped into the apartment, and blinked.

Sitting on a torn rug was an old man, wearing nothing but a red cloth gathered at the shoulder. The walls were covered by reed matting, and a noxious-smelling caldron bubbled in the fireplace. A torch provided the only illumination.

"What *is* this?" asked Meromo, ready to step back into the corridor if the old man appeared as irrational as his surroundings.

"Come sit across from me, Joseph Meromo," said the old man. "Surely this is less frightening than your nightmares."

"What do you know about my nightmares?" demanded Meromo.

"I know why you have them. I know what lies buried at the bottom of Olduvai Gorge."

Meromo shut the door quickly. "Who told you?"

"No one told me. I have peered into your dreams, and sifted through them until I found the truth. Come sit."

Meromo walked to where the old man indicated and sat down carefully, trying not to get too much dirt on his freshly pressed outfit.

"Are you Mulewo?" he asked.

The old man nodded. "I am Mulewo."

"How do you know these things about me?"

"I am a *laibon*," said Mulewo.

"A witch doctor?"

"It is a dying art," answered Mulewo. "I am the last practitioner."

"I thought *laibons* cast spells and created curses."

"They also remove curses—and your nights, and even your days, are cursed, are they not?"

"You seem to know all about it."

"I know that you have done a wicked thing, and that you are haunted not only by the ghost of it, but by the ghosts of the future as well."

"And you can end the dreams?"

"That is why I have summoned you here."

"But if I did such a terrible thing, why do you *want* to help me?"

"I do not make moral judgments. I am here only to help the Maasai."

"And what about the Maasai who live by the gorge?" asked Meromo. "The ones who haunt my dreams?"

"When they ask for help, then I will help them."

"Can you cause the material that's buried there to vanish?"

Mulewo shook his head. "I cannot undo what has been done. I cannot even assuage your guilt, for it is a just guilt. All I can do is banish it from your dreams."

"I'll settle for that," said Meromo.

There was an uneasy silence.

"What do I do now?" asked Meromo.

"Bring me a tribute befitting the magnitude of the service I shall perform."

"I can write you a check right now, or have money transferred from my account to your own."

"I have more money than I need. I must have a tribute."

"But—"

"Bring it back tomorrow night," said Mulewo.

Meromo stared at the old *laibon* for a long minute, then got up and left without another word.

He called in sick the next morning, then went to two of Dodoma's better antique shops. Finally he found what he was looking for, charged it to his personal account, and took it home with him. He was afraid to nap before dinner, so he simply read a book all afternoon, then ate a hasty meal and returned to Mulewo's apartment.

"What have you brought me?" asked Mulewo.

Meromo laid the package down in front of the old man. "A headdress made from the skin of a lion," he answered. "They told me it was worn by Sendayo himself, the greatest of all *laibons.*"

"It was not," said Mulewo, without unwrapping the package. "But it is a sufficient tribute nonetheless." He reached beneath his red cloth and withdrew a small necklace, holding it out for Meromo.

"What is this for?" asked Meromo, examining the necklace. It was made of small bones that had been strung together.

"You must wear it tonight when you go to sleep," explained the old man. "It will take all your visions unto itself. Then, tomorrow, you must go to Olduvai Gorge and throw it down to the bottom, so that the visions may lie side by side with the reality."

"And that's all?"

"That is all."

Meromo went back to his apartment, donned the necklace, and went to sleep. That night his dreams were worse than they had ever been before.

In the morning he put the necklace into a pocket and had a government plane fly him to Arusha. From there he rented a ground vehicle, and two hours later he was standing on the edge of the gorge. There was no sign of the buried material.

He took the necklace in his hand and hurled it far out over the lip of the gorge.

His nightmares vanished that night.

One hundred thirty-four years later, mighty Kilimanjaro shuddered as the long-dormant volcano within it came briefly to life.

One hundred miles away, the ground shifted on the floor of Olduvai Gorge, and three of the lead-lined containers broke open.

Joseph Meromo was long dead by that time; and, unfortunately, there were no *laibons* remaining to aid those people who were now compelled to live Meromo's nightmares.

I had examined the necklace in my own quarters, and when I came out to report my findings, I discovered that the entire camp was in a tumultuous state.

"What has happened?" I asked Bellidore.

"The Exobiologist has not returned from the gorge," he said.

"How long has she been gone?"

"She left at sunset last night. It is now morning, and she has not returned or attempted to use her communicator."

"We fear . . ."

". . . that she might . . ."

". . . have fallen and . . ."

". . . become immobile. Or perhaps even . . ."

". . . unconscious . . . ," said the Stardust Twins.

"I have sent the Historian and the Appraiser to look for her," said Bellidore.

"I can help, too," I offered.

"No, you have the last artifact to examine," he said. "When the Moriteu awakens, I will send it as well."

"What about the Mystic?" I asked.

Bellidore looked at the Mystic and sighed. "She has not said a word since landing on this world. In truth, I do not understand her function. At any rate, I do not know how to communicate with her."

The Stardust Twins kicked at the earth together, sending up a pair of reddish dust clouds.

"It seems ridiculous . . . ," said one.

". . . that we can find the tiniest artifact . . . ," said the other.

". . . but we cannot find . . ."

". . . an entire exobiologist."

"Why do you not help search for it?" I asked.

"They get vertigo," explained Bellidore.

"We searched . . ."

". . . the entire camp," they added defensively.

"I can put off assimilating the last piece until tomorrow and help with the search," I volunteered.

"No," replied Bellidore. "I have sent for the ship. We will leave tomorrow, and I want all of our major finds examined by then. It is *my* job to find the Exobiologist; it is *yours* to read the history of the last artifact."

"If that is your desire," I said. "Where is it?"

He led me to a table where the Historian and the Appraiser had been examining it.

"Even *I* know what this is," said Bellidore. "An unspent cartridge." He paused. "Along with the fact that we have found no human artifacts on any higher strata, I would say this in itself is unique: a bullet that a man chose *not* to fire."

"When you state it in those terms, it *does* arouse the curiosity," I acknowledged.

"Are you . . ."

". . . going to examine it . . ."

". . . now?" asked the Stardust Twins apprehensively.

"Yes, I am," I said.

"Wait!" they shouted in unison.

I paused above the cartridge while they began backing away.

"We mean . . ."

". . . no disrespect . . ."

". . . but watching you examine artifacts . . ."

". . . is too unsettling."

And with that, they raced off to hide behind some of the camp structures.

"What about you?" I asked Bellidore. "Would you like me to wait until you leave?"

"Not at all," he replied. "I find diversity fascinating. With your permission, I would like to stay and observe."

"As you wish," I said, allowing my body to melt around the cartridge until it had become a part of myself, and its history became my own history, as clear and precise as if it had all occurred yesterday . . .

"They are coming!"

Thomas Naikosiai looked across the table at his wife.

"Was there ever any doubt that they would?"

"This was foolish, Thomas!" she snapped. "They will force us to leave, and because we made no preparations, we will have to leave all our possessions behind."

"Nobody is leaving," said Naikosiai.

He stood up and walked to the closet. "You stay here," he said, donning his long coat and his mask. "I will meet them outside."

"That is both rude and cruel, to make them stand out there when they have come all this way."

"They were not invited," said Naikosiai. He reached deep into the closet and grabbed the rifle that leaned up against the back wall, then closed the closet, walked through the airlock, and emerged on the front porch.

Six men, all wearing protective clothing and masks to filter the air, confronted him.

"It is time, Thomas," said the tallest of them.

"Time for *you*, perhaps," said Naikosiai, holding the rifle casually across his chest.

"Time for all of us," answered the tall man.

"I am not going anywhere. This is my home. I will not leave it."

"It is a pustule of decay and contamination, as is this whole country," came the answer. "We are all leaving."

Naikosiai shook his head. "My father was born on this land, and his father, and his father's father. *You* may run from danger, if you wish; I will stay and fight it."

"How can you make a stand against radiation?" demanded the tall man. "Can you put a bullet through it? How can you fight air that is no longer safe to breathe?"

"Go away," said Naikosiai, who had no answer to that, other than the conviction that he would never leave his home. "I do not demand that you stay. Do not demand that I leave."

"It is for your own good, Naikosiai," urged another. "If you care nothing for your own life, think of your wife's. How much longer can she breathe the air?"

"Long enough."

"Why not let *her* decide?"

"*I* speak for our family."

An older man stepped forward. "She is *my* daughter, Thomas," he said severely. "I will not allow you to condemn her to the life you have chosen for yourself. Nor will I let my grandchildren remain here."

The old man took another step toward the porch, and suddenly the rifle was pointing at him.

"That's far enough," said Naikosiai.

"They are Maasai," said the old man stubbornly. "They must come with the other Maasai to our new world."

"You are not Maasai," said Naikosiai contemptuously. "Maasai did not leave their ancestral lands when the rinderpest destroyed their herds, or when the white man came, or when the governments sold off their lands. Maasai never surrender. *I* am the last Maasai."

"Be reasonable, Thomas. How can you not surrender to a world that is no longer safe for people to live on? Come with us to New Kilimanjaro."

"The Maasai do not run from danger," said Naikosiai.

"I tell you, Thomas Naikosiai," said the old man, "that I cannot allow you to condemn my daughter and my grandchildren to live in this hellhole. The last ship leaves tomorrow morning. They will be on it."

"They will stay with me, to build a new Maasai nation."

The six men whispered among themselves, and then their leader looked up at Naikosiai.

"You are making a terrible mistake, Thomas," he said. "If you change your mind, there is room for you on the ship."

They all turned to go, but the old man stopped and turned to Naikosiai.

"I will be back for my daughter," he said.

Naikosiai gestured with his rifle. "I will be waiting for you."

The old man turned and walked off with the others, and Naikosiai went back into his house through the airlock. The tile floor smelled of disinfectant, and the sight of the television set offended his eyes, as always. His wife was waiting for him in the kitchen, amid the dozens of gadgets she had purchased over the years.

"How can you speak with such disrespect to the Elders!" she demanded. "You have disgraced us."

"No!" he snapped. "*They* have disgraced us, by leaving!"

"Thomas, you cannot grow anything in the fields. The animals have all died. You cannot even breathe the air without a filtering mask. *Why* do you insist on staying?"

"This is our ancestral land. We will not leave it."

"But all the others—"

"They can do as they please," he interrupted. "En-kai will judge them, as He judges us all. I am not afraid to meet my creator."

"But why must you meet him so soon?" she persisted. "You have seen the tapes and disks of New Kilimanjaro. It is a beautiful world, green and gold and filled with rivers and lakes."

"Once Earth was green and gold and filled with rivers and lakes," said Naikosiai. "They ruined this world. They will ruin the next one."

"Even if they do, we will be long dead," she said. "I want to go."

"We've been through all this before."

"And it always ends with an order rather than an agreement," she said. Her expression softened. "Thomas, just once before I die, I want to see water that you can drink without adding chemicals to it. I want to see antelope grazing on long green grasses. I want to walk outside without having to protect myself from the very air I breathe."

"It's settled."

She shook her head. "I love you, Thomas, but I cannot stay here, and I cannot let our children stay here."

"No one is taking my children from me!" he yelled.

"Just because you care nothing for *your* future, I cannot permit you to deny our sons *their* future."

"Their future is here, where the Maasai have always lived."

"Please come with us, Papa," said a small voice behind him, and Naikosiai turned to see his two sons, eight and five, standing in the doorway to their bedroom, staring at him.

"What have you been saying to them?" demanded Naikosiai suspiciously.

"The truth," said his wife.

He turned to the two boys. "Come here," he said, and they trudged across the room to him.

"What are you?" he asked.

"Boys," said the younger child.

"What *else?*"

"Maasai," said the older.

"That is right," said Naikosiai. "You come from a race of giants. There was a time when, if you climbed to the very top of Kilimanjaro, all the land you could see in every direction belonged to us."

"But that was long ago," said the older boy.

"Someday it will be ours again," said Naikosiai. "You must remember who you are, my son. You are the descendant of Leeyo, who killed one hundred lions with just his spear; of Nelion, who waged war against the whites and drove them from the Rift; of Sendayo, the greatest of all the *laibons*. Once the Kikuyu and the Wakamba and the Lumbwa trembled in fear at the very mention of the word *Maasai*. This is your heritage; do not turn your back on it."

"But the Kikuyu and the other tribes have all left."

"What difference does that make to the Maasai? We did not make a stand only against the Kikuyu and the Wakamba, but against *all* men who would have us change our ways. Even after the Europeans conquered Kenya and Tanganyika, they never conquered the Maasai. When Independence came, and all the other tribes moved to cities and wore suits and aped the Europeans, we remained as we had always been. We wore what we chose and we lived where we chose, for we were proud to be Maasai. Does that not *mean* something to you?"

"Will we not still be Maasai if we go to the new world?" asked the older boy.

"No," said Naikosiai firmly. "There is a bond between the Maasai and the land. We define it, and it defines us. It is what we have always fought for and always defended."

"But it is diseased now," said the boy.

"If I were sick, would you leave me?" asked Naikosiai.

"No, Papa."

"And just as you would not leave me in my illness, so we will not leave the land in *its* illness. When you love something, when it is a part of what you are, you do not leave it simply because it becomes sick. You stay, and you fight even harder to cure it than you fought to win it."

"But—"

"Trust me," said Naikosiai. "Have I ever misled you?"

"No, Papa."

"I am not misleading you now. We are En-kai's chosen people. We live on the ground He has given us. Don't you see that we *must* remain here, that we must keep our covenant with En-kai?"

"But I will never see my friends again!" wailed his younger son.

"You will make new friends."

"Where?" cried the boy. "Everyone is gone!"

"Stop that at once!" said Naikosiai harshly. "Maasai do not cry."

The boy continued sobbing, and Naikosiai looked up at his wife.

"This is *your* doing," he said. "You have spoiled him."

She stared unblinking into his eyes. "Five-year-old boys are allowed to cry."

"Not Maasai boys," he answered.

"Then he is no longer Maasai, and you can have no objection to his coming with me."

"I want to go too!" said the eight-year-old, and suddenly he, too, forced some tears down his face.

Thomas Naikosiai looked at his wife and his children—really *looked* at them—and realized that he did not know them at all. This was not the quiet maiden, raised in the traditions of his people, that he had married nine years ago. These soft sobbing boys were not the successors to Leeyo and Nelion.

He walked to the door and opened it.

"Go to the new world with the rest of the black Europeans," he growled.

"Will you come with us?" asked his oldest son.

Naikosiai turned to his wife. "I divorce you," he said coldly. "All that was between us is no more."

He walked over to his two sons. "I disown you. I am no longer your father, you are no longer my sons. Now go!"

His wife put coats and masks on both of the boys, then donned her own.

"I will send some men for my things before morning," she said.

"If any man comes onto my property, I will kill him," said Naikosiai.

She stared at him, a look of pure hatred. Then she took the children by the hands and led them out of the house and down the long road to where the ship awaited them.

Naikosiai paced the house for a few minutes, filled with nervous rage. Finally he went to the closet, donned his coat and mask, pulled out his rifle, and walked through the airlock to the front of his house. Visibility was poor, as always, and he went out to the road to see if anyone was coming.

There was no sign of any movement. He was almost disappointed. He planned to show them how a Maasai protected what was his.

And suddenly he realized that this was *not* how a Maasai protected his own. He walked to the edge of the gorge, opened the bolt, and threw his cartridges into the void one by one. Then he held the rifle over his head and hurled it after them. The coat came next, then the mask, and finally his clothes and shoes.

He went back into the house and pulled out that special trunk that held the memorabilia of a lifetime. In it he found what he was looking for: a simple piece of red cloth. He attached it at his shoulder.

Then he went into the bathroom, looking among his wife's cosmetics. It took almost half an hour to hit upon the right combinations, but when he emerged his hair was red, as if smeared with clay.

He stopped by the fireplace and pulled down the spear that hung there. Family tradition had it that the spear had once been used by Nelion himself; he wasn't sure he believed it, but it was definitely a Maasai spear, blooded many times in battle and hunts during centuries past.

Naikosiai walked out the door and positioned himself in front of his house—his *manyatta*. He planted his bare feet on the diseased ground, placed the butt of his spear next to his right foot, and stood at attention. Whatever came down the road next—a band of black Europeans hoping to rob him of his possessions, a lion out of history, a band of Nandi or Lumbwa come to slay the enemy of their blood, they would find him ready.

They returned just after sunrise the next morning, hoping to convince him to emigrate to New Kilimanjaro. What they found was the last Maasai, his lungs burst from the pollution, his dead eyes staring proudly out across the vanished savannah at some enemy only he could see.

I released the cartridge, my strength nearly gone, my emotions drained.

So that was how it had ended for Man on earth, probably less than a mile from where it had begun. So bold and so foolish, so moral and so savage. I had hoped the last artifact would prove to be the final piece of the puzzle, but instead it merely added to the mystery of this most contentious and fascinating race.

Nothing was beyond their ability to achieve. One got the feeling that the day the first primitive man looked up and saw the stars, the galaxy's days as a haven of peace and freedom were numbered. And yet they came out to the stars not just with their lusts and their hatred and their fears, but with their technology and their medicine, their heroes as well as their villains. Most of the races of the galaxy had been painted by the Creator in pastels; Men were primaries.

I had much to think about as I went off to my quarters to renew my strength. I do not know how long I lay, somnolent and unmoving, recovering my energy, but it must have been a long time, for night had come and gone before I felt prepared to rejoin the party.

As I emerged from my quarters and walked to the center of camp, I heard a yell from the direction of the gorge, and a moment later the Appraiser appeared, a large sterile bag balanced atop an air trolley.

"What have you found?" asked Bellidore, and suddenly I remembered that the Exobiologist was missing.

"I am almost afraid to guess," replied the Appraiser, laying the bag on the table.

All the members of the party gathered around as he began withdrawing items: a blood-stained communicator, bent out of shape; the floating shade, now broken, that the Exobiologist used to protect her head from the rays of the sun; a torn piece of clothing; and finally, a single gleaming white bone.

The instant the bone was placed on the table, the Mystic began screaming. We were all shocked into momentary immobility, not only because of the suddenness of her reaction, but because it was the first sign of life she had shown since joining our party. She continued to stare at the bone and scream, and finally, before we could question her or remove the bone from her sight, she collapsed.

"I don't suppose there can be much doubt about what happened," said Bellidore. "The creatures caught up with the Exobiologist somewhere on her way down the gorge and killed her."

"Probably ate . . ."

". . . her too," said the Stardust Twins.

"I am glad we are leaving today," continued Bellidore. "Even after all these millennia, the spirit of Man continues to corrupt and degrade this world. Those lumbering creatures can't possibly be predators: there are no meat animals left on Earth. But given the opportunity, they fell upon the Exobiologist and consumed her flesh. I have this uneasy feeling that if we stayed much longer, we, too, would become corrupted by this world's barbaric heritage."

The Mystic regained consciousness and began screaming again, and the Stardust Twins gently escorted her back to her quarters, where she was given a sedative.

"I suppose we might as well make it official," said Bellidore. He turned to the Historian. "Would you please check the bone with your instruments and make sure that this is the remains of the Exobiologist?"

The Historian stared at the bone, horror-stricken. "She was my *friend!*" it said at last. "I cannot touch it as if it were just another artifact."

"We must know for sure," said Bellidore. "If it is not part of the Exobiologist, then there is a chance, however slim, that your friend might still be alive."

The Historian reached out tentatively for the bone, then jerked its hand away. "I can't!"

Finally Bellidore turned to me. "He Who Views," he said. "Have you the strength to examine it?"

"Yes," I answered.

They all moved back to give me room, and I allowed my mass to slowly spread over the bone and engulf it. I assimilated its history and ingested its emotional residue, and finally I withdrew from it.

"It is the Exobiologist," I said.

"What are the funeral customs of her race?" asked Bellidore.

"Cremation," said the Appraiser.

"Then we shall build a fire and incinerate what remains of our friend, and we will each offer a prayer to send her soul along the Eternal Path."

And that is what we did.

The ship came later that day, and took us off the planet, and it is only now, safely removed from its influence, that I can reconstruct what I learned on that last morning.

I lied to Bellidore—to the entire party—for once I made my discovery I knew that my primary duty was to get them away from Earth as quickly as possible. Had I told them the truth, one or more of them would have wanted to remain behind, for they are scientists with curious, probing minds, and I would never be able to convince them that a curious, probing mind is no match for what I found in my seventh and final view of Olduvai Gorge.

The bone was *not* a part of the Exobiologist. The Historian, or even the Moriteu, would have known that had they not been too horrified to examine it. It was the tibia of a *Man*.

Man has been extinct for five thousand years, at least as we citizens of the galaxy have come to understand him. But those lumbering, ungainly creatures of the night, who seemed so attracted to our campfires, are what Man has become. Even the pollution and radiation he spread across his own planet could not kill him off. It merely changed him to the extent that we were no longer able to recognize him.

I could have told them the simple facts, I suppose: that a tribe of these pseudo-Men stalked the Exobiologist down the gorge, then attacked and killed and, yes, ate her. Predators are not unknown throughout the worlds of the galaxy.

But as I became one with the tibia, as I felt it crashing down again and again upon our companion's head and shoulders, I felt a sense of power, of exultation I had never experienced before. I suddenly seemed to see the world through the eyes of the bone's possessor. I saw how he had killed his own companion to create the weapon, I saw how he planned to plunder the bodies of the old and the infirm for more weapons, I saw visions of conquest against other tribes living near the gorge.

And finally, at the moment of triumph, he and I looked up at the sky, and we knew that someday all that we could see would be ours.

And this is the knowledge that I have lived with for two days. I do not know who to share it with, for it is patently immoral to exterminate a race simply because of the vastness of its dreams or the ruthlessness of its ambition.

But this is a race that refuses to die, and somehow I must warn the rest of us, who have lived in harmony for almost five millennia.

It's not over.

Inspiration

BEN BOVA

Ben Bova began writing fiction in the late 1940s and has become one of science fiction's most notable writers and editors, with over eighty books of fiction and nonfiction to his credit. Among his best-known novels are *Colony, The Kinsman Saga, The Exiles Trilogy, The Voyagers Trilogy,* and *Mars;* recent novels include *Death Dream* and *Orion Among the Stars.* He worked for Project Vanguard during the 1950s and was a science writer for Avco Everett Research Laboratory before becoming editor of *Analog* in 1971 and winning six Hugo Awards as best editor. From 1978 to 1982, he was editor of *Omni* magazine.

Bova has won praise for his detailed, realistic, and carefully extrapolated visions of the future. "Inspiration," a finalist for the Nebula Award, displays his gift for realism in a moving story set in an alternative past. About this story, Ben Bova writes:

"I've always been fascinated by the interplay between scientific research and science fiction. Many academic papers have been written about the influence of 'real' science on science fiction, and vice versa. Whole books have been written on the subject. It struck me that it might be interesting to try a story that explores the theme.

"I did a bit of historical research. When H. G. Wells first published *The Time Machine,* Albert Einstein was sixteen. William Thomson, newly made Lord Kelvin, was the grand old man of physics and a stern guardian of the orthodox Newtonian view of the universe. Wells's idea of considering time as a fourth dimension would have been anathema to Kelvin; but it would have lit up young Albert's imagination.

"Who knows? Perhaps Einstein was actually inspired by Wells.

"At any rate, there was the kernel of a story. But how could I get Wells, Einstein, and Kelvin together? And why? To be an effective story, there must be a fuse burning somewhere that will cause an explosion unless the protagonist acts to prevent it.

"My protagonist turned out to be a time traveler, sent on a desperate mission to the year 1896, where he finds Wells, Einstein, and Kelvin and brings them together.

"And one other person, as well."

———

He was as close to despair as only a lad of seventeen can be. "But you heard what the professor said," he moaned. "It is all finished. There is nothing left to do."

The lad spoke in German, of course. I had to translate it for Mr. Wells.

Wells shook his head. "I fail to see why such splendid news should upset the boy so."

I said to the youngster, "Our British friend says you should not lose hope. Perhaps the professor is mistaken."

"Mistaken? How could that be? He is a famous man! A nobleman! A baron!"

I had to smile. The lad's stubborn disdain for authority figures would become world-famous one day. But it was not in evidence this summer afternoon in A.D. eighteen ninety-six.

We were sitting in a sidewalk café with a magnificent view of the Danube and the city of Linz. Delicious odors of cooking sausages and bakery pastries wafted from the kitchen inside. Despite the splendid warm sunshine, though, I felt chilled and weak, drained of what little strength I had remaining.

"Where is that blasted waitress?" Wells grumbled. "We've been here half an hour, at the least."

"Why not just lean back and enjoy the afternoon, sir?" I suggested tiredly. "This is the best view in all the area."

Herbert George Wells was not a patient man. He had just scored a minor success in Britain with his first novel and had decided to treat himself to a vacation in Austria. He came to that decision under my influence, of course, but he did not yet realize that. At age twenty-nine, he had a lean, hungry look to him that would mellow only gradually with the coming years of prestige and prosperity.

Albert was round-faced and plumpish; still had his baby fat on him, although he had started a mustache as most teenaged boys did in those days. It was a thin, scraggly black wisp, nowhere near the full white brush it would become. If all went well with my mission.

It had taken me an enormous amount of maneuvering to get Wells and this teenager to the same place at the same time. The effort had nearly exhausted all my energies. Young Albert had come to see Prof. Thomson with his own eyes, of course. Wells had been more difficult; he had wanted to see Salzburg, the birthplace of Mozart. I had taken him instead to Linz, with a thousand assurances that he would find the trip worthwhile.

He complained endlessly about Linz, the city's lack of beauty, the sour smell of its narrow streets, the discomfort of our hotel, the dearth of restaurants where one could get decent food—by which he meant burnt mutton. Not even the city's justly famous *Linzertorte* pleased him. "Not as good as a decent trifle," he groused. "Not as good by half."

I, of course, knew several versions of Linz that were even less pleasing, including one in which the city was nothing more than charred radioactive rubble and the Danube so contaminated that it glowed at night all the way down to the Black Sea. I shuddered at that vision and tried to concentrate on the task at hand.

It had almost required physical force to get Wells to take a walk across the Danube on the ancient stone bridge and up the Pöstlingberg to this little sidewalk café. He had huffed with anger when we had started out from our hotel at the city's central square, then soon was puffing with exertion as we toiled up the steep hill. I was breathless from the climb also. In later years a tram would make the ascent, but on this particular afternoon we had been obliged to walk.

He had been mildly surprised to see the teenager trudging up the precipitous street just a few steps ahead of us. Recognizing that unruly crop of dark hair from the audience at Thomson's lecture that morning, Wells had graciously invited Albert to join us for a drink.

"We deserve a beer or two after this blasted climb," he said, eying me unhappily.

Panting from the climb, I translated to Albert, "Mr. Wells . . . invites you . . . to have a refreshment . . . with us."

The youngster was pitifully grateful, although he would order nothing stronger than tea. It was obvious that Thomson's lecture had shattered him badly. So now we sat on uncomfortable cast-iron chairs and waited—they for the drinks they had ordered, me for the inevitable. I let the warm sunshine soak into me and hoped it would rebuild at least some of my strength.

The view was little short of breathtaking: the brooding castle across the river, the Danube itself streaming smoothly and actually blue as it glittered in the sunlight, the lakes beyond the city, and the blue-white snow peaks of the Austrian Alps hovering in the distance like ghostly petals of some immense unworldly flower.

But Wells complained, "That has to be the ugliest castle I have ever seen."

"What did the gentleman say?" Albert asked.

"He is stricken by the sight of the Emperor Friedrich's castle," I answered sweetly.

"Ah. Yes, it has a certain grandeur to it, doesn't it?"

Wells had all the impatience of a frustrated journalist. "Where is that damnable waitress? Where is our beer?"

"I'll find the waitress," I said, rising uncertainly from my iron-hard chair. As his ostensible tour guide, I had to remain in character for a while longer, no matter how tired I felt. But then I saw what I had been waiting for.

"Look!" I pointed down the steep street. "Here comes the professor himself!"

William Thomson, First Baron Kelvin of Largs, was striding up the pavement with much more bounce and energy than any of us had shown. He was seventy-one, his silver-gray hair thinner than his impressive gray beard, lean almost to the point of looking frail. Yet he climbed the ascent that had made my heart thunder in my ears as if he were strolling amiably across some campus quadrangle.

Wells shot to his feet and leaned across the iron rail of the café. "Good afternoon, your Lordship." For a moment I thought he was going to tug at his forelock.

Kelvin squinted at him. "You were in my audience this morning, were you not?"

"Yes, m'lud. Permit me to introduce myself: I am H. G. Wells."

"Ah. You're a physicist?"

"A writer, sir."

"Journalist?"

"Formerly. Now I am a novelist."

"Really? How keen."

Young Albert and I had also risen to our feet. Wells introduced us properly and invited Kelvin to join us.

"Although I must say," Wells murmured as Kelvin came round the railing and took the empty chair at our table, "that the service here leaves quite a bit to be desired."

"Oh, you have to know how to deal with the Teutonic temperament," said Kelvin jovially as we all sat down. He banged the flat of his hand on the table so hard it made us all jump. "Service!" he bellowed. "Service here!"

Miraculously, the waitress appeared from the doorway and trod stubbornly to our table. She looked very unhappy; sullen, in fact. Sallow pouting face with brooding brown eyes and downturned mouth. She pushed back a lock of hair that had strayed across her forehead.

"We've been waiting for our beer," Wells said to her.

"And now this gentleman has joined us—"

"Permit me, sir," I said. It *was* my job, after all. In German I asked her to bring us three beers and the tea that Albert had ordered and to do it quickly.

She looked the four of us over as if we were smugglers or criminals of some sort, her eyes lingering briefly on Albert, then turned without a word or even a nod and went back inside the café.

I stole a glance at Albert. His eyes were riveted on Kelvin, his lips parted as if he wanted to speak but could not work up the nerve. He ran a hand nervously through his thick mop of hair. Kelvin seemed perfectly at ease, smiling affably, his hands laced across his stomach just below his beard; he was the man of authority, acknowledged by the world as the leading scientific figure of his generation.

"Can it be really true?" Albert blurted at last. "Have we learned everything of physics that can be learned?"

He spoke in German, of course, the only language he knew. I immediately translated for him, exactly as he asked his question.

Once he understood what Albert was asking, Kelvin nodded his gray old head sagely. "Yes, yes. The young men in the laboratories today are putting the final dots over the i's, the final crossings of the t's. We've just about finished physics; we know at last all there is to be known."

Albert looked crushed.

Kelvin did not need a translator to understand the youngster's emotion. "If you are thinking of a career in physics, young man, then I heartily advise you to think again. By the time you complete your education there will be nothing left for you to do."

"Nothing?" Wells asked as I translated. "Nothing at all?"

"Oh, add a few decimal places here and there, I suppose. Tidy up a bit, that sort of thing."

Albert had failed his admission test to the Federal Polytechnic in Zurich. He had never been a particularly good student. My goal was to get him to apply again to the Polytechnic and pass the exams.

Visibly screwing up his courage, Albert asked, "But what about the work of Roentgen?"

Once I had translated, Kelvin knit his brows. "Roentgen? Oh, you mean that report about mysterious rays that go through solid walls? X rays, is it?"

Albert nodded eagerly.

"Stuff and nonsense!" snapped the old man. "Absolute bosh. He may impress a few medical men who know little of science, but his X rays do not exist. Impossible! German daydreaming."

Albert looked at me with his whole life trembling in his piteous eyes. I interpreted:

"The professor fears that X rays may be illusory, although he does not as yet have enough evidence to decide, one way or the other."

Albert's face lit up. "Then there is hope! We have not discovered *everything* as yet!"

I was thinking about how to translate that for Kelvin when Wells ran out of patience. "Where *is* that blasted waitress?"

I was grateful for the interruption. "I will find her, sir."

Dragging myself up from the table, I left the three of them, Wells and Kelvin chatting amiably while Albert swiveled his head back and forth, understanding not a word. Every joint in my body ached and I knew that there was nothing anyone in this world could do to help me. The café was dark inside, and smelled of stale beer. The waitress was standing at the bar, speaking rapidly, angrily, to the stout barkeep in a low venomous tone. The barkeep was polishing glasses with the end of his apron; he looked grim and, once he noticed me, embarrassed.

Three seidels of beer stood on a round tray next to her, with a single glass of tea. The beers were getting warm and flat, the tea cooling, while she blistered the bartender's ears.

I interrupted her vicious monologue. "The gentlemen want their drinks," I said in German.

She whirled on me, her eyes furious. "The *gentlemen* may have their beers when they get rid of that infernal Jew!"

Taken aback somewhat, I glanced at the barkeep. He turned away from me.

"No use asking him to do it," the waitress hissed. "We do not serve Jews here. *I* do not serve Jews and neither will he!"

The café was almost empty this late in the afternoon. In the dim shadows I could make out only a pair of elderly gentlemen quietly smoking their pipes and a foursome, apparently two married couples, drinking beer. A six-year-old boy knelt at the far end of the bar, laboriously scrubbing the wooden floor.

"If it's too much trouble for you," I said, and started to reach for the tray.

She clutched at my outstretched arm. "No! No Jews will be served here! Never!"

I could have brushed her off. If my strength had not been drained away I could have broken every bone in her body and the barkeep's, too. But I was nearing the end of my tether and I knew it.

"Very well," I said softly. "I will take only the beers."

She glowered at me for a moment, then let her hand drop away. I removed the glass of tea from the tray and left it on the bar. Then I carried the beers out into the warm afternoon sunshine.

As I set the tray on our table, Wells asked, "They have no tea?"

Albert knew better. "They refuse to serve Jews," he guessed. His voice was flat, unemotional, neither surprised nor saddened.

I nodded as I said in English, "Yes, they refuse to serve Jews."

"You're Jewish?" Kelvin asked, reaching for his beer.

The teenager did not need a translation. He replied, "I was born in Germany. I am now a citizen of Switzerland. I have no religion. But, yes, I am a Jew."

Sitting next to him, I offered him my beer.

"No, no," he said with a sorrowful little smile. "It would merely upset them further. I think perhaps I should leave."

"Not quite yet," I said. "I have something that I want to show you." I reached into the inner pocket of my jacket and pulled out the thick sheaf of paper I had been carrying with me since I had started out on this mission. I noticed that my hand trembled slightly.

"What is it?" Albert asked.

I made a little bow of my head in Wells's direction. "This is my translation of Mr. Wells's excellent story, *The Time Machine.*"

Wells looked surprised, Albert curious. Kelvin smacked his lips and put his half-drained seidel down.

"Time machine?" asked young Albert.

"What's he talking about?" Kelvin asked.

I explained, "I have taken the liberty of translating Mr. Wells's story about a time machine, in the hope of attracting a German publisher."

Wells said, "You never told me—"

But Kelvin asked, "Time machine? What on earth would a time machine be?"

Wells forced an embarrassed, self-deprecating little smile. "It is merely the subject of a tale I have written, m'lud: a machine that can travel through time. Into the past, you know. Or the, uh, future."

Kelvin fixed him with a beady gaze. "Travel into the past or the future?"

"It is fiction, of course," Wells said apologetically.

"Of course."

Albert seemed fascinated. "But how could a machine travel through time? How do you explain it?"

Looking thoroughly uncomfortable under Kelvin's wilting eye, Wells said hesitantly, "Well, if you consider time as a dimension—"

"A dimension?" asked Kelvin.

"Rather like the three dimensions of space."

"Time as a fourth dimension?"

"Yes. Rather."

Albert nodded eagerly as I translated. "Time as a dimension, yes! Whenever we move through space we move through time as well, do we not? Space and time! Four dimensions, all bound together!"

Kelvin mumbled something indecipherable and reached for his half-finished beer.

"And one could travel through this dimension?" Albert asked. "Into the past or the future?"

"Utter bilge," Kelvin muttered, slamming his emptied seidel on the table. "Quite impossible."

"It is merely fiction," said Wells, almost whining. "Only an idea I toyed with in order to—"

"Fiction. Of course," said Kelvin, with great finality. Quite abruptly, he pushed himself to his feet. "I'm afraid I must be going. Thank you for the beer."

He left us sitting there and started back down the street, his face flushed. From the way his beard moved I could see that he was muttering to himself.

"I'm afraid we've offended him," said Wells.

"But how could he become angry over an idea?" Albert wondered. The thought seemed to stun him. "Why should a new idea infuriate a man of science?"

The waitress bustled across the patio to our table. "When is this Jew leaving?" she hissed at me, eyes blazing with fury. "I won't have him stinking up our café any longer!"

Obviously shaken, but with as much dignity as a seventeen-year-old could muster, Albert rose to his feet. "I will leave, madame. I have imposed on your so-gracious hospitality long enough."

"Wait," I said, grabbing at his jacket sleeve. "Take this with you. Read it. I think you will enjoy it."

He smiled at me, but I could see the sadness that would haunt his eyes forever. "Thank you, sir. You have been most kind to me."

He took the manuscript and left us. I saw him already reading it as he walked slowly down the street toward the bridge back to Linz proper. I hoped he would not trip and break his neck as he ambled down the steep street, his nose stuck in the manuscript.

The waitress watched him too. "Filthy Jew. They're everywhere! They get themselves into everything."

"That will be quite enough from you," I said as sternly as I could manage.

She glared at me and headed back for the bar.

Wells looked more puzzled than annoyed, even after I explained what had happened.

"It's their country, after all," he said, with a shrug of his narrow shoulders. "If they don't want to mingle with Jews there's not much we can do about it, is there?"

I took a sip of my warm flat beer, not trusting myself to come up with a properly polite response. There was only one timeline in which Albert lived long enough to make an effect on the world. There were dozens where he languished in obscurity or was gassed in one of the death camps.

Wells's expression turned curious. "I didn't know you had translated my story."

"To see if perhaps a German publisher would be interested in it," I lied.

"But you gave the manuscript to that Jewish fellow."

"I have another copy of the translation."

"You do? Why would you—"

My time was almost up, I knew. I had a powerful urge to end the charade. "That young Jewish fellow might change the world, you know."

Wells laughed.

"I mean it," I said. "You think that your story is merely a piece of fiction. Let me tell you, it is much more than that."

"Really?"

"Time travel will become possible one day."

"Don't be ridiculous!" But I could see the sudden astonishment in his eyes. And the memory. It was I who had suggested the idea of time travel to him. We had discussed it for months back when he had been working for the newspapers. I had kept the idea in the forefront of his imagination until he finally sat down and dashed off his novel.

I hunched closer to him, leaned my elbows wearily on the table. "Suppose Kelvin is wrong? Suppose there is much more to physics than he suspects?"

"How could that be?" Wells asked.

"That lad is reading your story. It will open his eyes to new vistas, new possibilities."

Wells cast a suspicious glance at me. "You're pulling my leg."

I forced a smile. "Not altogether. You would do well to pay attention to what the scientists discover over the coming years. You could build a career writing about it. You could become known as a prophet if you play your cards properly."

His face took on the strangest expression I had ever seen: he did not want to believe me and yet he did; he was suspicious, curious, doubtful, and yearning—all at the same time. Above everything else he was ambitious; thirsting for fame. Like every writer, he wanted to have the world acknowledge his genius.

I told him as much as I dared. As the afternoon drifted on and the shadows lengthened, as the sun sank behind the distant mountains and the warmth of day slowly gave way to an uneasy deepening chill, I gave him carefully veiled hints of the future. A future. The one I wanted him to promote.

Wells could have no conception of the realities of time travel, of course. There was no frame of reference in his tidy nineteenth-century English mind of the infinite branchings of the future. He was incapable of imagining the horrors that lay in store. How could he be? Time branches endlessly and only a few, a precious handful of those branches manage to avoid utter disaster.

Could I show him his beloved London obliterated by fusion bombs? Or the entire northern hemisphere of Earth depopulated by man-made plagues? Or a devastated world turned to a savagery that made his Morlocks seem compassionate?

Could I explain to him the energies involved in time travel or the damage they did to the human body? The fact that time travelers were volunteers sent on suicide missions, desperately trying to preserve a timeline that saved at least a portion of the human race? The best future I could offer him was a twentieth century tortured by world wars and genocide. That was the best I could do.

So all I did was hint, as gently and subtly as I could, trying to guide him toward that best of all possible futures, horrible though it would seem to him. I could neither control nor coerce anyone; all I could do was to offer a bit of guidance. Until the radiation dose from my trip through time finally killed me.

Wells was happily oblivious to my pain. He did not even notice the perspiration that beaded my brow despite the chilling breeze that heralded nightfall.

"You appear to be telling me," he said at last, "that my writings will have some sort of positive effect on the world."

"They already have," I replied, with a genuine smile.

His brows rose.

"That teenaged lad is reading your story. Your concept of time as a dimension has already started his fertile mind working."

"That young student?"

"Will change the world," I said. "For the better."

"Really?"

"Really," I said, trying to sound confident. I knew there were still a thousand pitfalls in young Albert's path. And I would not live long enough to help him past them. Perhaps others would, but there were no guarantees.

I knew that if Albert did not reach his full potential, if he were turned away by the university again or murdered in the coming holocaust, the future I was attempting to preserve would disappear in a global catastrophe that could end the human race forever. My task was to save as much of humanity as I could.

I had accomplished a feeble first step in saving some of humankind, but only a first step. Albert was reading the time-machine tale and starting to think that Kelvin was blind to the real world. But there was so much more to do. So very much more.

We sat there in the deepening shadows of the approaching twilight, Wells and I, each of us wrapped in our own thoughts about the future. Despite his best English self-control, Wells was smiling contentedly. He saw a future in which he would be hailed as a prophet. I hoped it would work out that way. It was an immense task that I had undertaken. I felt tired, gloomy, daunted by the immensity of it all. Worst of all, I would never know if I succeeded or not.

Then the waitress bustled over to our table. "Well, have you finished? Or are you going to stay here all night?"

Even without a translation Wells understood her tone. "Let's go," he said, scraping his chair across the flagstones.

I pushed myself to my feet and threw a few coins on the table. The waitress scooped them up immediately and called into the café, "Come here and scrub down this table! At once!"

The six-year-old boy came trudging across the patio, lugging the heavy wooden pail of water. He stumbled and almost dropped it; water sloshed onto his mother's legs. She grabbed him by the ear and lifted him nearly off his feet. A faint tortured squeak issued from the boy's gritted teeth.

"Be quiet and do your work properly," she told her son, her voice murderously low. "If I let your father know how lazy you are . . ."

The six-year-old's eyes went wide with terror as his mother let her threat dangle in the air between them.

"Scrub that table good, Adolf," his mother told him. "Get rid of that damned Jew's stink."

I looked down at the boy. His eyes were burning with shame and rage and hatred. Save as much of the human race as you can, I told myself. But it was already too late to save him.

"Are you coming?" Wells called to me.

"Yes," I said, tears in my eyes. "It's getting dark, isn't it?"

Virtual Love

MAUREEN F. McHUGH

Maureen F. McHugh won a James Tiptree Jr. Memorial Award, a Locus Award, and a Lambda Literary Award for her first novel, *China Mountain Zhang,* which was also a Nebula and Hugo Award finalist and was widely praised for its detailed depiction of a future dominated by China. Her second novel, *Half the Day Is Night,* was published in 1994. She has lived in Loveland, Ohio; New York City; and Shijiazhuang, China; and now lives in a suburb of Cleveland.

"Virtual Love," nominated for the Nebula, is a lively exploration of technological escapism and human loneliness. About her short story, Maureen McHugh writes:

" 'Virtual Love' was written because *Time* magazine was going to use a science fiction short story in their special issue on the millennium. My agent heard about it and sent them a portion of my second novel to give them an idea of what I wrote. They said that it was interesting, but a little too dark for them. So I wrote 'Virtual Love,' trying to be a little lighter than my usual tone. *Time* decided to go with something by Arthur C. Clarke, and I sent the story to Kris Rusch."

The thing I like best about VR is that you can do anything. Not just the obvious things like murder someone or be an archaeologist in Peru, although that's fun once in a while. But just when you're hanging out, meeting people, you can be anything you want. I have twelve different personas. Some of them, like Lilith and Marty, I don't use very often, but I like to know that they're back there and if I want to be a vamp I can put on Lilith and go to a party, wear midnight blue sequins to show off my fox red hair, drink virtual martinis—did you ever taste a real martini? Jesus!—and sway my virtual hips all I want.

Being good in VR is a talent. When anybody can be anything, the competition for attention can get pretty fierce. Everybody can have a perfect figure, perfect legs, perfect hair, perfect lips, a wardrobe worth hundreds of thousands. You've got to have an edge and the really great thing, see, is that it isn't money and it isn't the genetic hand that mother nature dealt you and it isn't the accidents of fate and disease, it's really all mind. Out there, dressed as Lilith or Alicia or Terese, it's really pure energy, just the pure flame of a mind burning like an electron candle. Electrons dancing in the light. And who can tell the dancer from the dance?

Well, I can, baby, but *you* can't and that's really the whole point, isn't it?

I have a VR system in my place. It's not the best, it's a seated system, of course. My gloves are secondhand. They're good gloves, British made, DNRs. My helmet, I paid a lot for the helmet, you have no idea what that helmet cost. It's a Mitsubishi, not the most expensive but definitely high end. It's lightweight, and that's important to me if I'm going to wear it for any length of time. I put on the gloves and then the helmet and there's this moment before the system kicks on when everything is black inside the visor and there's no sound in my ears and I'm just floating there, suspended in the pre-virtual darkness as if I'm about to be born. Just time to take a breath and then the feed hooks in.

I'm in the dressing room. It's a dingy little green room, like actors use to get ready for a play. I can see the gloves on my hands, ruby red like the slippers in the *Wizard of Oz,* but there's no face in the mirror, which is exactly right because I haven't picked one yet.

Once in a while I go out invisible. It's called lurking. When I was eighteen and I first got full access to all the boards, including the adult boards, I used to do it all the time. For a couple of years I didn't have a body, never talked to anyone. I was just watching, learning the local customs so to speak. I became a connoisseur of people's personas. I could tell when the person was different from the body they'd picked, when they were really just an eighteen-year-old kid who was trying to pass for a thirty-five-year-old Cary Grant. What I really liked was watching someone do it right, so you forgot that they weren't the person they had put on and then there'd be a bit of stage business and I'd think, "ah-hah, I see you." Because that was just what I would have done in their place.

Eventually, I couldn't stand it anymore. That's when I set up the green room. I made Sulia, first. I didn't plan to wear Sulia but I knew she was amazing. Sulia's the most into the moment of my personas. She's tall and she's got cornrows all the way down her brown back in a waterfall of hair. She's muscular and sleek and innocently feral with a beautiful open smile. I'd wear her in the green room for hours, where no one could see me, just being her. Then, when I'd pull the helmet off there would be this moment when I had to remember I was just me. And I hated it.

But I have to be really riding high to wear Sulia. I built her first and she was inspired, but I didn't wear her first.

I started with Terese. Terese is a pale wisp of a thing in a soft, flowered dress, rose and pale green like spring to go with her pale hair. Terese doesn't overpower a room, she works on it like perfume. Terese listens a lot and people confide in her. People will say the most amazing, intimate things if you let them. It was easy to be Terese because one of her traits is that she's still. People think it means that she is calm. I can be very still.

Today I think I'll do Alicia. She's the persona I wear most often anymore.

There are a bunch of things besides makeup on the desk. There's a rose in a bud vase—that's Terese. If I pick up the rose I put on Terese. I pick up a fine gold chain and I am Alicia, a sleek woman with long warm brown hair swept up in a French braid. Almost all my personas have long hair. I worry about that, but my hair is mousy brown and thin and I always wanted long hair even though it would be so much trouble. Still, I am afraid it might become part of a signature. They should all be different, all be individual.

Alicia looks back at me from the mirror, her sun brown arms bare and smooth, her little ivory silk shift simple. That's Alicia, simple and unadorned and direct.

I point with the glove and I'm moving to the door. I open the door and go out into the world.

The access is always a big lobby, with menus posted. I study the menus, skipping the games, *Illuminati, Knights Templar, Cthulu, Voodoo Horsemen, International Spy,* looking for places. *Doc's* is all right, I've been there. *The Black Hole* is fun. *Nightmare* is a dud. *Madame Stael's* is one of my favorites, so I tap the menu, and the elevator door opens. Take a deep breath in the elevator.

The elevator opens and I'm looking down a long room, something like the Hall of Mirrors in Versailles. To the left are windows looking out on a garden, to the right are huge, gilt framed mirrors, and between the mirrors are doors to Salons. I head for the café, three doors down.

"Allô, Alicia," says Paul-Michel, the bartender. "Champagne?"

"A glass of Bordeaux." Paul-Michel is an eliza program. He'll let you pour out your troubles for hours and he always remembers your name. The only problem is that if the sysop is monitoring, she hears your problems, too.

There are half a dozen people in the café; sitting by the window is a guy I've never seen before. He's a nice job, and he looks like he belongs in a French café. He's sitting, either accidentally or on purpose, where the light falls on him like a figure in a Dutch painting. Vermeer. His face is the play of light and shadow, full-lipped and dark eyed and young. The face of an angel.

He's interesting. All the men are handsome, but right now there seems to be a lot of cynical, world-weary, charming matinee idol types running the virtual scene, sometimes it's like everybody shops for faces at the same store. His face doesn't seem made up, as if it might be his real face. Not that it is, of course. But *it seems to be.* That's skill.

He smiles at me, since I'm looking at him, a bit shy. So I take my glass of red wine and sit down across from him. To move, I point my finger and my system moves me through the environment, but the interface is configured so that for anyone watching I just walk. I've programmed different walks for all my personas using a bootleg spline program; Sulia walks like a cheetah, but Alicia has a subtle walk. I like to think she looks as if she might have taken dance when she was younger. I would have liked to have taken dance.

"Hi," he says. "I'm Ian."

"Hi, Ian," I say. "Alicia."

The table top is scarred wood. Outside the day is beautiful, the sky is clear blue, and people are out on the Champs Élysées. We can't see the Eiffel Tower from the window, but we could if we were outside.

Usually people ask something like, "Do you come here a lot?" or "Are you local?" meaning is this a local call for you or are you coming through a service. I always lie and say I'm coming through a service. But he doesn't ask, instead he says, "Seems like someone sitting here should be sketching or writing a poem or something."

"Are you an artist?" I ask. But of course, I know he is. Looking at him I can see his work, he is his work.

But he shakes his head. "I like this place," he says. I don't know if he means the Salon, or the café. Or maybe this place in the window. He looks out the window and I look out. A couple is strolling by arm in arm. She is pale and red-haired, the quintessential French girl, and he is dark-skinned, looks like a sailor. They are perfect, simple, uncomplicated. He stops to tie her scarf and for a moment I wish I were her—which is odd, because at this moment I am Alicia, and I am whole and graceful. I am what I wish to be. That couple is not even real, they are window dressing, generated by the sysop, the system operator, whose name is Cassia and who I have spoken to.

I look back and Ian is looking at me. I feel embarrassed, wondering if my feelings were written on my face.

"You are quite beautiful," he says.

My chest constricts, and I feel caught out, naked. What made him say that? "Here," I say, "everyone can be beautiful." I mean it to be nice, a way of saying that it doesn't mean anything, but it comes out sounding disparaging. He blushes.

That's a really nice touch, and I wonder how he does it; my program doesn't include blushing.

"Copies of beauty aren't really beautiful," he says. "They're perfect but all alike."

"What makes real beauty?" I ask, but I already have an idea what he's going to say. Something about originality.

"In real beauty," he says, "there is always something strange, an asymmetry."

Alicia isn't asymmetrical in any way. I made her to be like a dancer. And now he has me thinking of myself as not Alicia. "I'm just not sure I understand you," I say lightly.

He shakes his head. "I don't say things very well."

"Maybe you are a poet." I am trying to smile, trying to make the appropriate noises. Trying to keep things from becoming serious.

"No," he says sharply, abrupt, "I'm not."

Sometimes conversations in the Salon are very strange, suddenly intimate, because it's not oneself that is really talking, or more, it *is* oneself which is really talking, from behind the safety of the mask.

"I haven't seen you in the Salon before," I say.

"I've been lurking," he says. "Ghosting around. I've seen you before. Can I ask you a question?"

I shrug.

"Do you have more than one persona? If I'm out of line, tell me. But there is another woman who comes here and something about her reminds me of you. An older woman in a linen dress, all patterned, with her hair pulled back?"

Kristiana. Yes, she's my persona, but of all the personas to link together, Kristiana and Alicia. They're nothing alike; Kristiana is an old wise woman, tall and strong, with her gray-white hair pulled back in a knot tied with an ocher cord. "No," I lie. "No, I'm just me."

He smiles, but he looks perplexed. And I'm thinking, thinking, when was the last time that I wore Kristiana? I don't wear her often. Almost never to the Salon. I am almost tempted to ask if he is sure he saw her at the Salon. I could lie and say I have never seen anyone like that here.

He bites his lips. "There is a quality about her, that you have . . ."

Like a rabbit in headlights I sit still and listen.

"These people are all alike, but there is something about her. She, she is . . . beautiful. Like you."

"Thank you," I say. My foolishness, I am glad I can't blush. "Do you know the people here?" I ask, and I start pointing them out, telling him about them. Yellow Eyes and Greg, Lizabeth R. I'm just distracting him. And he smiles and nods and makes the appropriate noises but when I point to someone I can feel his eyes on me.

After a while I say, "I've got to meet some friends on another board, but it was very nice talking with you. Maybe we'll meet again."

"Wait a minute," he says, "how can I get in touch with you?"

"It's a small world," I say, "we'll run into each other again."

Alicia saunters out, but I know I'm fleeing.

Back in the green room I pick up the ocher hair tie that puts on Kristiana, grave Kristiana, how is she like Alicia? Kristiana who rarely smiles, who moves slowly—not because she is old but because she is grave and deliberate. Alicia isn't like her at all.

Maybe it is just a coincidence. He is new, he's been ghosting. Or maybe it's a gesture, maybe a slip, something of Alicia crossing over into Kristiana.

I put on Alicia. She is grave, too. I always thought she had a certain dignity, but maybe there is no difference between Alicia's dignity and Kristiana's deliberateness. And maybe Terese's stillness, maybe they are all the same.

No, Sulia is different, and Lilith the vamp with her fox hair, and Stork, who swears like a truck driver and drinks virtual scotch and plays poker.

Beautiful. He said they were both beautiful. Sulia is beautiful. Even Stork, with her freckles and her broad bones, Stork is not really pretty, but *I* think she is beautiful. They are all beautiful to me.

I take off Alicia and I'm invisible in the mirror. Open the door, ghosting through the lobby to pick *Madame Stael's,* back up the elevator and ghosting, lurking to the café. To watch him, sitting in the light. To see if he can see through other people. To watch him and see through him.

The bartender, Paul-Michel, doesn't look up as I ghost through the closed door.

The chair by the window is empty. He is gone.

And I notice that the light is different, not nearly so hot and white, when he is not sitting there.

He was beautiful, too.

For days and days I am a ghost. I haunt the Salon, I sit in Cairo in white linen under slow ceiling fans, I check all the local places where he might be. Places appropriate to his taste. But how do I know his taste? No one would ever guess that the same woman who is Alicia, who loves the Salon, could also be Stork, who loves the dirty talk of the Black Hole. Or Sulia, who lives in the flash of the Metro. He could be anywhere. Like anything. Maybe he has more than one persona.

Of course he has more than one persona.

So I start to look in all sorts of places.

I find him in the Rathskeller, talking politics. I know him the moment I see him, even though now he is a long-haired radical student wearing a coat out of the French revolution. He is vivid, interesting in the way that the pale copies around him are not. His signature is instant, apparent. It is not in any one thing, this student is as different from Ian as Kristiana is from Alicia, and yet they are both so intense, so original; they have style. He is an artist. He is someone I can talk to, who will understand the things I admire.

I slip back to the lobby, ghost back into the green dressing room—and pause. Who do I have for the Rathskeller? Who can sit in a brick basement and talk politics over the sound of the band?

I pick up a man's bracelet. Marty could go there. Marty looks back at me. Marty is small, neat, a bit natty. "System," I say out loud and do something I almost never do once I have finished a persona and named it; I change Marty. Instead of his natty suit, I give him a long sharkskin coat, just a bit roughed up. And I give him glasses, the kind you can look over. I raise his temples, take a little of his hair, working fast and knowing if I make a mistake it will take too long to fix, that I might miss *him*. I give Marty a narrow braid tail of hair, a pair of knee boots. He's a mix of eras and styles, scruffy and just right for the Rathskeller. I save him as Mick, and his icon becomes the glasses.

I cross the lobby and the elevator takes forever. He will be gone, I know it. I clump down a Berlin street, seeing myself reflected in the windows, moving wrong, moving in Marty's dapper way despite Mick's heavy boots, but it's too late to fix it. Past the green-haired whores shivering in the cold, calling "Hey Brit," because they think Mick looks British. So I decide maybe I'm a bit Irish, as I'm walking, flying high on adrenaline, improvising like mad, scared and excited.

He is still there. And he doesn't even notice me come in. The white-haired girl with the snake tattoo curling up her skinny arm draws me one of those tall beers, a virtual bier. And I lean on the bar and watch the people and wait for him to notice me, to see if he will.

His eyes slide across me once without recognition. That's okay, I'm patient. I look at the posters, Marlene on the wall in her Blue Angel pose. I glance back from a worker's movement poster and his eyes are on me again—not really looking at me; he is listening to someone else. His eyes wander away. They are radical blue.

And then they come back to me; we are looking at each other.

I have made a mistake. I should have avoided him. His hair is the wild gray-black of a storm cloud, soft and full around his face. He is a master. And he can see through the mask, can see underneath me, read all the insecurities and needs out of which I build my personas.

When he is looking at me, I forget Mick, just like I forgot Alicia. I know myself, a tiny woman in a chair, held in by seat restraints, wearing a VR visor and gloves. A woman who couldn't have a treadmill because she doesn't have a leg to stand on. Flipper babies they call us when we are little, seal babies, and even though I know I should be grateful that I was born with normal arms and hands, I'm not, I'm just not. I want to be normal. He is as beautiful and terrible as an angel, one of the thrones or seraphim, many-eyed, that surround God, and in the heat of his gaze, I feel the mask melt away and I am exposed for what I really am.

I reach up for the visor, because it is the fastest way to leave, because I am going to cry.

"Wait!" he says, interrupting the conversation. "Wait, I know you!"

That is the problem, I think, but I stop.

The chair clatters behind him as he stands—the sysop of the Rathskeller is good, things like that happen here—and he comes to me. "What is your name?" he asks.

"Mick," I say.

He is tall this time, very tall, over six feet I would say. He would be tall even to Sulia, who is the tallest of my personas.

"I've been looking for you," he says. "Ever since you left the French place. I looked on Tu Do Street, from the veranda of the Continental, and left a message for you on the moon."

I was in both of those places, but I was a ghost, so no one ever told me I had any messages.

"Tell me how you get your walk," he said. "Tell me how you make your people so . . . so, how do I explain it. Not flashy. Not like me, my people are all so obvious, but yours, it took me a while to realize just how good you are. You are more than good, you're . . . you're an artist. The more I look at you, the more things I see."

I shake my head. It was a mistake to see him, he's cruel without
meaning to be, he makes me know the illusion. I should ask him
about the white light in the café, the Vermeer light, and about how
he blushes. I can't, though.

"I can't talk to you," I say.

"You can't leave," he says. He grabs my hand and I feel his hand
through the glove. I jerk away.

"I can't," I say. "It was a mistake." Everybody in the bar is looking at us, but I don't care. When I turn and walk away, he doesn't
follow me.

Up the steps and out on the street, past the green-haired hookers
shivering in their shorts. I keep watching behind me, to see if he will
follow me, but he doesn't, back to the elevator, back to the safety of
the green room. Back to sit down in the chair and take off Mick and
cry. Sit, invisible, and cry and cry. I don't know what to do.

He has killed it for me. I can't go back out there; what if I run
into him again? But what am I going to do if I can't do VR? How
am I going to give them all up? How do I spend my days, sitting in
my chair, watching the vid, doing my word processing jobs and
dumping them into the modem, not talking to anyone for days at a
time and waiting for my parents to call to break the monotony? I
hate him. I hate what he has done to my life.

You are beautiful, he said. But I knew it wasn't true.

I can't stay away from the green room. I ghost about, start a new
personality; a copy, something no one would notice. But I can't stand
it, don't want to wear it. There's no magic to it, when I put it on I
don't forget. I don't come alive. So I don't bother to save it and I
drop out of the system, go watch something on the vid.

But in a little time I'm back again, rattling around in the green
room. Nothing to do, no one to talk to. I could find a service, pay
membership fees, and pay for the minutes of time I use. He is
local, like me. I wouldn't see him if I left the local net. But I
don't make enough, not to pay my bills, and my home help who
comes in to clean. It's too expensive. I need the local boards. Like
an addict.

I don't even dare pick up the icons. I don't want a reflection in
the mirror. Just the ruby red gloves, dancing around the room.

My system tells me I have a message. Mail.

I've never gotten anything but junk mail before. Nobody knows my system address. It's him, he's a magician. I look all over the green room, ignoring the message flag in the mirror, until I find it, tiny glittering scarab, blue-black beetle, hiding near the door. He must have attached it to me when he took my hand.

Now what? I look at the bug and try to decide what to do. Ignore the message? Accept it and never read it? He'll understand silence, won't he? (But he knows my address. What do I do, pay Ma Bell and change my access line? I'll have to, and that costs money.)

So I accept the message and play it. A screen rolls down in the dressing room, flat, like a window, like the vid. It is pearl gray for a moment, transition time, waiting to be born.

The little man in the wheelchair is all head, head with a sharp, pointed chin and thinning hair and quick eyes. He's not really all head, he has a body, and short stick legs, short muscular arms. Like something out of a Velásquez painting, a dwarf.

"Hi," he says.

It's a recording so I don't have to say anything back.

He twists a bit in his chair. I am very still. I am very good at still.

"I'm gambling," he says. "I have this terrible feeling that I'm wrong. But there was this theory about Toulouse-Lautrec, that one of the reasons he could paint his characters so unsparingly was that he wasn't one of them. The other people out on the board, they are all projecting something. But I'm not. I'm not projecting myself at all."

He pauses and wipes one hand over his mouth, his shoulder rolls. I wonder what screwed him up so badly that they couldn't fix his genes? Was he like me? Did the virus that was supposed to fix his genetic material screw up, only make things worse? There aren't very many of us.

"I don't know what makes you different," he says. "Maybe you're just some kind of genius at virtual reality. But I need to talk to you." Plaintively, "There's nobody else out there who would understand, but you do.

"I think this is a mistake," says the recording. "I'm not even sure I'm going to send it. But if I do, and if you want to get in touch with me, leave a message on the moon for Sam. Hell, I don't even know your name. Alicia."

And it ends without a good-bye.

Stork. She is the only person I could wear to the moon. Someone strong, and a little brash. She fits when she strides into the Tech Bar, with its windows looking out on the lunar landscape, all stark and blasted. Stork could be a rigger on a lunar station.

He knows me as soon as he sees me. He is still tall (of course, just like I almost always have long hair; it is something he wants so badly he can't keep from putting it in). He stands up from his solitaire game, he's a blue-eyed, red-haired Viking in a jumpsuit; it says "Sam" on the patch.

"Hi, Sam," I say. "I'm Stork. I think maybe your Toulouse-Lautrec theory is right." Not that I really do. I don't think I'm less likely than anyone else to project, any more objective than anyone else. But maybe people like Sam and me, we spend more time. We refine our art. "I want to ask you a bunch of stuff. Like how do you blush?"

Stork is like that, kind of in your face.

He doesn't say anything for a long moment. And then he laughs, a deep, big man belly laugh. I want to know how he does that, too.

"You are beautiful," he says.

None So Blind

JOE HALDEMAN

Joe Haldeman won a 1993 Nebula Award for his short story "Graves," which also won a World Fantasy Award. Among his other honors are Nebula Awards for his first science fiction novel, *The Forever War,* and his novella "The Hemingway Hoax"; three Hugo Awards; and two Rhysling Awards for his poetry. His books include *War Year, All My Sins Remembered, Tool of the Trade, Buying Time,* and his Worlds trilogy. His latest novel is *1968,* and another novel, *Forever Peace,* will soon be published. He divides his time between Florida and Cambridge, Massachusetts, where he teaches during the fall term at the Massachusetts Institute of Technology.

Of his Nebula Award finalist "None So Blind," which was honored with a Hugo Award, Joe Haldeman writes:

" 'None So Blind' was one of those ideas that just hang around waiting to be written. For about five years I had a note up on my bulletin board asking, 'Since so much of the brain is given over to processing visual information, why don't blind people take advantage of the unused gray matter and become geniuses?' I only write one or two short stories a year, so the idea gathered dust until a friend asked me to write a story for an anthology. I cranked it out and sent it to him. He didn't want it, though, so it wound up in *Asimov's.*

"The story has some personal meaning: my wife and I worked with the blind for several years when we lived in Daytona Beach, Florida, where the Library of Congress has a regional center for recording talking books. I recorded a number of my novels and hundreds of other things, from *Oedipus the King* to knitting instructions. I have a lot of admiration for the way blind people cope, and that's part of what this story's about."

I t all started when Cletus Jefferson asked himself, "Why aren't all blind people geniuses?" Cletus was only thirteen at the time, but it was a good question, and he would work on it for fourteen more years, and then change the world forever.

Young Jefferson was a polymath, an autodidact, a nerd literally without peer. He had a chemistry set, a microscope, a telescope, and several computers, some of them bought with paper route money. Most of his income was from education, though: teaching his class-mates not to draw to inside straights.

Not even nerds, not even nerds who are poker players nonpareil, not even nerdish poker players who can do differential equations in their heads, are immune to Cupid's darts and the sudden storm of testosterone that will accompany those missiles at the age of thirteen. Cletus knew that he was ugly and his mother dressed him funny. He was also short and pudgy and could not throw a ball in any direction. None of this bothered him until his ductless glands started cooking up chemicals that weren't in his chemistry set.

So Cletus started combing his hair and wearing clothes that mis-matched according to fashion, but he was still short and pudgy and irregular of feature. He was also the youngest person in his school, even though he was a senior—and the only black person there, which was a factor in Virginia in 1994.

Now if love were sensible, if the sexual impulse was ever tem-pered by logic, you would expect that Cletus, being Cletus, would assess his situation and go off in search of someone homely. But of course he didn't. He just jingled and clanked down through the Pachinko machine of adolescence, being rejected, at first glance, by every Mary and Judy and Jenny and Veronica in Known Space, going from the ravishing to the beautiful to the pretty to the cute to the plain to the "great personality," until the irresistible force of statistics brought him finally into contact with Amy Linderbaum, who could not reject him at first glance because she was blind.

The other kids thought it was more than amusing. Besides being blind, Amy was about twice as tall as Cletus and, to be kind, equally irregular of feature. She was accompanied by a guide dog who looked remarkably like Cletus, short and black and pudgy. Everybody was polite to her because she was blind and rich, but she was a new transfer student and didn't have any actual friends.

So along came Cletus, to whom Cupid had dealt only slings and arrows, and what might otherwise have been merely an opposites-attract sort of romance became an emotional and intellectual union that, in the next century, would power a social tsunami that would irreversibly transform the human condition. But first there was the violin.

Her classmates had sensed that Amy was some kind of nerd herself, as classmates will, but they hadn't figured out what kind yet. She was pretty fast with a computer, but you could chalk that up to being blind and actually needing the damned thing. She wasn't fanatical about it, nor about science or math or history or *Star Trek* or student government, so what the hell kind of nerd was she? It turns out that she was a music nerd, but at the time was too painfully shy to demonstrate it.

All Cletus cared about, initially, was that she lacked those pesky Y chromosomes and didn't recoil from him: in the Venn diagram of the human race, she was the only member of that particular set. When he found out that she was actually smart as well, having read more books than most of her classmates put together, romance began to smolder in a deep and permanent place. That was even before the violin.

Amy liked it that Cletus didn't play with her dog and was straightforward in his curiosity about what it was like to be blind. She could assess people pretty well from their voices: after one sentence, she knew that he was young, black, shy, nerdly, and not from Virginia. She could tell from his inflection that either he was unattractive or he thought he was. She was six years older than him and white and twice his size, but otherwise they matched up pretty well, and they started keeping company in a big way.

Among the few things that Cletus did not know anything about was music. That the other kids wasted their time memorizing the words to inane top-40 songs was proof of intellectual dysfunction if not actual lunacy. Furthermore, his parents had always been fanatical devotees of opera. A universe bounded on one end by puerile mumblings about unrequited love and on the other by foreigners screaming in agony was not a universe that Cletus desired to explore. Until Amy picked up her violin.

They talked constantly. They sat together at lunch and met between classes. When the weather was good, they sat outside before and after school and talked. Amy asked her chauffeur to please be ten or fifteen minutes late picking her up.

So after about three weeks' worth of the fullness of time, Amy asked Cletus to come over to her house for dinner. He was a little hesitant, knowing that her parents were rich, but he was also curious about that lifestyle and, face it, was smitten enough that he would have walked off a cliff if she asked him nicely. He even used some computer money to buy a nice suit, a symptom that caused his mother to grope for the Valium.

The dinner at first was awkward. Cletus was bewildered by the arsenal of silverware and all the different kinds of food that didn't look or taste like food. But he had known it was going to be a test, and he always did well on tests, even when he had to figure out the rules as he went along.

Amy had told him that her father was a self-made millionaire; his fortune had come from a set of patents in solid-state electronics. Cletus had therefore spent a Saturday at the university library, first searching patents and then reading selected texts, and he was ready at least for the father. It worked very well. Over soup, the four of them talked about computers. Over the calamari cocktail, Cletus and Mr. Linderbaum had it narrowed down to specific operating systems and partitioning schemata. With the beef Wellington, Cletus and "Call-me-Lindy" were talking quantum electrodynamics; with the salad they were on an electron cloud somewhere, and by the time the nuts were served, the two nuts at that end of the table were talking in Boolean algebra while Amy and her mother exchanged knowing sighs and hummed snatches of Gilbert and Sullivan.

By the time they retired to the music room for coffee, Lindy liked Cletus very much, and the feeling was mutual, but Cletus didn't know how much he liked Amy, *really* liked her, until she picked up the violin.

It wasn't a Strad—she was promised one if and when she graduated from Juilliard—but it had cost more than the Lamborghini in the garage, and she was not only worth it, but equal to it. She picked it up and tuned it quietly while her mother sat down at an electronic keyboard next to the grand piano, set it to "harp," and began the simple arpeggio that a musically sophisticated person would recognize as the introduction to the violin showpiece *Méditation* from Massenet's *Thaïs*.

Cletus had turned a deaf ear to opera for all his short life, so he didn't know the back story of transformation and transcending love behind this intermezzo, but he did know that his girlfriend had lost her sight at the age of five, and the next year—the year he was born!—was given her first violin. For thirteen years she had been using it to say what she would not say with her voice, perhaps to see what she could not see with her eyes, and on the deceptively simple romantic matrix that Massenet built to present the beautiful courtesan Thaïs gloriously reborn as the bride of Christ, Amy forgave her Godless universe for taking her sight, and praised it for what she was given in return, and she said this in a language that even Cletus could understand. He didn't cry very much, never had, but by the last high wavering note he was weeping into his hands, and he knew that if she wanted him, she could have him forever, and oddly enough, considering his age and what eventually happened, he was right.

He would learn to play the violin before he had his first doctorate, and during a lifetime of remarkable amity they would play together for ten thousand hours, but all of that would come after the big idea. The big idea—"Why aren't all blind people geniuses?"—was planted that very night, but it didn't start to sprout for another week.

Like most thirteen-year-olds, Cletus was fascinated by the human body, his own and others, but his study was more systematic than others' and, atypically, the organ that interested him most was the brain.

The brain isn't very much like a computer, although it doesn't do a bad job, considering that it's built by unskilled labor and programmed more by pure chance than anything else. One thing computers do a lot better than brains, though, is what Cletus and Lindy had been talking about over their little squids in tomato sauce: partitioning.

Think of the computer as a big meadow of green pastureland, instead of a little dark box full of number-clogged things that are expensive to replace, and that pastureland is presided over by a wise old magic shepherd who is not called a macroprogram. The shepherd stands on a hill and looks out over the pastureland, which is full of sheep and goats and cows. They aren't all in one homogenous mass, of course, since the cows would step on the lambs and kids and the goats would make everybody nervous, leaping and butting, so there are *partitions* of barbed wire that keep all the species separate and happy.

This is a frenetic sort of meadow, though, with cows and goats and sheep coming in and going out all the time, moving at about

3×10^8 meters per second, and if the partitions were all of the same size it would be a disaster, because sometimes there are no sheep at all, but lots of cows, who would be jammed in there hip to hip and miserable. But the shepherd, being wise, knows ahead of time how much space to allot to the various creatures and, being magic, can move barbed wire quickly without hurting himself or the animals. So each partition winds up marking a comfortable-sized space for each use. Your computer does that, too, but instead of barbed wire you see little rectangles or windows or file folders, depending on your computer's religion.

The brain has its own partitions, in a sense. Cletus knew that certain physical areas of the brain were associated with certain mental abilities, but it wasn't a simple matter of "music appreciation goes over there; long division in that corner." The brain is mushier than that. For instance, there are pretty well-defined partitions associated with linguistic functions, areas named after French and German brain people. If one of those areas is destroyed, by stroke or bullet or flung frying pan, the stricken person may lose the ability—reading or speaking or writing coherently—associated with the lost area.

That's interesting, but what is more interesting is that the lost ability sometimes comes back over time. Okay, you say, so the brain grew back—but it doesn't! You're born with all the brain cells you'll ever have. (Ask any child.) What evidently happens is that some part of the brain has been sitting around as a kind of backup, and after a while the wiring gets rewired and hooked into that backup. The afflicted person can say his name, and then his wife's name, and then "frying pan," and before you know it he's complaining about hospital food and calling a divorce lawyer.

So on that evidence, it would appear that the brain has a shepherd like the computer-meadow has, moving partitions around, but alas, no. Most of the time when some part of the brain ceases to function, that's the end of it. There may be acres and acres of fertile ground lying fallow right next door, but nobody in charge to make use of it—at least not consistently. The fact that it sometimes *did* work is what made Cletus ask, "Why aren't all blind people geniuses?"

Of course there have always been great thinkers and writers and composers who were blind (and in the twentieth century, some painters to whom eyesight was irrelevant), and many of them, like

Amy with her violin, felt that their talent was a compensating gift. Cletus wondered whether there might be a literal truth to that, in the micro-anatomy of the brain. It didn't happen every time, or else all blind people *would* be geniuses. Perhaps it happened occasionally, through a mechanism like the one that helped people recover from strokes. Perhaps it could be made to happen.

Cletus had been offered scholarships at both Harvard and MIT, but he opted for Columbia, in order to be near Amy while she was studying at Juilliard. Columbia reluctantly allowed him a triple major in physiology, electrical engineering, and cognitive science, and he surprised everybody who knew him by doing only moderately well. The reason, it turned out, was that he was treating undergraduate work as a diversion at best; a necessary evil at worst. He was racing ahead of his studies in the areas that were important to him.

If he had paid more attention in trivial classes like history, like philosophy, things might have turned out differently. If he had paid attention to literature he might have read the story of Pandora.

Our own story now descends into the dark recesses of the brain. For the next ten years the main part of the story, which we will try to ignore after this paragraph, will involve Cletus doing disturbing intellectual tasks like cutting up dead brains, learning how to pronounce cholecystokinin, and sawing holes in people's skulls and poking around inside with live electrodes.

In the other part of the story, Amy also learned how to pronounce cholecystokinin, for the same reason that Cletus learned how to play the violin. Their love grew and mellowed, and at the age of nineteen, between his first doctorate and his M.D., Cletus paused long enough for them to be married and have a whirlwind honeymoon in Paris, where Cletus divided his time between the musky charms of his beloved and the sterile cubicles of Institute Marey, learning how squids learn things, which was by serotonin pushing adenylate cyclase to catalyze the synthesis of cyclic adenosine monophosphate in just the right place, but that's actually the main part of the story, which we have been trying to ignore, because it gets pretty gruesome.

They returned to New York, where Cletus spent eight years becoming a pretty good neurosurgeon. In his spare time he tucked away a doctorate in electrical engineering. Things began to converge.

At the age of thirteen, Cletus had noted that the brain used more cells collecting, handling, and storing visual images than it used for all the other senses combined. "Why aren't all blind people geniuses?" was just a specific case of the broader assertion, "The brain doesn't know how to make use of what it's got." His investigations over the next fourteen years were more subtle and complex than that initial question and statement, but he did wind up coming right back around to them.

Because the key to the whole thing was the visual cortex.

When a baritone saxophone player has to transpose sheet music from cello, he (few women are drawn to the instrument) merely pretends that the music is written in treble clef rather than bass, eyeballs it up an octave, and then plays without the octave key pressed down. It's so simple a child could do it, if a child wanted to play such a huge, ungainly instrument. As his eye dances along the little fence posts of notes, his fingers automatically perform a one-to-one transformation that is the theoretical equivalent of adding and subtracting octaves, fifths, and thirds, but all of the actual mental work is done when he looks up in the top right corner of the first page and says, "Aw hell. Cello again." Cello parts aren't that interesting to saxophonists.

But the eye is the key, and the visual cortex is the lock. When blind Amy "sight-reads" for the violin, she has to stop playing and feel the Braille notes with her left hand. (Years of keeping the instrument in place while she does this has made her neck muscles so strong that she can crack a walnut between her chin and shoulder.) The visual cortex is not involved, of course; she "hears" the mute notes of a phrase with her fingertips, temporarily memorizing them, and then plays them over and over until she can add that phrase to the rest of the piece.

Like most blind musicians, Amy had a very good "ear"; it actually took her less time to memorize music by listening to it repeatedly, rather than reading, even with fairly complex pieces. (She used Braille nevertheless for serious work, so she could isolate the composer's intent from the performer's or conductor's phrasing decisions.)

She didn't really miss being able to sight-read in a conventional way. She wasn't even sure what it would be like, since she had never seen sheet music before she lost her sight, and in fact had only a vague idea of what a printed page of writing looked like.

So when her father came to her in her thirty-third year and offered to buy her the chance of a limited gift of sight, she didn't immediately jump at it. It was expensive and risky and grossly deforming: implanting miniaturized video cameras in her eyesockets and wiring them up to stimulate her dormant optic nerves. What if it made her only half blind, but also blunted her musical ability? She knew how other people read music, at least in theory, but after a quarter-century of doing without the skill, she wasn't sure that it would do much for her. It might make her tighten up.

Besides, most of her concerts were done as charities to benefit organizations for the blind or for special education. Her father argued that she would be even more effective in those venues as a recovered blind person. Still she resisted.

Cletus said he was cautiously for it. He said he had reviewed the literature and talked to the Swiss team who had successfully done the implants on dogs and primates. He said he didn't think she would be harmed by it even if the experiment failed. What he didn't say to Amy or Lindy or anybody was the grisly Frankensteinian truth: that he was himself behind the experiment; that it had nothing to do with restoring sight; that the little video cameras would never even be hooked up. They were just an excuse for surgically removing her eyeballs.

Now a normal person would have extreme feelings about popping out somebody's eyeballs for the sake of science, and even more extreme feelings on learning that it was a husband wanting to do it to his wife. Of course Cletus was far from being normal in any respect. To his way of thinking, those eyeballs were useless vestigial appendages that blocked surgical access to the optic nerves, which would be his conduits through the brain to the visual cortex. *Physical* conduits, through which incredibly tiny surgical instruments would be threaded. But we have promised not to investigate that part of the story in detail.

The end result was not grisly at all. Amy finally agreed to go to Geneva, and Cletus and his surgical team (all as skilled as they were unethical) put her through three twenty-hour days of painstaking but painless microsurgery, and when they took the bandages off and adjusted a thousand-dollar wig (for they'd had to go in behind as well as through the eyesockets), she actually looked more attractive than when they had started. That was partly because her actual hair had always been a disaster. And now she had glass baby-blues instead of the rather scary opalescence of her natural eyes. No Buck Rogers TV cameras peering out at the world.

He told her father that that part of the experiment hadn't worked, and the six Swiss scientists who had been hired for the purpose agreed.

"They're lying," Amy said. "They never intended to restore my sight. The sole intent of the operations was to subvert the normal functions of the visual cortex in such a way as to give me access to the unused parts of my brain." She faced the sound of her husband's breathing, her blue eyes looking beyond him. "You have succeeded beyond your wildest expectations."

Amy had known this as soon as the fog of drugs from the last operation had lifted. Her mind started making connections, and those connections made connections, and so on at a geometrical rate of growth. By the time they had finished putting her wig on, she had reconstructed the entire microsurgical procedure from her limited readings and conversations with Cletus. She had suggestions as to improving it, and was eager to go under and submit herself to further refinement.

As to her feelings about Cletus, in less time than it takes to read about it, she had gone from horror to hate to understanding to renewed love, and finally to an emotional condition beyond the ability of any merely natural language to express. Fortunately, the lovers did have Boolean algebra and propositional calculus at their disposal.

Cletus was one of the few people in the world she *could* love, or even talk to one-on-one, without condescending. His IQ was so high that its number would be meaningless. Compared to her, though, he was slow, and barely literate. It was not a situation he would tolerate for long.

The rest is history, as they say, and anthropology, as those of us left who read with our eyes must recognize every minute of every day. Cletus was the second person to have the operation done, and he had to accomplish it while on the run from medical ethics people and their policemen. There were four the next year, though, and twenty the year after that, and then two thousand and twenty thousand. Within a decade, people with purely intellectual occupations had no choice, or one choice: lose your eyes or lose your job. By then the "secondsight" operation was totally automated, totally safe.

It's still illegal in most countries, including the United States, but who is kidding whom? If your department chairman is secondsighted and you are not, do you think you'll get tenure? You can't even hold a conversation with a creature whose synapses fire six times as fast as yours, with whole encyclopedias of information instantly available. You are, like me, an intellectual throwback.

You may have a good reason for it, being a painter, an architect, a naturalist, or a trainer of guide dogs. Maybe you can't come up with the money for the operation, but that's a weak excuse, since it's trivially easy to get a loan against future earnings. Maybe there's a good medical reason for you not to lie down on that table and open your eyes for the last time.

I know Cletus and Amy through music. I was her keyboard professor once, at Juilliard, though now of course I'm not smart enough to teach her anything. They come to hear me play sometimes, in this rundown bar with its band of aging firstsight musicians. Our music must seem boring, obvious, but they do us the favor of not joining in.

Amy was an innocent bystander in this sudden evolutionary explosion. And Cletus was, arguably, blinded by love.

The rest of us have to choose which kind of blindness to endure.

Fortyday

DAMON KNIGHT

The Grand Master Nebula Award is given to a living writer for a lifetime of achievement. It is appropriate that, thirty years after the founding of SFWA, this honor should go to Damon Knight, SFWA's founder and its first president; but Damon Knight has done much more for science fiction than create an organization of its writers. He has contributed to the field as an editor, short fiction writer, novelist, critic, and as a teacher and discoverer of new talent.

Damon Knight was born in 1922 and grew up in Hood River, Oregon. By 1941, he was living in New York City, where he became a member of the Futurians, a group of aspiring science fiction writers that included such notable figures as Isaac Asimov, Cyril Kornbluth, Robert A. W. Lowndes, Donald A. Wollheim, James Blish, Judith Merril, and Frederik Pohl. (Knight has written about this period of his life in his 1977 memoir *The Futurians*.) Throughout the forties and fifties, he worked as an editor while honing his own considerable talents as a writer.

The Science Fiction Encyclopedia says about Knight that he "made his initial strong impact on the field as a book reviewer, and is generally acknowledged to have been the first outstanding genre-SF critic. . . . [He] reviewed books for a number of amateur and professional magazines . . . expressing throughout a sane and consistent insistence on the relevance of literary standards to SF." *In Search of Wonder,* a collection of Knight's reviews published in the fifties, won a Hugo Award.

Knight was to become one of the finest short story writers science fiction has produced. One of his most famous stories, the humorous but dark "To Serve Man," was adapted for television on Rod Serling's *Twilight Zone.* Other classic Knight tales include "The Country of the Kind," "Stranger Station," "Thing of Beauty," "The Handler," and "Masks." Knight is also an accomplished novelist; among his novels are *A for Anything, Beyond the Barrier, The World and Thorinn, The Man in the Tree, CV, The Observers, A Reasonable World,* and *Why Do Birds.* A new novel, *Humpty Dumpty,* will soon be published.

If Damon Knight's reputation rested solely on his fiction, his place in science fiction would be secure, but he has also been an extremely influential editor. His *Orbit* series of original anthologies, published from 1966 to 1980, showcased some of the finest work of Kate Wilhelm (Knight's wife since 1963), R. A. Lafferty, and Gene Wolfe, along with notable early work by Gardner Dozois, Joan D. Vinge, George Alec Effinger, Jack Dann, and Kim Stanley Robinson. (Writers submitting work to *Orbit* could learn a lot from Knight's concise and always pointed criticisms.) He has also edited a number of reprint anthologies, among them *A Century of Science Fiction, Thirteen French Science Fiction Stories* (for which he was also translator), *Cities of Wonder, A Science Fiction Argosy, The Golden Road, Science Fiction of the Thirties,* and *Nebula Award Stories 1965,* the first Nebula Awards anthology.

With Judith Merril and James Blish, Knight founded the Milford Science Fiction Writers' Workshop in 1956. This workshop was held annually for over twenty years and eventually led to the Clarion Workshop in Science Fiction and Fantasy, where many of the genre's best writers of the seventies, eighties, and nineties were trained; Damon Knight and Kate Wilhelm taught at Clarion for twenty-seven years. With such accomplishments to Knight's credit, Barry N. Malzberg has written that "a good case could be made for Damon Knight's being the most important literary figure to come out of science fiction to date."

"Fortyday," published in 1994 and included here, is a fine example of this Grand Master's gifts. About this story, Damon Knight has the following to say:

"In the window of a Hindu shop in Dublin I saw a long varnished board with about twenty painted Play-Doh figures arranged on it in a long arc, starting with a newborn child, then a toddler, a series of larger and larger schoolboys, then a series of young men getting thicker and balder as they became men of mature years, then old men, and finally a skeletal oldster on his deathbed. And I thought, isn't that terribly inefficient? Why wouldn't it be better if we grew older for forty years and then younger for forty more? (The subject was of interest to me because I was seventy at the time.) When we got back in the car I started making notes. At first I thought the story was going to be about two lovers, how their relationship changed from the time she was growing older and he younger, et cetera, but then when I got home I saw that it had to be the grandmother's story. Then I worked out what happened to the physical mass of people and plants as they dwindled. (What happens to the lost mass when people starve?) Most animals other than caged pets would not live long enough to dwindle to nothing; they would be eaten by predators first, just as they are in this world.

But human beings would be ceremonially cradled and kept alive in their second infancy—a nuisance, but much easier to handle than the senescent and terminally ill.

"The other part of this came from the same trip, when we visited the Roman villa at Fishbourne in Sussex. Some of the rooms have the mosaic floors almost intact. There is a sample or two of Roman furniture, so slender and light that it would look natural on a lawn. We saw the surviving parts of the hypocaust, the buried pipes that carried heat from the furnace under the floors. This was a first-century villa, like the one in the story, but I put mine in Tuscany because I wanted it to be closer to the latest news from Jerusalem.

"This is a what-if story, and the question is, what would history be like if a rebel like Jesus arose in one of the branches of this imaginary timeline? In order to answer the question, like any scientist trying to change only one thing at a time, I had to choose a branch that resembled the real first-century Rome as much as possible. It's true that that branch is improbable, but so are all the other branches, and your life is just as unlikely as Drusilla's, no more and no less."

Drusilla awoke in the little bed at the foot of the big bed, the matrimonial bed that she had occupied with three husbands, two of them at the same time. The lamp was smoking; she felt thick-headed, as she usually did in the mornings now. What had she forgotten? Oh, yes—this was to be her son's fortyday.

Her bladder was full. She put her feet down on the cold tiles, crossed to the commode and sat there; it was almost too high for her, but there was another, a little one, beside it. That was her future.

When she stood up and turned around, the stranger was standing just outside the lamplight. "Does it distress you that your son Rufus is older than you are?" he said.

"He is not older."

"Taller, then."

"He was always taller."

He looked at her. "Does it distress you that you now look like a child of ten?"

"Yes, but it's natural."

"If it's natural, why should it distress you?"

"Why do you keep asking these questions?"

But he was gone, and Numilia was coming in. The slave's hands were empty; where were the little gift baskets? "Are there no visitors today?" Drusilla asked. She was still not quite awake.

"Rufus is seeing the clients, by his order. He told me to tell you last night, but you were sleeping so nicely."

Drusilla said nothing for a moment. "I can have you thrashed."

"Oh, mistress, forgive me." Smiling, the slave made an exaggerated gesture of terror.

"Get out."

Numilia retreated, with a gleam of satisfied malice in her eye. Drusilla's reign as mistress of the house was over, the slave had just reminded her; well, she knew that, but Rufus could have waited one more day.

She took off the gown she had slept in and put on a clean one, and a cloak because the morning was cool. Perhaps she would dress herself from now on; she had noticed lately that she was embarrassed to let even a slave look at her boy's breasts and her downy pubis like the head of a chick.

She opened the door and went out into the colonnade. The farther half of the enclosed garden lay in deep shadow; in the nearer half, the trees and statues were glimmering with dew.

It was about the second hour; a thread of smoke rose from the kitchen. A few slaves were moving about on errands; the rest stood or squatted in the colonnade, waiting for orders.

Three sharecrop farmers, led by a slave, emerged from the atrium and started around the colonnade toward Rufus's room. Drusilla returned their greetings, but when two more appeared, she crossed the garden hurriedly to the passage beyond the kitchen, opened the outer door and went into the courtyard. She walked past the kitchen garden and the compost heap covered with the stalks of the summer's harvest, then past the dormitory, the kennels and stables, to the swine pen where a dozen shoats ran up to greet her.

Then across the dark creaking bridge, hearing the unseen water talking to itself underneath, and up again, a long uphill stride into the listening silence of the pines. From here she could look out over the meadows and the dawn-rimmed Etruscan hills, a view that always gave her pleasure.

The elder of her first two husbands had planted most of these trees; wood was the estate's chief source of income now, grapes and olives next, then the pottery and the sheep and swine, and their little plot of wheat last.

A bird called, clear and cold, somewhere up in the branches; then another.

Without turning her head she knew that the stranger was standing beside her. "Tell me," he said, "what happens to birds? Do they go back into the egg?"

"Don't you know? When they are too small to fly, other animals eat them. Except the swallow that buries itself in the mud until it is reborn in the spring."

"Where did you learn that?"

"Everybody knows it."

He was gone, and she felt lightheaded, perhaps because she had been angry before, or because she wanted her breakfast. A fragment of verse was drifting through her mind:

> The swallow tunnels in the mire;
> Shall I prefer the water, or the fire?
> Speak, Muses . . .

She turned to go down the hill, and after a few steps found that she had broken into a run without meaning to. It was indecorous at her age, but perhaps no one would see her, and after all, what if they did? The exercise warmed her and made her limbs supple; she was smiling when she reached the bottom.

In part of the kitchen garden, where beanstalks among the scattered straws had begun their retreat into the earth, slaves were putting up trestle tables. She watched them a moment, then entered the house and went to the larder.

As she emerged carrying her herbs and spices, Thessalus the cook came out into the colonnade in his soiled gown and burst into a complaint, "Lady, no 'elp good in kitchen. 'Ow I do?—"

"Oh, for heaven's sake, talk in Greek. You sound like an owl."

He said with dignity, "You asked me before not to speak Greek to you, in order to practice my Latin which offends you, but as you wish, it doesn't matter, I only want to say that these swineherds are of no use in the kitchen and only hinder me. I have asked you to buy another kitchen helper, but I really need two. It is bad enough on ordinary days, but now, when we are at heads and tails getting ready for the banquet . . ."

"Is the bread doughy again?"

He glared at her. "The bread? He is trying hard to make it better. It is good bread. It is not yet excellent, but he is doing his best, mistress. Please don't begin that again. I will see to it that he does his best."

"See that you do yours, too."

The cook turned with a muttered exclamation and hurled himself into the kitchen, where she heard him shouting at the other slaves. She moved off down the colonnade toward the front of the house.

She had sent a message nine days ago to a neighbor, asking for the loan of his cook, and he had agreed, but there was some difficulty—the slave was ill, and might not be able to come. But she could hardly tell Thessalus all that without seeming to apologize.

On the way to the atrium she looked in for a moment on her last husband, Quinctius, who lay red and wrinkled on the folded cloth in his basket. A pregnant young slave, kneeling beside him with a fly-whisk, watched her without speaking. She reminded herself to speak to Rufus later: was the child his, and would he raise or expose it when it was born?

In the corner gleamed the seated life-size carving of Priapus, where Quinctius would go when he was small enough to rest in the hollow at the tip of the god's erect wooden pizzle.

It was understood that Calpurnia would do the honors, making it possible for Quinctius to be reborn as her next child. It was not considered likely that she would have another child, but the alternative would be a slave or a prostitute. At any rate, Calpurnia might enjoy the god's phallus well smeared with goose grease; she complained often enough that she never saw Rufus's.

The arms and legs of the little red person moved feebly; his eyes were closed, those fierce eyes; his mouth opened and shut, but there was no sound. That was better; for almost six months he had roared incessantly, and nothing could be done to soothe him.

She had been fifty-one when they married, and he fifty-six, a man in his full strength. For ten years he had astonished her with his vigor in bed. It was the best time for both of them, because they were both past forty and growing younger. When the ten years were over, she had been to all appearance a young matron not yet twenty, he a youth of fourteen.

After that they had another few years of tender dalliance, gradually more condescending on her part. Then the last years came, and they were difficult for him, especially so because of all the trouble he had with his teeth. She had borne his rages as best she could; after a time he seemed to forget who he was, and ran and shouted with the children. Now she visited him several times a day; she felt that she could talk to him in his stillness as she never had been able to do when he was moving about.

Of her first two husbands, one had been older than she and one younger. Portius, the younger one, had suffered an affliction in his right arm just before he turned forty; afterward, instead of healing he died and was cremated; it was a great disgrace to the family and his name was not spoken.

Behind her the stranger said, "Do you wish things were otherwise? Would it be better to die as Portius did, without warning?"

"No, of course not. Death is for animals." The slave glanced up incuriously, then returned her attention to the fly-whisk.

"There are accidents," he said, "and soldiers sometimes die in battle."

"That's different. Soldiers try not to kill each other, but they know the risk they take."

"But you, you take no risk. You know what's going to happen and when."

"Yes. Don't you?"

"Oh, no. In my country, no one grows young after forty. We all grow older instead, until we are so sick that we die. But no man knows the day and hour."

"How absurd! Wasteful, too. Why do you stand for it?"

There was no reply; he was gone again.

In the atrium, smoke was going everywhere except through the hole in the roof. She arranged her offerings before the little household goddess in her niche, and lighted the incense with a twig from the fire. When she left, slaves were coming in with ladders and pails to clean the blackened frescoes on the ceiling, although the smoke was so dense that they could barely see.

It was now the third hour, and slaves and children were gathering around the sunlit garden to watch the priest's two assistants putting stakes in the ground to build the Janus hut.

It was always the same, a round hut of wattle roofed with straw, with a hide curtain for a door. There was nothing especially mysterious about it, in Drusilla's view, but only those dedicated to Janus could build it or take it down.

The last of the clients were coming out of Rufus's room now. She went into the family dining room, where slaves were laying the table for breakfast; she sat down and took some bread and olives. Presently Rufus's wife Calpurnia entered with her two children and their nanny, and finally Rufus himself, who sat down and helped himself to cheese with a great stir. "You might have waited," he said to Drusilla when he saw her eating.

"So might you," she said.

Rufus took a bite and chewed, staring at her, then rose from his chair and walked around the table. "Get up," he said to his daughter Prima, who was sitting beside Drusilla. Rufus sat down in the vacated chair (Prima meanwhile giving him a reproachful glance), and said, "Mother, we've got to live together in this house, and it's better to have an understanding."

"Yes," she said.

"There can't be two masters."

"No."

"But I'll ask your advice whenever I need it, and you can be of great help to me, as long as you understand. Is it agreed?"

"Yes, Rufus."

"Good, then." He leaned nearer and said, "Give me just a word before the ceremony. After all, you're my mother. How much does it really hurt?"

She kept her mouth closed and did not look at him.

"Oh, well, if *you* lived through it, I suppose I can too." He went back to his seat, displacing Prima again, and spoke sharply to little Secundus, who had a sulky expression and was pounding the cheese with his fist.

"I don't care," Secundus shouted, and kicked the table. Rufus gestured to the nanny, who rose and took Secundus away screaming. Then the butler appeared with his accounts. Drusilla got up, and Calpurnia did too.

"He kept me awake all night," Calpurnia said as they left. She was pale and looked more haggard than usual.

"Rufus was always a fearful child. It will be all right when it's over."

In the courtyard a little slave girl was weaving flowers into straw hats for the banquet. Clattering sounds came from the kitchen. "I'll be glad, too, when it's over," said Calpurnia.

At noon when Rufus and Calpurnia retired for their nap, Drusilla stayed awake and made sure the door slaves were at their posts. Toward the eighth hour guests began to arrive: landowners from neighboring estates, and the same farmers who had come in the morning, now with their wives and children in tow.

Marcus Pollio bustled toward her with elaborate apologies. "Dear Drusilla, about my cook—well, to tell you the truth it wasn't he who was indisposed, it was my wife, who felt she could not do without the special meals he prepared for her. She sends her regrets. She is feeling better now, but preferred not to travel. I hope you were not inconvenienced."

"No, it was nothing. Please give it no more thought, Marcus."

"You're very kind." Bowing and smiling, he went away to talk to Rufus. Then the carriages from more distant places began to roll up, and for a while the vestibule was full of guests complaining about the bad roads, while foot slaves helped them off with traveling shoes and into sandals. Gifts were piling up on a table in the atrium.

Drusilla's sister Serena from Rome appeared, and they embraced; they had been companions in first childhood, and still felt a great affection for each other although they seldom met. There was no time to talk, because Calpurnia's mother and father, both in their vigorous second youth, were bustling through the entrance.

The courtyard was full of drivers and outriders unharnessing their horses, slave children running about underfoot, dogs barking and women shouting. One of the carriages had broken an axle and was blocking the way of others. Rufus had gone to his room with Calpurnia and her parents. Drusilla, summoned by the butler, got four husky slaves to support the leaning carriage at one corner while other slaves dragged it out of the way. Somehow in the confusion one of the dogs was run over, and yelped piercingly until one of the outriders killed it with his sword.

On the way back, she noticed Rufus's daughter sitting in a corner of the courtyard, almost hidden behind the carriages. Drusilla hesitated; she really did not have time, but she went to the child and sat down beside her. They were almost the same height. "Well, what is it, has someone been cruel to you?"

"No, it isn't that."

"Then it must be something else. You may as well tell me."

The child bit her lip. "Will he be different afterward?"

"After the ceremony? No, there's nothing magical about it. The ceremony won't change him."

"Nanny says it will."

"Nanny is a fool. Your father will be just the same to you as he always was, no better, no worse. Besides, you'll be going to school next year. Will you like that?"

"I don't know. Sometimes I'm afraid."

"And your breasts hurt? And you wake up sometimes in the night, and cry?"

"Yes. Grandmother, sometimes I'm afraid of *everything*." Tears filled her eyes, and she leaned against Drusilla.

The closeness of the sweaty young body called up memories; it was pleasant and repugnant at the same time. Drusilla said, "Do you remember when you were much younger, how you were afraid of things that don't frighten you now?"

The girl's head nodded. "But then I was a baby."

"The rest will be just the same. We're always afraid before something happens, and then we see that it was nothing. When you go to bed, tell yourself, 'This won't matter by tomorrow night.' "

The girl released her and smiled. "I'll try. Thank you, Grandmother."

Drusilla arose and went into the colonnade, where the household and all the guests were gathering. It was a little before the tenth hour. One of the priest's assistants walked out into the garden, stood in front of the Janus hut, and beat a gong for silence. Then the second assistant appeared, carrying the sacred implements. These were wrapped to conceal them from profane eyes, but it was not hard to see what Drusilla already knew, that one was a rod, one a basin, one a lantern, and the fourth a sword. The assistants entered the hut and came out empty-handed. One of them went to the kitchen and returned with two jugs, which he deposited inside the hut as well.

Then the priest appeared with Rufus, who was wearing a robe so tattered and dirty that he must have borrowed it from the cook. The priest was carrying a bundle that Drusilla recognized: it was the new toga made from wool spun, dyed, and woven here on the estate.

Rufus conferred with the priest a moment; then the priest and the two assistants closed around him and marched him into the hut while the guests and household looked on.

The hide curtain fell, and there was silence, but Drusilla remembered and knew what was going on in the darkness. First they would strip him bare, and make him sit on a low stool between them, with the priest in front and the slaves behind. They would let him wait a while.

Now the priest would be saying, "In this warm water were you born naked, and this milk was your first food." Here the slaves drenched Rufus with water from the basin, then pulled his head back and poured milk into his face.

"These bitter herbs made you weep." One of the slaves would rub a paste of onions and garlic into his eyes. "Weep now for your first childhood, your first youth, and your first manhood, for they are done. Out of the darkness you came . . ." (here the slave uncovered the lantern and shone it into his face) ". . . and into the darkness you go . . ." (the slave covered the lamp again), ". . . but not until you have had your second manhood, your second youth, and your second childhood."

Blinded and weeping, he was made to get up and stand on the stool. "You stand now at the summer of your life, looking backward and looking forward. This moment will not come again. Remember it."

Then a blow on the back that made him cry out (they heard the cry where they stood watching), and the salt rubbed into the wound. (Another cry, more anguished than the first.)

Now the slave would be wiping his face with a cloth dipped in water, then drying it until he could see again.

"Will you loyally serve the tribe, your family, your household, and the city and empire? Think before you speak." Here the lantern was opened again, and the second slave held up his sword.

"Do you know and understand the penalty for breaking this oath?"

He would respond, as he had been taught, "If I break this oath, I must be cut off from tribe, family, household, city, and empire."

"Remember it." Another blow, another rubbing of salt. This time he was silent. Good.

"Will you serve the gods of your mothers, never blaspheming or neglecting them?"

"I will."

A third blow, the last. The priest would dip another cloth in the basin and begin to wash his body. "In this water I wash away your old life and begin the new."

Now the slaves would be dressing him in the toga sapientis with its purple, green, and white stripes. "Wear this garment in token of new life. From this day you join the company of men, women, and gods."

The door of the hut opened, and here he was now, looking splendid in his new toga, but sober and red-eyed. The guests surged into the garden and surrounded him. When her turn came, Drusilla embraced him and said a word or two. "Thanks," said Rufus, seeming to look beyond her. Then the press of people forced her out, and she went back to the colonnade.

The priest was there, pulling off his gloves. "It went very well, very well," he was saying. "Might I have a drop of something to drink?"

One of the slaves dipped him a cup of tempered wine; he poured a little on the ground and drank the rest thirstily. "It's dry work, you know," he said.

Because of the unexpected guests the dining room was more crowded than was proper; even though most of the local people were being fed outside, there were twelve at table, four on each side. Luckily Serena and Drusilla were together at the head couch. "At last we can talk," Drusilla said. "Tell me all your news."

"Well, I wrote you last year that I was going to Jerusalem to visit Gaius, didn't I?"

"Yes, but I never heard a word afterward, until somebody told me you were safely back in Rome."

"And lucky to get there, too; the ship just before mine was lost in the Internal Sea."

"Thank the gods it wasn't yours, but you always were lucky. How did you like Judea?"

"Well, I'd been there before, of course. It's not so bad, apart from the natives. Do you remember that Jew who was sent to Rome and crucified about five years ago?"

"Which one?"

"Jeshua, the one who prophesied the end of the world and said the Emperor ought to repent."

"They all say that. What about him?"

"Well, they cut him down when he had finished his time, of course, and sent him home in fair condition to Buggerall or wherever he came from, but now his followers are saying that he died on the cross and then came back to life."

"How absurd. Does anyone believe that?"

"Only his little clique, but they're all loud and abusive. We may have to round them up and crucify a few more to teach them manners."

"It won't work. Well, what did you do when you got back to Rome?"

"I was just in time for the farewell to Cloaca—pardon me, I mean, of course, Clodia."

"Oh, yes, I heard she was due. Were many people there?"

Serena smiled. "The consul attended, and about half the Committee, and the G.G. knows who. The temple was full, there must have been at least a thousand people outside. Everybody was smiling when they left."

"She *was* an awful person."

"Yes, and her daughters are just like her, I'm afraid. Well, and what is life going to be for you now?"

"Whatever Rufus chooses to make of it."

Serena looked at her keenly. "When things get too much for you, come and visit me. Promise."

"Yes, I promise. You're a good friend, Serena. The last one I have."

"Let us be all the closer then."

After the first course of little cakes, herbs, and cheeses, the slaves brought around thrushes and songbirds, sugared pork, ham, cutlets, goose, and fat hen. Rufus began drinking wine without water, and when the dessert came he was singing joyfully.

Afterward, when the eating stopped but the drinking went on, Drusilla took Serena away to her room. In the light of a single lamp, they sat listening to the sounds of revelry. "Seven is a banquet, nine is a brawl," Serena quoted.

"Well, Rufus was worried. Men take these things too seriously. Do you remember, when the boys were practicing with their javelins, how we used to wade down the brook, and try to catch rivernymphs in the shallows?"

"Yes, and we collected the brightest pebbles and took them home in baskets. What did you do with yours?"

"I kept them in a bowl of water to look at, but of course I had to throw them out when I dedicated all my toys to the Lar."

"You look just as you did then. It gave me a queer feeling when I saw you."

"And I you. It seems a long time ago."

"Except in sleep."

"Do you dream of those days too?"

"Often, lately. Were we as happy then as I think?"

"Probably not. Memory gilds everything, doesn't it?"

"Well, not *everything*. When I dream about Father, he's as awful as ever."

"You know what I mean."

"Yes, I do know. And nobody else understands; that's very sad in a way, isn't it?"

After a moment the door opened and the butler looked in. "Pardon, mistress, but your son is ill and Calpurnia has gone to bed with orders not to disturb her."

"What's the matter with him?"

"He is vomiting, and can't be roused."

"Bring him here."

The butler withdrew and came back; behind him were four men carrying Rufus; he was groaning and white-faced. "He looks poisoned to me," Serena said. "You'd better have your slaves tortured just to make sure."

"He drank too much. It's not the first time."

"As you wish." Serena yawned. "I'm for bed, then, it's been a long day."

Alone with Rufus, she sent for purgatives, and made him vomit again and again. After all, it was possible, even likely, that slaves had put something in his wine, but torturing them would prove nothing. Toward dawn, when he fell into a natural sleep, she left him, crossed the silent courtyard, unbarred the door, and slipped out into darkness. It was about the eleventh hour of night; except for a cock crowing in the farmyard, the world was empty.

When she was halfway down to the bridge, she heard a distant discordant trumpeting overhead. Up there, so high that they were in daylight although the rest of the world was dark, two Vs of white cranes were flying home to Africa. She stood without moving until they were gone.

Under the bridge she removed her sandals, tied up her robe, and stepped into the fast shallow water. The pebbles were unexpectedly hard to her bare feet. She walked downstream between arching willows and ferns that dropped icy sprays on her fingers.

Soon enough she found the little streamside meadow where she and Serena had often sat plaiting wreaths of flowers. She climbed up on the bank and dried her feet with grass. She was shivering, and wished she had brought her cloak, but it was glorious to be here, alone, out of sight and sound of the whole world.

As she sat there, the sky gradually brightened, then dawn came in streamers of copper and red, the sun rose higher, gilding the willows, and she could hardly breathe, and now, now, light touched the brook and laid bare all the wonders under the rushing ice-clear water: the pebbles of brown, green, and ivory, the threads of grass, the many-legged rivernymphs hiding in the shadows.

In Memoriam: Robert Bloch

FRANK M. ROBINSON

Robert Bloch (1917–1994), to many, will forever be known as "the author of *Psycho*," a phrase repeated in just about every obituary of this gifted and versatile writer. This particular claim to fame obscures the fact that Bloch was also one of the most loved figures in science fiction and fantasy, a man valued for his warmth and generosity. Stephen King called him "a man of wit and gentleness and great, great talent." Peter Straub said about him that "being around Bob in a crowded social scene was always an object lesson in how to enjoy oneself while remaining a decent human being. Bob is the only person I can think of who could make *dignity* lighthearted." Harlan Ellison, remembering Bloch, wrote: "He was the exemplar of what my father told me a man should always strive to be: a *mensch*. There is no higher accolade."

I first met Robert Bloch in 1973 in Toronto, where he was Guest of Honor at that year's World Science Fiction Convention. His wit was on display during his speech at the Hugo Awards banquet, during which he held up a sheaf of reviews of his work, announced that he was going to read a few passages, thought better of it, and then scattered the offending reviews, thus winning the applause of every writer in the room. His kindness was also evident; he introduced himself to me, a shy fledgling writer of only a few stories, and spent a few moments conversing with me while throngs were clamoring for his attention—solely because we had both had stories published recently in the same anthology.

A few years ago, at another convention where Bob Bloch was an honored guest, I wandered into the inn's dining room early in the morning in desperate need of coffee and had the happy experience of being invited to join Bob for breakfast (eggs and bacon, with plenty of coffee and a few cigarettes) and listen to his tales of Hollywood. Later, I was sitting with writer George Zebrowski autographing books when Bob arrived for his signing and took a seat next to us. Immediately long lines of people anxious for a Bloch autograph formed. "Get some of their books, too!" he said to the crowd, pointing in our direction, and a few people actually did. He was at the top of his form; I expected, as did others, that the world would be graced with his presence much longer than it was.

Robert Bloch created classics of fantasy, science fiction, mystery, suspense, and horror, winning almost every award for lifetime achievement bestowed in these various genres. Among his many novels and short story collections are *The Scarf, It's All in Your Mind, Spiderweb, The Dead Beat, Night-World, Psycho II, The Night of the Ripper, Psycho House,* and the three-volume *The Selected Stories of Robert Bloch.* He also wrote many teleplays for such programs as *Alfred Hitchcock Presents, Thriller, I Spy, Run for Your Life, Star Trek,* and *Night Gallery.* He is remembered here, in a summary of his life and work, by Frank M. Robinson, author of the novels *The Power* (made into a movie in the late fifties) and *The Dark Beyond the Stars,* a *New York Times* Notable Book for 1991. With Thomas N. Scortia, Robinson is also the author of *The Glass Inferno* (filmed as *The Towering Inferno*), *The Prometheus Crisis,* and *The Gold Crew.*

Robert Bloch, one of the best-loved authors in the field of fantasy and suspense, died Friday, September 23, of cancer of the esophagus and kidneys. He was seventy-seven years old. His career spanned an amazing sixty years in seven decades.

Services were held at the Pierce Brothers Mortuary in Westwood, California. Many of the hundred friends and fellow writers in attendance made short remarks, and Richard Matheson read tributes from Peter Straub, Stephen King, William Peter Blatty, and Ray Bradbury (who could not be present), among others. Sally Francy, Bloch's daughter, read a poem about a daughter's love for her father.

Bloch had been diagnosed early in June when he sought treatment for difficulty in swallowing. His doctors, as he confided to friends later, "told me I could play with fireworks, but I shouldn't plan on trick-or-treating." Shortly after diagnosis, he wrote a final piece for *Omni* (October 1994) about death and dying and his fear of it.

The article was an eerie echo of an early interview with Bloch that ran in the *Milwaukee Journal Green Sheet* for April 6, 1935, when Bloch was eighteen. The *Journal* mentioned the horror stories he had recently written for *Weird Tales,* then concluded: "And still—this same young man confesses to an inexplicable and profound fear of death." Quoting Bloch: "I can write horror tales very impersonally but I can't view death impersonally. The more I read of it, the more I fear it."

The *Journal,* discussing Bloch and his future career, mentioned that writing terror tales was only to help him achieve his real ambition—to be a comedian. Apparently, scarcely a day went by that Bloch didn't write four or five gags that he stored away for future use. When he was older, according to the paper, the young Bloch hoped to act in sketches that he wrote. Luckily for us, Bloch didn't move completely onstage.

Though he started as a writer of weird and horror stories, and later varied the mix with forays into humor, fantasy, science fiction, and even westerns, he was to achieve his real fame and importance pioneering the psychological horror story. During the war years, his interest in writing supernatural stories of the type popularized by H. P. Lovecraft had begun to pall. He was becoming more interested in the monsters within than the monsters without.

"By the mid-1940s I had pretty well mined the vein of ordinary supernatural themes. I realized as a result of what went on during World War Two and from reading . . . psychology that the real horror is not in the shadows but in the twisted world inside our own skulls."

Bloch's first effort in exploring that "twisted world" was *The Scarf* (The Dial Press, 1947), a short novel told from the viewpoint of a psychopathic strangler. It was followed by *The Kidnapper* (Lion, 1954)—Bloch's personal favorite of his novels and another first-person narrative of a psychopath—*Spiderweb* (Ace, 1954), and in 1959, the novel that was to make him famous, *Psycho* (Simon & Schuster).

Unlike most of his short fiction, his psychological horror novels were terse and clinical, with little of the humor that usually marked a Bloch story. His earliest tales were pastiches of Lovecraft, but even they had humorous undertones. He couldn't resist killing off a thinly disguised Lovecraft—to whom he dedicated the story—in "The Shambler from the Stars" (*Weird Tales,* September 1935). Lovecraft retaliated by writing a story in which he killed one "Robert Blake" of Milwaukee ("The Haunter of the Dark," *Weird Tales,* December 1936). He dedicated the story to Bloch, for which Bloch was forever grateful.

But it was psychological horror that made Bloch's literary

reputation. In many respects, his novels were ahead of their time, but they paved the way for many of the later books by Stephen King, Thomas Harris, and others. Norman Bates and Hannibal Lecter might differ in degrees of sophistication and depravity, but most readers would have little difficulty in identifying them as inmates of the same asylum.

Robert Bloch was born in Chicago in 1917, the son of Raphael and Stella Loeb Bloch. His father was a cashier in a bank, his mother a former schoolteacher and social worker who had once turned down a career in light opera. They were Jewish but not particularly religious, and for the most part Bloch was raised as a Methodist. A chance meeting with magician Howard Thurston sparked an early interest in show business. Family members were already enthusiasts of vaudeville, and Bloch also attended movies regularly, especially comedies. His childhood idols were Buster Keaton (whom he was to meet much later in life) and Harold Lloyd.

But the defining moment in his experience of the performing arts came when, as a small boy, he attended a nighttime production of *The Phantom of the Opera* starring Lon Chaney. The scene where the Phantom removes his mask to reveal his skull-face was to stay with him the rest of his life. In one interview he said he'd peed in his pants, ran home from the theater, and slept with the light on for the next two years. (In his autobiography, he denied it all—though he admitted he became a Chaney fan as well as a fan of other horror pictures of the period.)

An interest in Egyptology, picked up from his numerous visits to the Art Institute and Chicago's Field Museum, led him to buy his first copy of *Weird Tales*. He'd been browsing through the newsstand at Chicago's huge Northwestern Railroad Station and spotted the issue featuring Otis Adelbert Kline's "The Bride of Osiris" on the cover (August 1927). An indulgent aunt bought the issue for him and changed his life forever. He was nine years old.

Bloch's father lost his bank job in the early twenties at about the same time his mother was offered a position by the Abraham Lincoln House in Milwaukee, where she'd been employed as a social worker prior to her marriage. The family relocated to Milwaukee. While in junior high school, Bloch discovered science fiction in *Amazing Stories* and became a fan of H. P. Lovecraft through his stories in *Weird Tales*.

In 1933, Bloch started a long correspondence with Lovecraft, which continued until the latter's death. Lovecraft introduced the young fan to other writers for *Weird Tales* such as Clark Ashton Smith, E. Hoffmann Price, and August Derleth. Lovecraft also encouraged the young Bloch to try his hand at writing stories and offered to read and criticize the results. His first efforts were published by William L. Crawford, who printed Bloch's story "Lillies" in *Marvel Tales* and "The Black Lotus" in *Unusual Stories*.

The only drawback was that Crawford paid no money to contributors. By this time, Bloch was serious about writing. It was the middle of the Depression, there were few jobs available for high school graduates, and writing for a living was worth a gamble. He bought a secondhand typewriter, a used card table, paper and carbon from the local Woolworths, and set up shop in his bedroom.

A month after graduating from high school, Bloch sold his first story to *Weird Tales,* "The Secret of the Tomb." But the first published story was the second one he sold, "The Feast in the Abbey" (*Weird Tales,* January 1935). Others quickly followed, and Bloch soon became a familiar and popular name in the magazine. But he had yet to find his own voice.

One of the side effects of his early writing career was his introduction to the Milwaukee Fictioneers, an organization whose members included Stanley G. Weinbaum, Raymond A. Palmer, Roger Sherman Hoar ("Ralph Milne Farley"), and others. Bloch was making friends through the mails as well, among them Henry Kuttner, with whom he later collaborated on a story ("The Black Kiss," *Weird Tales,* June 1937). He took a trip to Chicago to meet Farnsworth Wright, the editor of *Weird Tales.*

Bloch didn't restrict his creative efforts to writing horror stories. He had written gags in high school, acted in skits for the drama club, and appeared in a minstrel show and the senior play. Later, with high school friend Harold Gauer, he wrote a mock radio broadcast and collaborated on an unpublished—and unpublishable—novel, *In the Land of the Sky-Blue Ointment.*

Through it all, he was turning into a journeyman writer with experience in a number of different forms, all of which would stand him in good stead. He was analytical about his writing, realizing that his penchant for horror sprang from his own fear of death. "I was terribly susceptible to fear of death. . . . I decided I'm not going to let them scare me, I'm going to scare them. And that's exactly what I did. I put on a fright mask myself and it worked. . . . Familiarity didn't breed contempt, but it made it . . . much easier . . . to see how you manipulate the props to make the audience scream."

He was an avid reader of fantasy and read extensively in the fields of Freudian and Jungian psychology. Later in life, when asked to analyze the connection between comedy and horror, he wrote: "To me, horror and comedy are two sides of the same coin. Both of them involve a common denominator. Both of them involve the grotesque, the unexpected. In most cases, humor relies upon the twist, just as the shock in horror relies upon some kind of twist. . . ."

When Lovecraft died, Bloch was devastated by the loss of his mentor. When Henry Kuttner invited him to spend a month in Los Angeles, he jumped at the chance. Hollywood was the home of many of his childhood heroes. In addition, he finally met Kuttner, Fritz Leiber Jr., Catherine Moore, and the members of the Los Angeles Fantasy Society.

It was a trip he never forgot.

Back in Milwaukee, he discovered that Ziff-Davis had purchased *Amazing Stories* and Ray Palmer, his friend from the Fictioneers, was the editor. Ray needed new stories in a hurry, and Bloch hastened to oblige. The resulting increase in income enabled him to rent an office in downtown Milwaukee and hire a secretary. Trips to New Orleans and Sauk City, Wisconsin (where he met August Derleth for the first time), followed. He now expanded his writing base still further, selling gags to Stoopnagle and Budd, a radio team, and one of his own monologues to comic Roy Atwell, who had appeared on the Fred Allen radio show. He also took on a side job as a stand-up comic, emcee, and mimic in various taverns and nightclubs.

None of these efforts produced much money, and when, in 1939, an offer came for him and Harold Gauer to mastermind a political campaign, he accepted. Their candidate was an assistant city attorney named Carl Zeidler—tall and blond, with a firm handshake and a good singing voice and few other obvious qualifications. Their opponent was the "dean of American mayors," Daniel Webster Hoan, the Socialist mayor of Milwaukee for twenty-three years.

With little in the way of money, though much in the way of promises, Bloch and Gauer trusted to wit and innovation. They slanted the campaign to women (Zeidler was a bachelor and handsome) and youth (Zeidler was young), with a heavy reliance on photographs. They wrote Zeidler's platform as well as his speeches, held rallies at which pretty girls passed out campaign booklets, showcased their candidate standing in front of a huge American flag, and at the end of his speech yanked on strings backstage that flooded the auditorium with balloons.

Early in the campaign, Bloch and Gauer had decided that politics was just another form of show business, and designed the campaign along those lines. None of what they did is unusual today, but it was in 1939. They got extensive press coverage, generated intense political excitement, and when it was all over, their no-talent candidate was in the runoff for mayor.

In the general election that followed, Zeidler won by twelve thousand votes. He also stiffed Bloch and Gauer for their fees, doubtlessly contributing to Bloch's sardonic take on politics in particular and life in general.

Bloch married Marion Ruth Holcombe in October 1940, tried his hand at another political campaign with little financial reward, and was faced with making a living for two. Returning to writing short stories, he lifted a character from the unpublished *In the Land of the Sky-Blue Ointment*. The character was Lefty Feep, a petty gambler with overtones of Damon Runyon. Feep, along with other characters from the original Bloch/Gauer novel, was to star in twenty-three short stories and novelettes.

Bloch now paid frequent visits to Chicago to visit editors, meet other writers, and play poker at Ray Palmer's house in Evanston, where he met William P. McGivern, Howard Browne, and William Hamling. He was an average poker player, but invariably managed to fleece this naive Ziff-Davis office boy invited to the poker parties for just that reason.

Despite his success with Lefty Feep and other fiction, money was still tight. Marion was not in good health, and medical bills began to eat up their income. Bloch's solution was to go to work for the Gustav Marx advertising agency, consisting at the time of Marx and a secretary. Marx had been a member of the Milwaukee Fictioneers, had heard of Bloch's straitened circumstances, and offered him a job—at no salary. After six months experience, Marx claimed, Bloch could find a decent job with any agency in town.

Bloch had written copy for the several political campaigns he had masterminded, and writing copy for the ad agency was not so different—or difficult. At the end of the six months, Marx asked him to stay on at a generous salary and with the option of writing his own fiction when he wasn't involved with agency work.

Bloch stayed for eleven years.

But writing fiction and ad copy weren't his only sources of income. He was soon offered a freelance job writing scripts for a radio show titled *Stay Tuned for Terror*. Bloch agreed to write thirty-nine fifteen-minute shows and deliver them within three months. It amounted to doing three scripts a week while holding down his full-time job at the agency.

It was a stretch. Bloch adapted many of his stories from *Weird Tales*, though the twelve minutes of airtime (fifteen minutes minus commercials) made condensing them a problem. So did commuting to Chicago, where the shows were frequently recorded back to back.

Probably Bloch's most famous story of the forties, one he considered an average story but which turned out to be a legend, was "Yours Truly, Jack the Ripper" (*Weird Tales,* July 1943). Julius Schwartz, his then-agent, sold the story to a hardcover anthology. Subsequently, it was dramatized on the CBS radio show *The Kate Smith Hour,* and starred Laird Cregar, soon to be seen in the film *The Lodger* playing . . . Jack the Ripper. The story has since been anthologized and presented on radio and television more than fifty times (by Bloch's own estimate—he may have missed a few).

In 1944, Bloch's first book was published. August Derleth asked him to review his one hundred or more published stories and pick out enough for a collection. (This was the same August Derleth who had once told a younger Robert Bloch that he would never be a writer.) *The Opener of the Way* garnered good reviews but didn't produce much in the way of royalties—some $600, most of it paid out over the years.

Bloch was now invited to join in still another political campaign, this time on behalf of Senator Robert M. La Follette Jr. Bloch urged the senator to spend more time in the state shaking the hands of his constituents, especially the younger voters to whom he was a legend but not much more. The senator listened quietly, thanked him, then made a few cursory stops around the state and spent most of his campaign sitting it out in Washington. He lost by a very narrow margin.

The new senator from Wisconsin was Joe McCarthy.

In 1946, Bloch wrote a short novel about a serial killer, a psychopathic strangler, titled *The Scarf* (Dial Press, 1947). It was to be the first of a number of novels dealing with serial killers and psychiatric themes. The style was not typical Bloch. It was terse, gritty, and avoided the humor that he frequently used in short stories. It received good reviews, including one by Dr. Frederic Wertham in a psychiatric journal and another in *The New Yorker*. The book went through several hardcover printings and promptly sold to paperback. Bloch should have been on his way to fame and fortune, except Dial bounced his next proposal, his editor quit to get married, and the literary agency (A. & S. Lyons) that had handled the sale of the novel suddenly went out of business.

A film company in Hollywood subsequently produced a film titled *The Scarf* with a storyline remarkably similar to Bloch's, but he had neither agent nor publisher to help him contest the similarity.

It was six years before Bloch published another novel, though a condensed version of an initially unsuccessful attempt ran in the August '52 *Bluebook* under the title "Once a Sucker." (The original version, possibly rewritten, appeared in 1954 as *Spiderweb,* half of an Ace Double.)

Of the shorts that now followed, perhaps the best known was "The Man Who Collected Poe" (*Famous Fantastic Mysteries,* October 1951), in which he directly inserted lines from Poe's own "The Fall of the House of Usher." Professor Thomas Olive Mabbott of Hunter College was impressed by it and invited Bloch to finish Poe's last, never-completed story, "The Lighthouse." Bloch did so (it was published in *Fantastic,* January 1953), and was very proud that few people could tell where Poe left off and he began.

Marion's physical condition continued to worsen, and in 1953, the Blochs moved to Weyauwega, Wisconsin, Marion's hometown. Marion was now among family and friends, but Bloch was something of a fish out of water. He had gotten used to cities, and a rural community with a population of twelve hundred became a social prison. He was cut off from normal contact with his friends and other writers.

Something of a relief was offered by an invitation to appear as a panelist on a cartoon quiz show out of Milwaukee titled *It's a Draw.* The money from the show, and the social contact it offered, was a godsend. It was also during this period that his correspondence with other writers and with fandom increased greatly. He contributed hundreds of articles and letters to fanzines and even edited several one-shots of his own (primarily for FAPA), and coedited six issues of a professional fanzine published by Gnome Press, *The Science Fiction World*, with Wilson Tucker. He became a frequent toastmaster at Worldcons and was honored at a number of them.

In 1959, at the Worldcon in Detroit, he and Isaac Asimov were co-toastmasters and handed out the Hugo Awards. Asimov would introduce the categories and Bloch would open the sealed envelopes and read the names of the winners. He was in shock when he read out his own name as the author of the Best Short Story, "The Hell-Bound Train" (*F&SF*, September 1958).

Bloch was breaking into magazines outside the genre now, including appearances in *Alfred Hitchcock's Mystery Magazine, Ellery Queen, Mike Shayne's Mystery Magazine, The Saint Mystery Magazine*, and *Playboy*. The pulps may have died, but the digests and the men's magazines were picking up the slack.

In 1959, the world changed enormously for Bloch. Several years before, in the little town of Plainfield, forty miles from Weyauwega, the local sheriff had walked into a barn owned by a farmer named Ed Gein and discovered a woman's torso hanging on hooks, much as if it had been the carcass of a deer. The seemingly innocuous Gein had prowled the lonely hearts columns, and a steady stream of widows and lonely middle-aged women had disappeared into his barn.

The Gein case was an overnight sensation, and Bloch was convinced there was material in it for a novel. But while the big cities covered the story in detail, the papers in Weyauwega and surrounding towns had only limited coverage. *Psycho* was based upon the murders but not upon Gein himself, about whom Bloch knew little. The character of Norman Bates sprang full-blown from Bloch's own imagination; the very name Norman was a pun, the murderer being "neither woman nor man." (Years later, when he did an article about the murders for editor Anthony Boucher—*The Quality of Murder*, Dutton, 1962—he was astonished how close he'd come to the real character of Gein.)

Psycho was published by Simon & Schuster in 1959 to good reviews. Shortly afterward, Bloch's agent—Harry Altschuler—received a "blind" offer of $5,000 for the film rights. The purchaser was unknown. Bloch refused to sell, and the offer was raised to $9,500, which he accepted. Of the total price, Altschuler received his ten percent, Simon & Schuster their fifteen percent, and after taxes Bloch received about $6,250. Not an unusual offer for the time, but a miserable one in light of what the film was to make. Unfortunately, few authors who sold movie rights during the fifties were offered a piece of the action.

The real wonder, perhaps, is that the film was made at all. The story was replete with transvestism, hints of incest, and the definitely un-American suggestion (as Bloch put it) that a boy's best friend might not be his mother. Paramount hated everything about it, starting with the title. But the purchaser was Alfred Hitchcock's production company, and Hitchcock badly wanted to make the film. Paramount cut his budget and told Hitchcock no sound stages would be available during his projected shooting schedule. Hitchcock, in retaliation, put up some of his own money and filmed the movie in black and white on the Universal lot (though Paramount still released the film), using the cinematographer from his television show.

At a screening of the rough cut, Hitchcock asked Bloch what he thought of the film and Bloch said, "I think it's either going to be your biggest hit or your biggest disaster."

The critics were initially unkind, but *Psycho* soon became the largest-grossing black-and-white film ever made. Only *The Birth of a Nation* had grossed more (and today, of course, *Schindler's List*).

Oddly, *Psycho* did not bring Bloch out to Hollywood—he was already there. He had been invited to Hollywood to write a segment of *Lock Up*, and by the time *Psycho* was released, he had already written six or seven teleplays and had five or six more assignments.

He now became famous as the author of *Psycho*, but somehow the fame didn't translate into money. The big bucks for another book never materialized until years later when he wrote *Psycho II* (1982), a volume that had nothing at all to do with the sequel to the movie released at about the same time.

Bloch continued to write the occasional novel and short story, but more and more, his work was for films and television. During the sixties, he wrote extensively for *Alfred Hitchcock Presents*, *Thriller*, and *The Alfred Hitchcock Hour*, as well as doing three segments of the original *Star Trek* ("Wolf in the Fold" was a Jack the Ripper story set hundreds of years in the future). He also did work for *I Spy, Whispering Smith, Night Gallery,* and others. In addition, other writers adapted some of his stories for these and other shows.

Like Ray Bradbury, Charles Beaumont, Harlan Ellison, and a few others, Bloch had discovered Hollywood and Hollywood had discovered him. The stars whom he had idolized while watching them on theater screens in Chicago and Milwaukee were now personal friends. Buster Keaton, Boris Karloff, Joan Crawford, Dick Foran. . . . He moved the family out to California and settled down to relative peace and prosperity. He hadn't made a fortune on *Psycho,* but soon *Psycho* and Robert Bloch were synonymous, and that didn't hurt.

But as the years went by, the situation at home became increasingly untenable. Marion's physical condition worsened, and while Bloch enjoyed the atmosphere of Hollywood and socializing with his movie star friends, Marion did not. Bloch had warned her that life in Hollywood would be far different from the life they'd led in Weyauwega. But Marion couldn't adjust, and in October 1963 Bloch received an interlocutory decree of divorce and moved into his own apartment. Marion eventually sold the house he bought her and moved to Desert Hot Springs, where she became active in the life of the small community.

Bloch had resolved never to marry again, a resolve that crumbled almost immediately after meeting Eleanor Alexander at a party. Her writer-husband had died of a heart attack three months before, and this was the first party she'd attended since. In his autobiography, Bloch states that he proposed marriage to her after twenty-two minutes of talking to her. She wasn't quite as ready as he was, but five days after he received his final divorce decree in October of 1964, they were married.

The story had a happy ending after all.

Ellie's life and Bloch's meshed without difficulty, and Bloch's friends quickly became Ellie's as well. His circle of friends and acquaintances among writers and actors and in fandom expanded still further, if such a thing was possible.

He wasn't quite as prolific now, but he had reached that stage of life marked by honors and awards. He had been the first Guest of Honor at a convention outside the United States, the Sixth World Science Fiction Convention in Toronto (1948). Once again he was Guest of Honor at Torcon II in 1973. In 1975, he was Guest of Honor at Bouchercon I, the San Diego Comicon, and the World Fantasy Convention. He had received the Hugo for Best Short Story in 1958 and the World Fantasy Life Award in 1975, and twice won the Ann Radcliffe Award, once for Television in 1966, and once for Literature in 1969. He won a World Science Fiction Convention Special Lifetime Career Award in 1984, the Bram Stoker Award in 1990, and the World Horror Convention Grand Master Award in 1991. He served as President of the Mystery Writers of America for 1970–71.

He would never have denied that he had a somewhat sardonic view of life, encouraged by his experiences in politics, where shallow candidates and the ease of manipulating the public had largely turned him off. His views became more intense in later years, when the story lines in horror films, the genre he loved, were replaced by special effects and copious amounts of gore. "You might just as well go to a slaughterhouse and pick out a few animals and carve them up screaming and squealing on camera." He was sickened by the audiences that laughed at the blood and sadism in the "splatter" films.

He regretted that despite *Psycho* he had never received the critical acclaim nor the fortune bestowed on other writers in the genre (hardly an unusual complaint). But he never forgot that he'd elected to become a public entertainer early in life, and took great pride in the fact that probably no other writer in the genre had had so many stories published, reprinted, and shown on television or presented as theatrical films. He attributed his television and theatrical film popularity to the fact that his stories could be easily translated to the visual medium, not that they were necessarily better than those of other authors.

He was a journeyman writer and entertainer, and had more experience in various writing forms—from political speeches to advertising to short stories, novels, articles, teleplays, and film scripts—than probably any other genre writer.

But all of his stories, all of his movies, and all of his teleplays didn't account for the feelings of affection that both fans and writers felt for him. When he was a struggling young writer, H. P. Lovecraft had helped him with his craft. Bloch never forgot that, nor did he hesitate to "pass it on" when he became the experienced professional and beginning writers approached him for aid and advice.

In one sense, he was a contradiction in terms. He was one of the most beloved figures in the field, but never tried to disguise his disappointment in humanity as a whole. "When you really get to know people, you don't need to invent monsters. . . . I believe a majority of mankind is violent. . . . Modern horror fiction . . . has provided virtually everyone with a 'Devil' theory. As Flip Wilson says, 'The Devil made me do it.' . . . No one is individually responsible."

When it came to fandom, he was the most accessible of all the professional writers. He was a fan himself and had joined the ranks for the same reasons that most fans do—he was lonely and sought social contact. He wrote extensively for fanzines, he published his own, he was the most sought-after toastmaster and emcee in fandom. His presence at a convention was enough to turn it into a family party. Once, when asked what he considered the highlights of his writing career, he replied: "My first sales—of a short story, of a novel . . . the sale of *Psycho* to films and its subsequent success. But the most satisfying and memorable moments have come with the conventions where I was invited to appear as guest of honor, the winning of various awards . . . the continuing interest of fans. . . ."

During the last few months of his life, Bloch received hundreds of calls and notes of appreciation. For as long as he could, he took all the calls and read all the notes and letters. When he could no longer do so, they were read to him.

It was typical of Bloch that he wrote the notes for his own obituary for distribution to various media. At the end of them, he typed: "Always interested in giving readers a 'surprise ending,' Bloch wrote these obituary notes himself." His personal memorabilia were donated to the American Heritage Center at the University of Wyoming. His ashes will also be at the center in a book-shaped urn. According to several reports, the legend on the urn will read: "Here lie the collected works of Robert Bloch."

Despite his sardonic view of the world, Robert Bloch was a man without malice. Almost everybody who met him sensed that, and almost everybody who met him loved him for it. It was impossible not to.

Bob is survived by his wife Ellie and his daughter Sally.

And by a multitude of friends who never realized how much they were going to miss him until the day he died.

The Martian Child

DAVID GERROLD

David Gerrold first achieved renown for "The Trouble with Tribbles," a famous *Star Trek* episode first broadcast in 1967, for which he wrote the script. He soon received critical praise and several Nebula and Hugo Award nominations for his novels and stories during the 1970s. Among his published books are *The Flying Sorcerers* (written with Larry Niven), *When Harlie Was One, With a Finger in My I, The Man Who Folded Himself,* and *Moonstar Odyssey;* recent novels include *Voyage of the Star Wolf, Under the Eye of God, A Covenant of Justice, The Middle of Nowhere,* and *The War Against the Chtorr* sequence of novels. Gerrold teaches screenwriting at Pepperdine University and writes a regular column for *PC-Techniques* magazine; he also writes screenplays, nonfiction, teleplays, computer programs, and comic books.

David Gerrold's Nebula Award–winning "The Martian Child" may be one of the most personal stories this writer has ever written; among its other honors are the Locus Award and the Hugo Award. He says about his novelette:

" 'The Martian Child' is semiautobiographical. It's about a storyteller like me who adopts a little boy like the one I adopted, only to discover that the child might be a Martian. It's sort of about myself and my son, but not really. When I asked Sean if he was a Martian, he said he wasn't allowed to tell. (That was my first clue.)

"It wasn't until a long time after I finished the story that I realized what it was actually about. There's a moment of disrecognition that I think occurs for all new parents. One minute you're looking at your child lovingly, marveling how lucky you are; the very next instant you're wondering, 'Who let this loathsome reptilian thing into my life? Whose good idea was this?' Eventually the perception shifts again, this time stabilizing into a more natural and permanent state. This isn't a loathsome reptilian thing after all; it's just a short person with some serious opinions of its own. And it expects to be listened to. Parenting is the acceptance of that other person's existence as a person, not a thing.

"Maybe all of our little Martians have mind-wiped us into loving them and that's all that keeps us from strangling them in their cribs, but I prefer to believe that as human beings we're delighted beyond words to have our lives so wonderfully expanded by our children, no matter what planet they come from."

Toward the end of the meeting, the caseworker remarked, "Oh—and one more thing. Dennis thinks he's a Martian."

"I beg your pardon?" I wasn't certain I had heard her correctly. I had papers scattered all over the meeting room table—thick piles of stapled incident reports, manila-foldered psychiatric evaluations, Xeroxed clinical diagnoses, scribbled caseworker histories, typed abuse reports, bound trial transcripts, and my own crabbed notes as well: Hyperactivity. Fetal Alcohol Syndrome. Emotional Abuse. Physical Abuse. Conners Rating Scale. Apgars. I had no idea there was so much to know about children. For a moment, I was actually looking for the folder labeled *Martian.*

"He thinks he's a Martian," Ms. Bright repeated. She was a small woman, very proper and polite. "He told his group home parents that he's not like the other children—he's from Mars—so he shouldn't be expected to act like an Earthling all the time."

"Well, that's okay," I said, a little too quickly. "Some of my best friends are Martians. He'll fit right in. As long as he doesn't eat the tribbles or tease the feral Chtorran."

By the narrow expressions on their faces, I could tell that the caseworkers weren't amused. For a moment, my heart sank. Maybe I'd said the wrong thing. Maybe I was being too facile with my answers.

—The hardest thing about adoption is that *you have to ask someone to trust you with a child.*

That means that you have to be willing to let them scrutinize your entire life, everything: your financial standing, your medical history, your home and belongings, your upbringing, your personality, your motivations, your arrest record, your IQ, and even your sex life. It means that *every* self-esteem issue you have ever had will come bubbling right to the surface like last night's beans in this morning's bathtub.

Whatever you're most insecure about, that's what the whole adoption process will feel like it's focused on. For me, it was that terrible familiar feeling of being *second best*—of not being good enough to play with the big kids, or get the job, or win the award, or whatever was at stake. Even though the point of this interview was simply to see if Dennis and I would be a good match, I felt as if I was being judged again. What if I wasn't good enough this time?

I tried again. I began slowly. "Y'know, you all keep telling me all the bad news—you don't even know if this kid is capable of forming a deep attachment—it feels as if you're trying to talk me out of this match." I stopped myself before I said too much. I was suddenly angry and I didn't know why. These people were only doing their job.

And then it hit me. That was it—these people were *only* doing their job.

At that moment, I realized that there wasn't anyone in the room who had the kind of commitment to Dennis that I did, and I hadn't even met him yet. To them, he was only another case to handle. To me, he was . . . the possibility of a family. It wasn't fair to unload my frustration on these tired, overworked, underpaid women. They cared. It just wasn't the same kind of caring. I swallowed my anger.

"Listen," I said, sitting forward, placing my hands calmly and deliberately on the table. "After everything this poor little guy has been through, if he wants to think he's a Martian—I'm not going to argue with him. Actually, I think it's charming. It's evidence of his resilience. It's probably the most rational explanation he can come up with for his irrational situation. He probably feels alienated, abandoned, different, *alone.* At least, this gives him a reason for it. It lets him put a story around his situation so he can cope with it. Maybe it's the wrong explanation, but it's the only one he's got. We'd be stupid to try to take it away from him."

And after I'd said that, I couldn't help but add another thought as well. "I know a lot of people who hide out in fantasy because reality is too hard to cope with. Fantasy is my business. The only difference is that I write it down and make the rest of the world pay for the privilege of sharing the delusion. Fantasy isn't about escape; it's a survival mechanism. It's a way to deal with things that are so much bigger than you are. So I think fantasy is special, something to be cherished and protected because it's a very fragile thing and without it, we're so defenseless, we're paralyzed.

"I know what this boy is feeling *because I've been there.* Not the same circumstances, thank God—but I know this much, if he's surrounded by adults who can't understand what he really needs, he'll never have that chance to connect that everyone keeps talking about." For the first time I looked directly into their eyes as if they had to live up to *my* standards. "Excuse me for being presumptuous—but he's got to be with someone who'll tell him that it's all right for him to be a Martian. Let him be a Martian for as long as he needs."

"Yes. Thank you," the supervisor said abruptly. "I think that's everything we need to cover. We'll be getting back to you shortly."

My heart sank at her words. She hadn't acknowledged a word of what I'd said. I was certain she'd dismissed it totally. I gathered up all my papers. We exchanged pleasantries and handshakes, and I wore my company smile all the way to the elevator. I didn't say a word, neither did my sister. We both waited until we were in the car and headed back toward the Hollywood Freeway. She drove, guiding the big car through traffic as effortlessly as only a Los Angeles real estate agent can manage.

"I blew it," I said. "Didn't I? I got too . . . full of myself again."

"Honey, I think you were fine." She patted my hand.

"They're not going to make the match," I said. "It would be a single-parent adoption. They're not going to do it. First they choose married couples, Ward and June. Then they choose single women, Murphy Brown. Then, only if there's no one else who'll take the kid, will they consider a single man. I'm at the bottom of the list. I'll never get this kid. I'll never get *any* kid. My own caseworker told me not to get my hopes up. There are two other families interested. This was just a formality, this interview. I know it. Just so they could prove they'd considered more than one match." I felt the frustration building up inside my chest like a balloon full of hurt. "But this is the kid for me, Alice, I know it. I don't know how I know it, but I do."

I'd first seen Dennis's picture three weeks earlier; a little square of colors that suggested a smile in flight.

I'd gone to the National Conference of the Adoptive Families of America at the Los Angeles Airport Hilton. There were six panels per hour, six hours a day, two days, Saturday and Sunday. I picked the panels that I thought would be most useful to me in finding and raising a child and ordered tapes—over two dozen—of the sessions I couldn't attend in person. I'd had no idea there were so many different issues to be dealt with in adoptions. I soaked it up like a sponge, listening eagerly to the advice of adoptive parents, their grown children, clinical psychologists, advocates, social workers, and adoption resource professionals.

But my *real* reason for attending was to find *the child.*

I'd already been approved. I'd spent more than a year filling out forms and submitting to interviews. But approval doesn't mean you get a child. It only means that your name is in the hat. Matching is done to meet the child's needs first. Fair enough—but terribly frustrating.

Eventually, I ended up in the conference's equivalent of a dealer's room. Rows of tables and heart-tugging displays. Books of all kinds for sale. Organizations. Agencies. Children in Eastern Europe. Children in Latin America. Asian children. Children with special needs. Photo listings, like real-estate albums. Turn the pages, look at the eyes, the smiles, the needs. "Johnny was abandoned by his mother at age three. He is hyperactive, starts fires, and has been cruel to small animals. He will need extensive therapy . . ." "Janie, age nine, is severely retarded. She was sexually abused by her stepfather, she will need round-the-clock care . . ." "Michael suffers from severe epilepsy . . ." "Linda *needs* . . ." "Danny *needs* . . ." "Michael *needs* . . ." So many *needs.* So much hurt. It was overwhelming.

Why were so many of the children in the books "special needs" children? Retarded. Hyperactive. Abused. Had they been abandoned because they weren't perfect, or were these the leftovers after all the good children were selected? The part that disturbed me the most was that I could understand the emotions involved. I wanted a child, not a case. And some of the descriptions in the book did seem pretty intimidating. Were these the only kind of children available?

Maybe it was selfish, but I found myself turning the pages looking for a child who represented an easy answer. Did I really want another set of *needs* in my life—a single man who's old enough to be considered middle-aged and ought to be thinking seriously about retirement plans?

This was the most important question of all. "Why do you want to adopt a child?" And it was a question I couldn't answer. I couldn't find the words. It seemed that there was something I couldn't write down.

The motivational questionnaire had been a brick wall that sat on my desk for a week. It took me thirty pages of single-spaced printout just to get my thoughts organized. I could tell great stories about what I thought a family should be, but I couldn't really answer the question why *I* wanted a son. Not right away.

The three o'clock in the morning truth of it was a very nasty and selfish piece of business.

I didn't want to die alone. I didn't want to be left unremembered.

All those books and TV scripts . . . they were nothing. They used up trees. They were exercises in excess. They made other people rich. They were useless to me. They filled up shelves. They impressed the impressionable. But they didn't prove me a real person. They didn't validate my life as one worth living. In fact, they were about as valuable as the vice presidency of the United States.

What I *really* wanted was to make a difference. I wanted someone to know that there was a real person behind all those words. A dad.

I would lie awake, staring into the darkness, trying to imagine it, what it would be like, how I would handle the various situations that might come up, how I would deal with the day-to-day business of daddying. I gamed out scenarios and tried to figure out how to handle difficult situations.

In my mind, I was always kind and generous, compassionate and wise. My fantasy child was innocent and joyous, full of love and wide-eyed wonder, and grateful to be in my home. He was an invisible presence, living inside my soul, defying reality to catch up. I wondered where he was now, and how and when I would finally meet him—and if the reality of parenting would be as wonderful as the dream.

—But it was all fantasyland. The books were proof of that. These children had histories, brutal, tragic, and heartrending.

I wandered on to the next table. One of the social workers from the Los Angeles County Department of Children's Services had a photo book with her. I introduced myself, told her I'd been approved—but not matched. Could I look through the book? Yes, of course, she said. I turned the pages slowly, studying the innocent faces, looking for one who could be my son. All the pictures were of black children, and the county wasn't doing transracial adoptions anymore. Too controversial. The black social workers had taken a stand against it—I could see their point—but how many of these children would not find homes now?

Tucked away like an afterthought on the very last page was a photo of the only white child in the book. My glance slid across the picture quickly, I was already starting to close the album—and then as the impact of what I'd seen hit me, I froze in midaction, almost slamming the book flat again.

The boy was riding a bicycle on a sunny tree-lined sidewalk; he was caught in the act of shouting or laughing at whoever was holding the camera. His blond hair was wild in the wind of his passage, his eyes shone like stars behind his glasses, his expression was raucous and exuberant.

I couldn't take my eyes off the picture. A cold wave of certainty came rolling up my spine like a blast of fire and ice. It was a feeling of *recognition*. This was *him*—the child who'd taken up permanent residence in my imagination! I could almost hear him yelling, "Hi, Daddy!"

"Tell me about this child," I said, a little too quickly. The social worker was already looking at me oddly. I could understand it. My voice sounded odd to me too. I tried to explain. "Tell me. Do you ever get people looking at a picture and telling you that this is the one?"

"All the time," she replied. Her face softened into an understanding smile.

His name was Dennis. He'd just turned eight. She'd just put his picture in the book this morning. And yes, she'd have the boy's caseworker get in touch with my caseworker. But . . . she cautioned . . . remember that there might be other families interested too. And remember, the department matches from the child's side.

I didn't hear any of that. I heard the words, but not the cautions.

I pushed hard and they set up a meeting to see if the match would work. But they cautioned me ahead of time—"This might not be the child you're looking for. He's classified as 'hard-to-place.' He's hyperactive and he's been emotionally abused and he may have fetal alcohol effects and he's been in eight foster homes, he's never had a family of his own . . ."

I didn't hear a word of it. I simply refused to listen. The boy in the picture had grabbed my heart so completely that I'd suddenly expanded all my definitions of what I was willing to accept.

I posted messages on CompuServe asking for information and advice on adoption, on attention deficit hyperactivity disorder, on emotional abuse recovery, on everything I could think of—what were this child's chances of becoming an independent adult? I called the Adoption Warm Line and was referred to parents who'd been through it. I hit the bookstores and the libraries. I called my cousin, the doctor, and he faxed me twenty pages of reports. And I came into the meeting so well-papered and full of theories and good intentions that I must have looked the perfect jerk.

And now . . . it was over.

I leaned my head against the passenger side window of my sister's car and moaned. "Dammit. I'm so *tired* of being pregnant. Thirteen months is long enough for any man! I've got the baby blues so bad, I can't even go to the supermarket anymore. I find myself watching other people with their children and the tears start welling up in my eyes. I keep thinking, 'Where's *mine?*'"

My sister understood. She had four children of her own, none of whom had ended up in jail; so she had to have done something right. "Listen to me, David. Maybe this little boy isn't right for you—"

"Of course he's right for me. He's a Martian."

She ignored the interruption. "And if he isn't right, there'll be another child who is. I promise you. And you said it yourself that you didn't know if you could handle all the problems he'd be bringing with him."

"I know—it's just that . . . I feel like—I don't know what I feel like. This is worse than anything I've ever been through. All this wanting and not having. Sometimes I'm afraid it's not going to happen at all."

Alice pulled the car over to the curb and turned off the engine. "Okay, it's my turn," she said. "Stop beating yourself up. You are the smartest one in the whole family—but sometimes you can be awfully stupid. You are going to be a terrific father to some very lucky little boy. Your caseworker knows that. All of those social workers in that meeting saw your commitment and dedication. All that research you did—when you asked about the Apgar numbers and the Conners scale, when you handed them that report on hyperactivity, which even they didn't know about—you *impressed* them."

I shook my head. "Research is easy. You post a note on CompuServe, wait two days, and then download your E-mail."

"It's not the research," Alice said. "It's the fact that you did it. That demonstrates your willingness to find out what the child needs so you can provide it."

"I wish I could believe you," I said.

She looked deeply at me. "What's the matter?"

"What if I'm really *not* good enough?" I said. "That's what I'm worried about—I can't shake that feeling."

"Oh, that—" she said, lightly. "*That's* normal. That's the proof that you're going to do okay. It's only those parents who don't worry who need to."

"Oh," I said. And then we both started laughing.

She hugged me then. "You'll do fine. Now let's go home and call Mom before she busts a kidney from the suspense."

Two centuries later, although the calendar insisted otherwise, Ms. Bright called me. "We've made a decision. If you're still interested in Dennis, we'd like to arrange a meeting—" I don't remember a lot of what she said after that; most of it was details about how we would proceed; but I remember what she said at the end. "I want to tell you the two things that helped us make the decision. First, all that research you did shows that you're committed to Dennis's needs. That's very important in any adoption, but especially in this one. The other thing was what you said at the end of the meeting—about understanding his need to be a Martian. We were really touched by your empathy for his situation. We think that's a quality that Dennis is going to need very much in any family he's placed in. That's why we decided to try you first."

I thanked her profusely; at least, I think I did; I was suddenly having trouble seeing, and the box of tissues had gone empty.

I met Dennis three days later, at the Johnson Group Home in Culver City. He was one of six children living at the facility; four boys, two girls. Because the caseworkers didn't want him to know that he was being *auditioned,* I would be introduced as a friend of the group home parents.

The child who came home from school was a sullen little zombie, going through the motions of life. He walked in the door, walked past me with no sign of recognition, and headed straight to his room. I said, "Hi." He grunted something that could have been "H'lo" and kept on going. For a moment, I felt somehow cheated. I recognized him, why hadn't he recognized me? And then I had to remind myself with a grin that I was the grown-up, not him. But, after a bit, he came out from his retreat and asked me to play electric hockey.

For the first few minutes, he was totally intent on the game. I didn't exist to him. Then I remembered an exercise from one of my communications courses—about simply *being with* another person. I stopped trying so hard to do it *right,* and instead just focused my attention on Dennis, letting it be all right with me for him to be exactly the way he was.

And yet, I couldn't turn off the analytical part of my mind. After reading all those reports, and hearing all the opinions of the caseworkers, I couldn't help but watch for evidence. I couldn't see it. None of it. All I could see was a child. And then that thing happened that always happens to an adult who is willing to play with a child. I rediscovered my own childhood again. I got involved in the game, and very shortly I was smiling and laughing when he did, returning the same delight and approval at every audacious play. And that's when it happened. He began to realize that there was a real human being on the opposite side of the game board. Something sparked. He started reacting to me instead of to the puck. I could feel the sense of connection almost as a physical presence.

Then, abruptly, it was time for him to do his chores. We loaded up the wagon with the cans from the recycling bin and walked them over to the nearby park. We talked about stuff. He talked, I listened. Sometimes I asked questions, sometimes he did. On the way back, he insisted that I pull the wagon so he could ride in it. By now, he was glowing. He was the boy in the photograph.

When we got back to the group home, however, the other children had arrived home from school and were already playing together in the backyard. As soon as he saw them, Dennis broke away from me and ran to the back of the yard. He flung himself into the corner of a large old couch and curled up in a ball. He was as apart from the other children—indeed the whole world—as it was possible to get.

What had suddenly triggered his unhappiness? Was it the thought that now that there were other children to play with, I would reject him? Did he have to reject me first? Or was there something else going on? From inside the house, I watched him as he sat alone. He was a very unhappy little boy. And he had stopped glowing. At that moment, I knew I couldn't leave him here. Whatever other problems he might have, my commitment was bigger. Or so I believed.

The group home parents invited me to stay to dinner with the children. I hadn't planned on it, but all the children insisted that I stay, so I did, specifically making a point of sitting next to Dennis. He didn't talk at all, he was subdued, as if he was afraid of losing something that he wanted very much—or maybe that was only my perception. He ate quietly and timidly. But then Tony, one of the more excitable children, suddenly piped up, "Do you know what Dennis said?"

Tony was sitting directly across from me. He had that look of malicious mischief common to children who are about to betray a confidence. "What?" I asked, with a queasy foreboding.

"Dennis said he wishes you were his dad." Even without looking, I could see that beside me, Dennis was cringing, readying himself for the inevitable politely worded rejection.

Instead, I turned to Dennis, focusing all my attention on him, and said, "Wow, what a great wish. Thank you!" There was more I wanted to add, but I couldn't. Not yet. The "game plan" required me to be Dennis's "special friend" for at least six weeks before I made any kind of commitment to him. He couldn't know that I had the same wish he did. I felt cheated at not being able to add, "So do I." But I understood the rationale, and I would follow it.

"Better watch out," Tony said. "He might make it a Martian wish, and then you'll *have* to."

At the time, I didn't understand what Tony had meant. So I forgot about it.

The next time I heard about Martians happened thirteen months later.

I was in Arizona, at a party at Jeff Duntemann's sprawling house. Jeff is a two-time Hugo nominee who gave up science fiction to write books about computer programming. Apparently, it was far more profitable than science fiction; now he was publishing his own magazine, *PC-Techniques*. I write a regular column for the magazine, an off-the-wall mix of code and mutated zen. It was the standing joke that my contribution to the magazine was the "Martian perspective."

I was sitting on the patio, watching Dennis splash enthusiastically across the pool. He was doing cannonballs into the deep end. A year ago, I couldn't pry him loose from the steps in the shallow end; he wouldn't even let me teach him how to dog paddle—now he was an apprentice fish. He spent more time swimming across the bottom of the water than the top.

A year ago, he'd been a waif—capable of joy, the picture proved that—but more often sad, uncertain, alienated, and angry. A year ago, he'd told his caseworker, "I don't think God listens to my prayers. I prayed for a dad and nothing happened." On the day he moved in, I asked his caseworker to remind him of that conversation and then tell him that sometimes it takes God a little while to make a miracle happen.

A miracle—according to my friend Randy Macnamara—is something that wouldn't have happened anyway. Now, after the fact, after the first giddy days of panic and joy, after the days of bottomless fears, after the tantrums and the testing, after a thousand and one peanut butter and jellyfish sandwiches, I understood what he meant. And more. A miracle takes real commitment. It never happens by accident. I'd had other miracles happen in my life—one which I'd written about, one which I may never write about—but this one was the best. I had the proof of it framed on my wall.

One afternoon I'd opened Dennis's lunch kit to see how much he'd eaten and found the note I'd packed that morning. It said, "Please eat your whole lunch today! I love you! Daddy." On the other side, written in a childish scrawl, was Dennis's reply: *"I love you to. you are very specil to me. I realy think your the best. I love you very much dady I never loved eneyone more than you. I never new anyone nicer than you."* At the bottom, he'd drawn three hearts and put the word "dady" in the biggest of them.

So the miracle was complete. Dennis *could* form a deep attachment. And he could express it. And all I had to do was sit and glow and realize that despite all my doubts and all my mistakes, I was getting the important part of the job done right. I had passed from wannabe to gonnabe to finding-how-to-be to simply be-ing. I was glowing as brightly as the warm Arizona evening. Pink clouds were striped across the darkening twilight sky.

I didn't know anyone else at the party besides Jeff and Carol—and the world-famous Mr. Byte who was in the kitchen begging scraps he wasn't supposed to have. But that was all right. I was content just to sit and watch my son enjoying himself. And then I heard the word "Martian" in back of me, and without moving, my attention swiveled 180 degrees.

Four of the wives were sitting together—it was that kind of party; the programmers were talking code, the wives were talking children. I didn't know enough about either subject, I still felt like a dabbler in both fields, so I made the best kind of listener. One of the women was saying, "No, it's true. Since she was old enough to talk she's insisted that she's a Martian. Her mother has never been able to convince her otherwise. She asked her, 'How do you explain that I remember going to the hospital and giving birth to you?' and she said, 'I was implanted in your tummy.' She's twelve now and she still believes it. She has a whole story, an explanation for everything. She says UFOs are implanting Martian babies all the time."

The other women laughed gently. I found myself smiling to myself and watching Dennis. Remembering for the first time in a long while what he'd once told his caseworker—that he was a Martian too. Interesting coincidence.

Then, one of the others said, "We had a boy in my daughter's school who wore a T-shirt to school almost every day that said, 'I am a Martian.' He took a lot of teasing about it. The principal tried to make him stop wearing it, but he refused. All the kids thought he was crazy."

"That was probably the only way he could get the attention he needed."

"Well," said the fourth voice, "it's a common childhood fantasy—that the child is really a changeling or an orphan and that you're not her real mother. Adding Mars to it is just a way to take advantage of the information in the real world to make it more believable."

I didn't hear any more of that conversation; we were interrupted by Carol announcing that dessert was served; but a seed of inquiry had been planted. If nothing else, I thought it might make an interesting story. If only I could figure out an ending for it. Let's see, a man adopts a little boy and then discovers that the child is a Martian.

Hmm. But what's the hook?

Horror story? Too easy. Too obvious—the Martian children are going to murder us in our beds. Besides, Richard Matheson could do it better, if he hadn't already. John Wyndham already had. A hidden invasion? The Martians will take us over without our ever knowing? Fred Brown had beaten me to it by four decades. His story had even ended up as an episode on Hitchcock. Maybe something tender and gentle instead? Parenting a starlost orphan? That would be the hardest to write—and Zenna Henderson had already written it several times over. Sturgeon was another one who could handle that angle. I wished I could pick up the phone and call him. He would have had the most interesting insight for the ending, but the connect charges would have been horrendous. I could call Harlan, of course, but he'd probably bitch at me for interrupting him during *Jeopardy*. Besides, I didn't think he would take this question seriously. "Harlan, listen—I think my son's a Martian, and I'm trying to write it up as a story . . ." Yeah, right, David. Have you had your medication checked recently?

I made a mental note to think about it later. Maybe my subconscious would think about it during the drive home. Maybe I'd stumble across an ending by accident. I really couldn't do anything at all without an ending in mind. It's easy to start a story, but if you don't know the ending, you don't know what you're writing toward and after a while the story goes adrift, the energy fails, and you've got one more thing to be frustrated about. I had a file cabinet full of unfinished stories to prove that this was not the best way to generate pay copy.

The next day . . . we were slicing across the desolate red desert, seemingly suspended between the blazing sky and the shimmering road, not talking about anything, just listening to a tape of Van Dyke Parks and sipping sodas from the cooler. The tape came to an end and the white noise of the wind rushed in to envelop us. Convertibles are fun, but they aren't quiet.

Abruptly, I remembered last night's conversation.

"Hey," I asked. "Are you a Martian?"

"What?"

"Are you a Martian?" I repeated.

"Why do you ask that?"

"Ah, obviously you're a Jewish Martian. You answer a question with a question."

"Who told you I was a Martian?"

"Kathy did. Before I met you, we had a meeting. She told me all about you. She said that you told her you were a Martian. Do you remember telling her that?"

"Yes."

"Are you still a Martian?"

"Yes," he said.

"Oh," I said. "Do you want to tell me about it?"

"Okay," he said. "I was made on Mars. I was a tadpole. Then I was brought to Earth in a UFO and implanted in my mommy's tummy. She didn't know. Then I was borned."

"Ahh," I said. "That's how I thought it happened. Is that all?"

"Uh-huh."

"Why did the Martians send you here?"

"So I could be a Earth-boy."

"Oh."

"Can we go to Round Table Pizza for dinner?" he asked, abruptly changing the subject as if it was the most natural thing to do.

"Do Martians like pizza?"

"Yes!" he said excitedly. Then he pointed his fingers at me like a funny kind of ray gun. Most children would have pointed the top two fingers to make a pretend gun, but Dennis pointed his index and little fingers, his thumb stood straight up for the trigger. "If you don't take me out for pizza tonight, I'll have to disneygrade you."

"Ouch, that sounds painful. I definitely do not want to be dis-neygraded. Then I'd have to stand in the dark and sing that awful song forever while boatloads of Japanese tourists take pictures of me. But we're not going tonight. Maybe tomorrow, if you have a good day at school."

"No, tonight!" He pointed his fingers menacingly—both hands now—and for a moment I wondered what would happen if he pressed his thumbs forward. Would I be turned into a giant three-fingered mouse?

"If you disneygrade me," I said, "for sure you won't get any pizza."

"Okay," he said. Then he closed up both weapons, first one hand, then the other. First the little finger of his left hand, then the index finger; then the little finger of his right hand, then the index finger. Each time he made a soft clicking sound with his mouth. Finally he folded his thumbs down—and abruptly he had hands again.

Later, I tried to do the same thing myself. A human can do it, but it's like the Vulcan salute. It takes practice.

I have pinched a nerve in my back. If I do my twisting exercises a couple of times a week, and if I take frequent breaks from the keyboard, and if I remember to put myself into the spa every couple days and let the bubbles boil up around me, then I can keep myself functioning pretty much like a normal person. It's a fair trade. Usually I wait until after dinner to sit in the spa. After the sun sets is a perfect time for a little skinnydipping.

Several days after the Phoenix trip, Dennis and I were alone in the pool. The pool has a blue filter over the light, the spa has a red one; when the bubbles are on, it looks a little like a hot lava bath. Sometimes we talk about nothing important, sometimes we just sit silently letting the bubbles massage our skins, sometimes we stare up into the sky and watch for meteors; once we'd seen a bright red starpoint streak across the sky like a bullet.

But tonight, as he splashed in the bubbles, I found myself studying the way the light shaped his features. I'm not an expert on the development of children's skulls, but abruptly I was struck by the odd proportions of his forehead and eyes.

Before I'd adopted him, I'd been given copies of various doctor's reports. One doctor, who was supposed to be looking for fetal alcohol effects, had described the five-year-old Dennis as "an unusual-looking" child. I couldn't see what he was talking about. To me, Dennis had always been an unusually good-looking boy.

There are only two shapes of faces—pie and horse. Dennis was a pie-face, I'm a horse. In that, he was lucky because his smile was so wide he *needed* a round face to hold it all. He was blessed with dark blond hair which was growing steadily toward shoulder-length. His eyes were puppy-brown and hidden behind lashes long enough to trouble the sleep of mascara manufacturers. His complexion was as luminous and gold as an Arizona sunset.

His body was well proportioned too; he had long legs and a swimmer's torso. He was thin, but not skinny. He looked like a Disney child. I expected him to be a heartbreaker when he grew up. The girls were going to chase him with lassos. Already I wondered what kind of a teenager he would become—and if I would be able to handle it.

Now . . . seeing him in the reflected red light of the spa—is this the same color light they have on Mars?—he did look a little *alien* to me. His forehead had a roundish bulge toward the crown. His cheekbones seemed strangely angled. His eyes seemed narrow and reptilian. Probably it was the effect of the light coming from underneath instead of above, combined with the red filter, but it was momentarily unnerving. For a moment, I wondered what kind of a *thing* I'd brought into my life.

"What?" he asked, staring back.

"Nothing," I said.

"You were looking at me."

"I was admiring you. You're a beautiful kid, do you know that?"

"Uh-huh." And suddenly he was Dennis again.

"How do you know that?"

"Everybody says so. They all like my eyelashes."

I laughed. Of course. Here was a child who'd learned to work the system. He was a skilled manipulator. He'd learned real fast how to turn on his special smile and get what he wanted out of people. Of course he knew how much attention his eyelashes attracted.

But—for a moment there, he hadn't been Dennis the little boy. He'd been something else. Something cold and watchful. He'd noticed me studying him. He'd sensed the suspicion. Or was it just the power of suggestion at work? Most of the books on parenting advised not to feel guilty for wondering if your child is going to suddenly catch a fly with his tongue. It's a very common parental fear.

And then . . . whenever I had doubts about Dennis and my ability to keep up with him, all I had to do was ask myself one simple question. How would I feel if Kathy Bright said she had to remove him from my home? *Ripped apart* was the simplest answer. The truth was, I didn't care if he was a Martian or not, I was as *bonded* to him as he was to me.

But out of curiosity, and possibly just to reassure myself that I was imagining things, I logged on to CompuServe. The ISSUES forum has a parenting section. I left a message under the heading, "Is your child a Martian?"

> My little boy says he's a Martian. I've heard of two other children who claim to be Martians as well. Has anyone else heard of children who believe that they're from Mars?

Over the course of the next few days—before the message scrolled off the board and into the bit bucket—I received thirty-three replies.

Several of the messages were thoughtful analyses of why a child might say such a thing; it was pretty much what that mother in Phoenix had surmised; it's common for children to fantasize that they have glamorous origins. In the past, children might have believed they were secretly princes and princesses and one day their real parents would arrive to take them to their golden castles. But because that mythology has now been superseded by starships and mutants, it's more appropriate for children to fantasize about traveling away on the *Millennium Falcon* or the *Enterprise.* But if a child was experienced enough to know that those stories were just fiction, he would also know that Mars was a real planet; therefore . . . Mars gave credibility to the fantasy. Et cetera. Et cetera. Local mileage may vary, but if the delusion persists, see a good therapist. It may be evidence of some deeper problem. Et cetera some more.

I knew what Dennis's deeper problems were. He'd been bounced around the foster care system for eight years before landing in my arms. He didn't know *where* he came from or *where* he belonged.

Several of the replies I received were from other parents sharing pieces of weirdness their own children had demonstrated. Interesting, but not particularly useful to my inquiry.

But . . . there were over a dozen private messages.

> "My sister's little girl used to insist that she'd been brought to Earth in a UFO and implanted in her mommy's tummy while her mommy was

asleep. She kept this up until she was about fourteen, then abruptly stopped. After that, she wouldn't answer questions about it at all."

"My next door neighbors had a boy who said he wasn't from Earth. He disappeared when he was twelve. Without a trace. The police assumed he was kidnapped."

"My ex-wife was a child psychologist. She used to joke about her Martian children. She said she could tell how crazy New York was by the number of Martians she saw in any given year. At first she used to tell the parents that same old same old about children needing to fantasize about a glamorous background, but later on she began to wonder. The stories the kids told were all very similar. They began life as Martian tadpoles brought to Earth and implanted in the uteruses of Earth women. She always wanted to do a study on Martian children, but she could never get a grant."

"I dated a girl once who said she was from Mars. She was very insistent on it. When I tried to get serious with her, she turned me down flat. She said she really liked me, but it wouldn't work out between us. When I asked her why, she said it was because she was from Mars. That's all. I guess Martians have a rule against marrying outside their species."

"I heard about a Martian when I was in high school. He killed himself. I didn't know him. I only heard about it afterward."

"I thought I was from Mars once. I even had memories of being on Mars. It had a pink sky. That's how I knew it was Mars. When the photos came in from JPL showing that Mars really did have a pink sky, just like in my memories, I thought that proved something. When I told my parents, they took me to see a doctor. I was in therapy for a long time, but I'm fine now. Maybe you should get your son into therapy too."

It was the last one that really got to me. I knew the person who sent it meant to be reassuring, but instead, his message had the opposite effect.

Okay, maybe it's me. Maybe it's because I'm a writer. I read subtext where none is intended. And maybe the cumulative effect of all these messages, especially the wistful, almost plaintive tone of the last one, left me with a very uncomfortable feeling.

I replied to all of these messages.

I know this sounds silly, but please indulge me. What did your Martian friend/relative look like? Did he/she have any special physical characteristics or medical problems? What was his/her personality like? Do you know what happened to him or her? Does he/she still believe that he/she is from Mars?

It took a week or two to compile the responses. Of the ten Martians specifically mentioned, two had committed suicide. One was successful in business. Three refused to talk about Mars. Two were "cured." The whereabouts of the others were unknown. Three were missing. Two of the missing had been repeated runaways during their teen years. I wondered where they thought they were running *to*.

Of the ten Martians, six were known to have had golden-brown skin, round faces, brown eyes, and very long eyelashes. The hair color was generally dark blond or brown. That was an interesting statistical anomaly.

Of the ten Martians, five were hyperactive, two were epileptic. The other three weren't known.

I asked the fellow whose ex-wife had been a child psychologist if she'd ever noticed any statistical patterns among her Martians. He said he didn't know and he didn't even know her whereabouts anymore. She had disappeared two years earlier.

I called my friend Steve Barnes. He'd written one of the character references I'd needed to adopt Dennis, and because of that I regarded him as an unofficial godfather to the boy. We chatted about this and that and the other thing for a while. And then, finally, I said, "Steve—do you know about the Martian phenomenon?" He didn't. I told him about it. He asked me if I was smoking dope again.

"I'm serious, Steve."

"So am I."

"I haven't touched that crap since I kicked out she-who-must-not-be-named." I said it angrily.

"Just checking. You gotta admit that's a pretty bizarre story, though."

"I know that. That's why I'm telling you. You're one of the few people I know who will actually consider it fairly. Geez—why is it that science fiction writers are the most skeptical animals of all?"

"Because we get to deal with more crazies than anyone else," Steve replied without missing a beat.

"I don't know what to do with this," I said, admitting my frustration. "I know it sounds like one more crazy UFO mystery. Only this one is something that can actually be validated. This is the kind of statistical anomaly that can't be explained away by coincidence. And I bet there's a lot more to it too. Like, what was the blood type of all those children? What was the phase of the moon? What are their favorite foods? How well did they do in school? What if there's something really going on here?—maybe not Martians, maybe some kind of social phenomenon or syndrome—I don't know what it is, I don't know what else to ask, and I don't know who to tell. Most of all, I don't want to end up on the front page of the *Enquirer*. Can't you just see it? 'SCI-FI WRITER HAS MARTIAN CHILD!' "

"It might be good for your career," Steve said thoughtfully. "I wonder how many new readers you could pick up."

"Oh, yeah, sure. And I wonder how many old readers I'll lose. I'd like to be taken seriously in my old age, Steve. Remember what happened to what's-his-name."

"I'll never forget old what's-his-name," Steve said. "Yeah, that was a real sad story."

"Anyway . . . ," I said. "You see my point? Where do I go from here?"

"You want my *real* advice?" Steve asked. He didn't wait for my reply. "Don't go anywhere with it. Drop it. Let someone else figure it out. Or no one. You said it yourself, David. 'It's almost always dangerous to be right too soon.' Don't go borrowing trouble. Turn it into a story if you must and let people think it's a harmless fantasy. But don't let it screw up your life. You wanted this kid, didn't you? Now you have him. Just parent him. That's the only thing that's really wanted and needed."

He was right. I knew it. But I couldn't accept it. "Sure. That's easy for you to say. You don't have a Martian in the house."

"Yes I do." He laughed. "Only mine's a girl."

"Huh—?"

"Don't you get it? *All* children are Martians. We get thirteen years to civilize the little monsters. After that, it's too late. Then they start eating our hearts out for the rest of our lives."

"You sound like my mother now."

"I'll take that as a compliment."

"It's a good thing you don't know her, or you wouldn't say that."

"Listen to me, David," and his tone of voice was so serious that six different jokes died before they could pass my lips. "You're right on schedule. Have you ever really looked at the faces of new parents? Most of them are walking around in a state of shock, wondering what happened—what is this loathsome reptilian thing that has suddenly invaded their lives? It's part of the process of assimilation. The only difference is that you have a more active imagination than most people. You know how to name your fears. Trust me on this, Toni and I went through it too with Nicki. We thought she was a—never mind. Just know that this normal. There are days when you are absolutely certain that you've got a cute and stinky little alien in your house."

"But *every* day?"

"Trust me. It passes. In a year or two, you won't even remember what your life was like before."

"Hmm. Maybe that's how long it takes a Martian to brainwash his human hosts . . ."

Steve sighed. "You've got it bad."

"Yes, I do," I admitted.

The Martian thing gnawed at me like an ulcer. I couldn't get it out of my head. No matter what we did, the thought was there.

If we went out front to swat koosh balls back and forth, I wondered if the reason he was having trouble with his coordination was the unfamiliar gravity of Earth. If we went in the backyard and jumped in the pool together, I wondered if his attraction to water was because it was so scarce on Mars. I wondered about his ability to hear a piece of music a single time and still remember the melody so clearly that he could sing it again, note for note, a month later; he would walk through the house singing songs that he could not have heard except on the tapes I occasionally played; how many nine-year-olds know how to sing *My Clone Sleeps Alone* like Pat Benatar? I wondered why he had so little interest in comic books, but loved to watch television dramas about the relationships of human beings. He hated *Star Trek;* he thought it was "too silly." He loved the Discovery channel—especially all the shows about animals and insects.

There was no apparent pattern to his behavior, nothing that could be pointed to as evidence of otherworldliness. Indeed, the fact that he was making his father paranoid was a very strong argument that he was a normal Earth kid.

And then, just when I'd forgotten . . . something would happen. Maybe he'd react to something on television with an off-the-wall comment that would make me look over at him curiously. There was that Bugs Bunny cartoon, for instance, where the rabbit is making life difficult for Marvin the Martian, stealing the detonator so he can't blow up the Earth. In the middle of it, Dennis quietly declared, "No, that's wrong. Martians aren't like that." Then he got up and turned the television set *off.*

"Why did you do that?" I asked.

"Because it was wrong," he said blandly.

"But it's only a cartoon." One of my *favorite* cartoons, I might add.

"It's still wrong." And then he turned and went outside as if the whole concept of television would never be interesting to him again.

And now, almost two years to the day since I'd filled out the first application, the nickel finally dropped and I sat up in bed in the middle of the night. Why were so many adopted children *hyper-active?*

The evidence was all around me. I just hadn't noticed it before. It was there in the photo-listing books. It seemed as if every third child was hyperactive. It was acknowledged in the books, the articles, the seminars, the tapes . . . that a higher proportion of foster children have Attention Deficit Disorder, also called hyperactivity. Why was that?

Some theorists suggested that it was the result of substance abuse by the parents, which is why we saw it more in abandoned and unwanted children. Some doctors believed that hyperactivity was the result of the body's failure to produce certain key enzymes in response to physical stimulation; therefore the child needed to over-stimulate himself in order to produce an equivalent amount of calming. Still others postulated that there was an emotional component to the disorder; that it was a response to a lack of nurturing. Most interesting of all to me was the offhand note in one article that some theorists believed that many cases of ADD were actually misdiagnoses. If you were unattached and didn't know who you were or where you had come from or where you were going, you'd have a lot to worry about; your attention might be distracted too.

Or . . . what if the behavior that was judged abnormal for Earth children was perfectly normal for Martian children? What if there was no such thing as ADD . . . in Martians?

At this point, I'd reached the limits of my ability to research the question. Who could I tell? Who would have the resources to pursue this further? And who would take me seriously?

Suppose I picked up the *Los Angeles Times* tomorrow and saw that Ben Bova had called a press conference to announce that he'd been kidnapped by aliens and taken into space where they'd performed bizarre sexual experiments on him . . . would I believe him? Ben is one of the most believable men in the world. Once, he almost talked me into voting for Ronald Reagan. But if I saw a report like that in the newspaper, the first thing I'd do would be to call Barbara and ask if Ben were all right.

In other words . . . there was simply no way for me to research this question without destroying all of my credibility as a writer.

Even worse, *there was no way to research it without also destroying my credibility as a parent.*

Up until this time, I'd always been candid with the caseworkers and therapists; I'd talked to them about our discipline problems, about my feelings of frustration, about every little step in the right direction and every major victory. But . . . suddenly, I realized this was something I couldn't talk to them about. Suppose I called Kathy Bright. What could I say? "Uh, Kathy, it's David. I want to talk to you about Dennis. You know how he says he's a Martian? Well, I think he might *really* be a Martian and . . ."

Uh-huh.

If the adoptive father was starting to have hallucinations about the child, how long would the Department of Children's Services leave the child in that placement? About twenty minutes, I figured. About as long as it took to get out there and pick him up. She'd pull him out of my house so fast they'd be hearing sonic booms in Malibu. And I wouldn't even be able to argue. She'd be right to do so. A child needs a stable and nurturing environment. How stable and nurturing would it be for him to be living with an adult who suspects he's from another planet and is wondering about his ultimate motives?

If I pursued this, I'd lose my son.

The thought was intolerable. I might never recover. I was sure that he wouldn't. For the first time in his life, he'd finally formed an attachment. What would it do to him to have it broken so abruptly? It would truly destroy his ability to trust any other human being.

I couldn't do that to him. I couldn't do *anything* that might hurt him.

And what about me? I had my own "attachment issues." I couldn't stand the thought of another failure. Another brick in the wall, as they say.

That was where I stayed stuck for the longest time. I walked around the house in physical pain for three weeks. My chest hurt. My head hurt. My legs hurt. My back hurt. My eyes hurt. My throat hurt. The only part of me that didn't hurt was my brain. That was so numb, I couldn't think.

I didn't know if he was a Martian or not. But something weird was going on. Wasn't it? And if it was just me—if I was going insane—then what right do I have to try to parent this child anyway? Either way I lose. If he's a Martian, I can't tell anyone. And if he isn't a Martian, then I'm going crazy.

I started looking for local evidence. I began browsing through my journal. I'd been making daily notes of interesting incidents, in case I ever wanted to write a book about our experiences. At first, I couldn't find anything. Most of the incidents I'd written about were fairly mundane. Not even good *Reader's Digest* material.

For instance, the week after he moved in, I'd taken him to the baseball game at Dodger Stadium. For the first part of the game,

he'd been more interested in having a pennant and getting some
cotton candy than in what was going on down on the stadium floor
But along about the fifth inning, he'd climbed up onto my lap and I
began explaining the game to him. "See that man at home plate
holding the bat. Wish for him to hit the ball right out of the park."

"Okay," said Dennis.

Cra-a-ack! The ball went sailing straight out into the right field
stands. Someone in the lower deck caught it and the runner saun-
tered easily around the bases while the organist played, "Glory, glory
Hallelujah."

"You're a good wisher, Dennis. That was terrific. Want to try it
again?"

"No."

"Okay."

Two innings later, the Dodgers were one run behind. I asked
Dennis to wish for hits again. Four pitches later, there were runners
at first and third. It didn't matter to me who came up to bat now; I
hadn't remembered the names of any ballplayers since Roy Cam-
panella was catching for Don Drysdale and Sandy Koufax. As far as
I was concerned, Who was on first, What was on second, and I Don't
Know still played third. I liked baseball only so long as I didn't have
to be an expert; but I'd never seen the Dodgers win a game. Every
time I came to the stadium they lost; so I'd made it a point to stay
away from Dodger Stadium to give them a fair chance at winning. I
didn't expect them to win tonight; but Dennis's wishes had brought
them from three runs behind.

"Okay, Dennis," I said, giving him a little squeeze. "It's time for
one last wish. See that guy at the home plate, holding the bat. You
gotta wish for him to hit a home run. All the way out of the park.
Just like before. Okay?"

"Okay."

And just like before—*cra-a-ack*—the ball went sailing deep into
right field, triggering a sudden cluster of excited fans scrambling
down across the seats.

The Dodgers won that night. All the way home, I kept praising
Dennis for his excellent wishing.

A couple of weeks after that, we were stopped at a light, waiting for
it to change. It was one of those intersections that existed slightly

sideways to reality. Whenever you stopped there, time slowed down to a crawl. Without even thinking, I said, "Dennis, wish for the light to turn green, please."

"Okay," he said.

—and abruptly the light turned green. I frowned. It seemed to me the cycle hadn't quite completed.

Nah. I must have been daydreaming. I eased the car through the intersection. A moment later, we got caught at the next red light. I said a word.

"Why'd you say that?"

"These lights are supposed to be synchronized," I said. "So you only get green ones. We must be out of synch. Why don't you wish for this light to change too, please."

"Okay."

—green.

"Boy! You are really a *good* wisher."

"Thank you."

A minute later, I said, "Can you wish this light to turn green too?"

"No," he said, abruptly angry. "You're going to use up all my wishes."

"Huh?" I looked over at him.

"I only have so many wishes and you're going to use them all up on stoplights." There was a hurt quality in his voice.

I pulled the car over to the side of the road and stopped. I turned to him and put my hand gently on his shoulder. "Oh, sweetheart. I don't know who told you that, but that's not so. The wish bag is bottomless. You can have as many wishes as you want."

"No, you can't," he insisted. "I have to save my wishes for things that are important."

"What's the most important thing you ever wished for?" I asked, already knowing the answer.

He didn't answer.

"What's the most important wish?" I repeated.

Very softly, he admitted, "I wished for a dad. Someone who would be nice to me."

"Uh-huh. And did you get your wish?"

He nodded.

"So, you see, sweetheart. There's no shortage of miracles."

I didn't know if he believed me. It was still too early in the process. We were still learning who each other was. I noted the conversation in my journal and let the matter slide. But it left me with an uncomfortable feeling. What has to happen to a child to make him believe there's a limit to wishes?

A year later, I looked at the words I'd written glowing on the computer screen, and *wondered* about Dennis's ability to wish. It was probably a coincidence. But maybe it wasn't. That time we'd matched four out of six numbers in the lottery and won eighty-eight dollars—was that the week I'd asked him to wish real hard for us to win?

Maybe Martians have precognitive or telekinetic powers . . . ?

Dennis likes cleaning things. Without asking, he'll go out and wash the car, or the patio. He'll give the dogs baths. He'll vacuum the rugs and take the Dustbuster to the couch. He'll mop the floors. His favorite toys are a sponge and a squirt bottle of Simple Green. I've seen him take a rusty old wrench he found in a vacant field and scrub the rust off of it until it shone like new. One night after dinner, after he finished methodically loading the dishwasher, I sat him down at the kitchen table and told him I had a surprise for him.

"What?"

"It's a book of puzzles."

"Oh." He sounded disappointed.

"No, listen. Here's the game. You have twenty minutes to do these puzzles, and then when you finish, I add them up and we'll find out how smart you are. Do you want to do this?"

"It'll really tell you how smart I am?"

"Uh-huh."

He grabbed for the book and a pencil.

"Wait a minute—let me set the timer. Okay? Now once you start, you can't stop. You have to go all the way through to the end. Okay?"

"Okay."

"Ready?"

"Ready."

"One, two, three . . . go."

He attacked the first three puzzles with a vengeance. They were simple. Pick the next shape in a series: triangle, square, pentagon . . . ? Which object doesn't belong: horse, cow, sheep, scissors? Feather is to Bird as Fur is to: dog, automobile, ice cream . . . ?

Then the puzzles started getting harder and he started to frown. He brushed his hair out of his eyes and once he stopped to clean his glasses; but he stayed interested and involved and when the timer went off, he didn't want to stop. He insisted that he be allowed to finish the puzzle he was working on. What the hell. I let him.

"What does it say?" Dennis asked as I computed the percentile. He wanted to grab the test book out of my hand.

"Well . . . let me finish here." I held it out of his reach as I checked the table of percentiles.

The test showed that he had above-average intelligence—not unexpected; hyperactive kids tend to be brighter than average—but well within the normal range for a nine-year-old. "It says that you are fifty-two inches high, that you weigh sixty-six pounds, and that your daddy loves you very much. It also says that you are very smart."

"How smart?"

"Well, if this test were given to one hundred children, you would be smarter than ninety-two of them."

"How good is that?"

"That's *very* good. You can't get much better. And it means we should go out for ice cream after dinner. What do you think?"

"Yeah!"

Oh, that was another thing. He didn't like chocolate. He preferred rainbow sherbet. I'd never seen that in a kid before.

A couple of weeks later, we played another game. I made sure to pick a quiet evening, one with no distractions. "This game is even harder," I explained. "It's a kind of card game," I explained. "See these cards? There are six different shapes here. A circle, a square, a star, three squiggly lines, a cross, and a figure eight. All you have to do is guess which one I'm looking at. See if you can read my mind, okay?"

He frowned at me, and I had to explain it two or three more times. This was not a game he wanted to play. I said okay and started to put the deck away. If he didn't want to cooperate, the results would be inconclusive. "Can we go for ice cream after we do this?" he asked abruptly.

"Sure," I said.

"Okay, let's do it then."

"All right. We have to do it five times. Do you think you can do it that many times?"

He shrugged. I laid out a paper in front of him, showing him the shapes so he would be able to remember them all. I told him he could close his eyes if it would help him concentrate. The test conditions were less than perfect, but if there were any precognitive or telepathic powers present, five trials should be enough to demonstrate them.

Half an hour later, I knew.

Martians aren't telepathic.

But they do like rainbow sherbet. A lot.

There were other tests. Not many. Not anything too weird. Just little ones that might indicate if there was something worth further investigation. There wasn't. As near as I could determine, there was nothing so unusual about Dennis that it would register as a statistical anomaly in a repeatable testable circumstance. He couldn't levitate. He couldn't move objects. He couldn't make things disappear. He didn't know how to *grok*. He could only hold his breath for thirty-three seconds. He couldn't *think* muscles. He couldn't see around corners.

But—

He *could* predict elevators. Take him into any building, anywhere. Take him to the elevator bank. Let him push the up button. Don't say a word. Without fail, the door he stands in front of will be the one where the first elevator arrives. Was he wishing them or predicting them? I don't know. It's useful only at science fiction conventions, which are legendary for recalcitrant elevators. It has little value anywhere else in the world.

He could make stoplights turn green—sometimes. Mostly, he waited until he saw the lights for the cross street turn yellow before he announced his wish. Maybe he could still make the Dodgers score four runs in two innings—but it wasn't consistent. We went back to Dodger Stadium in May, and either Dennis wasn't wishing or he really had used up all his wishes.

He *could* sing with perfect pitch, especially if the lyrics were about Popeye's gastrointestinal distress. He could play a video game for four hours straight without food or water. He could invent an amazing number of excuses for not staying in bed. He could also hug my neck so hard that once I felt a warning crack in my trachea. My throat hurt for a week afterward.

I began to think that *maybe* I had imagined the whole thing.

On school nights, I tucked him in at 9:30. We had a whole ritual. If there was time, we read a storybook together; whatever was appropriate. Afterward, prayers—

"I'm sorry God for . . . I didn't do anything to be sorry for."

"How about sassing your dad? Remember you had to take a time-out?"

"Oh, yeah. I'm sorry God for sassing my dad. Thank you God for . . . um, I can't think of anything."

"Going swimming."

"No. Thank you God for Calvin, my cat."

"Good. Anything else you want to say to God?"

"Does God hear the prayers of Martians?"

"Uh . . . of course he does. God hears everybody's prayers."

"Not Martians."

"Yes, even Martians."

"Uh-uh."

"Why do you say no?"

"Because God didn't make any Martians."

"If God didn't make the Martians, then who did?"

"The devil."

"Did the devil make you?"

"Uh-huh."

"How do you know?"

"Because . . . I'm a Martian."

"Mmm," I said, remembering a little speech I'd made just about a year ago. *Let it be all right for him to be a Martian for as long as he needs to be.* "All right," I said. "But let me tell you a secret," I whispered. "The devil didn't make any Martians. That's just a lie the devil wants you to believe. God made the Martians."

"Really?"

"Cross my heart and hope to die. Stick a noodle in my eye."

"How do you know?" He was very insistent.

"Because I talk to God every night," I said. "Just like you, I say my prayers. And God made everything in the world."

"But Martians aren't from this world—"

"That's right. But God made Mars too. And everything on it. Just like she made this world, she made a whole bunch of others, and Mars was one of them. Honest."

"How come you say 'she' when you talk about God?"

"Because sometimes God is female and sometimes God is male. God is everything. And now it's time for you to stop asking questions and go to sleep. Hugs and kisses—?"

"Hugs and kisses."

"G'night. No more talking."

"I love you."

"I love you too. Now no more talking."

"Dad?"

"What?"

"I have to tell you something."

"What?"

"I love you."

"I love you too. Now, shhh. No more talking, Dennis."

"G'night."

"Sleep tight—"

Finally, I got smart. I stopped answering. Control freaks. We each wanted to have the last word.

I padded barefoot down the hall. I stopped in the living room long enough to turn off the television set, the VCR, and the surround-sound system. I continued on through the dining room and finally to my office. Two computers sat on my desk, both showing me that it was 9:47. The monster-child had manipulated an extra seventeen minutes tonight.

I sat down in my chair, leaned back, put my feet up on my desk, and stared out at the dark waters of the swimming pool in the back-yard. The pool glowed with soft blue light. The night was . . . silent. Somewhere, a dog, barked.

Somewhere—that was his name, yes; he was a writer's dog—lived under my desk. When I said, "Let's go to work," wherever he was in the house, Somewhere would pick himself up and laboriously pad-pad-pad into my office where he'd squelch himself flat and scrooch his way under the desk, with a great impassioned Jewish sigh of "I hope you appreciate what I do for you."

He'd stay there all day—as long as the computer was on. Somewhere would only come out for two things: cookies and the doorbell . . . and the doorbell was broken. It had been broken for as long as I'd lived in this house. I'd never had the need to get it fixed. If someone came to the door, the dog barked.

Somewhere, the dog, barked.

That was why I loved him so much. He was a living cliché. He was the only possible justification for one of the most infamous sentences in bad writing. It was just a matter of placing the commas correctly.

Somewhere had just enough intelligence to keep out of the way and more than enough intelligence to find his dinner dish—as long as no one moved it. He spent his mornings resting under my desk, his afternoons snoozing behind the couch, his evenings snoring next to Dennis; he spent the hours before dawn in the dark space underneath the headboard of my bed, dreaming about the refrigerator.

Almost every night, just as Dennis began saying his prayers, Somewhere would come sighing down the hall, a shaggy, absent-minded canine-American. He'd step over everything that was in his way, uncaring if he knocked over a day's worth of Lego construction. He'd climb onto the bed, over my lap, over Dennis, grumbling softly as he found his position next to Dennis. With his prehensile tongue, he could slurp the inside of Dennis's right ear from the left side of his head, taking either the internal or external route.

Tonight, though, he knew I wasn't finished working. I had some serious thinking to do. He remained under the desk, sighing about the overtime. "You're in super-golden hours," I said to him; he shut up.

Whenever I'm in doubt about something, I sit down and start writing. I write down everything I'm feeling or thinking or worrying about. I say everything there is to say until there's nothing left to say. The first time I did this was the day after my dad died. I sat and wrote for two days. When I was finished, I had a Nebula-nominated story, *In the Deadlands.* To this day I still don't fully understand what the story was about, but the emotional impact of it is undeniable. It still gives me the shudders.

But the lesson I learned from that experience was the most important thing I've ever learned about storytelling. Effective writing isn't in the mechanics. Anyone can master the mechanical act of stringing together words and sentences and paragraphs to make a character move from A to B. The bookstores are full of evidence. But that's not writing. Writing isn't about the words, it's about the experience. It's about the *feeling* that the story creates inside of you. If there's no feeling, there's no story.

But sometimes, there's only the feeling without any meaning or understanding. And that's not a story either. What I was feeling about Dennis was so confusing and troubling and uncertain that I couldn't even begin to sort it out. I needed to write down all the separate pieces—as if in the act of telling, it would sort itself out. Sometimes the process worked.

When I looked up again, three hours had passed. My back and shoulders ached. The dog had gone to bed, and I felt I had accomplished nothing at all except to delineate the scale of my frustration.

Why would an alien species come to this planet? The last time I spent that much time on this question, I came up with giant pink man-eating slugs in search of new flavors. Why would Martians send their children to Earth?

The most logical idea that I came up with was that they were here as observers. Spies.

Haven't you ever been pulling on your underwear and realized that your dog or your cat is watching you? Haven't you ever considered the possibility that the creature is sharing your secrets with some secret network of dogs and cats? *"Oh, you think that's weird? My human wears underwear with pictures of Rocky and Bullwinkle on them."*

But dogs and cats are limited in what they can observe. If you *really* want to know a culture, you have to be a member of it. But an alien couldn't step in and pretend to be a member of this culture, could he? He'd have to learn. He'd have to be taught . . .

Where could a Martian go to get lessons in being a human? Who gives lessons in human beingness?

Mommies and daddies. That's right.

"You're too paranoid," said my sane friend. He asked me to leave his name out of this narrative, so I'll just call him my sane friend.

"What do you mean?"

"You think that aliens are all motivated by evil intentions. You've written four novels about evil aliens eating our children, and you're working on a fifth. Isn't it possible that you're wrong?"

"*Moi?* Wrong?"

"Do you ever think about the cuckoo?" my sane friend asked.

"No," I said.

"Well, think about the cuckoo for a moment."

"Okay."

"How do you feel about the cuckoo?" he asked.

"It's an evil bird," I said. "It lays its egg in the sparrow's nest. The cuckoo chick pushes the other babies out of the nest. The sparrow ends up raising it—even at the expense of her own young. It's a parasite."

"See, that's your judgment talking—"

"That's the truth—" I started to object.

"Is it? Is that what you tell Dennis about his birth-mother?"

"Uh—I tell him that his birth-mom couldn't take care of him. And that she loves him and misses him. And that's the truth. Sort of . . . whitewashed."

My sane friend grinned at me.

"Okay," I admitted. "I'm protective of my son. So what?"

My sane friend shrugged. "How do you think the cuckoo feels?"

"Birds don't feel."

"If it could feel, how do you think it would feel?"

I thought about it. The first image that came to mind was the silly little bird from the Dr. Seuss story; the one who flew off, leaving Horton the elephant to hatch her egg. I shook my head. "I'm not getting anything useful—"

"How do you think Dennis's mother feels?"

I shook my head again. "Everything I've heard about her . . . I can't empathize."

"All right, try it this way. Under what circumstances would *you* give Dennis up?"

"I'd die before I'd give him up," I said. "He makes me happier than anybody I've ever known before. Just looking at him, I get an endorphin rush. If anybody started proceedings to take him out of my home, I'd have him on a plane to New Zealand so fast—" I stopped. "Oh, I see what you mean." I thought about it. "If I wasn't able to take care of him, or if I thought I was hurting him, or if I thought I wasn't doing a good enough job—" There was that old *familiar* twinge again. "If I thought he'd *really* be better off with someone else, I'd want him to have the best chance possible. But I just can't see that happening."

"Uh-huh . . ." My sane friend grinned. "*Now,* how do you think the Martians feel?"

"Huh?"

He repeated the question.

I thought about it for a while. "I'd have to assume that if they have the capability to implant their children in human wombs that they would have a highly developed science and technology and that implies—to me anyway—a highly developed emotional structure and probably a correspondingly well-developed moral structure as well. At least, that's what I'd like to believe."

"And if what you believe is true . . . ," he started to say.

I finished the thought for him. ". . . then the Martians are trusting us with their children."

"Aren't they?" he asked.

I didn't answer. I didn't like where that train of thought might lead. But I followed it anyway.

"Would you trust your child to apes or wolves?" my sane friend asked.

"No," I said. "You know what happens to feral children."

He nodded. "I've read the same books you have."

"So, if the Martians are trusting us with their children . . . then that implies that either they don't care about their children very much—or they do."

"You want my best guess?"

"This is where you resolve everything for me, isn't it?"

"No. This is where I tell you what I think. I think they're engaged in a long-term breeding experiment . . . to upgrade the level of intelligence and compassion in the human race."

"Yeah?" I gave him my best raised-eyebrow look. "Remember what happened to Spock? He was a half-breed too. His parents wanted to breed a logical human. Instead, they got an emotional Vulcan."

"Have you got a better guess?"

"No," I admitted. "But what kind of Martians *are* we raising?"

"What kind of Martian are *you* raising?" he corrected.

And that really did it for me. That was the question. "I don't know," I finally admitted. "But—he is mine to raise, isn't he?"

"Yep," my sane friend agreed.

That thought echoed for a long long moment. Finally, I acknowledged the truth of it with a grin. "Yeah," I said. "I can live with that . . ."

As a literary puzzle, this is incomplete. As a story, it doesn't work. There's no ending.

There isn't enough evidence for me to even *suggest* a conclusion. What do we know about the Martians? For that matter, what do we really know about ourselves? There's nothing to extrapolate. And if the Martians are really engaged in some kind of large-scale genetic engineering, we won't really know what their intentions are until the Martian children start reaching adulthood. Dennis will be old enough to vote in 2005. (And that raises *another* question. *How long* have the Martians been planting their babies in human homes? Maybe we *already* live in a Martian-influenced world?)

Maybe the Martian children will be super geniuses, inventing cold fusion and silicon sentience and nanotechnological miracles— Stephen Hawking and Buckminster Fuller. Maybe they'll be spiritual saviors, bringing such superior technology of consciousness that those of us brave enough to follow will achieve the enlightenment of saints. Maybe they'll be demagogues and dictators. Or maybe they'll be madmen and all end up in institutions. And maybe they'll be monsters, giving us a new generation of serial killers and cult leaders— Jack the Ripper and Charles Manson.

All we can do is wait and see how it works out.

There's one more thing.

In reviewing the material for this story, I came across a curious coincidence. Kathy Bright had given me several huge stacks of reports on Dennis, written by various therapists and counselors. I hadn't had time to read them all, and after the first few, I stopped —I didn't want *their* experience of Dennis; I wanted to make up my own mind. But as I paged through the files, looking for Martian stuff, one of them caught my eye. On Saturday, June 27, 1992, Carolyn Green (his counselor) had noted, "Dennis thinks God doesn't hear his prayers, because he wished for a dad and nothing happened."

I first saw Dennis's picture on Saturday, June 27, 1992, at about two in the afternoon. According to Carolyn Green's report, that was the exact time of his weekly session. I cannot help but believe that he was wishing for a dad at the exact moment I first saw his picture. *A Martian wish.* Was that what I felt so strongly?

Does it mean anything? Maybe. Maybe not. In any case, I know better than to argue with Martian wishes. Tonight, at bedtime, he wished for me to be happy.

I had to smile. "Was that a Martian wish?" I asked.

"Yes," he said, in a voice that left no room for disagreement.

"Then, I'm happy," I said. And in fact, I was.

I hadn't realized it before, because I hadn't acknowledged it, not even to myself; but as I walked back down the hall to my office, I had to admit that I was glowing. I'd gotten everything I'd wanted, a wonderful son, a profound sense of family, a whole new reason for waking up in the morning. So what if he's a Martian, it really doesn't matter, does it? He's my *son,* and I love him. I'm not giving him up. He's *special.*

When Dennis puts his mind to it, he can predict elevators and make stoplights turn green and help the Dodgers win baseball games. He can make lottery tickets pay off (a little bit, four numbers at a time) and he can wish a father into his life. That's pretty powerful stuff.

I think we might experiment with that a little bit more. We haven't bought any lottery tickets in a while. Maybe we should buy a couple tonight. And if that works, who knows what else he could wish for. I was thinking of asking him to wish for a Hugo Award for his dad—just a test, you understand—but this morning, he announced he was going to wish for a mom instead. I'll be *very* interested to see how that one works out.

Rhysling Award Winners

W. GREGORY STEWART and ROBERT FRAZIER
JEFF VANDERMEER
BRUCE BOSTON

The Rhysling Awards, named after the Blind Singer of the Spaceways featured in Robert A. Heinlein's "The Green Hills of Earth," are given each year by the members of the Science Fiction Poetry Association in two categories, Best Long Poem and Best Short Poem.

The 1994 Rhysling Award for Best Long Poem went to W. Gregory Stewart and Robert Frazier for their poem "Basement Flats." Robert Frazier is a previous winner of the Rhysling Award whose poetry and fiction have appeared in *The Magazine of Fantasy & Science Fiction, Amazing Stories, Asimov's Science Fiction, Synergy, Omni,* and other magazines and anthologies. In the past, he edited *T.A.S.P. (The Anthology of Speculative Poetry)*. W. Gregory Stewart is a three-time Rhysling Award winner whose poetry has appeared in *Amazing Stories, Star*Line, Thin Ice,* and *Asimov's Science Fiction*. His first collection, *Antepenult, the Selected Works of W. Gregory Stewart,* has been published.

About "Basement Flats," the first coauthored poem to win a Rhysling, W. Gregory Stewart writes:

"The seed of 'Basement Flats' was the phrase 'time facs,' which was also the original title. Time facs, time fax—just the phrase at first. And then the idea of a time-traveling archaeologist who could NOT send back specimens (for whatever reasons of side-stepped science . . .). No specimens, but information as to where to find potentially rich fossil troves, certain prize pieces, based on the time traveler's direct observations, even intervention—this could be sent back. It built from there. And then it deconstructed from *there*.

"When I had something to work with, I sent it off to Robert Frazier, then editor of *Star*Line* and a writer whose work I had long admired. I asked if he would be interested in taking 'Time Facs' and working with it—he was agreeable. 'Basement Flats' (Bob's title, by the way) is the result of that happy collaboration."

Robert Frazier adds:

"Greg and I started with rough ideas, several fragmentary stanzas of the original, and research on the Burgess Shale and those strange creatures it enfossiled. We eventually adopted separate voices of husband and wife, but later worked over each other's lines until our collaboration blurred into higher narrative. Part skull-buzz temporal science. Part f-word sentimentality. Along came *Air Fish,* a kind of indie *Dangerous Visions* thing, and it was no longer our love child. Again, here, it is yours."

Jeff VanderMeer's short fiction has appeared in *Asimov's Science Fiction, Fear* magazine, *Dark Voices 5: The Pan Book of Horror, Amazing Stories, Pulphouse, Weird Tales, Midnight Shadows, Darker Voices,* and many other publications in the U.S. and abroad. His nonfiction, including his highly praised essays about the work of Angela Carter, has been published in *SF Eye, Tangent, Carnage Hall,* and *Magill's Guide to SF/Fantasy Literature.* He has published a short story collection, *The Book of Frog,* and a collection of poetry, *Lyric of the Highway Mariner;* another collection, *The Book of Lost Places,* came out in 1995. VanderMeer recently won a $5,000 1995–96 Florida Individual Artist's Grant for fiction.

About his poem "Flight Is for Those Who Have Not Yet Crossed Over," he writes:

"The poem had two sources of inspiration—first, the songs of Freedy Johnson and second, a short story of mine also called "Flight . . ." I was stuck on the short story, which is told from the point of view of the guard in the poem, so I decided to write from the perspective of the prisoner, and out came the poem. Because the poem made me understand the very simplified and ironic world of the prisoner, I was then able to complete the short story. I do not write poetry very much, but when I do, it is to catch an instant of transformation, that critical moment in which something of great beauty and yet great pain is happening or is about to happen. I enjoy also the compression of words, the sense that every word must have a particular weight and a particular sound in order for the poem to work. Working on poetry often helps my fiction because, at least in certain short stories, that same compression can be used to devastating effect."

Bruce Boston, a four-time winner of the Rhysling Award, has also won a Pushcart Prize for Fiction, the *Asimov's Science Fiction* Readers' Poll (twice), and the *Aboriginal SF* Readers' Poll. He is the author of twenty-one books and has published fiction, poetry, and articles in hundreds of magazines and anthologies, among them *Amazing Stories, Cavalier, Pulphouse, Twilight Zone* magazine, *Science Fiction Age,* and *The Year's Best Fantasy and Horror;* his work has been translated into German, Japanese, Polish, and Spanish. His latest novel is *Stained Glass Rain,* and his *Sensuous Debris: Selected Poems 1970–1995* was recently published.

About his poem "Spacer's Compass," he has this to say:

" 'Spacer's Compass' is part of an ongoing series of poems I've been writing about an unnamed galactic traveler. The first poem in the series, 'For Spacers Snarled in the Hair of Comets,' won the 1986 Rhysling Award for short poem and appeared in *Nebula Awards 21.* In a symbolic and more contemporary sense, the 'spacer' stands for any individual who stands apart from society and consensual wisdom, who, like Colin Wilson's outsider, sees too much and too deeply, and consequently seeks answers to life and reality through behavior that defies/transcends the norm."

Basement Flats:
Redefining the Burgess Shale

W. GREGORY STEWART and
ROBERT FRAZIER

You were downtime—one way on a simplex link
hoarding observations & lucky guesses
waiting to timeburn
back through the millennia, to where I waited
& read it all
(I called heads, you got tails—
they sent *you* down . . .)

> *The creatures here are low form*
> *bottom rung*

> *true, but they too follow strict rules*
> *mating habits that seem to mimic marriage—*
> *or at least corporate law*

love in this prehistoric age
is no less detailed
it is still a language of bump and run

Downtime
doing Burgess reconnaissance
you got to see where the weird things are
you watched them die
you saw them settle
taking extensive notes for me to find them later
I got to chip their carcasses from stone
time faxes I began to call them
a fossil is a time fax

I find the water here
difficult to drink
no choice really but
my civilized stomach flora
are not adapted and I get sick
kind of the reverse of
savages lacking immunity to smallpox
I hope in turn my germs are weak

the irony hurts
literally

I remember the night before you left—
In our basement flat you said
Anomalocaris would be your favorite nightmare
I opted for *Opabinia*
we'd met as students, below ground then as well
recataloging the Walcott collection
in the Smithsonian dungeons
in the long flat trays & drawers & cabinets
oh, we innocently promised to redefine Walcott
& I remember how we hardly slept
that last night together—you drove alone
to the lab & the next morning you woke about

530 million years before I did
with no coffee

> *Time paradox is not a simple matter*
> *is it the paradox that history is immutable*
> *I'm not sure*
> *I feel I could change things easily—*
> *though how is not yet clear to me*

You did the time well because
you did *time* well—
hell, better than I could have

> *The true paradox may be that*
> *whatever changes*
> *timeburning might cause*
> *are anticipated*
> *and so the changes are there already—*
> *or else how could I travel back*

& I studied what you *lived* each day
& I found your landmarks
& I found your fossils
& I found the phyla you found
we did good science together—
or so it seemed—
for a good long month

> *I am pregnant*
> *nothing is less a paradox*
> *for it was by my will and choice*
> *that it happened before my downtime*
> *in case it was you going down*
> *possibility swims before me*
> *makes me dizzy with wavy lines*

Then came Retrieval
only they couldn't pinpoint you

& they didn't dare send me back
the project closed, bloody fools
"timeburning halted for investigation"
I wake up each morning
530 million years after you
to yet another day . . .

> *My dear husband*
> *soul mate*
> *there are conventions which time*
> *cannot account for*
>
> *so*
> *I'll not be seeing you again*
> *(after two full months*
> *that much is obvious)*
> *I feel like emptiness distilled*
> *who before has ever been this lonely*
>
> *I have lost everything*
> *I have no context for living*
> *except my child*

Only last Easter, my wife
(& twenty Easters since I lost you)
did I think to do EMR/CAT
on the Walcott specimens
was there something we missed
inside, yes, inside the fossil remains
indeed
in just a few I found
these chips encoded with your notes

& with your personal entries
& your endearments
& too your thin gold ring
battered, worn to nothing

hardened in one
an *Anomalocaris*

>   *My concentrates are exhausted*
>   *I cannot sustain on these creatures*
>   *they do not agree*
>   *nor boost my energy*
>   *I fear I will not reach*
>   *the time to birth our baby*
>   *I've come this far and can't get that far*
>   *and I could have told her*
>   *or him, looking like you*
>   *I suppose*
>   *I could have said what no one can say*
>   *"your father lives millions of years*
>   *in the future"*

>   *paradox is a game, I have decided*
>   *a goddamned philosopher's convention*
>   *timeburning is possible*
>   *because all things are probable*
>   *blinking or not blinking—both*
>   *change history*
>   *whatever*
>   *goes unseen in the moment*
>   *or seen*
>   *is forever invaluable*

>   *each of us burns time*
>   *in a moment-to-moment speed chase*
>   *no matter the era*

>   *a big jump offers*
>   *no guarantee that it won't be another*
>   *basement flat back there*
>   *and poorly furnished*

a bigger jump guarantees
no fucking special circumstance at all
except mortality

I live in a penthouse now   one wall
Is tiled in shale
I wear both bands—
you survived so long just to find me
once again
I am the change that you left behind

Flight Is for Those Who Have Not Yet Crossed Over

JEFF VANDERMEER

You never thought
it could happen this way,
in a Guatemalan prison
among men armed
with rubber hoses, scalpels,
piano wire, and propaganda;
men who scream at you
to tell what you cannot tell,
until you mark the days by
the visits of your interrogators,
muttered prayers to God,
and the screams which echo
down the hall.

In a dream on a moonless night
it came to you from beyond the window,
mixed with the smell of palm trees,
sea salt, and rotting wood;
it came to you like a whisper
from your dead lover,
an exhalation of her breath.
You woke sprawled against

the wall opposite your bed
and the guard said, "Dios mio!"
it was a miracle, a visitation,
the work of saints or devils.
You had flown around the cell
like an eagle, your arms
outstretched, fingers reaching
for the sky.

Miraculous, and yet you
laughed along with the guard,
because to fly in your cell
cannot save you, because
the only flight you desire
is the flight of an angel,
spiraling upward, freed
from the sharp, clarifying
edge of pain.

Spacer's Compass

BRUCE BOSTON

South I shipped . . . galactic south
        spanning the reaches of unbounded space
           through the moss stars and beyond
   hanging with this crew or that
           a rough lot they were
           or some just strange
  stranger than you'd care to know
        for a light-year or two on the fly

West I wandered . . . galactic west
           leaving lovers changing friends
     past clusters hanging in the heavens
       like burning ingots and bands of flame
    landing always in a different land
       a ready cup for alien ways

seeking never so much an answer
as a fix . . . a frame of reference
to sift my strangeness from

East I flew . . . galactic east
against the words of wiser souls
to decaying grandeurs steeped in fog
and cultures deadly spent
to language worlds and pleasure worlds
and the mother world or fabled so
a desolation of rust and snow
heir only to its past

Old I grow . . . galactic old
the polar night now calls my name
and still I tramp the stellar routes
from burning white to burning red
jump cutting lives and lands
fixing no frame of reference
beyond the passage itself
adrift in the passages
yet to be taken

Space has no directions
and holds all directions at once
a well of radiant possibilities
all matter of strangeness

. . . and the stars are for the living

Understanding Entropy

BARRY N. MALZBERG

Barry N. Malzberg won the first John W. Campbell Memorial Award for his novel *Beyond Apollo* and a Locus Award for his nonfiction book *The Engines of the Night*. He has been one of science fiction's most prolific writers and, over the years, has become one of its most influential. He has been a Nebula finalist five times; among his highly praised novels and collections are *Final War and Other Fantasies*, *The Falling Astronauts*, *Herovit's World*, *Guernica Night*, *Underlay*, *Down Here in the Dream Quarter*, *Galaxies*, *The Man Who Loved the Midnight Lady*, *The Cross of Fire*, and *The Remaking of Sigmund Freud*. *The Encyclopedia of Science Fiction* has called his writing "unparalleled in its intensity and in its apocalyptic sensibility."

About his Nebula finalist "Understanding Entropy," Barry Malzberg writes:

" 'Understanding Entropy' was written in memory of Henry Walter Weiss (2/10/40–11/3/91), who I knew for more than forty years and who was for a substantial part of my life my best friend. A graduate of Dartmouth and Oxford colleges, Henry graduated from Harvard Law in 1965 and practiced in New York and New Jersey for a quarter of a century. He died in Florida very bravely, after a long illness. He was not only my best friend but my attorney, and if that isn't an oxymoron there is no such thing as the Science-fiction and Fantasy Writers of America . . .

"I miss Henry a lot. I hope the story does not dishonor him."

So I go to Martin Donner's bedside in the room they have staked out for him in Florida, and I ask him the crucial question: If you had known? I say, if you had known that it would end this way, that you would be dying of a hundred wounds, of the tuberculosis, of the pneumocystitis, of the parasites and the kidney breakdown and the hepatitis, the jaundice, the venerium and the shattering of the pancreas, if you had known that five years after the positive diagnosis and three years after the first episode of the pneumonia you would be lying here, eighty-two pounds, filled with morphine which does not work anymore—oh, nothing works but that isn't quite the point, is it, they are trying—with your lover and your daughters and your wife and the doctors circling in the outer room and coming in now and then to inspect your reeking corpus, some of them weeping, others taking your pulse and monitoring your breathing: if you had known this fifteen years ago, Martin Donner, if you had known everything that would happen to you and that it would end this way, would you have left your wife and children to their lives and your history and gone out to Fire Island, Cherry Groves, the baths and the bathhouses and the quick and the scuffled, the long and the grievous affairs full time, no longer sneaking it around? Would you if you had known? Or would you have stayed in your marriage in the suburbs, Martin Donner, and played with your daughters and watched them grow and claimed your wife with closed eyes in the marriage bed and nothing more, *nothing* more because you would never know when the dogs truly came into the basement and snuffled up the stairs? Oh maybe once a year you might let some man tend to you with rubber gloves in a bank vault, but otherwise nothing, nothing, nothing at all? If you could have seen that it would have ended this way, Martin, what would you have done? Tell me the truth now. Do you know the truth? Is there any such thing as the truth? Because I need, I need, I need to know now, it affects my own situation.

He stares at me. He is relatively lucid now, it comes and it goes, in and out, back and forth, the pounding on the chest has loosened the phlegm, the morphine has momentarily quelled the cough, he thinks that he can think, although this is not necessarily the issue, and he thinks, of course, that I am a hallucination. Hallucination is common in this late-life condition, although the dementia has not affected him as fully as it might in a few more hours or (if he lasts that long, he probably will not) days. I don't know, he says. His eyes are strangely lustrous, the only motion, the only thing in his face not quiescent; the rest is dead, bland, sunken, a canvas upon which has been embedded the full and perfect features of the dead, the valley of the dead, the shades and valleys and small tablelands upon which the dead walk until at last they sleep. Yes, Martin Donner says, yes I do know. I can answer that. He thrashes weakly, the ganglia in his shattered nerves trying to pull into alignment. I wouldn't have done it, he said. I would not have died this way. It is not worth it. I *thought* it was worth it, that it was worth any price to be what you are, to live expressly and fully, but it is not; this is unbearable, I am sinking, I am sinking in disgrace, I wet myself, I humiliate myself, I seethe with visions and dreams of such inextinguishable horror . . . no, he says, *no,* and his voice is momentarily stronger, he screams in the room, *no,* he says, I would not have left them, I would have stayed there and I would have died, I would have died in a thousand ways, but it is the difference between metaphor and truth, they are *not* the same, once I thought they were but no, no, no, no, no, no, he says uncontrollably, the word ratcheting uncontrollably, and he sinks into the steaming sheets, his eyes fluttering, closed and the coughing, the moaning, the turgid phlegm passes again through his desiccated and shattered cavities. *No,* he says, and *no;* I think, his answer is no and momentarily there is a kind of settling; I can feel my own re-alignment and a sense of history colliding with imminence merging with the steaming and impenetrable future, but of course this fusion cannot last and I am in Martin Donner's bedroom fifteen years earlier, the bedroom on the second floor of the suburban colonial in one of the nicest areas of a nicer suburb in these sets of anterooms to the city, and I have put the question again. I have put it to him calmly and without sinister intent and then have used my powers— the powers granted me by the old and terrible antagonist who nonetheless, and this is undeniable, always plays fair, as fairly as Martin did not with his wife and daughters and friends and family through all of the years up to this point. I show him the bottles, the tubing, the arc and density of the room, the harsh and desperate light and it is uncommonly vivid; I have placed all my powers in the service of this adumbration. Oh yes, Martin says, seeing it all, oh yes, I see now. Yes, he says, it is worth it. I would do this. I would not be deterred. It is worth it. It is worth anything to expressly enact what you are, what you must be, the full and alarming necessities of the soul. So I do not care, he says. I am going, I am going to leave, if this is my destiny, so be it. His features congeal with conviction, unlike his face in the room of his death, they recede and pulsate, project and flutter with light, there is light all through him. Worth it, he says, worth it to be what one is. How many years until this happens? he says. Not that it matters. But I want to know.

Seventeen, I say. Seventeen years and not all of them will be happy. Your daughters will weep and one of them will hate you, there will be many betrayals, also other illnesses, earlier illnesses, small and larger betrayals, a terrible bout with hepatitis. Disgraceful venereal conditions. I don't care, he says, seventeen years is a good time. In seventeen years here, lying here, sneaking around, pounding myself into myself, I will be dead, I will have killed myself anyway. No, he says, there is no question, there is no argument. I have made my choice. He closes his eyes, smiles, thinking evidently that he is dreaming. Such dialogues are common inside Martin in this crucial time; he thinks that he is constructing a worst case venue but is nonetheless being firm. Yes, he says, I will do this. His breathing, irregular, levels out. As I withdraw, he thinks that he is making passage into dreamless slumber. As he recedes he feels, I know, some kind of imminence, and perhaps it is my question, no less than anything else, which has led him to this resolution. Or perhaps not. It is difficult to work within such difficult and speculative borders without being overwhelmed by my own relative helplessness and stupor.

But of course this is in only partial quest of verification. I move through the channels of recorded (and possible) time, asking Martin Donner this question at various places within the continuum. I discuss this with him at Cherry Grove in 1978 at a tea dance while he is hanging shyly against the walls, yes, he says, of course it is worth it; I ask him this in 1986 when, thunderously, the implications of the positive diagnosis begin to come through to him and he closes his eyes as I make the forced pictures in his head, showing him what it would be like: I don't know, he says, I don't know, I am in shock, I am in agony here, I can't give you a false or a real answer, can take no position, how can I tell? Maybe I shouldn't have done it, I don't know, I don't know. Take the question to him in Chicago two years later; he is attending a class reunion with his lover, partial remission, he feels in control of himself, some benignity, perhaps illusory but the moment can be extended, he feels, as so many other moments have been extended. I would have done it again, he says, knowing what I know, I would have wanted it this way still; I would not have treated it differently, I would not exchange these years for anything.

Ask him and ask him, up and down the line, sometimes an enthusiastic, desperate yes, other times more tentative, a no at the end and tracking back from that *no* mostly for the six to eight months before this special, spectacular extended agony; his position then is not fixed any more than it might have been twenty, thirty years ago when Martin refused to respond to the messages flicking like trap shots from the basement of his sensibility. Nothing is sure, nothing is firm. Mostly yes, an occasional no, more *no* as the end is approached, but even then at some of the moments in between the moments of the worst anguish, a soft, insistent yes. It is not fixed, nothing is fixed, the human condition is not fixed. The price we will pay for fully expressing what we are does seem indeterminate then. It resonates, this confusion, against my own uncertainty, and I understand then, staring at and through all of this, that there can be no answers from Martin, none at all. If Martin is the voice and tensor of all possibility, then there is *no* possibility, no singularity.

Understanding this does not surprise me but fills me with a desperate and irreparable weakness; I would not have had it this way, I would have wanted surer answers. Everyone wants answers if not *the* answer, even I. I return to my old antagonist on the desert and hand him the helmet and the simulating device and the other armaments of our translation, our bargain, our possibility. I have wrestled and wrestled, I say, I have wrestled you through all the avenues of this life and I do not know, I am stunned and pinned, dislocated and shattered. Martin is not the answer; he can provide me with no firm basis at all.

Of course, my old antagonist says. His ruddy skin glows with sympathy or perhaps it is only health. Or vindication. You see, he says, you are left with it just as I said, you are left with all of this on your own. *You* must decide what price to pay and whether that is correct and no one can know. He backs away from me, horns a rapier, fine eyes glints of purpose in the night. Now, he says, *now* you must decide. *You,* not Martin Donner, who is only a paradox or a metaphor, *you* must make that decision. It is the fortieth day, he says. Soon it will be the fortieth night. You must now turn in the way you must, and there will be no returning.

Yes, I say, yes, I understand that. Before me, closing my eyes like Martin in the hallucinatory daze, I see the traps, the sights, the visions of my own circumstance: the donkey, the cobblestones, the crowds, Pilate's smooth and terrible judgment, the hanging and the darkness. I see and I see and I see and in the iron spikes of the sun of Gologotha, alone and under the darkness, I see too the expanding and necessitous heart of God.

I Know What You're Thinking

KATE WILHELM

Kate Wilhelm has won the Nebula Award three times for her short fiction, and the Hugo Award once, for her novel *Where Late the Sweet Birds Sang*. She is one of science fiction's finest writers, whose stories and novels are rooted in the familiar patterns of everyday life while revealing how shaky the underpinnings of those lives can be. Wilhelm is equally accomplished as a novelist and as an author of short fiction; her books include *The Mile-Long Spaceship; The Downstairs Room; The Infinity Box; The Clewiston Test; Welcome, Chaos; Huysman's Pets; Death Qualified: A Mystery of Chaos; Cambio Bay; Naming the Flowers;* and with her husband, Damon Knight, *Better Than One*.

About "I Know What You're Thinking," a finalist for the Nebula, Kate Wilhelm writes:

"See, I'm cleaning muck out of the fishpond, good black oozy stuff, hauling it up, putting it in a bucket to toss on the compost, and koi, goldfish, and golden orfes swarm around my hands, which are freezing because it's no longer summertime, kiddo, and I say, forget it, I know what you're thinking and you're wrong, it's not feeding time, and besides if I never fed you again, you'd be OK because there are bugs, larvae, plants, algae, and like that for you to eat, so just get lost, OK, but they swarm, and I think, yeah, I know what you're thinking, and what the cats are thinking when I walk outside carrying anything at all: feed me, that's the message they're all transmitting, a message I'm receiving just fine, and when I'm in the kitchen and human types come through at six or later when it's my day to cook, just passing through without saying anything, sniffing like crazy, knowing better than to whine or beg or snivel or anything—who has to when it's after six? I ask you—I sort of glower and they pass on by and pretend that what they're really after is to watch TV or look at the African violet or something, even though that's a lie and they know it and so do I, but—whatthehell, don't we all live with lies and by lies all the time anyway?—we all pretend they just happen to be passing this way, although I know they suspect I see through their air of nonchalance as if they were wearing plastic wrap; they don't dare ask, and I'll never tell, but, believe me, neither they nor you have any secrets, none, zilch, whatsogoddamever, because Iknowwhatyou/they'rethinking. So sue me."

Dinner parties were always the worst. In big noisy groups no one paid much attention to me since I was quiet and smiled a lot. But at dinner parties everyone became the focus of attention if only for a moment. The white noise became real noise and I moved in fear verging on panic that I might slip and drown in it.

"Honey, you have to come," Cal said. "His people don't invest in just the company, but the ones behind it, and their families. They look for stability, in the business and in the personal lives of people they're interested in."

It was as bad as I had known it would be. When Mr. Davies shook my hand he said, "And finally I get to meet the charming Mrs. Paterson. How do you do?"

He smiled affably through an appraisal as cold as a mortician's. So this is the kid with the money, pretty, but not all there, touched, he was thinking, doesn't really look it, but who ever can tell. Wondering if Cal played around much, how I was in bed, if I kept a tight rein on the money. Tomorrow he'd be out of here, do something about his lower back, and if Gloria had messed up again, he'd take off her head. ". . . such an impressive young man, your Cal. Very good presentation today, one of the best I've seen." . . . doing numbers about the company finances . . .

I smiled at him and moved away. All evening I smiled a lot, and said as little as possible and I thought I had succeeded beautifully until we were in the car on our way home.

"Why in God's name did you start talking about chemical warfare in the Persian Gulf?" Cal asked in a harsh low voice.

Muscles I had thought already tense drew up even tighter until I felt I couldn't move. I had done it again.

He was driving too fast, so angry he was hoping something would get in front of him, something he could smash. Never again, he was thinking, make excuses, illness . . . come on, slow down, I'll ram you . . .

I was shivering as I realized that no one else was pretending anything; neither was it practice and self-control; they didn't hear each other. It wasn't that they had all learned to live in such a noisy world; rather, the world they lived in was silent. I was too frightened

and stunned to speak. Cal wanted me to try to explain so he could
have an excuse to yell at me. I had detected impatience, irritation,
dislike from time to time, and love, passion, lust, amusement, and I
had felt those same things about him; everyone went through such
violent swings. On the drive home he hated me, he wished I was
dead, that he was dead, that we all were dead, especially Davies, the
slob . . . I sat with my chin tucked in, my eyes closed, trying to bring
back the white noise.

The drive home was short, out of Portland on the interstate, then
onto the twisting country road to our house. While he paid the baby-
sitter I went upstairs to check on the girls. Donna was eight, Patty
seven. Patty's covers were all over, part on her, most on the floor;
Donna looked as if she had not moved since going to bed. I straightened out Patty's bedding, kissed them both, and then went downstairs.

"Cal, we have to talk," I said. He was on the couch in the living
room with a drink in his hand, thinking of Davies, and his own coming presentation to a board of directors down in Los Angeles, thinking about Harry who should be the one to go and wouldn't, about
guidance systems and he couldn't just walk out and Florence had
been in the liquor again and Donna's books were all over the kitchen
table . . .

He hardly glanced at me. "So talk."

"I heard him, Cal. I heard Davies talking about chemical warfare."

"He was talking about guidance systems, airplane control."

"In his head he was talking about systems to deliver things too
dangerous for people to handle, chemical agents, nerve gas."

"And you heard him talking in his head," Cal said sarcastically.
"I know you have a problem with your ears, but isn't that pushing it
just a little?"

"I did, though." I didn't know how else to describe it. I didn't
hear words; I simply knew what people were thinking, as if their
thoughts were mine, all mixed together, random, disjointed, like my
own but always separate. There was no way to explain it if he didn't
do it also, and until that night I had believed everyone did it exactly
the way I did, but with control and pretense that I had not yet
mastered.

He looked up at me. His face changed, and for a time his mind was numb, then fear came. I shut my eyes. He thought I was crazy, that my parents had known, that's why they tied up the money the way they did, why they kept me home all those years, not fair, he should have been told . . . I turned and ran to the kitchen.

Cal went upstairs; soon there was the distant sound of water rumbling in the bathtub. Our house was ninety years old, and in spite of remodeling, the pipes still announced water running anywhere. Dad had bought the house when I was twelve, I had lived in it ever since—fifteen years. My mother and father had moved out here because they had known there was something wrong with me. Abruptly I started a pot of coffee. I had to rethink my entire life; it would be a long night.

But my thoughts were as jumbled as Cal's had been. Snatches of conversations came, phrases, ideas that had not been mine, answers that had been wrong, questions asked of me that had no answers . . . A carpenter had worked on the house when I was young; he hadn't known he was colorblind, he had told Mother, until they examined him for the Air Force. Mother said he believed he saw exactly what everyone else saw, and maybe no two people saw the same thing when they said green or blue or red. There was no way to tell. Later I read an article that claimed what we saw or heard was culturally determined, that the Japanese were culturally trained not to hear sounds made by others separated by nothing more than a paper wall. The article went on to say that people in major cities had to learn not to see others, not to see the chaos about them. I didn't know why people who wrote such lies were allowed to have them printed.

I began having school trouble in the fifth grade, and I failed sixth grade. They took me in for a medical checkup, an eye test; they took me to a psychologist. Did I hear voices? Did I see strange things? Did shapes change and become other things? I said the world was too noisy. She suggested a hearing test. The ear doctor said it was a problem with filtering; we have to learn how to filter noise, be attentive to what is important, squelch what isn't. I was giving everything the same attention. The problem wasn't in my ears, but in my brain.

Cal came back down in his robe and stood in the doorway, thinking Davies must have subvocalized what was really on his mind.

"He might have been subvocalizing," I said faintly.

I shared his relief. He was tired, the bath had relaxed him, too much stress recently, and tonight had been hard. He didn't linger; weak with relief, he went to bed.

How many times had I heard my mother say in exasperation, "I know what you're thinking, and you're wrong. You think . . ." I believed she really knew. Later, when I realized what she said was not what Father was thinking, or what I was thinking, I concluded it was part of the same pattern that let people think certain words and voice others.

I drank coffee and paced through the downstairs: living room with antiques, dining room large enough to seat twelve, a den, laundry room . . . It was a very large house. They had bought and furnished it so that I never would have to go buy anything.

They decided to keep me home the year I was twelve, to tutor me themselves. Father was ill with Lou Gehrig's disease; he sold his share in an advertising agency in Seattle and we moved to this house, centered in six acres of woodland, eleven miles out of Portland. I could sleep at night again, and I stopped going into a near-paralytic state three or four times a day when the noise overcame me. There was no noise.

The phrase *acute adolescent schizophrenia* was in the air for a time, but they didn't take me for treatment. As long as I was home, I was perfectly well, and I was learning to cope with the world gradually. The process of turning the noise into white noise continued through the next few years until I could go to the library, go shopping or to the zoo or a movie with Mother, places where people were not thinking about me. But if the focus turned to me, I froze, or I made a mistake and responded to a thought instead of a spoken word.

I gathered Donna's school books and put them in her backpack. Now what? I asked myself, but I couldn't form a thought about the future yet, not until I finished reexamining the past.

Father died when I was sixteen. I met Cal a year later, and his thoughts were clear, focused on me, and welcome. He was ten years older than I was, and he loved me. We married the day I turned eighteen, and Donna was born ten months later. I knew the instant I became pregnant; the noise faded to a murmurous hum far off in the distance. I told Mother it was gone, I was at peace, and we wept together.

She got an apartment in town, and talked about changing her

will. She and Father had tied up everything in such a way that I would have an income for the rest of my life, and the house, with a trust to take care of it. If I sold the house, or took out a mortgage, the money would go into the trust fund. I had been provided for. With that act they had proclaimed what I now knew: they called it a problem with hearing, but they thought I was crazy.

The nine months of pregnancy were blissful; we entertained, and started to make friends; we lived just like other young couples. The day after Donna was born, I woke up drowning in the noise again. They took me home and Mother moved back in.

Mother was killed in a four-car collision on the interstate when Donna was nine months old, and I was pregnant again a month later. As before, the pregnancy curbed the noise, and, as before, the noise was back louder, more insistent than ever the day after Patty was born.

I had accepted that people considered me a social klutz, a little strange, weird even, but I thought of it as the sort of pity swimmers showed to nonswimmers; it was something anyone could do if they tried hard enough. Everyone else controlled the noise; I could learn to control it too.

It was four in the morning when I fell into bed, with no answer to Now what?

The clock rang at seven; I was so groggy I stumbled through making breakfast and told Donna she didn't need her hair braided, and didn't even try to respond to Cal's thoughts and words because I was not sure which was which.

A doctor, I thought, maybe a brain specialist. Maybe there was a treatment, a cure. I moved zombielike through the usual morning chores—making beds, loading the dishwasher, picking up towels—and abruptly I stopped. Why? I found myself asking. Why should I risk doing such a thing?

I had only one answer: Cal was getting tired of a wife who was a social liability. But I couldn't tell anyone, because I would become a menace to be ostracized, or a medical curiosity to be studied and probed, or, I forced myself to follow the thought through, I would be put away under one pretense or another.

I shuddered thinking of what would happen if they put me in a hospital, tranquilized me; they would open the floodgates and listen to me scream.

Nothing had changed, I thought then; people would still consider me a little weird, a hearing problem, you know, but very intuitive. Funny how when a person is challenged in one area, a different area compensates, like the blind developing such a good sense of smell, the hearing impaired becoming more intuitive . . . How many times I had heard such thoughts, both voiced and unvoiced. I repeated to myself, nothing had changed, except, I added, now I was aware.

Cal went to Los Angeles for three days. I did my stint at the school library, and I went to the public library twice while he was gone. I concentrated on psychology, on brain physiology, brain abnormalities . . . I read about aversion therapy, neurolinguistics theory on phobia handling, other theories, and I sat in the reading room and thought: *Here I am. Someone hear me. Make a sign that you hear me. I know what you're thinking.* People moved in and out of the book stacks, sat at the computers, talked to each other and the librarians. No one paid any attention to me.

Cal was tense and jumpy when he returned. He lied about his trip, about his meals, the presentation, everything. All went well, he said, but when he sank into silence, I learned just how badly it had gone. At first he blamed a bad hotel and bad food; then he blamed himself for not preparing better, for stumbling over some of the questions they had asked, and then he was blaming me. If I had come on better, not left Davies with the impression that I was a neurotic wife heading for a nervous breakdown, the rest would have worked okay. I listened to it happening in his head and could not say a word. For all I knew he was right.

After he went to bed, I began to analyze how I had handled his thoughts. They had been as jumbled as ever, but I had sifted through them, disregarding the irrelevant ones—he liked the chicken, his foot hurt, crush at the airport, bumpy landing, slob in the middle seat . . . I could do it automatically with Cal, just as I had done it with my parents. I knew their processes, could pick out their thoughts from the dense fog. If I had learned to do it with them, I could do it with others.

I started the next day. I chose a small coffee shop with half a dozen people in it at ten-thirty in the morning. For twenty minutes I nursed a cup of coffee and for the first time in my life I deliberately listened to the flow of thoughts that filled the air like radio waves.

Not trying to squelch them, or turn them into white noise, but paying attention, I found that I could almost make them coherent. At the end of twenty minutes, my hands were shaking, my head hurt, and I had to leave, but I knew I had succeeded.

That night almost as soon as the girls were sleeping Cal and I went to bed. He had swung from dark pessimism to near euphoric optimism, and our lovemaking was exuberant and unrestrained. Our sex life had always been passionate, uninhibited. I knew exactly what he liked, and when he was joyous, delirious, so was I. That night, floating in the aftermath, I wondered suddenly what it would be like if both partners knew, and I was shocked by the thought. I was shocked again when I realized he was fantasizing a real woman. He sometimes fantasized while making love; usually his fantasy lover was a movie star, or someone from television, or an exotic dancer, someone unattainable and beautiful. Sometimes it was me in a foreign setting, on a beach, in a tent, sometimes even tinged with sadomasochism. That night it was a woman from the office who was in his mind as he drifted into deeper sleep.

People lived rich fantasy lives; I had grown used to that fact. Most of what people thought was never voiced. No one could control their flow of thoughts and ideas, impressions and feelings, desires and dislikes, hatreds, jealousies, loves; only their actions counted, and their spoken words. I knew this the way I knew people had dark hair or blond, or were tall or short, or fat or thin.

I had considered telling Cal about me; it really wasn't fair not to, he had a right to know. Lying there awake, I knew I couldn't. He wouldn't be able to live with me. And I knew that now, after nine years of marriage, he was thinking of other women in a way he never had before. I wasn't a good wife for him and never had been. Sex wasn't enough. That and the children were all that tied us together. It annoyed him if I mentioned something he was certain he had not talked about, like the time recently that I made a dental appointment for him. A tooth had been bothering him, but he didn't want to believe I knew it. He didn't want me to tell him things if he couldn't understand how I knew them, especially when I was right.

He was still denying to himself that it was getting harder to contain his frustration with a weird wife who was not good in company, and who made him uneasy in ways he couldn't comprehend. I had known for years that he was more relaxed with the children than with me, but I had assumed his reasons were like mine: the children weren't in his head.

What if they turned out to be like me, I thought, and this time my startlement made me get out of bed, slip on my robe, and go downstairs.

Would they be like me? Cal believed my parents should have had me treated, not kept me hidden away and let whatever my problem was develop into a phobia about crowds. He would insist on a doctor who would drug the girls, tranquilize them, hospitalize them . . . They would go insane, or die.

But I might not know for years. This hadn't started with me until I was nearly twelve. Then, finally, I began to plan seriously for the future.

I began going out nearly every day, small coffee shops at first, places where there would be few people, then a bigger restaurant, and finally a clothing store where I bought a few things. Constantly I repeated, I can do it. I can do it. I thought Cal would be pleased that I had bought myself a pant suit, but he was only annoyed. If I could shop, why had I messed around with catalogs for years? Why had he wasted so much time shopping? The company Davies represented had turned Cal and Harry down, no financial help was available although they had a good product, maybe in a year or two . . . he blamed me.

Donna's birthday came and I had a party for her; a few mothers came along with their children, and I had a tea party for them. I can do it, I told myself. I can do it.

When school was out I took the children to the coast for a month as usual. Before, Cal had joined us every weekend, but that year he was too busy. He was having his affair finally. She was Audrey, the woman at work. And he was bitterly disappointed. I took a great deal of malicious satisfaction in his disappointment, and I wouldn't let him touch me until I was certain they had used condoms. They were together only three times; afterward he was overcome with guilt and shame that lasted for months.

At the coast, watching the girls play in the waves, I heard a man thinking about a boy. I had heard thoughts like this before, but always generalized, and he was very specific. I sat unmoving, terrified, and only gradually began to search for him. I had learned to track the droplets to their source part of the time, not reliably, and I thought I would not be able to locate him, but then I knew who it was. About thirty, thin, he was lying back on the sand supported by his elbows, less than twenty feet away, paying no attention to me, intent on the child. I located the boy next, a slight child of nine or ten, playing Frisbee with his father.

The man was thinking of various scenarios when suddenly his thoughts turned more murderous, and he stood up. A woman and a large black dog had joined in the Frisbee game. The boy threw the disk and the dog leaped up to catch it, trotted to the child to drop it at his feet, and stood tense and expectant waiting for the next throw. The predatory man was leaving, moving through the soft sand as fast as he could to the packed wet sand where he started to jog down the beach. I watched him out of sight.

But he would focus on another child, I thought, shivering. I lost control of the noise then. I had to get up and join the girls at the edge of the water, out of range of the dozen or so people who were clamoring for attention in my head.

That night I paced until I ached. I couldn't turn my back on such things, I told myself, but neither could I do anything about them. I thought bitterly of taking on the role of avenger, swooping down on unsuspecting criminals and dispatching them, or joining forces with the police, sniffing out evil and preventing crimes. I sat down and stared at the tabletop. Plastic with unlikely roses on trellises crisscrossed it. We had rented this same cottage every summer for eight years; the tablecloth had been here all that time.

The next day I bought a camera small enough to fit in my purse. If it happened again, I would take a picture and send it to the police along with information about whatever the person was planning. I was afraid to try to do more than that. For the first time it occurred to me that someone, gangsters, the FBI, police, CIA, someone might decide to make use of me if they ever found out. Watching Donna and Patty trying to catch crabs in a tidepool, I knew how malleable I would be if they were ever threatened.

I practiced taking pictures, hiding the camera in my hand, behind my purse. I had six rolls of film developed when we returned home and they were mostly terrible. I told the puzzled clerk the children had played with the camera and he thought that was a pretty expensive toy. I would learn photography, developing, printing, all of it, I decided on the spot.

When school started again, I enrolled in a photography class where several times I was desperate to drop out, but each time I was able to bring back the white noise and continue. Privately I learned my range, about forty feet; I learned how to turn the noise into coherent patterns; I learned how to track thoughts to a source reliably. I had a darkroom built in the basement and practiced taking pictures, developing, and printing them. I took hundreds of pictures of the trees on our property, and then began taking pictures of strangers in stores, in restaurants. Twice I sent a picture to the police with a note. Patty had her eighth birthday, Donna her tenth.

Cal and Harry found another potential backer and this time I gave the dinner party; I was charming, attentive, ignored all thoughts as if they were not there, and later I told Cal that Mr. Hendrickson was out to steal the program he and Harry were working on. Furious, he stalked out to spend the night with a woman named Jean.

When he came back the next evening, I had moved my things into my old childhood room. He glared at me in disbelief.

"What's that supposed to mean?"

"You know as well as I do. You didn't even use a condom, did you? Who did she sleep with last week, last month? Did you ask? I believe they say you have to wait about six months and then do the blood test. Until then, separate rooms."

For the first time ever he wanted to hit me. "I don't know what you're talking about."

"Do I have to spell it out? You're screwing around. There. Six months. Or you can leave now, tonight."

His old fear flashed back. He turned away. "You've changed," he muttered, walking toward the den where we kept the liquor.

We never had fought really. After our first argument I had realized that I would be too destructive. I knew exactly how to devastate him and if we argued I might say something awful and irreversible. For many years I had thought he could do the same to me, admired him for not giving in to the urge.

Now, after eleven years of not fighting with each other, his guilt was too strong for him to start. He thought of the house, no worries about food, about day-to-day living, my monthly allowance that made it possible. About Harry and June struggling along. About the girls, how much he loved them. Admit to a mistake, beg me to forgive him? But six months! Deny everything, he decided. I was suspicious, but I couldn't know for sure. I had always been a little crazy; there had been a few remissions, but here it was back, worse than before because now I was paranoid. Schizophrenic and paranoid.

By the time he had thought out his strategy, I was upstairs in my old room with the door locked.

We didn't mention it again. He continued to see Jean, and I slept with my door locked. I didn't want to force a confrontation with him, force him to leave. He was very good with the girls, and they loved him fiercely, and I felt oddly protective of him. It wasn't his fault that I knew what he was thinking, that he couldn't hide anything from me.

Donna turned twelve and was as normal as any little twelve-year-old girl could be; she cried at slights, or was manic, and experimented with makeup, and talked about boys with her friends, and thought about boys and makeup and dating. The day I realized I was hearing her thoughts, I knew she was not like me.

Now my attention turned to Patty, but again it was a waiting game. Cal and Harry had broken off their negotiations with Hendrickson. But then they licensed the program that had occupied them so long, and suddenly they were making a great deal of money. I was very happy for them.

Cal and Jean had a fight and broke up, and for several months he was as celibate as I was, and the thought crossed his mind now and then that the six months I had given him would be easy. But, he thought in surprise one night, he liked living the way he was. He didn't want to leave me exactly, but neither did he want to have to be on guard all the time, uneasy around me all the time. He liked sharing the house and the children, liked his meals, liked our inane conversations, liked everything about his life except being celibate, and eventually he took care of that.

I was strangely content also. It was all so much easier this way. Unexpectedly I had become involved with photography and worked at getting good at it. And every once in a while I took a picture of a stranger and wrote a note on the computer, printed it out, and sent it to the police. A man planning a big drug delivery. A woman robbing nursing home patients. A man planning murder. A child molester . . .

Patty had her eleventh birthday and was growing moody, exactly the way Donna had, the way I had in the distant past.

I had been in the back of the lot, photographing a certain tree I had concentrated on for months, getting it in every possible light, because no matter how often I looked at it, it was a different tree I saw. I was trying to capture that elusive changeable aspect of all living things, the constant flux that seemed to bolster the notion that reality was being reinvented moment by moment.

I was taking off my boots at the back door when the doorbell rang. It was March; the boots were very muddy, my hands were frozen, my face numb. I finished with the boots before I went to answer the bell, still with my jacket on. I stopped short of the front door, policemen! Two of them. Detectives in plainclothes, cold and miserable. One of them was angry, the other was remote, thinking about the setting of our house, nice with so many trees, smart to keep them cleared back in case of fire . . .

I opened the door.

The older one said, "Mrs. Paterson? Detective Sergeant Lauria, and this is Detective Neilson." He held out identification. "May we have a few words with you?"

He was in his forties, heavyset, nearly bald. He was thinking I looked like a kid in my socks and jacket, pink cheeks. The other one was young and lean, in his thirties, and very angry.

I stepped back. "Why? Is something wrong? Has there been an accident?" I knew better, but they expected something like that.

"Nothing happened," Lauria said. "We're trying to locate someone."

I led them into the living room and took off my jacket and we all sat down.

"What do you mean?"

"Mrs. Paterson, we're trying to find a connection among a group of people. Maybe you can help us. Would you mind telling us if you know any of the people whose names I'll mention?"

I shook my head. Neilson was furious because he was on this wild-goose chase. Two teenage girls had been slashed on Burnside, a gang shooting, goddamn Spaulding, chief had a hole in his head big enough to drive trucks through . . .

Lauria began to read from a list of names. I shook my head each time. But I was learning what they were after. I had sent in eleven pictures over a two-year period; he had seven of the names in his notebook. As he read the names, he made the connections in his head: the nursing-home attendant stealing patients' money; a child molester; a murderer . . . They had investigated seven of eleven. One of the names was Gerald Spaulding, who was stealing industrial secrets, selling them to the Japanese. At the mention of his name Neilson filled in the rest: someone had leaked to Spaulding that a nut had accused him, had taken his picture. Spaulding was a lobbyist, important, knew important people, he had demanded an investigation which had started four months earlier. Four months! Then Neilson began to fume again about this waste of time . . .

When Lauria asked me to look at some pictures, I agreed, because I didn't yet know how they had traced anything to me. I found out as he opened a briefcase, extracted a manila envelope, and took out the first picture. In my photography class we had done a series of sports shots, using fast action film, ISO 1600, what the instructor called recording film. Now I found out that it was rarely used, that it usually was specially ordered, but kept in stock by the store I had gone to because our classes asked for it. They had been tracking down everyone in Portland and the surrounding area who had bought it over the past three years. I was one of dozens of people they were following up on. Not just me, then, I realized, relieved.

I shook my head at the first picture, a late one. Then an earlier one, and another. The quality improved, I thought distantly, studying them, as I got better with the camera and darkroom technique. Finally I said, "I don't know any of those people." I stood up.

Something was bothering Lauria; he was dissatisfied with me for no reason he could think of except that I was taking this too calmly. "Mrs. Paterson, do you use ISO 1600 film?" he asked, getting to his feet. He agreed with his partner that this was a waste of time, but still, there was something . . .

"No," I said sharply. "And I don't intend to answer any more questions unless you tell me what you want, why you're here." His suspicions eased a little.

"Could we have a quick look at your darkroom?" he asked.

"No. I'm going to call my lawyer if you don't leave now."

I walked to the door with them, but suddenly Lauria was thinking about another case of a nut informer who was said to have been right with every suspect he fingered. I caught my breath.

"Sergeant, wait a minute," I said with my hand on the doorknob. "I guess I don't care if you look at my darkroom, or my photographs, if that's part of your job." Neither of them noticed how strange I sounded.

Neilson was furious with this new delay, and Lauria was less than enthusiastic now that I had agreed to show them everything. He knew at a glance that my trees were not at all like the grainy head shots, but I kept showing them more and more trees and bushes and blades of grass, and all the time getting a snippet here, another there.

When they left I sat down to think. I was in no danger of discovery. Early on I had found my own reflection in a car bumper in a practice photograph; after that I examined them very carefully, and cropped them if there was anything to give me away. I wore thin vinyl gloves in the darkroom, no fingerprints. None on the computer paper or the envelopes, bought in a discount store.

At first the police had paid little attention to the tips. The third picture, of a bank embezzler, had made them change their minds and reexamine the first two. By now they had found six of the people, had made arrests in five instances, and were investigating the sixth. Four remained elusive, and then there was Spaulding.

There had been high-level meetings. Not an extortion setup, they had decided, although that was what Spaulding claimed to believe. At one of the meetings someone had mentioned the similiarity to a case back east, except that nut had not used pictures, but gave actual names. And he was right every time. I had been desperate to find out where back east, and finally Lauria had thought about how they had handled it in Cincinnati. They had decided it was the work of an insider, and made everyone in the department from the chief down take a polygraph test; there had been resignations and general turmoil since most of the force had no idea why.

I didn't know when all that happened. Cincinnati. As foreign as India or Morocco. Was she still there, still doing it? I didn't know.

I felt feverish and more than a little crazy then, thinking about someone like me out there. I had broadcast my message over and over: *Look at me, hear me. I'm here. I know what you're thinking.* Then I had given up; no one could hear me.

I couldn't remember the last time I had had a real conversation with anyone; I felt stupid responding to half-truths, evasions, lies as if I believed them. But there was someone in Cincinnati, I thought all through the afternoon, into the evening. I made dinner as usual and listened to the girls chatter, and to Cal going on about a car he had test driven earlier that week, and I felt like a spectator in my own house, watching my life erode away.

I spent time in the library again; I read about Cincinnati, about Ohio, studied a map of the city. Where did she live? Had she gained as much control as I had? Was she married? Had she stopped tipping off the police? How had she got the actual names of the suspects? Most people hardly ever thought of their own names. What if it was a man? The idea made my legs give, I had to sit down. *What would it be like if they both knew?*

For several years I had known that Donna was trying to hide her ambivalent feelings about me, and I had accepted that as the normal growing up process of an adolescent girl. They get critical of their mothers, I told myself; they get judgmental; they prefer their fathers . . . Both girls knew Cal and I weren't sleeping together; they knew he had a girlfriend, and had even met her, and we all pretended none of that was true, although the girls talked about it privately, and Donna thought about it a lot.

They were in their room one afternoon in May; I was on my way to my room when I passed their door and came to a stop. Their voices were too low to carry, but I realized I was hearing both of them in my head. I leaned against the wall with my eyes closed; the waiting was over. Now I knew.

Donna was thinking that if we got divorced she wanted to live with her father, and Patty was thinking about Stella, the girlfriend, how easy it was to talk to her, how she understood. For the first time I realized they were as uneasy around me as Cal was, it was not simply adolescence driving a wedge.

I wanted to cry as the realization came. I had failed Cal and my children alike. In spite of all my care, they knew there was something wrong. Donna thought I was a little crazy. She thought I spied on her, read her diary; I couldn't tell her otherwise since I wasn't supposed to know that. Now Patty thought she didn't blame Cal: I was a little creepy, not a bit like Stella. I moved away, but then it hit me: I was free.

It was all very civilized. I waited until school was out to tell Cal I was leaving him; he was grateful that I was the one to bring it up. We discussed it calmly with the girls and they said they wanted to go with him. We talked about custody, visitation rights, college tuition costs, everything, and left little for an attorney to do. Just like that, it was over. The girls cried and I did, and Cal was uncomfortably near tears, but we all were relieved.

The next day I packed suitcases, packed my camera bags, and I left for Ohio. I would take a long trip, I told them all, leave them in peace to make their arrangements. We all cried again, but when I drove off, I felt a great excitement, exhilaration even.

The enormity of the land amazed me, the desert, mountains, then the plains that stretched forever. I drove until I got tired, ate when I got hungry, slept in motels or hotels, and drove again. I had thought I would plan everything during the days of driving, the restless nights wishing it were morning again. My excitement mounted but the only plan that formed was simply to visit public places—the library, the zoo, parks, and keep calling until you answered: *Hear me. See me. Speak to me. I know you're here. I know what you're thinking.*

A Defense of the
Social Contracts

MARTHA SOUKUP

Martha Soukup is an alumna of the Clarion Workshop in Science Fiction and Fantasy whose short fiction has appeared in *Universe, Asimov's Science Fiction, Amazing Stories, The Magazine of Fantasy & Science Fiction, Xanadu 2, Aboriginal SF, Full Spectrum, Alternate Presidents, Analog,* and other magazines and anthologies. Several of her stories have been nominated for Nebula and Hugo awards; her Nebula finalist "Over the Long Haul" was adapted as a short film for the Showtime television channel by director Danny Glover. She lives in San Francisco.

Of her Nebula Award–winning "A Defense of the Social Contracts," Martha Soukup says the following:

"Actually, I didn't mean to write 'A Defense of the Social Contracts' at all. I meant to write a story about how obsession can feed into revenge that can loop back to reinforce the obsession, but the notion I had for telling that story was a fantasy notion, and this time I felt like writing science fiction. I found a voice for the story and started writing in a far future in which the fantasy element could be made into a science-fictional element; but in the process of putting that future together, I found it had taken over the story, and the original story would have to go on hold.

"Instead of a story about the ambiguities of revenge, I found myself writing a story about the ambiguities of utopia. Humans are complex, and any human system will have noise: noise in a culture is someone's pain. . . . I made up the best future I could think of. I just couldn't make up a utopia.

"The other answer to how I wrote this story is: surprisingly easily. I wrote it over a long weekend, finishing Monday afternoon in time to post it to my workshop group and, I learned later, barely miss an appearance by candidate Bill Clinton two blocks from my door. Each morning I got up, put Réné Dupéré's *Saltimbanco* soundtrack on the stereo, on infinite loop, and wrote. During breaks I treated myself to most of Steven Brust's Taltos books, a lot of reading. You want to read something good—and unlike your own work—when writing, so it doesn't creep in. (*Saltimbanco* crept in.) When I got tired, I turned off the stereo and the computer and went to bed, and when I woke up, I started all over again, all day. Three days later, I had a different story than I'd expected. I wish they all went like that."

He flirted with all and he meant it with none, but Anli had been foolish enough to think he meant it with her.

That is the language of the bad old days. In these times we may be more fair than that to Anli and Derren. Derren was a registered nonmonogamist, than which little could be more clear. He was scrupulous enough to keep his preference license by the doorway of his privacy room, under his certificate of health, though this was not required. Who could ask more of Derren than that? Watch his movements, listen to his words in the context he has placed them in. Be rational.

Anli had recently withdrawn a registration of celibacy. It had stood two years and more, which is a long time for a citizen who has not taken celibacy as a life choice, but it is not unheard of.

Before her celibacy, she had offered three contracts of monogamy, two to men and one to a woman, which had not been accepted. Her friends suggested she brooded too much over the third rejection, by the second man, who took instead the offer of a group family. Anli had obliged their urgings and taken erotic rebalancing: through a combination of nano and of tailored drugs, the doctors remapped her responses so she would not find men of his size, shape, coloring, and vocal characteristics attractive. After the procedure she no longer woke in the middle of the night, breath-starved and sweat-drenched, the dream-touch of a blond, smooth, brown-eyed man fading too slowly to forget; she told her friends this so they would no longer worry.

She did not tell them that she still brooded. She did not tell them of her unhealthy resentment at the loss of her fantasy.

In this light, we may say Anli was wise when she chose to register celibate. Or we may wonder why she did not go back to the doctors. Should not her decisions be judged by their results? These are not the dark old days, after all, when citizens approached each other as across a field of buried mines: whether blindfolded or not, still never able to entirely avoid danger when they touched. These are modern times, mapped and rational, and avoiding heartache is a simple matter of taking responsibility for oneself. The social contracts have been made clear. Who would argue otherwise?

Anli did not go back to the doctors, but she stayed celibate for two years, until she considered she was no longer brooding, or perhaps until brooding no longer made celibacy compelling. She reregistered as she had been before: open. After two weeks from an open registration, she could switch again to whatever she desired: non-monogamy, single or group partnership, or a dozen other, more arcane classifications and subclassifications.

Her friends held a party in her honor. Derren was at that party.

So were many men and women, nearly all registered open or nonmonogamous, a few registered to group families that were not full. Her friends had taken care to supply Anli with a full palette of human potential to celebrate her departure from celibacy. They gathered in the common hall of Anli's cooperative, making matches among each other or not as they chose, all polite enough to introduce themselves first to their guest of honor.

Derren himself did not arrive until near the end of the party. Had the party before worked out differently, he would not have stayed after it was over.

But for the first hour, two men from a group family flirted with her, and while she thought the first was funny and the second intriguing, she did not want to think about group families. And for the second hour she became engrossed in a discussion of jai-alai with another man, who followed the same team she did, and while they exchanged access numbers and agreed to attend a game together soon, they also agreed to call each other Brother and Sister. And at the end of the third hour, she nearly asked a wry and intense woman to stay after, but something familiar and carefully uninteresting about the woman's blond hair and brown eyes and rich contralto voice changed her mind. Anli generally preferred men anyway, and did not demur when the woman, watching her, suddenly said she thought she might as well make an early night of it.

So by the fourth and last hour of her party, Anli sat in a corner of the hall trading word jokes with the remaining guests, reflecting that a change from celibacy to noncelibacy was more symbolic than predictive. It would be fair to Anli to say that she was not brooding on this, or did not see herself to be brooding: she laughed with her friends and argued about which turn of phrase scored the most points in the game and had put aside any thought of exercising her new license that night.

"I'm sorry to be so late," said a tall man with dark hair and hazel eyes, a man Anli did not know. "Will someone tell me who our hostess is so I may apologize properly?" His soft voice teased and danced.

Anli stood and extended her hand. He stood looking at her for a long moment, then took her hand and kissed it, not dropping his eyes. He grinned and said, "With the beauty of the hostess and the circumstances of the party, it's my great luck she's still here to apologize to."

"I wouldn't abandon my guests before the party was over," Anli said lightly.

"The party is not over," he said. He had not released her hand.

They went to her privacy room, not across town to his, and made love under her certificate of openness rather than his of nonmonogamy, but he told her how he was registered beforehand, as a good citizen should. His nonmonogamous status, as she knew, meant he could not directly enter a partnership even if he wanted: he would have to pass through a two-month transition, registered open, first.

Derren's practice and experience stood him in good stead. Within an hour Anli had forgotten to even wonder if she was brooding.

Two citizens with an open registration may spend ten nights together without having to change their registration. After that, or before if things move quickly, they must discuss whether they will change their registrations to monogamy or provisional monogamy, or if they will list each other as nonexclusive partners, or start a group family.

These are all decisions Anli would have had to discuss with a lover who was open, as she was, but Derren's nonmonogamy gave him more latitude.

Perhaps it is ironic that Derren's nonmonogamy allowed Anli to see Derren more often without either of them reconsidering their registration. But we must note that most citizens understand that nonmonogamy is exactly what it says on the face of it. Most citizens do not have the difficulty facing straightforward reality, written on a certificate beside a bed, that Anli had. Society cannot be held to blame.

It is precisely because Anli did know that Derren was committed to being uncommitted that he could take her to his bed, or she take him to hers, so frequently. In that month, it was twenty times.

"Anli," he gasped as he shuddered into her. "Ah, you fit sweetly. No other the same."

Anli shuddered herself, a shudder of warmth and happiness, and rolled to his side. "No other?" she teased. "Of your hundred women?"

"Not a hundred," he said, and chuckled, "not this year, but if it were a hundred, none of them like you."

How did Anli hear these words? Was she bearing in mind the social contracts, as every schoolchild knows to? Should we offer her sympathy for remembering those words only, and not what he had said three nights before? "Ah, Anli, you're a change from any other woman I know," he'd said. "How nice to be surprised again after all these years. If you change your registration again, love, you should think about registering as I have. There's nothing like the thrill of discovery."

She may have remembered part of that, but not the parts we would note. She may have placed undue weight on his use of the word "love." Understanding this does not mean approving this. The very fact that she teased him about a hundred women must mean she herself understood he was, indeed, exactly as the social contract presented him.

In that month Derren slept twenty times with Anli and a dozen or more times with old friends, most of them also nonmonogamous, and a few new friends, some nonmonogamous and some open. Derren was in the higher percentiles for sexual activity, as are many who register nonmonogamous. You will assume he mentioned some of this other activity to Anli; you will assume correctly. He only mentioned it a few times, but why should he have mentioned it more?

Anli slept twice with other men, one of whom irked her by too soon mentioning that he was looking for a partnership, and one of whom had skills she thought compared unfavorably to Derren's. She contacted Derren and was with him an hour after the second man left.

"We should keep doing this," she said after Derren had confirmed her judgment.

"I'll have to stop for at least ten minutes, love," he joked, running the back of his hand gently down her sweat-dampened side.

She smiled back at him. "I mean that we should keep seeing each other," she said.

"I'll happily keep seeing you, no fear. Not as often as we have been. I've been neglecting some of my other friends too much, they tell me."

Anli paused. "I was thinking of a contract," she said.

Derren sat up. Of course this would be a surprise to him. "Anli, love, I'm nonmonogamous."

"You could reregister."

"After first reregistering open, for two months, before I would be allowed to take a contract—and why would I? I'm nonmonogamous, Anli. I've been nonmonogamous for twelve years. You can see the dates on my certificate. You know who I am."

"You like me, you like being with me," Anli said. "You could be happy in a partnership with me."

"I like many people, Anli," said Derren. He was frowning now. He pulled the sheet up past his waist.

"But you don't need them."

"I want them all, yes," Derren said. He spoke slowly, watching her. "I want many women, but I don't need any one of them. I am not monogamous. I do not need any one of you."

Did he see Anli flinch? He did.

"We have, perhaps, seen too much of each other, love," he said. "You were open. I thought perhaps open to my way of living. Perhaps I misjudged. I've never slept with someone who had been so long celibate before. Does that make a difference? Have you seen anyone other than I?"

"Several people," Anli said, exaggerating, and then she said, "I think you're right about my registration. I'll think about it. I'll call you." She dressed then and left.

Derren's adherence to responsibility cannot be denied. Anli, however—

Anli appeared at Derren's doorway three days later with a piece of paper in her hand. She glanced only once at the woman sitting up in Derren's bed, peering curiously around him at her, then said, "I decided you have the best idea. I've changed my registration."

He looked at the paper. It read nonmonogamous. He looked at her.

"So, I'll give you a call sometime, all right?" Anli said.

"All right. I have company—"

"I won't keep you." She left his building and went back to her own. She took her certificate off the wall and carefully smoothed the forged one over it. She waited to see if she would hear from Derren.

If any of you is vulnerable to backward thinking, you may say this was a small crime. But it is well said that the smallest breach in the social contracts leads to dangerous rifts: plunging, deadly chasms of conflict and misunderstanding: insanity. It is not for nothing that our forebears set up our system of social contracts. Eternal vigilance is the price of sociability.

Learn from Anli's errors.

When Derren did not call for several days, Anli contacted him and, keeping her voice as casual as she could, arranged for him to come to her privacy room.

She found her thoughts strangely divided while he was there. She was glad to see him and triumphant at the success of her fraud. (Derren did not even glance at the false certificate on her wall. Who would falsify a certificate?)

And yet, as she kissed him and he stroked her hips and breathed into her ear, she was tormented by the thought that he would as soon be with the redheaded woman she had seen in his bed as with her. She had conceived, so she thought, a true passion for him, while to him she was an interchangeable partner, one among many.

She found this thought unbearable.

It was, she thought, even as she moved in complex rhythms with the man, worse than being rejected for partnership by someone registered open. It was infinitely worse, because he did not even look at her as the material for a partnership.

This, though Derren was nonmonogamous from the start of things.

We see that, so soon after her first crime, Anli had begun to slip into what we can only call insanity. Backward-thinking people might call it jealousy, or insecurity, or even love, but we know there is no place for love that is not law-abiding. And we can see this from Anli's desperate actions to follow.

She now saw Derren only every week or two. Between times, she thought about little but the next time she would see him. When they spent an hour together, it seemed to her Derren was reserved, much more cautious in his dealings with her than he had been before. She brooded.

She brooded, and she did not take this as a sign to change her ways: instead, she plotted how to change Derren's ways. This is a violation of all the principles of the social contracts. The social contracts were designed to help Anli and all citizens easily find those others who could suit their needs, so they would not violate the rights of other citizens by trying to change them.

Anli had had failures, but who of us has not? Her error was in brooding. Her error was in turning criminal against the principles of social contracts. Her error was in not keeping faith with the system.

Anli tried arranging surprises of dress, food, or activity with Derren; she tried reading the latest poems and being witty; she tried seven fashions of styling her hair and coloring her eyes. She stuck to her lie of nonmonogamy but slept only with Derren, when she could.

Which was not often.

Although she had broken the contracts and broken her word, giving a fellow citizen no understanding of her desires or intentions, Derren pulled back. We may look at it as though he saw her true self under the false, a rough skin under the soft, her real certificate under the forgery.

Which, of course, he could not. No citizen could be prepared for such dissemblance. Perhaps we should blame the doctors Anli went to two years before, that they did not find her flaw. Or perhaps we can still only blame her, who knew her own flaw and did not strive to have it removed.

But, as he pulled back, whatever ancient instinct guiding him, Anli grew more desperate, and as she grew more desperate, more criminal.

Each citizen devotes twenty hours a week to her work (Anli had a technical position with the weather service, tracking which storms were likely and which necessary, and determining when to alter their patterns), and ten hours to social services, which at this time she spent removing old broadsheets and flyers from walls and kiosks. Neither occupation, we can see, afforded her much interaction with her fellow citizens. Her weather analysis she conducted alone, in her own privacy room; the flyer removal was a simple task that took her out in public but did not require her to as much as speak to anyone. It also gave her every opportunity to brood, which she did, even in good sunlight and surrounded by adjusted, normal people.

It is not good for someone with retrogressive tendencies to shun societal contact, but just as she did in her work, she stayed to herself in her free hours.

Somewhere in the midst of this unhealthy solitude, she conceived her desperate plan.

In this one area the city might be held accountable. There obviously were insufficient safeguards on the personal files of its citizens. Yet there is no record that anyone before had attempted to alter the parts of those files Anli now compromised. Perhaps some had tried before and failed. Perhaps she found an untapped genius within herself.

Through trickery, finesse, and deceit, she found a way to change the files, from her own home workstation. Within a week of her determination to make it so, Derren's registration was changed to open, backdated six weeks.

The certificate on his wall was the same as ever. Anli could see it on the occasions she was there, as she smiled at him, lying to him by the very way she carried herself, breaking the social contracts.

Only twice she saw him in the next two weeks, but on these occasions, she relaxed and smiled. Their sex was much better, relaxed, as perhaps Derren sensed that the brooding cloud she had carried was gone. He mentioned something about taking a day to visit the summer fair with her.

"That would be perfect," said Anli. The fair was to begin two weeks and two days after she had altered his records.

We are all rightly proud of our famous summer fair, that fabulous gathering of jugglers, clowns, acrobats, holo-illusionists, personality readers, contests, and music. A hundred different foods are flash-grown in tanks of colorful fluids, cooked, and served in the open air. Nearly the whole city attends at least a full day, and others come from thousands of miles away to see it.

Anli met Derren at a roast-apple stand and offered him one.

They strolled arm in arm down the street. Derren pointed out a group of acrobats tumbling up and down invisible rappelling lines along a building's side. Two leapt unexpectedly ten meters through empty air to the next building over, causing Anli and Derren to gasp and laugh. Anli pulled him to a stand where a musical trio she liked, horn, viola, and a gene-modified canary controlled by a trainer, was playing. They ate again, chopped potatoes with herbs and sausage.

And for an hour Anli thought she would not do what she had planned to do. She took Derren's arm, leaned against his side, and drifted through the crowds feeling perfectly right in the world. She was, as we understand, deluding herself. She allowed herself to feel Derren's falsified social contract status was his true one, that he was open to a partnership; but the truth could not be plastered over.

For Derren removed her arm from his and said, "Wait just a moment, please?" And went over to a tall, fair woman pouring cider at a booth; Anli could hear them laughing as old friends do and setting a date for later in the week. Her fingers stiffened, clenched, and marked her palms with her nails. She did not notice. She watched Derren and the tall woman, her breath painful in the back of her throat.

She stood back. She pulled the device from her belt that linked her to her systems at home and to the citywide systems. She issued an instruction.

The results of further planning, deceit, and trickery fell into place.

When Derren returned, Anli said, "I'm tired of walking. Could we go back to my place now?"

"I'd rather see more of the fair," Derren said. "There's a pantomime I want to watch that begins in less than an hour."

"I don't feel well. Please help me home."

Anli pulled Derren away, between the stilts of performers who moved slowly through the crowd, dipping as low as three meters and soaring as high as ten on the telescoping stilts; red satin capes rippled in the breeze high over the pair's heads, meter-wide butterflies with wings patterned to match the capes flying evanescently among them.

"Anli, love," Derren was saying, as she twisted them quickly toward her building through waves of smiling people moving in the other direction, "Anli, I think we should talk. You don't really seem the sort of person suited to nonmonogamy. You say you've been see-ing other people, but no one I know has seen you with anyone else for months." So we can see that Derren was not himself a fool. He understood the social contracts and had some intuition of Anli's re-sistance to them. Could he have expected the lengths to which she would go? No one could have.

Anli did not reply. She quickened her pace, so that Derren had to lengthen his stride to keep up. He said, "You're a special woman and our time has been sweet, but perhaps you should register as open again and find someone who wants a partnership, Anli." They reached her building and Anli signaled the door to open. "Love, I'll see you to your room, but then I think I should go."

Anli nodded impatiently. The door opened; they were inside. She shut it.

"Are you all right now? I should leave."

"You have to see something."

Derren frowned as Anli pulled at the mail drawer by her work-station. She removed an envelope and took two sheets of paper from it. Her eye was bright, her cheeks flushed. She showed them to him.

"I don't need a partnership. I have one."

Derren looked at the papers. They were not simple forgeries like the certificate of nonmonogamy Anli had fooled him with earlier, the one he had never thought to examine skeptically. They were freshly delivered from the city's record-keeping center itself, when Anli had triggered her mad plan from the fair. They were as legal and legiti-mate as any contracts in the city—if we can say that anything is le-gitimate with deliberate error and deceit at its base.

"What is this?"

"We have a partnership," Anli said, and the calm satisfaction in her voice could only be called quite mad.

Imagine what Derren felt then. Imagine yourself, if the foun-dations on which you had built your life were with no warning per-verted against you: if your parent or coparent called you stranger; if you came home and found your room a factory filled with silk-spinning vats instead of your own comfortable furniture and belong-ings, and the building manager insisted it was ever so; if you found yourself arrested for the crime of performing the ordinary job you had worked for three years.

So must Derren have felt, and we cannot be surprised that he found no words at first, that his knees weakened so he must sit dizzily on the chair Anli pushed up behind him.

"We do not," he finally said. "That is madness."

"I have the certificates. I can show you the city records," she said, stepping past him to her workstation. Derren shook his head in stunned disbelief at what she showed him.

He said it was not true, and Anli made him call up the records from his own link. He said he had not so registered, and she smiled. He said the city records must have misfunctioned somehow, and she reminded him that such a thing had not happened in thirty years. He said he would reregister, and she asked if he had forgotten the minimum partnership term was three months.

He said he was not her partner.

Anli said, "You are."

He stood, with a near violence rarely seen in a modern citizen, staring at her wildly. Then he slumped back into the chair and pulled at his hair. "I don't understand, I don't understand."

"I applied and it went through. You must have applied as well."

"I couldn't have! I'm nonmonogamous! I always have been!"

"That's not what the city said," Anli said, her voice clear and innocent.

"You were registered nonmonogamous!"

"I changed my registration back two months ago. Didn't I tell you? I thought I'd told you." She gestured at the wall, where her certificate hung. The forged paper had been removed from over her true certificate, but now her true certificate was a forgery as well: its beginning date altered to two months, two days before.

"It makes no sense," he said, moaning, "no sense."

She paused. "We're in a partnership now. Three months, that's all. Such a little time. Why not try it, Derren?"

"I will live my life as I always have," he said. The anger in his voice would have caused any normal person to step back. Anli stepped forward and brushed slack hair from his forehead with the edge of her hand.

"You will not," she said. "You cannot."

He got up and left then without another word. We might have expected Anli would have locked her door against his exit, but she had not. She watched him leave, and sat in the chair he had unwillingly warmed, and waited. In a while she ordered some food to her door; in a while she did a little work, approving a hurricane's deflection away from the coast. She hummed sometimes to herself. She did not brood. She waited.

The madness was ripe. It was full.

The next day Derren returned. His breath was short and his eye wild, but he kept his voice low. "They have all been informed. Every woman I know. They all received official notice that I am partnered. They all congratulated me!"

"They must be polite and gracious women," Anli said. "I'm sure they're very happy for you."

"They will not receive me!"

"Of course not," said Anli. "It's the social contract."

"How can I live my life?" he cried. "I am not made for celibacy!"

"I am here, my partner."

For the first time he looked at her with something like hatred. For a normal citizen to feel hatred, he must have been driven to an extreme. Anli met his glare and did not flinch.

"It will not be," he said, and left again.

Anli took two hours away from home to perform her social duties. She slid through the crowds of the fair with a sprayer of defixative, examining kiosks for outdated notices, spraying them and peeling them off. She smiled; she fairly glowed with satisfaction. Other citizens caught her eye and smiled back. Some laughing clowns grabbed her hands and pulled her into their troupe; she danced with them down the street on a platform atop a giant slow-moving ball that swirled with colors in time to the dance. She dismounted and went back to work, humming in counterpoint to the strains of the street musicians. She rolled up the old flyers, dropped them into a recycling bin, and returned to her home.

The next night Derren returned. "You did something," he accused.

"I? I agreed to a partnership with you," she said. "You're lucky I'm an understanding woman. Another might have notified the city that you are derelict in your duties."

Derren made a wordless noise and fled. He did not come back that night, or the night after. Anli did her work and watched the days go by.

After a week and some days, she went to his room. She signaled the door and it let her in. "You!" said Derren, sitting up groggily, one person in a bed made for two. "How did—"

"We are partnered," said Anli. "The city knows that. Your building knows that. I have entry here."

A sob broke from Derren.

"I understand," she said. "You've been alone. That's hard for you. I am your partner: I am here."

"No," said Derren.

She sat on the bed beside him. "You shouldn't have to feel like this," she said. She was wearing a scent he had given her.

"No." He pulled away.

She pulled her legs up onto the bed and removed her light evening jacket. Under it she wore a thin, sheer camisole. "Yes," she said.

Derren closed his eyes and shuddered. We must understand what Anli did, what we noted earlier: as most citizens who choose lifelong nonmonogamy, Derren was in the highest percentiles for sexual need. He had not been two weeks without a bedmate since he was fifteen. We can only speculate on the pressures within him, in a position the social contracts should never have allowed, unwilling to submit to a lie made real in the city records about his very nature. But a man battered by abstinence. "No."

Anli brushed a finger, feather soft, around his ear, and the fingertips of her other hand up his opposite thigh, in a manner he had always moaned to feel. He moaned now, in agony more than pleasure.

"No—"

She kissed him on the jawline. He trembled. Tears rolled from his eyes.

"No," he said, a last time.

When he woke in the morning she was asleep, curled beside him smiling, both her arms wrapped around his, her leg across his leg.

We must find sympathy for Derren. The madness had not been his. He had not first cracked and then shattered the social contracts to serve his own selfish ends: Anli had shattered those, and his life, his public and thus his private self, with them.

What happened then was appalling, but it stemmed naturally from Anli's crimes, and not from Derren himself.

Still, the city might not have found out for days, not until far too late, if Derren had not been so broken, so driven to his own reflective madness, moon to Anli's sun, that he went out, wildly searching the fair until he found a woman from a distant city whom he had met once years ago, one who would not have received notice of his changed status. He stayed with her at her hostel; only the next morning did she idly link up to her host city's records to check on his status. He had not said if he was still nonmonogamous, and she herself, open to partnership, looked to see if he now was.

She notified the authorities, of course. They came to arrest Derren before he woke.

Someone backward-thinking might call him a broken man, but he was performing his duty as a citizen by telling the city representatives everything that had happened. An ambulance was immediately dispatched to his privacy room, an override ordered for the lock on his door.

They found Anli on the floor beside the bed, neck broken, but still breathing. Still smiling.

It was a simple matter to repair her broken body, grow nerves back to touch nerves, mend a shattered vertebra. Within days this was done.

Her madness was another matter. The city gives each citizen every opportunity to reconcile with its principles. While her record of mental health was examined, while her erotic remapping studied to see if errors had been made, Anli appeared before a hearing of the city elders. They listened as she put her words on record, words that would become part of her file.

"There can be no contract to make everyone happy," she said. "There are no rules for love. You're fools, all of you, all of us, for thinking we can sort everyone by some kind of emotional taxonomy. Do you think you can order everyone to lie down neatly in rows for you?"

She stood and shook her fist. She thought herself heroic and defiant at this moment. We can only picture her thin arm waving, her strained voice spouting irrationalities.

"If my heart is broken, it is mine to be broken. If I am a fool, there can be no sane law against it."

But how may the insane speak of sanity? How may the criminal claim she damages no one but herself?

"However you made it my duty to be happy, you could not compel it from me. However many cozy boxes you designed for me, I could not fit into one. Is this my fault? Yours? Nature's? I call on the people to erase their registrations. Walk into chaos as human beings, not social components! Stumble blindly among your fellow blind men and women! Collide, confuse, hurt each other. You're fooling yourselves if you think everyone can herd their feelings like domestic animals. Why try? Why submit? Why—"

The council looked silently down at her.

"Revolt!" Anli said, but her voice was cracked, and she let them take her away.

No citizen may be treated against her will. Ours is a society of freedom and democracy. Derren's treatment was simple—his madness only temporary and reactive—and he was released to live a life as adjusted as it had been before. At his request, he forgot Anli entirely.

Anli had the stubbornness of true madness. But madness will burn itself out after enough years of protective custody; if it doesn't, society is patient. The social contracts will out, in the end.

So finally, with caring help, Anli was erotically rebalanced, socially adjusted, and sent back into society.

Her home had been held empty for her return by the generosity of the city. Her friends welcomed her with open arms, and a party as warm as the one that had marked the beginning of her criminal path. A new post was created for her at the weather bureau, awaiting only the completion of one small task, which she happily completed for society's sake.

Learn from her errors: her story is published herewith as a caution to all citizens. Had she sought help when she showed the signs of early madness, the uncontrolled brooding, the first small crimes, society would have been spared much labor, Anli much pain.

Learn from her errors: all her mad rebellion bought was that pain.

Learn from her errors: in the design of the social contracts, in our agreement to them, are the tools to keep us all on a calm and healthy path. Society is perfectable: it is a simple matter of codifying it to meet every human need.

If society is perfectable, it is the responsibility of the individual to be perfectable. It would be madness to think madness cannot be made obsolete, defeatism to think citizens might continue to deny themselves the proffered means to be calm and fulfilled. It would be the worst sort of defeatism to deny the perfectability of humankind.

Who could disagree?

Submitted to the Council of City Elders
Anli Vinnera, Citizen

From a Park Bench to the Great Beyond: The Science Fiction and Fantasy Films of 1994

KATHI MAIO

There is no Nebula Award for filmed or televised science fiction, but it is customary to include an essay in this volume about the year's most important science fiction and fantasy in visual form. Kathi Maio, the author of *Feminist in the Dark* and *Popcorn and Sexual Politics*, writes columns on film for *The Magazine of Fantasy & Science Fiction* and *Sojourner*. In the spring of 1995, I was in the audience at a conference on film held at the State University of New York at Binghamton when Kathi Maio gave a lecture, interspersed with film clips, on images of working women in movies; the audience was treated to an entertaining, informative, and wide-ranging presentation covering movies, changing social attitudes, and the disappearance of the working-class woman (as opposed to the career woman) as a heroine in American films.

In a recent column, Maio asked: "When was it that the hero and the villain of science fiction and fantasy films became nearly inter-changeable? I can't seem to tie it to an exact date. . . . I only know that far too many of the speculative films I'm seeing these days seem morally empty. . . . Remember when science fiction films explored social and political and moral issues through stories just on the other side of our perception of present-day reality? I remember movies like that. I just don't see them very often anymore." Kathi Maio views films both as a lover of movies and as a social critic, as her essay on movies of 1994 demonstrates.

The biggest live-action film of 1994 was not a science fiction film. Nor was it a fantasy film. Or was it? *Forrest Gump*, which was still in very active release at year's end, pulled in more than $300 million in 1994—doubling the grosses of its nearest nonanimated competitor. It was told in a realistic style, as one (not very bright) man's experience as a witness to, and active participant in, forty turbulent years of modern American history.

But the film was more than a naif's picaresque saga through twentieth-century life. Viewers responded with almost religious fervor to Forrest's telling of his own story because it was a fairy tale with healing powers. (Distressing things happen "for no particular reason," but goodness is amply rewarded.) In the end, they clapped because they believed. Or wanted badly to.

An oblivious mover and shaker, Forrest inspired two generations of rock legends and helped to topple a presidency. And that was just on his off days. His life was so wonderful, it would have given Jimmy Stewart's George Bailey suicidal feelings of inferiority—again. And yet, Mr. Gump hadn't a clue how important he was.

Good simple Forrest (the always endearing Tom Hanks) was like the white feather that floated and flew through the film's opening (and closing) shots. He was acted upon by the violent winds of America at midcentury. And yet he survived and miraculously prospered. A man without anger or guilt, he was the epitome of "go with the flow." Therein lay his greatness.

The politics of the film are debatable, but movie audiences weren't arguing with how good they felt after watching it. And the fable of *Forrest Gump* sprang forth from movie wizards who informed their realistic style with the techniques of science fiction and fantasy filmmaking.

Director Robert Zemeckis (*Back to the Future, Who Framed Roger Rabbit?*) used a delicate hand to integrate rather spectacular special effects into his story. With the help of a frequent collaborator, visual effects supervisor Ken Ralston, and his crews at Industrial Light & Magic, Zemeckis did away with the lower legs of actor Gary Sinise (in the film's best performance), and added Mr. Hanks to events as varied as a champion Ping-Pong match in China and George Wallace's segregationist grandstanding at the University of Alabama in 1963.

Despite its heavy use of FX, and the mystical quality of its story line, *Forrest Gump* is a fantasy film only if you're inclined to see it that way. For the purposes of this overview, I'm willing to give it the benefit of the doubt. No doubts exist, however, about the status of the other mega-blockbuster of the year, the animated family film *The Lion King*.

Disney animation has never looked better than in this fable about a cub named Simba who is born to rule his African homeland. It has all the standard House of Mouse classic elements, a dastardly villain, comic sidekicks, tragic separation from a parent figure, great musical interludes, and the ultimate triumph of a brave (if, in this case, self-doubting and guilt-ridden) hero. All this in a multicultural, anthropomorphic fantasy that delights the eye with its majestic vistas.

Disney wiped the sticky floor of the nation's movie theaters with the competition this year. Not only did box office grosses for *The Lion King* break $300 million by the end of 1994 (even though Disney removed the film from general release during the early autumn to boost holiday receipts), but a 1994 direct-to-tape sequel to 1992's *Aladdin* also broke records. The vastly inferior but nonetheless entertaining musical/action romp entitled *The Return of Jafar* sold seven million tape units in its first months of release. And that's without the vocal lunacy of Robin Williams as the Genie.

Could it be that Disney has cornered the market on animation? Certainly, the big success of their recent animated fantasies, including (besides *Aladdin*) *The Little Mermaid* and *Beauty and the Beast,* has given the studio the kind of track record that brings little tykes and their adult friends to any full-length cartoon that has the name Disney attached to it. A hit-making audience appears to be a given. With all its fast-food tie-ins and synergistic merchandising, Disney has to blow it big-time to lose the moviegoing masses.

Not so for non-Disney projects in family-style animation. Two romantic fairy tales, Don Bluth's *Hans Christian Andersen's Thumbelina,* and *The Swan Princess* from (another Disney escapee) Richard Rich's Animation Studio, both did very poorly in 1994. More surprising, perhaps, was the miserable $12 million showing of *The Pagemaster,* a live-action/animated fantasy starring Macaulay Culkin as a timid little boy who learns how to be a daredevil from spending quality time with good books.

It's an illogical (even for a fantasy) premise, compromised further by a plodding delivery. Christopher Lloyd is lovable in the combined role of librarian Mr. Dewey and the wizard Pagemaster. But we see far too little of him and far too much of three other animated entities.

Called Adventure, Fantasy, and Horror, they are drawn as books—a real mistake, that. Books are wonderful things, but they don't make for interesting or colorful cartoon characters. And even the voice work of Whoopi Goldberg (always a delight) and Patrick Stewart could not save this movie from being a tedious disappointment.

I found another cartoon pretty disappointing, but movie audiences did not apparently agree. The live-action feature based on the classic Hanna-Barbera animated sitcom *The Flintstones* was a summer 1994 smash. This despite an insignificant plot that would have worked well as a half-hour show, but which dragged badly in a two-hour movie.

The cast, especially John Goodman (Fred) and Rosie O'Donnell (Betty), did the best they could with the silliness. (Hard to believe it took thirty-plus writers to come up with a screenplay like this!) But by far and away the best thing this visit to Bedrock had going for it are the characters created by the artists, technicians, and puppeteers at Jim Henson's Creature Shop.

An energetic Dino, a delightfully officious Dictabird (voiced by Harvey Korman), as well as a steady stream of rock puns, could not, unfortunately, keep the fun in this picture. But with its nostalgia-enhanced wide appeal for both baby boomers and their cartoon-crazed offspring, *The Flintstones* hit it big anyway.

The success of *The Crow* was more of a surprise. Based on J. O'Barr's not exactly cheery comic books, the project didn't have nearly the name recognition of *The Flintstones*. Although it achieved considerable infamy when the film's star, Brandon Lee, was accidentally shot and killed (at the age of twenty-eight) during the filming of a gunfight on the set.

At first there was some question as to whether the film could, or should, be completed. And when director Alex Proyas, with the help of Dream Quest Image's digital compositing skills and a body double, found ways to complete the project, the original distributor, Paramount, dropped it. Miramax eventually distributed, in what turned out to be a lucrative move. *The Crow* ended up a summer hit.

The story of a young man who is murdered but cannot rest until he avenges his own death and that of his beloved is undeniably monotonous. One episode of hunt-and-kill is followed by another. And another. If the film works at all—and it does—it is because of Brandon Lee's considerable charisma and Mr. Proyas's darkly stylish (and drenched to the bone) vision. A driving soundtrack featuring the likes of Nine Inch Nails, The Cure, and Stone Temple Pilots didn't hurt, either.

Another modern comic book found a happy home on the big screen with *The Mask,* starring the smokin' Jim Carrey (who had two other hits, *Ace Ventura: Pet Detective* and *Dumb and Dumber,* in 1994). Here was the perfect melding of man and material. The rubber-faced, flex-jointed Carrey is a dynamo of whacked-out comedy. Yet he is very capable of projecting a kind of shy innocence as well.

Who better to play a mild-mannered bank clerk transformed into a ingratiating demon by a rustic mask? The violence and bite of Mike Richardson's Dark Horse Comic was toned down by director Charles Russell and screenwriter Mike Werb to make a movie both kids and adults could love. And they did. Carrey's performance is a manic delight, and the special effects makeup by Greg Cannom and computer animation effects by IL&M made it a sure-win entertainment.

If some of the animation seems stolen directly from Tex Avery's 1940s classic cartoons, at least the film acknowledges its debts honestly. *The Mask* took old and new and made something audiences worldwide could enjoy. But not all variations upon the classics work so well.

The Shadow is a film that bored young viewers and outraged many older audiences with an abiding love of the pulp hero of their youth. Not surprisingly, it was the high-profile fantasy failure of the summer.

Russell Mulcahy's film was a misguided project, starting with the casting. Although I personally liked Alec Baldwin in the title role, I nonetheless recognized him as a little *too* leading mannish for the part. And what can be said about Penelope Ann Miller as Margo Lane, British actor Ian McKellen as her dad, and Jonathan Winters as Wainwright Barth? To put it generously, they were curious choices.

The film's oddly erratic tone—alternately existential, wise ass, limply romantic, and just plain dumb—is the death of the movie, even more than its harebrained plot. Oh, *The Shadow* is pretty to look at. But looks aren't everything.

Special effects are, needless to say, the meat and potatoes of science fiction and fantasy film. But they should complement the story line, and not dominate the film as showboating frills. The fact that FX bits (like a message flying through a pneumatic tube system and a demonic dancing dagger taunting our hero) are, along with the sumptuous production design, what you most remember about *The Shadow* sadly illustrates what a dud it turned out to be.

Mary Shelley's Frankenstein was another costly, high-profile loser. It wasn't as bad a botch-up as *The House of the Spirits*, in which a passionate Chilean saga of magic realism got a chilly Scandinavian treatment by a Danish director and an uncomfortable assortment of European and North American actors. Nonetheless, it was an undeniable mess.

Kenneth Branagh should have known not to get involved with a production team headed by Francis Ford Coppola. (Didn't he see the self-important nonsense known as *Bram Stoker's Dracula?*) The screenplay by Steph Lady and Frank Darabont allowed the talented Mr. Branagh to indulge all his worst tendencies.

Pumped up and full of himself, Branagh (the actor) couldn't seem to keep his shirt on as Dr. F., despite the chilly climate of Switzerland and Germany. And Branagh (the director) couldn't keep his mind on the simple power of Shelley's tale. He continually got caught up in Shakespearean pretension and operatic flourishes.

There's plenty of blood and dismemberment, but precious little suspense in the film. And there is something—shades of Karloff—faintly comical about Robert DeNiro's monster. He's like rubberized roadkill with a New York accent. Perhaps that's in the grand cinematic tradition of the story, but I couldn't fathom why the good doctor would have done just as bad a stitching job on his own beloved. Guess he should have taken a good home ec class when he was a boy.

I hope that Kenneth Branagh learns an important lesson about the dangers of hubris from the character he played in *Frankenstein*—and from the less than enthusiastic reception his heavily hyped film received from the moviegoing public.

Even big brawny names had a rough year in 1994. Although Arnold Schwarzenegger did well as the Bondian macho hero of James Cameron's extremely expensive but explosively entertaining flick, *True Lies,* audiences found him much more resistible in a warm and fuzzy science fiction film directed by Ivan Reitman called *Junior*.

The movie's high concept—Preggers Terminator—came with a few built-in laughs, but the film (originally scripted by Chris Conrad, and then multirevised by Kevin Wade) had no sustainable humor to back up the poster of Ah-nuld with a gigantic tummy.

Forget about the shaky science of a man being able to carry a fetus to term without a uterus and placenta of some sort. Movie viewers are happy enough to forget such things if they genuinely enjoy a film. But that was the catch. *Junior* gave men the willies. They didn't want to see their favorite action hero experiencing morning sickness and complaining of sensitive nipples.

And women, who might have been expected to enjoy such a turnabout revenge fantasy, didn't like it any better. The movie's insulting commentary about what estrogen does to a rational human being—that is, it makes them weepy, domestic, insecure, and possessive—didn't set well with female viewers. And neither did the depiction of the brilliant Emma Thompson as Arnie's buffoonish love interest.

Most audiences prefer their action stars to be manly men, through and through. That was one of several difficulties facing *Blankman,* an attempt at a comic crimefighter fantasy. As the geeky title character, Damon Wayans seemed to be doing a Jerry Lewis impersonation—but with considerably less verve than Jim Carrey in *The Mask*—and with an incomplete transformation into a truly intrepid action figure.

The film's low-energy performances clearly stem from the lethargic direction, by Mike Binder, and less than sparkling writing, by Mr. Wayans and J. F. Lawton. But whatever the cause, this one was a major waste of talent and resources. And, worse, it represents another bungled bid to create an African-American superhero.

Another action actor stayed true to his greatest (or, according to your viewpoint, *only*) talent by making sure that there was plenty of macho kick to his SF storyline. Martial arts heartthrob Jean-Claude Van Damme zipped through the present, near future, and recent past as the *Timecop,* a man who'd much rather use his feet than a zap gun on a rambunctious bad guy.

Time travel has become a reality. And with the invention of a bulky prototype time machine, Van Damme becomes an officer for the Time Enforcement Commission, an elite government agency dedicated to keeping history honest. You might wonder why the TEC doesn't just post a guard or two at the extremely massive vehicle. But if you wonder that, you will probably shake your head throughout the film over its loony logic and self-contradictory morals.

Van Damme is still no actor. He can, however, do a mean split on a kitchen counter, and he kickboxes with real grace. It would be easy to argue that the SF trappings of Peter Hyams's workmanlike film are mere window dressing. Unquestionably, audiences primarily went to see *Timecop* so as to enjoy a good-looking guy kicking up his heels.

But even action audiences are discriminating. Van Damme closed out the year by bringing the video game *Street Fighter* to life. Sort of. Even the splendor of an ailing Raul Julia couldn't save that garish film. And another video-game-to-film, *Double Dragon,* was even more of a dud.

With too much repetitive violence and too little in the way of engaging plot, video games just have not, to date, translated well into big-screen entertainment. For that matter, a 1994 film about playing an interactive video game, *Brainscan,* was no improvement. In it, a young lad played by Edward Furlong is enticed into becoming a serial killer by a beyond-VR game and its accompanying punkish monster, who calls himself Trickster.

The biggest problem with *Brainscan* was its schizoid personality. It wanted to be a high-tech gaming horror fable *and* a slasher monster movie that could be franchised as an ongoing series. The two did not mix well. And the film just doesn't work, despite a good performance by Furlong as an alienated computer junkie.

Creating a memorable, bring-'em-back-for-more horror monster is harder than it looks. Many a Trickster has tried and failed to find an audience. Only a handful of modern boogeymen, like Jason and especially Freddy Krueger, have truly sparked the public's imagination. Having done so, they've been able to go back to the well time after time to drink in fame and fortune.

Therein lies the rub. Even with a world-famous fiend ripping up entrails for you, going back into production too many times usually results in a jaded audience, decreasing box office returns, and increasingly caustic critical response. Eventually, filmmakers, studios, and actors want to move on. And so, the monster is laid to rest. For a time.

Still, hobgoblins (who resemble cash cows) have a nasty habit of coming back from the dead. And so it was with Freddy Krueger, who returned from *Freddy's Dead: The Final Nightmare* (1991) in *Wes Craven's New Nightmare.* As the title indicates, Freddy was finally back in the hands of the man who created him.

But Mr. Craven wasn't really interested in creating a honestly hair-raising horror movie with his *New Nightmare.* Instead he wanted to contemplate the world of horror filmmaking. Craven's original heroine, Heather Langenkamp, appears as a fictionalized version of herself, and Robert Englund plays both himself and the eternal Freddy. Craven even plays a role as The (Slasher) Player with a troubling script to shoot.

From an admirably spooky opening of a dismembered blade-hand running amok on a movie set, *Wes Craven's New Nightmare* rapidly loses its pace and coherence. Fans of the Elm Street series still tended to find it a witty, self-referential romp by a master of horror. Others characterized it as an unsatisfying Hollywood ego trip.

Despite the disappointing grosses of his last theatrical outing, it would be foolish to count Freddy out. He's a horror tradition—and a still-viable franchise. The trick will be to make the next Nightmare seem really New.

The Star Trek movie and television empire does it by constantly creating new product: new crews facing new adventures. *Star Trek Generations* was an important step in that direction. This surefire addition to the Trek canon was designed as a feature film transition between the first and second series.

The cast list is crowded with sentimental favorites from both shows—which causes frustrations aplenty. For the majority of the crewmembers of both *Enterprise*s have little more than walk-on parts. But at least our two favorite captains, Kirk and Picard, are provided with a jolly ride in this one. Perhaps too jolly, in fact.

You can almost see writers Rick Berman, Ronald D. Moore, and Brannon Braga brainstorming their stars' wish list of enjoyable scenes and antics. Oh yes, give Shatner a chance to do one of his favorite things, ride a horse. And, after winning awards for his one-man *Christmas Carol,* why not set Stewart loose in a Dickensian Christmas paradise with a tragic undercurrent?

These personalized touches aren't exactly essential to the film's story. But what of it? At this point, none of us go to a Star Trek movie for original, challenging writing. We go to visit with old friends. And, in the case of *Star Trek Generations,* there was the added pull of getting to say good-bye forever (or so they say) to Jim Kirk.

We, therefore, didn't waste much time pondering the plot involving an energy ribbon called the Nexus, which provides such powerful druglike fantasies that a rabid villain like Malcolm McDowell's Dr. Soran is willing to destroy a planet or two to get back into it. Instead, we enjoyed the sojourn, shed a tear or two at the leave-taking, and watched a Hollywood baton being passed from one generation to the Next.

For those who wanted a good, old-fashioned science fiction film without any emotional baggage, there was *StarGate,* an original movie that borrowed from every SF, adventure, and pop psychology tradition. Interplanetary exploration becomes a healing ritual for injured manhood when a discredited and lonely Egyptologist (James Spader) and grieving, suicidal career soldier (Kurt Russell) unlock and enter another world.

Although the natives are fairly friendly when they arrive, the resident god is less welcoming. Ra (Jaye Davidson, in another gender-nonspecific and elegantly campy performance) is really an alien dependent on the slave labor of the people of the planet Abydos. He wants to destroy the interlopers before they can foment a rebellion.

Liberation is a small job Russell and his unit take on while Spader shyly romances a local beauty and works to break the code on the StarGate's other side, so that the earthlings can get back home. If you can sit back and enjoy the film as if it were a Cecil B. DeMille *Raiders of the Lost Chariots of the Gods* with a few nifty, nineties-style special effects, you will enjoy Roland Emmerich's film immensely. Most critics couldn't do that. But most moviegoers could. And *StarGate* was an unexpected fall hit.

Less unanticipated was the boffo box office of *Interview with the Vampire.* The screen adaptation of Anne Rice's best-seller spent nearly two decades in Development Hell as a hot (unproduced) property. When it, at long last, went before the cameras, controversy fueled audience interest even more. First, author Rice groused over the casting of the wholesome, boyish Tom Cruise as Lestat. Then, strategically, she recanted just prior to the film's release with paid ads telling her millions of fans that she "simply loved it."

Star power and big buzz are, if you will, the life's blood of Hollywood. And there was enough of both associated with this project to ensure lines around the block. In some ways, the film even lived up to the hype. Neil Jordan (who made the underrated *The Company of Wolves* as well as *The Crying Game*) and his cinematographer, Philippe Rousselot, deserve kudos for their good-looking, if gruesome, film. The performances are adequate to excellent. (In my opinion, the best work was done by the least-known performer: little Kirsten Dunst as the eternal child, Claudia.)

As the vampire story has become "modern," its violence has become more and more eroticized. And, as in the case of *Interview*'s monsters, we are encouraged to identify and sympathize with murderous demons. Louis's avowed aversion to his killing ways is, of course, a poor excuse for real scruples. Because he continues to annihilate others.

That is why the decadent splendor of *Interview with the Vampire* thrilled me not in the least. I enjoyed much more a $2 million Mexican film that made very little splash in the U.S. when it was released in 1994, after taking the Grand Prize of Critics' Week at Cannes a year earlier. The film was entitled *Cronos,* and it was the work of a gifted, young makeup effects artist turned writer/director, Guillermo del Torro.

The title refers to a device invented by an alchemist centuries earlier as a means toward eternal life. In present-day Mexico, it is accidentally discovered by a benign old antiques dealer (played by Argentina's Federico Luppi), who has no idea what it is. The gadget's bite has a rejuvenating effect on the old man. And, too late, Juan Gris realizes there is a horrible curse attached to his youthful feelings.

There is a great deal of dark, fresh humor in *Cronos*—some of which is provided by *Beauty and the Beast*'s Ron Perlman as the goon nephew of an ailing industrialist hunting for the Cronos device. But del Torro also explores the pathos of his story with great honesty. Gris, a man of principles who accidentally becomes a ghoul, will not gracefully glide through the centuries like Louis. But while he fills the screen, he indeed captures our sympathy and regard.

It just wasn't that good of a year for the Hollywood creature feature, however. Mike Nichols, improbably enough, tried his hand with a rather pointedly sophisticated lycanthropic legend in *Wolf.*

Jack Nicholson, who has always seemed like a disreputable fiend—remember his devil in *Witches of Eastwick?*—plays a mild-mannered New York editor who gets in touch with his inner hellhound after being bitten by a wolf.

The first half of the movie isn't bad, as Nicholson's character is transformed from the meek to the ruthless in publishing politics. (Although the metaphor of business being a dog-eat-dog world might be just a tad obvious.) The love story with Nicholson's *Witches* costar, Michelle Pfeiffer, is where the film falls down.

Not enough attention is given to her motivations and responses. We never learn why she chooses to be a woman who runs with the wolves. I suspect the film was trying to say something profound about emasculation in nineties society and healing the primal self. If so, the movie's rather melodramatic and confused ending—with lots of fangs and fur by Rick Baker—spoils the impact.

There were several other SF/horror films about human transmogrification that suffered even more at the box office than old feral Jack. Released to only a few theaters and festivals in 1993, Abel Ferrara's *Body Snatchers* finally got a slightly wider release in 1994 and still failed to fill theaters. It was a competent retelling of a familiar parable of righteous paranoia, although those conversant with the 1956 and 1978 versions of the same tale will probably find this the weakest of the three.

The problem lies with the film's (more youthful than prior) protagonist, this time played by a woman, Gabrielle Anwar. Ms. Anwar is sufficiently alienated as the daughter of an EPA inspector, she looks good in a bathtub and even better naked on a gurney, and she plays fear well. But she's not spirited enough to carry our interest throughout the film. You wonder why this particular young woman bothered to resist the creeping tendrils—very convincing creations of Tom Burman and Bari Dreiband-Burman—of the alien force. And you wonder why Mr. Ferrara bothered to toil on yet another film version of Jack Finney's novel.

The human factor is always the catching point in alien possession flicks. And so it was, too, with *Robert A. Heinlein's The Puppet Masters*. I thought the slimy stingray creatures were rather impressive. Not so the human characters, who were underwritten and (especially in the case of the young male hero played by Eric Thal) rather tedious. Thal's romance with a scientist played by Julie Warner was hastily developed in ways that have nothing to do with love at first sight and everything to do with sloppy writing and directing. And even more disastrously sketchy was the father-son angst between Thal and Donald Sutherland, as members of the same investigative unit.

Parent-child discord was also the theme of two unfortunate children's fantasies. *North* and *Trading Mom* were both about children so dissatisfied with their parents that they decide to trade them in for new ones. The talented Elijah Wood almost makes *North* worth watching. But his globe-trotting jaunt to look over a succession of trial parents is only an excuse for scores of ethnic jokes that are decidedly unfunny. And sketch after sketch of bad humor, awkwardly delivered, makes for a miserable movie.

Worse is *Trading Mom* in which each of the ridiculous maternal figures at a Mommy Market is played by Sissy Spacek, who happens to play the trio of disgruntled kids' original mother. Kiddie farce is not Ms. Spacek's strong suit. But I don't know who could have made this particular movie work.

Everybody seems to love Tim Allen, however. And the *Home Improvement* star's feature debut, *The Santa Clause,* about a dad who literally becomes Saint Nick, was the holidays' top-grossing hit—despite the critics. A remake (retooled for maximum male bonding) of *Angels in the Outfield* also did deservedly well with family audiences.

But no one knew what to make of *Cabin Boy*, a seafaring fantasy starring Letterman player and *Get A Life* star Chris Elliott. Written and directed by Adam Resnick and produced by Tim Burton and Denise Di Novi, the film is a pastiche of *Captains Courageous*–style boy adventure stories. In this case, though, the "Fancy Lad" boy hero is played by the thirty-something, bearded Elliott.

The movie struggled toward a surreal humor, with characters that included an enchanted ship figurehead, a menacing giant, and a seductive, six-armed goddess, Calli (played well by Ann Magnuson). But, alas, much of the comedy of *Cabin Boy* falls flat on its (which is to say, Mr. Elliott's dopey) face.

Cabin Boy is a bad movie with excellent production values. Not an unusual occurrence in Hollywood these days. But Tim Burton, as a director, explored another movie manifestation with his award-winning, box office flop *Ed Wood.*

Edward D. Wood Jr. is known the world over as a man who made bad movies with equally poor production values. The writing was loopy, the direction clumsy, and the sets and actors look like they were borrowed from a school for the criminally insane. And yet, Wood's science fiction and horror films are unforgettable cinematic experiences.

(I ask you: Who else would have made an autobiographical film calling for compassion and understanding toward transvestism . . . and included in it Bela Lugosi, seated in a chair, acting as a puppet-master "Spirit" who warns of a "big green dragon" and exclaims "Pull the string!" while stock footage of a buffalo stampede thunders across the screen below his tired face?)

It makes perfect sense that one of the most talented oddball directors of modern science fiction and fantasy should be drawn to a biopic meant to celebrate one of the least talented oddball directors of the science fiction and fantasy films of his youth. Screenwriters Scott Alexander and Larry Karaszewski cinched the deal by emphasizing the relationship between Wood and his ailing actor hero, Bela Lugosi. (How could that not resonate with Mr. Burton's own feelings for that great gentleman of horror, Vincent Price?)

I could ask, too, how Americans could fail to embrace such an affectionate, funny, beautifully performed film. But the answers are easy to come by. The studios (Columbia, and finally, Disney) feared that audiences would no longer sit still for black-and-white cinematography. They were probably right, although Stefan Czapsky's photography in *Ed Wood* is absolutely exquisite.

But the failure of Tim Burton's best film has more to do with the psychology of moviegoing.

Ed Wood is, in fact, an intriguing inversion of *Forrest Gump*. Society held not very great expectations for both men. But Ed believed in his own limitless potential. He dreamed big, he worked feverishly toward his goals—and he failed miserably. Forrest, on the other hand, was content to just get by. He demanded little from life—and ended up a national hero with phenomenal wealth.

In a sense, all movies are fantasies. Is it any wonder which of these two America fell in love with?

The Matter of Seggri

URSULA K. LE GUIN

Ursula K. Le Guin has won four Nebula Awards and five Hugo Awards. She is one of the most admired and widely respected writers of science fiction and fantasy, whose other honors include the National Book Award, the Locus Award, the Janet Heidinger Kafka Award, the Pilgrim Award, and the Pushcart Prize. Among her most popular works are *The Left Hand of Darkness*, *The Dispossessed*, *The Lathe of Heaven*, *Always Coming Home*, the Earthsea trilogy, and *Tehanu: The Last Book of Earthsea*. Her most recent collections of short fiction are *Searoad: The Chronicles of Klatsand*, *A Fisherman of the Inland Sea*, and *Four Ways to Forgiveness*.

About her Nebula finalist "The Matter of Seggri," which also won the James Tiptree Jr. Award (the first piece of short fiction to be so honored), Ursula Le Guin says:

" 'The Matter of Seggri' is one of the stories I have been writing the last couple of years which I call the Swiving Across the Cosmos series. That is, it has to do with gender; and gender does seem often to bring us right up face-to-face with sex, as well as love, and stuff like that, and the functioning of society, and the conditions of freedom. It was a hard story to write because it was so painful. I had no idea that just changing the demographics would hurt so much."

The first recorded contact with Seggri was in year 242 of Hainish Cycle 93. A Wandership six generations out from Iao (4-Taurus) came down on the planet, and the captain entered this report in his ship's log.

Captain Aolao-olao's Report

We have spent near forty days on this world they call Se-ri or Ye-ha-ri, well entertained, and leave with as good an estimation of the natives as is consonant with their unregenerate state. They live in fine great buildings they call castles, with large parks all about. Outside the walls of the parks lie well-tilled fields and abundant orchards, reclaimed by diligence from the parched and arid desert of stone that makes up the greatest part of the land. Their women live in villages and towns huddled outside the walls. All the common work of farm and mill is performed by the women, of whom there is a vast superabundance. They are ordinary drudges, living in towns which belong to the lords of the castle. They live amongst the cattle and brute animals of all kinds, who are permitted into the houses, some of which are of fair size. These women go about drably clothed, always in groups and bands. They are never allowed within the walls of the park, leaving the food and necessaries with which they provide the men at the outer gate of the castle. The women evinced great fear and distrust of us, and our hosts advised us that it were best for us to keep away from their towns, which we did.

The men go freely about their great parks, playing at one sport or another. At night they go to certain houses which they own in the town, where they may have their pick among the women and satisfy their lust upon them as they will. The women pay them, we were told, in their money, which is copper, for a night of pleasure, and pay them yet more if they get a child on them. Their nights thus are spent in carnal satisfaction as often as they desire, and their days in a diversity of sports and games, notably a kind of wrestling, in which they throw each other through the air so that we marvelled that they seemed never to take hurt, but rose up and returned to the combat with marvelous dexterity of hand and foot. Also they fence with blunt swords, and combat with long light sticks. Also they play a game with balls on a great field, using the arms to catch or throw the ball and the legs to kick the ball and trip or catch or kick the men of the other team, so that many are bruised and lamed in the passion of the sport, which was very fine to see, the teams in their contrasted garments of bright colors much gauded out with gold and finery seething now this way, now that, up and down the field in a mass, from which the balls were flung up and caught by runners breaking free of the struggling crowd and fleeting towards the one or the other goal with all the rest in hot pursuit. There is a "battlefield" as they call it of this game lying without the walls of the castle park, near to the town, so that the women may come watch and cheer, which they do heartily, calling out the names of favorite players and urging them with many uncouth cries to victory.

Boys are taken from the women at the age of eleven and brought to the castle to be educated as befits a man. We saw such a child brought into the castle with much ceremony and rejoicing. It is said that the women find it difficult to bring a pregnancy of a boy child to term, and that of those born many die in infancy despite the care lavished upon them, so that there are far more women than men. In this we see the curse of GOD laid upon this race as upon all those who acknowledge HIM not, unrepentant heathens whose ears are stopped to true discourse and blind to the light.

These men know little of art, only a kind of leaping dance, and their science is little beyond that of savages. One great man of a castle to whom I talked, who was dressed out in cloth of gold and crimson and whom all called Prince and Grandsire with much respect and deference, yet was so ignorant he believed the stars to be worlds full of people and beasts, asking us from which star we descended. They have only vessels driven by steam along the surface of the land and water, and no notion of flight either in the air or in space, nor any curiosity about such things, saying with disdain, "That is all women's work," and indeed I found that if I asked these great men about matters of common knowledge such as the working of machinery, the weaving of cloth, the transmission of holovision, they would soon chide me for taking interest in womanish things as they called them, desiring me to talk as befit a man.

In the breeding of their fierce cattle within the parks they are very knowledgeable, as in the sewing up of their clothing, which they make from cloth the women weave in their factories. The men vie in the ornamentation and magnificence of their costumes to an extent which we might indeed have thought scarcely manly, were they not withal such proper men, strong and ready for any game or sport, and full of pride and a most delicate and fiery honor.

The log including Captain Aolao-olao's entries was (after a twelve-generation journey) returned to the Sacred Archives of The Universe on Iao, which were dispersed during the period called The Tumult, and eventually preserved in fragmentary form on Hain. There is no record of further contact with Seggri until the First Observers were sent by the Ekumen in 93/1333: an Alterran man and a Hainish woman, Kaza Agad and Merriment. After a year in orbit mapping, photographing, recording and studying broadcasts, and analysing and learning a major regional language, the Observers landed. Acting upon a strong persuasion of the vulnerability of the planetary culture, they presented themselves as survivors of the wreck of a fishing boat, blown far off course, from a remote island. They were, as they had anticipated, separated at once, Kaza Agad being taken to the Castle and Merriment into the town. Kaza kept his name, which was plausible in the native context; Merriment called herself Yude. We have only her report, from which three excerpts follow.

From Mobile Gerindu'uttahayudetwe'menrade Merriment's Notes for a Report to the Ekumen, 93/1334.

34/223. Their network of trade and information, hence their awareness of what goes on elsewhere in their world, is too sophisticated for me to maintain my Stupid Foreign Castaway act any longer. Ekhaw called me in today and said, "If we had a sire here who was worth buying or if our teams were winning their games, I'd think you were a spy. Who are you, anyhow?"

I said, "Would you let me go to the College at Hagka?"

She said, "Why?"

"There are scientists there, I think? I need to talk with them."

This made sense to her; she made their "Mh" noise of assent.

"Could my friend go there with me?"

"Shask, you mean?"

We were both puzzled for a moment. She didn't expect a woman to call a man 'friend,' and I hadn't thought of Shask as a friend. She's very young, and I haven't taken her very seriously.

"I mean Kaza, the man I came with."

"A man—to the college?" she said, incredulous. She looked at me and said, "Where *do* you come from?"

It was a fair question, not asked in enmity or challenge. I wish I could have answered it, but I am increasingly convinced that we can do great damage to these people; we are facing Resehavanar's Choice here, I fear.

Ekhaw paid for my journey to Hagka, and Shask came along with me. As I thought about it I saw that of course Shask was my friend. It was she who brought me into the motherhouse, persuading Ekhaw and Azman of their duty to be hospitable; it was she who had looked out for me all along. Only she was so conventional in everything she did and said that I hadn't realised how radical her compassion was. When I tried to thank her, as our little jitney bus purred along the road to Hagka, she said things like she always says—"Oh, we're all family," and "People have to help each other," and "Nobody can live alone."

"Don't women ever live alone?" I asked her, for all the ones I've met belong to a motherhouse or a daughterhouse, whether a couple or a big family like Ekhaw's, which is three generations: five older women, three of their daughters living at home, and four children— the boy they all coddle and spoil so, and three girls.

"Oh yes," Shask said. "If they don't want wives, they can be single women. And old women, when their wives die, sometimes they just live alone till they die. Usually they go live at a daughterhouse. In the colleges, the *vev* always have a place to be alone." Conventional she may be, but Shask always tries to answer a question seriously and completely; she thinks about her answer. She has been an invaluable informant. She has also made life easy for me by not asking questions about where I come from. I took this for the incuriosity of a person securely embedded in an unquestioned way of life, and for the self-centeredness of the young. Now I see it as delicacy.

"A *vev* is a teacher?"

"Mh."

"And the teachers at the college are very respected?"

"That's what *vev* means. That's why we call Eckaw's mother Vev Kakaw. She didn't go to college, but she's a thoughtful person, she's learned from life, she has a lot to teach us."

So respect and teaching are the same thing, and the only term of respect I've heard women use for women means teacher. And so in teaching me, young Shask respects herself? And/or earns my respect? This casts a different light on what I've been seeing as a society in which wealth is the important thing. Zadedr, the current mayor of Reha, is certainly admired for her very ostentatious display of possessions; but they don't call her Vev.

I said to Shask, "You have taught me so much, may I call you Vev Shask?"

She was equally embarrassed and pleased, and squirmed and

said, "Oh no no no no." Then she said, "If you ever come back to Reha I would like very much to have love with you, Yude."

"I thought you were in love with Sire Zadr!" I blurted out.

"Oh, I am," she said, with that eye roll and melted look they have when they speak of the Sires, "aren't you? Just think of him fucking you, oh! Oh, I get all wet thinking about it!" She smiled and wriggled. I felt embarrassed in my turn and probably showed it. "Don't you like him?" she inquired with a naivety I found hard to bear. She was acting like a silly adolescent, and I know she's not a silly adolescent. "But I'll never be able to afford him," she said, and sighed.

So you want to make do with me, I thought, nastily.

"I'm going to save my money," she announced after a minute. "I think I want to have a baby next year. Of course I can't afford Sire Zadr, he's a Great Champion, but if I don't go to the Games at Kadaki this year I can save up enough for a really good sire at our fuckery, maybe Master Rosra. I wish, I know this is silly, I'm going to say it anyway, I kept wishing you could be its lovemother. I know you can't, you have to go to the college. I just wanted to tell you. I love you." She took my hands, drew them to her face, pressed my palms on her eyes for a moment, and then released me. She was smiling, but her tears were on my hands.

"Oh, Shask," I said, floored.

"It's all right!" she said. "I have to cry a minute." And she did. She wept openly, bending over, wringing her hands, and wailing softly. I patted her arm and felt unutterably ashamed of myself. Other passengers looked round and made little sympathetic grunting noises. One old woman said, "That's it, that's right, lovey!" In a few minutes Shask stopped crying, wiped her nose and face on her sleeve, drew a long, deep breath, and said, "All right." She smiled at me. "Driver," she called, "I have to piss, can we stop?"

The driver, a tense-looking woman, growled something, but stopped the bus on the wide, weedy roadside; and Shask and another woman got off and pissed in the weeds. There is an enviable simplicity to many acts in a society which has, in all its daily life, only one gender. And which, perhaps—I don't know this but it occurred to me then, while I was ashamed of myself—has no shame?

———

34/245. (Dictated) Still nothing from Kaza. I think I was right to give him the ansible. I hope he's in touch with somebody. I wish it was me. I need to know what goes on in the Castles.

Anyhow I understand better now what I was seeing at the Games in Reha. There are sixteen adult women for every adult man. One conception in six or so is male, but a lot of nonviable male fetuses and defective male births bring it down to 1 in 16 by puberty. My ancestors must have really had fun playing with these people's chromosomes. I feel guilty, even if it was a million years ago. I have to learn to do without shame but had better not forget the one good use of guilt. Anyhow. A fairly small town like Reha shares its Castle with other towns. That confusing spectacle I was taken to on my tenth day down was Awaga Castle trying to keep its place in the Maingame against a castle from up north, and losing. Which means Awaga's team can't play in the big game this year in Fadrga, the city south of here, from which the winners go on to compete in the *big* big game at Zask, where people come from all over the continent— hundreds of contestants and thousands of spectators. I saw some holos of last year's Maingame at Zask. There were 1,280 players, the comment said, and forty balls in play. It looked to me like a total mess, my idea of a battle between two unarmed armies, but I gather that great skill and strategy is involved. All the members of the winning team get a special title for the year, and another one for life, and bring glory back to their various Castles and the towns that support them.

I can now get some sense of how this works, see the system from outside it, because the college doesn't support a Castle. People here aren't obsessed with sports and athletes and sexy sires the way the young women in Reha were, and some of the older ones. It's a kind of obligatory obsession. Cheer your team, support your brave men, adore your local hero. It makes sense. Given their situation, they need strong, healthy men at their fuckery; it's social selection reinforcing natural selection. But I'm glad to get away from the rah-rah and the swooning and the posters of fellows with swelling muscles and huge penises and bedroom eyes.

I have made Resehavanar's Choice. I chose the option: Less than the truth. Shoggrad and Skodr and the other teachers, professors we'd call them, are intelligent, enlightened people, perfectly capable of understanding the concept of space travel, etc., making decisions about technological innovation, etc. I limit my answers to their questions to technology. I let them assume, as most people naturally assume, particularly people from a monoculture, that our society is pretty much like theirs. When they find how it differs, the effect will be revolutionary, and I have no mandate, reason, or wish to cause such a revolution on Seggri.

Their gender imbalance has produced a society in which, as far as I can tell, the men have all the privilege and the women have all the power. It's obviously a stable arrangement. According to their histories, it's lasted at least two millennia, and probably in some form or another much longer than that. But it could be quickly and disastrously destabilised by contact with us, by their experiencing the human norm. I don't know if the men would cling to their privileged status or demand freedom, but surely the women would resist giving up their power, and their sexual system and affectional relationships would break down. Even if they learned to undo the genetic program that was inflicted on them, it would take several generations to restore normal gender distribution. I can't be the whisper that starts that avalanche.

34/266. (Dictated) Skodr got nowhere with the men of Awaga Castle. She had to make her inquiries very cautiously, since it would endanger Kaza if she told them he was an alien or in any way unique. They'd take it as a claim of superiority, which he'd have to defend in trials of strength and skill. I gather that the hierarchies within the Castles are a rigid framework, within which a man moves up or down issuing challenges and winning or losing obligatory and optional trials. The sports and games the women watch are only the showpieces of an endless series of competitions going on inside the Castles. As an untrained, grown man Kaza would be at a total disadvantage in such trials. The only way he might get out of them, she said, would be by feigning illness or idiocy. She thinks he must have done so, since he is at least alive; but that's all she could find out—"The man who was cast away at Taha-Reha is alive."

Although the women feed, house, clothe, and support the Lords of the Castle, they evidently take their noncooperation for granted. She seemed glad to get even that scrap of information. As I am.

But we have to get Kaza out of there. The more I hear about it from Skodr the more dangerous it sounds. I keep thinking "spoiled brats!" but actually these men must be more like soldiers in the training camps that militarists have. Only the training never ends. As they win trials they gain all kinds of titles and ranks you could translate as "generals" and the other names militarists have for all their power grades. Some of the "generals," the Lords and Masters and so on, are the sports idols, the darlings of the fuckeries, like the one poor Shask adored; but as they get older apparently they often trade glory among the women for power among the men, and become tyrants within their Castle, bossing the "lesser" men around, until they're overthrown, kicked out. Old sires often live alone, it seems, in little houses away from the main Castle, and are considered crazy and dangerous—rogue males.

It sounds like a miserable life. All they're allowed to do after age eleven is compete at games and sports inside the Castle, and compete in the fuckeries, after they're fifteen or so, for money and number of fucks and so on. Nothing else. No options. No trades. No skills of making. No travel unless they play in the big games. They aren't allowed into the colleges to gain any kind of freedom of mind. I asked Skodr why an intelligent man couldn't at least come study in the college, and she told me that learning was very bad for men: it weakens a man's sense of honor, makes his muscles flabby, and leaves him impotent. " 'What goes to the brain takes from the testicles,' " she said. "Men have to be sheltered from education for their own good."

I tried to "be water," as I was taught, but I was disgusted. Probably she felt it, because after a while she told me about "the secret college." Some women in colleges do smuggle information to men in Castles. The poor things meet secretly and teach each other. In the Castles, homosexual relationships are encouraged among boys under fifteen, but not officially tolerated among grown men; she says the "secret colleges" often are run by the homosexual men. They have to be secret because if they're caught reading or talking about ideas they may be punished by their Lords and Masters. There have been some interesting works from the "secret colleges," Skodr said, but she had to think to come up with examples. One was a man who had smuggled out an interesting mathematical theorem, and one was a painter whose landscapes, though primitive in technique, were admired by professionals of the art. She couldn't remember his name.

Arts, sciences, all learning, all professional techniques, are *haggyad,* skilled work. They're all taught at the colleges, and there are no divisions and few specialists. Teachers and students cross and mix fields all the time, and being a famous scholar in one field doesn't keep you from being a student in another. Skodr is a vev of physiology, writes plays, and is currently studying history with one of the history vevs. Her thinking is informed and lively and fearless. My School on Hain could learn from this college. It's a wonderful place, full of free minds. But only minds of one gender. A hedged freedom.

I hope Kaza has found a secret college or something, some way to fit in at the Castle. He's very fit, but these men have trained for years for the games they play. And a lot of the games are violent. The women say don't worry, we don't let the men kill each other, we protect them, they're our treasures. But I've seen men carried off with concussions on the holos of their martial-art fights, where they throw each other around spectacularly. "Only inexperienced fighters get hurt." Very reassuring. And they wrestle bulls. And in that melee they call the Maingame they break each other's legs and ankles deliberately. "What's a hero without a limp?" the women say. Maybe that's the safe thing to do, get your leg broken so you don't have to prove you're a hero anymore. But what else might Kaza have to prove?

I asked Shask to let me know if she ever heard of him being at the Reha fuckery. But Awaga Castle services (that's their word, the same word they use for their bulls) four towns, so he might get sent to one of the others. But probably not, because men who don't win at things aren't allowed to go to the fuckeries. Only the champions. And boys between fifteen and nineteen, the ones the older women call *dippida,* baby animals, like puppies or kitties or lambies. They like to use the dippida for pleasure, and the champions when they go to the fuckery to get pregnant. But Kaza's thirty-six, he isn't a puppy or a kitten or a lamb. He's a man, and this is a terrible place to be a man.

Kaza Agad had been killed; the Lords of Awaga Castle finally disclosed the fact, but not the circumstances. A year later, Merriment radioed her lander and left Seggri for Hain. Her recommendation was to observe and avoid. The Stabiles, however, decided to send another pair of observers; these were both women, Mobiles Alee Iyoo and Zerin Wu. They lived for eight years on Seggri, after the third year as First Mobiles; Iyoo stayed as Ambassador another fifteen years. They made Resehavanar's Choice as "all the truth slowly." A limit of two hundred visitors from offworld was set. During the next several generations the people of Seggri, becoming accustomed to the alien presence, considered their own options as members of the Ekumen. Proposals for a planetwide referendum on genetic alteration were abandoned, since the men's vote would be insignificant unless the women's vote were handicapped. As of the date of this report the Seggri have not undertaken major genetic alteration, though they have learned and applied various repair techniques, which have resulted in a higher proportion of full-term male infants; the gender balance now stands at about 12:1.

The following is a memoir given to Ambassador Eritho te Ves in 93/1569 by a woman in Ush on Seggri.

You asked me, dear friend, to tell you anything I might like people on other worlds to know about my life and my world. That's not easy! Do I want anybody anywhere else to know anything about my life? I know how strange we seem to all the others, the half-and-half races; I know they think us backward, provincial, even perverse. Maybe in a few more decades we'll decide that we should remake ourselves. I won't be alive then; I don't think I'd want to be. I like my people. I like our fierce, proud, beautiful men, I don't want them to become like women. I like our trustful, powerful, generous women, I don't want them to become like men. And yet I see that among you each man has his own being and nature, each woman has hers, and I can hardly say what it is I think we would lose.

When I was a child I had a brother a year and a half younger than me. His name was Ittu. My mother had gone to the city and paid five years' savings for my sire, a Master Champion in the Dancing. Ittu's sire was an old fellow at our village fuckery; they called him "Master Fallback." He'd never been a champion at anything, hadn't sired a child for years, and was only too glad to fuck for free. My mother always laughed about it—she was still suckling me, she didn't even use a preventive, and she tipped him two coppers! When she found herself pregnant she was furious. When they tested and found it was a male fetus she was even more disgusted at having, as they say, to wait for the miscarriage. But when Ittu was born sound and healthy, she gave the old sire two hundred coppers, all the cash she had.

He wasn't delicate like so many boy babies, but how can you keep from protecting and cherishing a boy? I don't remember when I wasn't looking after Ittu, with it all very clear in my head what Little Brother should do and shouldn't do and all the perils I must keep him from. I was proud of my responsibility, and vain, too, because I had a brother to look after. Not one other motherhouse in my village had a son still living at home.

Ittu was a lovely child, a star. He had the fleecy soft hair that's common in my part of Ush, and big eyes; his nature was sweet and cheerful, and he was very bright. The other children loved him and always wanted to play with him, but he and I were happiest playing by ourselves, long elaborate games of make-believe. We had a herd of twelve cattle an old woman of the village had carved from gourd-shell for Ittu—people always gave him presents—and they were the actors in our dearest game. Our cattle lived in a country called Shush, where they had great adventures, climbing mountains, discovering new lands, sailing on rivers, and so on. Like any herd, like our village herd, the old cows were the leaders; the bull lived apart; the other males were gelded; and the heifers were the adventurers. Our bull would make ceremonial visits to service the cows, and then he might have to go fight with men at Shush Castle. We made the castle of clay and the men of sticks, and the bull always won, knocking the stickmen to pieces. Then sometimes he knocked the castle to pieces too. But the best of our stories were told with two of the heifers. Mine was named Op and my brother's was Utti. Once our hero heifers were having a great adventure on the stream that runs past our village, and their boat got away from us. We found it caught against a log far downstream where the stream was deep and quick. My heifer was still in it. We both dived and dived, but we never found Utti. She had drowned. The Cattle of Shush had a great funeral for her, and Ittu cried very bitterly.

He mourned his brave little toy cow so long that I asked Djerdji the cattleherd if we could work for her, because I thought being with the real cattle might cheer Ittu up. She was glad to get two cowhands for free (when Mother found out we were really working, she made Djerdji pay us a quarter-copper a day). We rode two big, good-natured old cows, on saddles so big Ittu could lie down on his. We took a herd of two-year-old calves out onto the desert every day to forage for the edta that grows best when it's grazed. We were supposed to keep them from wandering off and from trampling stream banks, and when they wanted to settle down and chew the cud we were supposed to gather them in a place where their droppings would nourish useful plants. Our old mounts did most of the work. Mother came out and checked on what we were doing and decided it was all right, and being out in the desert all day was certainly keeping us fit and healthy.

We loved our riding cows, but they were serious-minded and responsible, rather like the grown-ups in our motherhouse. The calves were something else; they were all riding breed, not fine an-imals of course, just village-bred; but living on edta they were fat and had plenty of spirit. Ittu and I rode them bareback with a rope rein. At first we always ended up on our own backs watching a calf's heels and tail flying off. By the end of a year we were good riders, and took to training our mounts to tricks, trading mounts at a full run, and hornvaulting. Ittu was a marvelous hornvaulter. He trained a big three-year-old roan ox with lyre horns, and the two of them danced like the finest vaulters of the great Castles that we saw on the holos. We couldn't keep our excellence to ourselves out in the desert; we started showing off to the other children, inviting them to come out to Salt Springs to see our Great Trick Riding Show. And so of course the adults got to hear of it.

My mother was a brave woman, but that was too much for even her, and she said to me in cold fury, "I trusted you to look after Ittu. You let me down."

All the others had been going on and on about endangering the precious life of a boy, the Vial of Hope, the Treasurehouse of Life and so on, but it was what my mother said that hurt.

"I do look after Ittu, and he looks after me," I said to her, in that passion of justice that children know, the birthright we seldom honor. "We both know what's dangerous and we don't do stupid things and we know our cattle and we do everything together. When he has to go to the Castle he'll have to do lots more dangerous things, but at least he'll already know how to do one of them. And there he has to do them alone, but we did everything together. And I didn't let you down."

My mother looked at us. I was nearly twelve, Ittu was ten. She burst into tears, she sat down on the dirt and wept aloud. Ittu and I both went to her and hugged her and cried. Ittu said, "I won't go. I won't go to the damned Castle. They can't make me!"

And I believed him. He believed himself. My mother knew better.

Maybe someday it will be possible for a boy to choose his life. Among your peoples a man's body does not shape his fate, does it? Maybe some day that will be so here.

Our Castle, Hidjegga, had of course been keeping their eye on Ittu ever since he was born; once a year Mother would send them the doctor's report on him, and when he was five Mother and her wives took him out there for the ceremony of Confirmation. Ittu had been embarrassed, disgusted, and flattered. He told me in secret, "There were all these old men that smelled funny and they made me take off my clothes and they had these measuring things and they measured my peepee! And they said it was very good. They said it was a good one. What happens when you descend?" It wasn't the first question he had ever asked me that I couldn't answer, and as usual I made up the answer. "Descend means you can have babies," I said, which, in a way, wasn't so far off the mark.

Some Castles, I am told, prepare boys of nine and ten for the Severance, woo them with visits from older boys, tickets to games, tours of the park and the buildings, so that they may be quite eager to go to the Castle when they turn eleven. But we "outyonders," villagers of the edge of the desert, kept to the harsh old-fashioned ways. Aside from Confirmation, a boy had no contact at all with men until his eleventh birthday. On that day everybody he had ever known brought him to the Gate and gave him to the strangers with whom he would live the rest of his life. Men and women alike believed and still believe that this absolute severance makes the man.

Vev Ushiggi, who had borne a son and had a grandson, and had been mayor five or six times, and was held in great esteem even though she'd never had much money, heard Ittu say that he wouldn't go to the damned Castle. She came next day to our motherhouse and asked to talk to him. He told me what she said. She didn't do any wooing or sweetening. She told him that he was born to the service of his people and had one responsibility, to sire children when he got old enough; and one duty, to be a strong, brave man, stronger and braver than other men, so that women would choose him to sire their children. She said he had to live in the Castle because men could not live among women. At this, Ittu asked her, "Why can't they?"

"You did?" I said, awed by his courage, for Vev Ushiggi was a formidable old woman.

"Yes. And she didn't really answer. She took a long time. She looked at me and then she looked off somewhere and then she stared at me for a long time and then finally she said, 'Because we would destroy them.' "

"But that's crazy," I said. "Men are our treasures. What did she say that for?"

Ittu, of course, didn't know. But he thought hard about what she had said, and I think nothing she could have said would have so impressed him.

After discussion, the village elders and my mother and her wives decided that Ittu could go on practicing hornvaulting, because it really would be a useful skill for him in the Castle; but he could not herd cattle any longer, nor go with me when I did, nor join in any of the work children of the village did, nor their games. "You've done everything together with Po," they told him, "but she should be doing things together with the other girls, and you should be doing things by yourself, the way men do."

They were always very kind to Ittu, but they were stern with us girls; if they saw us even talking with Ittu they'd tell us to go on about our work, leave the boy alone. When we disobeyed—when Ittu and I sneaked off and met at Salt Springs to ride together, or just hid out in our old playplace down in the draw by the stream to talk—he got treated with cold silence to shame him, but I got punished. A day locked in the cellar of the old fiber-processing mill, which was what my village used for a jail; next time it was two days; and the third time they caught us alone together, they locked me in that cellar for ten days. A young woman called Fersk brought me food once a day and made sure I had enough water and wasn't sick, but she didn't speak; that's how they always used to punish people in the villages. I could hear the other children going by up on the street in the evening. It would get dark at last and I could sleep. All day I had nothing to do, no work, nothing to think about except the scorn and contempt they held me in for betraying their trust, and the injustice of my getting punished when Ittu didn't.

When I came out, I felt different. I felt like something had closed up inside me while I was closed up in that cellar.

When we ate at the motherhouse they made sure Ittu and I didn't sit near each other. For a while we didn't even talk to each other. I went back to school and work. I didn't know what Ittu was doing all day. I didn't think about it. It was only fifty days to his birthday.

One night I got into bed and found a note under my clay pillow: *in the draw to-nt.* Ittu never could spell; what writing he knew I had taught him in secret. I was frightened and angry, but I waited an hour till everybody was asleep, and got up and crept outside into the windy, starry night, and ran to the draw. It was late in the dry season and the stream was barely running. Ittu was there, hunched up with his arms round his knees, a little lump of shadow on the pale, cracked clay at the waterside.

The first thing I said was, "You want to get me locked up again? They said next time it would be thirty days!"

"They're going to lock me up for fifty years," Ittu said, not looking at me.

"What am I supposed to do about it? It's the way it has to be! You're a man. You have to do what men do. They won't lock you up, anyway, you get to play games and come to town to do service and all that. You don't even know what being locked up is!"

"I want to go to Seradda," Ittu said, talking very fast, his eyes shining as he looked up at me. "We could take the riding cows to the bus station in Redang, I saved my money, I have twenty-three coppers, we could take the bus to Seradda. The cows would come back home if we turned them loose."

"What do you think you'd do in Seradda?" I asked, disdainful but curious. Nobody from our village had ever been to the capital.

"The Ekkamen people are there," he said.

"The Ekumen," I corrected him. "So what?"

"They could take me away," Ittu said.

I felt very strange when he said that. I was still angry and still disdainful but a sorrow was rising in me like dark water. "Why would they do that? What would they talk to some little boy for? How would you find them? Twenty-three coppers isn't enough anyway. Seradda's way far off. That's a really stupid idea. You can't do that."

"I thought you'd come with me," Ittu said. His voice was softer, but didn't shake.

"I wouldn't do a stupid thing like that," I said furiously.

"All right," he said. "But you won't tell. Will you?"

"No, I won't tell!" I said. "But you can't run away, Ittu. You can't. It would be—it would be dishonorable."

This time when he answered his voice shook. "I don't care," he said. "I don't care about honor. I want to be free!"

We were both in tears. I sat down by him and we leaned together the way we used to, and cried a while; not long; we weren't used to crying.

"You can't do it," I whispered to him. "It won't work, Ittu."

He nodded, accepting my wisdom.

"It won't be so bad at the Castle," I said.

After a minute he drew away from me very slightly.

"We'll see each other," I said.

He said only, "When?"

"At games. I can watch you. I bet you'll be the best rider and hornvaulter there. I bet you win all the prizes and get to be a Champion."

He nodded, dutiful. He knew and I knew that I had betrayed our love and our birthright of justice. He knew he had no hope.

That was the last time we talked together alone, and almost the last time we talked together.

Ittu ran away about ten days after that, taking the riding cow and heading for Redang; they tracked him easily and had him back in the village before nightfall. I don't know if he thought I had told them where he would be going. I was so ashamed of not having gone with him that I could not look at him. I kept away from him; they didn't have to keep me away anymore. He made no effort to speak to me.

I was beginning my puberty, and my first blood was the night before Ittu's birthday. Menstruating women are not allowed to come near the Gates at conservative Castles like ours, so when Ittu was made a man I stood far back among a few other girls and women, and could not see much of the ceremony. I stood silent while they sang, and looked down at the dirt and my new sandals and my feet in the sandals, and felt the ache and tug of my womb and the secret movement of the blood, and grieved. I knew even then that this grief would be with me all my life.

Ittu went in and the Gates closed.

He became a Young Champion Hornvaulter, and for two years, when he was eighteen and nineteen, came a few times to service in our village, but I never saw him. One of my friends fucked with him and started to tell me about it, how nice he was, thinking I'd like to hear, but I shut her up and walked away in a blind rage which neither of us understood.

He was traded away to a Castle on the east coast when he was twenty. When my daughter was born I wrote him, and several times after that, but he never answered my letters.

I don't know what I've told you about my life and my world. I don't know if it's what I want you to know. It is what I had to tell.

The following is a short story written in 93/1586 by a popular writer of the city of Adr, Sem Gridji. The classic literature of Seggri was the narrative poem and the drama. Classical poems and plays were written collaboratively, in the original version and also by rewriters of subsequent generations, usually anonymous. Small value was placed on preserving a "true" text, since the work was seen as an ongoing process. Probably under Ekumenical influence, individual writers in the late sixteenth century began writing short prose narratives, historical and fictional. The genre became popular, particularly in the cities, though it never obtained the immense audience of the great classical epics and plays. Literally everyone knew the plots and many quotations from the epics and plays, from books and holo, and almost every adult woman had seen or participated in a staged performance of several of them. They were one of the principal unifying influences of the Seggrian monoculture. The prose narrative, read in silence, served rather as a device by which the culture might question itself, and a tool for individual moral self-examination. Con-

*servative Seggrian women disapproved of the genre as antagonistic
to the intensely cooperative, collaborative structure of their society.
Fiction was not included in the curriculum of the literature departments of the colleges and was often dismissed contemptuously—"fiction is for men."*

*Sem Gridji published three books of stories. Her bare, blunt style
is characteristic of the Seggrian short story.*

Love Out of Place
by Sem Gridji

Azak grew up in a motherhouse in the Downriver Quarter, near the
textile mills. She was a bright girl, and her family and neighborhood
were proud to gather the money to send her to college. She came
back to the city as a starting manager at one of the mills. Azak worked
well with other people; she prospered. She had a clear idea of what
she wanted to do in the next few years: to find two or three partners
with whom to found a daughterhouse and a business.

A beautiful woman in the prime of youth, Azak took great pleasure in sex, especially liking intercourse with men. Though she saved
money for her plan of founding a business, she also spent a good
deal at the fuckery, going there often, sometimes hiring two men at
once. She liked to see how they incited each other to prowess beyond
what they would have achieved alone, and shamed each other when
they failed. She found a flaccid penis very disgusting, and did not
hesitate to send away a man who could not penetrate her three or
four times an evening.

The Castle of her district bought a Young Champion at the
Southeast Castles Dance Tournament, and soon sent him to the fuckery. Having seen him dance in the finals on the holovision and been
captivated by his flowing, graceful style and his beauty, Azak was
eager to have him service her. His price was twice that of any other
man there, but she did not hesitate to pay it. She found him handsome and amiable, eager and gentle, skillful and compliant. In their
first evening they came to orgasm together five times. When she left
she gave him a large tip. Within the week she was back, asking for
Toddra. The pleasure he gave her was exquisite, and soon she was
quite obsessed with him.

"I wish I had you all to myself," she said to him one night as they lay still conjoined, langorous and fulfilled.

"That is my heart's desire," he said. "I wish I were your servant. None of the other women that come here arouse me. I don't want them. I want only you."

She wondered if he was telling the truth. The next time she came, she inquired casually of the manager if Toddra were as popular as they had hoped. "No," the manager said. "Everybody else reports that he takes a lot of arousing, and is sullen and careless towards them."

"How strange," Azak said.

"Not at all," said the manager. "He's in love with you."

"A man in love with a woman?" Azak said, and laughed.

"It happens all too often," the manager said.

"I thought only women fell in love," said Azak.

"Women fall in love with a man, sometimes, and that's bad too," said the manager. "May I warn you, Azak? Love should be between women. It's out of place here. It can never come to any good end. I hate to lose the money, but I wish you'd fuck with some of the other men and not always ask for Toddra. You're encouraging him, you see, in something that does harm to him."

"But he and you are making lots of money from me!" said Azak, still taking it as a joke.

"He'd make more from other women if he wasn't in love with you," said the manager. To Azak that seemed a weak argument against the pleasure she had in Toddra, and she said, "Well, he can fuck them all when I've done with him, but for now, I want him."

After their intercourse that evening, she said to Toddra, "The manager here says you're in love with me."

"I told you I was," Toddra said. "I told you I wanted to belong to you, to serve you, you alone. I would die for you, Azak."

"That's foolish," she said.

"Don't you like me? Don't I please you?"

"More than any man I ever knew," she said, kissing him. "You are beautiful and utterly satisfying, my sweet Toddra."

"You don't want any of the other men here, do you?" he asked.

"No. They're all ugly fumblers, compared to my beautiful dancer."

"Listen, then," he said, sitting up and speaking very seriously. He was a slender man of twenty-two, with long, smooth-muscled limbs, wide-set eyes, and a thin-lipped, sensitive mouth. Azak lay stroking his thigh, thinking how lovely and lovable he was. "I have a plan," he said. "When I dance, you know, in the story-dances, I play a woman, of course; I've done it since I was twelve. People always say they can't believe I really am a man, I play a woman so well. If I escaped—from here, from the Castle—as a woman—I could come to your house as a servant—"

"What?" cried Azak, astounded.

"I could live there," he said urgently, bending over her. "With you. I would always be there. You could have me every night. It would cost you nothing, except my food. I would serve you, service you, sweep your house, do anything, anything, Azak, please, my beloved, my mistress, let me be yours!" He saw that she was still incredulous, and hurried on, "You could send me away when you got tired of me—"

"If you tried to go back to the Castle after an escapade like that they'd whip you to death, you idiot!"

"I'm valuable," he said. "They'd punish me, but they wouldn't damage me."

"You're wrong. You haven't been dancing, and your value here has slipped because you don't perform well with anybody but me. The manager told me so."

Tears stood in Toddra's eyes. Azak disliked giving him pain, but she was genuinely shocked at his wild plan. "And if you were discovered, my dear," she said more gently, "I would be utterly disgraced. It is a very childish plan, Toddra: please never dream of such a thing again. But I am truly, truly fond of you, I adore you and want no other man but you. Do you believe that, Toddra?"

He nodded. Restraining his tears, he said, "For now."

"For now and for a long, long, long time! My dear, sweet, beautiful dancer, we have each other as long as we want, years and years! Only do your duty by the other women that come, so that you don't get sold away by your Castle, please! I couldn't bear to lose you, Toddra." And she clasped him passionately in her arms, and arousing him at once, opened to him, and soon both were crying out in the throes of delight.

Though she could not take his love entirely seriously, since what could come of such a misplaced emotion, except such foolish schemes as he had proposed?—still he touched her heart, and she felt a tenderness toward him that greatly enhanced the pleasure of their intercourse. So for more than a year she spent two or three nights a week with him at the fuckery, which was as much as she could afford. The manager, trying still to discourage his love, would not lower Toddra's fee, even though he was unpopular among the other clients of the fuckery; so Azak spent a great deal of money on him, although he would never, after the first night, accept a tip from her.

Then a woman who had not been able to conceive with any of the sires at the fuckery tried Toddra, and at once conceived, and being tested found the fetus to be male. Another woman conceived by him, again a male fetus. At once Toddra was in demand as a sire. Women began coming from all over the city to be serviced by him. This meant, of course, that he must be free during their period of ovulation. There were now many evenings that he could not meet Azak, for the manager was not to be bribed. Toddra disliked his popularity, but Azak soothed and reassured him, telling him how proud she was of him, and how his work would never interfere with their love. In fact, she was not altogether sorry that he was so much in demand, for she had found another person with whom she wanted to spend her evenings.

This was a young woman named Zedr, who worked in the mill as a machine-repair specialist. She was tall and handsome; Azak noticed first how freely and strongly she walked and how proudly she stood. She found a pretext to make her acquaintance. It seemed to Azak that Zedr admired her; but for a long time each behaved to the other as a friend only, making no sexual advances. They were much in each other's company, going to games and dances together, and Azak found that she enjoyed this open and sociable life better than always being in the fuckery alone with Toddra. They talked about how they might set up a machine-repair service in partnership. As time went on, Azak found that Zedr's beautiful body was always in her thoughts. At last, one evening in her singlewoman's flat, she told her friend that she loved her, but did not wish to burden their friendship with an unwelcome desire.

Zedr replied, "I have wanted you ever since I first saw you, but I didn't want to embarrass you with my desire. I thought you preferred men."

"Until now I did, but I want to make love with you," Azak said.

She found herself quite timid at first, but Zedr was expert and subtle, and could prolong Azak's orgasms till she found such consummation as she had not dreamed of. She said to Zedr, "You have made me a woman."

"Then let's make each other wives," said Zedr joyfully.

They married, moved to a house in the west of the city, and left the mill, setting up in business together.

All this time, Azak had said nothing of her new love to Toddra, whom she had seen less and less often. A little ashamed of her cowardice, she reassured herself that he was so busy performing as a sire that he would not really miss her. After all, despite his romantic talk of love, he was a man, and to a man fucking is the most important thing, instead of being merely one element of love and life as it is to a woman.

When she married Zedr, she sent Toddra a letter, saying that their lives had drifted apart, and she was now moving away and would not see him again, but would always remember him fondly.

She received an immediate answer from Toddra, a letter begging her to come and talk with him, full of avowals of unchanging love, badly spelled and almost illegible. The letter touched, embarrassed, and shamed her, and she did not answer it.

He wrote again and again, and tried to reach her on the holonet at her new business. Zedr encouraged her not to make any response, saying, "It would be cruel to encourage him."

Their new business went well from the start. They were home one evening busy chopping vegetables for dinner when there was a knock at the door. "Come in," Zedr called, thinking it was Chochi, a friend they were considering as a third partner. A stranger entered, a tall, beautiful woman with a scarf over her hair. The stranger went straight to Azak, saying in a strangled voice, "Azak, Azak, please, please let me stay with you." The scarf fell back from his long hair. Azak recognised Toddra.

She was astonished and a little frightened, but she had known Toddra a long time and been very fond of him, and this habit of affection made her put out her hands to him in greeting. She saw fear and despair in his face, and was sorry for him.

But Zedr, guessing who he was, was both alarmed and angry. She kept the chopping knife in her hand. She slipped from the room and called the city police.

When she returned she saw the man pleading with Azak to let him stay hidden in their household as a servant. "I will do anything," he said. "Please, Azak, my only love, please! I can't live without you. I can't service those women, those strangers who only want to be impregnated. I can't dance anymore. I think only of you, you are my only hope. I will be a woman, no one will know. I'll cut my hair, no one will know!" So he went on, almost threatening in his passion, but pitiful also. Zedr listened coldly, thinking he was mad. Azak listened with pain and shame. "No, no, it is not possible," she said over and over, but he would not hear.

When the police came to the door and he realised who they were, he bolted to the back of the house seeking escape. The policewomen caught him in the bedroom; he fought them desperately, and they subdued him brutally. Azak shouted at them not to hurt him, but they paid no heed, twisting his arms and hitting him about the head till he stopped resisting. They dragged him out. The head of the troop stayed to take evidence. Azak tried to plead for Toddra, but Zedr stated the facts and added that she thought he was insane and dangerous.

After some days, Azak inquired at the police office and was told that Toddra had been returned to his Castle with a warning not to send him to the fuckery again for a year or until the Lords of the Castle found him capable of responsible behavior. She was uneasy thinking of how he might be punished. Zedr said, "They won't hurt him, he's too valuable," just as he himself had said. Azak was glad to believe this. She was, in fact, much relieved to know that he was out of the way.

She and Zedr took Chochi first into their business and then into their household. Chochi was a woman from the dockside quarter, tough and humorous, a hard worker and an undemanding, comfortable lovemaker. They were happy with one another, and prospered.

A year went by, and another year. Azak went to her old quarter to arrange a contract for repair work with two women from the mill where she had first worked. She asked them about Toddra. He was back at the fuckery from time to time, they told her. He had been named the year's Champion Sire of his Castle, and was much in demand, bringing an even higher price, because he impregnated so many women and so many of the conceptions were male. He was not in demand for pleasure, they said, as he had a reputation for roughness and even cruelty. Women asked for him only if they wanted to conceive. Thinking of his gentleness with her, Azak found it hard to imagine him behaving brutally. Harsh punishment at the Castle, she thought, must have altered him. But she could not believe that he had truly changed.

Another year passed. The business was doing very well, and Azak and Chochi both began talking seriously about having children. Zedr was not interested in bearing, though happy to be a mother. Chochi had a favorite man at their local fuckery to whom she went now and then for pleasure; she began going to him at ovulation, for he had a good reputation as a sire.

Azak had never been to a fuckery since she and Zedr married. She honored fidelity highly, and made love with no one but Zedr and Chochi. When she thought of being impregnated, she found that her old interest in fucking with men had quite died out or even turned to distaste. She did not like the idea of self-impregnation from the sperm bank, but the idea of letting a strange man penetrate her was even more repulsive. Thinking what to do, she thought of Toddra, whom she had truly loved and had pleasure with. He was again a Champion Sire, known throughout the city as a reliable impregnator. There was certainly no other man with whom she could take any pleasure. And he had loved her so much he had put his career and even his life in danger, trying to be with her. That irresponsibility was over and done with. He had never written to her again, and the Castle and the managers of the fuckery would never have let him service women if they thought him mad or untrustworthy. After all this time, she thought, she could go back to him and give him the pleasure he had so desired.

She notified the fuckery of the expected period of her next ovulation, requesting Toddra. He was already engaged for that period, and they offered her another sire; but she preferred to wait till the next month.

Chochi had conceived, and was elated. "Hurry up, hurry up!" she said to Azak. "We want twins!"

Azak found herself looking forward to being with Toddra. Regretting the violence of their last encounter and the pain it must have given him, she wrote the following letter to him:

"My dear, I hope our long separation and the distress of our last meeting will be forgotten in the joy of being together again, and that you still love me as I still love you. I shall be very proud to bear your child, and let us hope it may be a son! I am impatient to see you again, my beautiful dancer. Your Azak."

There had not been time for him to answer this letter when her ovulation period began. She dressed in her best clothes. Zedr still distrusted Toddra and had tried to dissuade her from going to him; she bade her "Good luck!" rather sulkily. Chochi hung a mother-charm round her neck, and she went off.

There was a new manager on duty at the fuckery, a coarse-faced young woman who told her, "Call out if he gives you any trouble. He may be a Champion but he's rough, and we don't let him get away with hurting anybody."

"He won't hurt me," Azak said smiling, and went eagerly into the familiar room where she and Toddra had enjoyed each other so often. He was standing waiting at the window just as he had used to stand. When he turned he looked just as she remembered, long-limbed, his silky hair flowing like water down his back, his wide-set eyes gazing at her.

"Toddra!" she said, coming to him with outstretched hands.

He took her hands and said her name.

"Did you get my letter? Are you happy?"

"Yes," he said, smiling.

"And all that unhappiness, all that foolishness about love, is it over? I am so sorry you were hurt, Toddra, I don't want any more of that. Can we just be ourselves and be happy together as we used to be?"

"Yes, all that is over," he said. "And I am happy to see you." He drew her gently to him. Gently he began to undress her and caress her body, just as he had used to, knowing what gave her pleasure, and she remembering what gave him pleasure. They lay down naked together. She was fondling his erect penis, aroused and yet a little reluctant to be penetrated after so long, when he moved his arm as if uncomfortable. Drawing away from him a little, she saw that he had a knife in his hand, which he must have hidden in the bed. He was holding it concealed behind his back.

Her womb went cold, but she continued to fondle his penis and testicles, not daring to say anything and not able to pull away, for he was holding her close with the other hand.

Suddenly he moved onto her and forced his penis into her vagina with a thrust so painful that for an instant she thought it was the knife. He ejaculated instantly. As his body arched she writhed out from under him, scrambled to the door, and ran from the room crying for help.

He pursued her, striking with the knife, stabbing her in the shoulder blade before the manager and other women and men seized him. The men were very angry and treated him with a violence which the manager's protests did not lessen. Naked, bloody, and half-conscious, he was bound and taken away immediately to the Castle.

Everyone now gathered around Azak, and her wound, which was slight, was cleaned and covered. Shaken and confused, she could ask only, "What will they do to him?"

"What do you think they do to a murdering rapist? Give him a prize?" the manager said. "They'll geld him."

"But it was my fault," Azak said.

The manager stared at her and said, "Are you mad? Go home."

She went back into the room and mechanically put on her clothes. She looked at the bed where they had lain. She stood at the window where Toddra had stood. She remembered how she had seen him dance long ago in the contest where he had first been made champion. She thought, "My life is wrong." But she did not know how to make it right.

Alteration in Seggrian social and cultural institutions did not take the disastrous course Merriment feared. It has been slow and its direction is not clear. In 93/1602 Terhada College invited men from two neighboring Castles to apply as students, and three men did so. In the next decades, most colleges opened their doors to men. Once they were graduated, male students had to return to their Castle, unless they left the planet, since native men were not allowed to live anywhere but as students in a college or in a Castle, until the Open Gate Law was passed in 93/1662.

Even after passage of that law, the Castles remained closed to women; and the exodus of men from the Castles was much slower than opponents of the measure feared. Social adjustment to the Open Gate Law has been slow. In several regions programs to train men in basic skills such as farming and construction have met with moderate success; the men work in competitive teams, separate from and managed by the women's companies. A good many Seggri have come to Hain to study in recent years—more men than women, despite the great numerical imbalance that still exists.

The following autobiographical sketch by one of these men is of particular interest, since he was involved in the event which directly precipitated the Open Gate Law.

Autobiographical Sketch by Mobile Ardar Dez.

I was born in Ekumenical Cycle 93, Year 1641, in Rakedr on Seggri. Rakedr was a placid, prosperous, conservative town, and I was brought up in the old way, the petted boychild of a big motherhouse. Altogether there were seventeen of us, not counting the kitchen staff—a great-grandmother, two grandmothers, four mothers, nine daughters, and me. We were well off; all the women were or had been managers or skilled workers in the Rakedr Pottery, the principal industry of the town. We kept all the holidays with pomp and energy, decorating the house from roof to foundation with banners for Hillalli, making fantastic costumes for the Harvest Festival, and celebrating somebody's birthday every few weeks with gifts all round. I was petted, as I said, but not, I think, spoiled. My birthday was no grander than my sisters', and I was allowed to run and play with them just as if I were a girl. Yet I was always aware, as were they, that our mothers' eyes rested on me with a different look, brooding, reserved, and sometimes, as I grew older, desolate.

After my Confirmation, my birthmother or her mother took me to Rakedr Castle every spring on Visiting Day. The gates of the Park, which had opened to admit me alone (and terrified) for my Confirmation, remained shut, but rolling stairs were placed against the Park walls. Up these I and a few other little boys from the town climbed, to sit on top of the Park wall in great state, on cushions, under awnings, and watch demonstration dancing, bull-dancing, wrestling, and other sports on the great Gamefield inside the wall. Our mothers waited below, outside, in the bleachers of the public field. Men and youths from the Castle sat with us, explaining the rules of the games and pointing out the fine points of a dancer or wrestler, treating us seriously, making us feel important. I enjoyed that very much, but as soon as I came down off the wall and started home it all fell away like a costume shrugged off, a part played in a play; and I went on with my work and play in the motherhouse with my family, my real life.

When I was ten I went to Boys' Class downtown. The class had been set up forty or fifty years before as a bridge between the motherhouse and the Castle, but the Castle, under increasingly reactionary governance, had recently withdrawn from the project. Lord Fassaw forbade his men to go anywhere outside the walls but directly to the fuckery, in a closed car, returning at first light; and so no men were able to teach the class. The townswomen who tried to tell me what to expect when I went to the Castle did not really know much more than I did. However well-meaning they were, they mostly frightened and confused me. But fear and confusion were an appropriate preparation.

I cannot describe the ceremony of Severance. I really cannot describe it. Men on Seggri, in those days, had this advantage: they knew what death is. They had all died once before their body's death. They had turned and looked back at their whole life, every place and face they had loved, and turned away from it as the gate closed.

At the time of my Severance, our small Castle was internally divided into "collegials" and "traditionals," a liberal faction left from the regime of Lord Ishog and a younger, highly conservative faction. The split was already disastrously wide when I came to the Castle. Lord Fassaw's rule had grown increasingly harsh and irrational. He governed by corruption, brutality, and cruelty. All of us who lived there were of course infected, and would have been destroyed if there had not been a strong, constant, moral resistance, centered around Ragaz and Kohadrat, who had been protégés of Lord Ishog. The two men were open partners; their followers were all the homosexuals in the Castle, and a good number of other men and older boys.

My first days and months in the Scrubs' dormitory were a bewildering alternation: terror, hatred, shame, as the boys who had been there a few months or years longer than I were incited to humiliate and abuse the newcomer, in order to make a man of him—and comfort, gratitude, love, as boys who had come under the influence of the collegials offered me secret friendship and pro tection. They helped me in the games and competitions and took me into their beds at night, not for sex but to keep me from the sexual bullies. Lord Fassaw detested adult homosexuality and would have reinstituted the death penalty if the Town Council had allowed it. Though he did not dare punish Ragaz and Kohadrat, he punished consenting love between older boys with bizarre and appalling physical mutilations—ears cut into fringes, fingers branded with red-hot iron rings. Yet he encouraged the older boys to rape the eleven- and twelve-year-olds, as a manly practice. None of us escaped. We particularly dreaded four youths, seventeen or eighteen years old when I came there, who called themselves the Lordsmen. Every few nights they raided the Scrubs' dormitory for a victim, whom they raped as a group. The collegials protected us as best they could by ordering us to their beds, where we wept and protested loudly, while they pretended to abuse us, laughing and jeering. Later, in the dark and silence, they comforted us with candy, and sometimes, as we grew older, with a desired love, gentle and exquisite in its secrecy.

There was no privacy at all in the Castle. I have said that to women who asked me to describe life there, and they thought they understood me. "Well, everybody shares everything in a motherhouse," they would say, "everybody's in and out of the rooms all the time. You're never really alone unless you have a singlewoman's flat." I could not tell them how different the loose, warm commonalty of the motherhouse was from the rigid, deliberate publicity of the forty-bed, brightly lighted Castle dormitories. Nothing in Rakedr was private: only secret, only silent. We ate our tears.

I grew up; I take some pride in that, along with my profound gratitude to the boys and men who made it possible. I did not kill myself, as several boys did during those years, nor did I kill my mind and soul, as some did so their body could survive. Thanks to the maternal care of the collegials—the resistance, as we came to call ourselves—I grew up.

Why do I say maternal, not paternal? Because there were no fathers in my world. There were only sires. I knew no such word as father or paternal. I thought of Ragaz and Kohadrat as my mothers. I still do.

Fassaw grew quite mad as the years went on, and his hold over the Castle tightened to a death grip. The Lordsmen now ruled us all. They were lucky in that we still had a strong Maingame team, the pride of Fassaw's heart, which kept us in the First League, as well as two Champion Sires in steady demand at the town fuckeries. Any protest the resistance tried to bring to the Town Council could be dismissed as typical male whining, or laid to the demoralising influence of the Aliens. From the outside Rakedr Castle seemed all right. Look at our great team! Look at our champion studs! The women looked no further.

How could they abandon us?—the cry every Seggrian boy must make in his heart. How could she leave me here? Doesn't she know what it's like? Why doesn't she know? Doesn't she want to know?

"Of course not," Ragaz said to me when I came to him in a passion of righteous indignation, the Town Council having denied our petition to be heard. "Of course they don't want to know how we live. Why do they never come into the Castles? Oh, we keep them out, yes; but do you think we could keep them out if they wanted to enter? My dear, we collude with them and they with us in maintaining the great foundation of ignorance and lies on which our civilisation rests."

"Our own mothers abandon us," I said.

"Abandon us? Who feeds us, clothes us, houses us, pays us? We're utterly dependent on them. If ever we made ourselves independent, perhaps we could rebuild society on a foundation of truth."

Independence was as far as his vision could reach. Yet I think his mind groped further, towards what he could not see, the body's obscure, inalterable dream of mutuality.

Our effort to make our case heard at the Council had no effect except within the Castle. Lord Fassaw saw his power threatened. Within a few days Ragaz was seized by the Lordsmen and their bully boys, accused of repeated homosexual acts and treasonable plots, arraigned, and sentenced by the Lord of the Castle. Everyone was summoned to the Gamefield to witness the punishment. A man of fifty with a heart ailment—he had been a Maingame racer in his twenties and had overtrained—Ragaz was tied naked across a bench and beaten with "Lord Long," a heavy leather tube filled with lead weights. The Lordsman Berhed, who wielded it, struck repeatedly at the head, the kidneys, and the genitals. Ragaz died an hour or two later in the infirmary.

The Rakedr Mutiny took shape that night. Kohadrat, older than Ragaz and devastated by his loss, could not restrain or guide us. His vision had been of a true resistance, long-lasting and nonviolent, through which the Lordsmen would in time destroy themselves. We had been following that vision. Now we let it go. We dropped the truth and grabbed weapons. "How you play is what you win," Kohadrat said, but we had heard all those old saws. We would not play the patience game anymore. We would win, now, once for all.

And we did. We won. We had our victory. Lord Fassaw, the Lordsmen, and their bullies had been slaughtered by the time the police got to the Gate.

I remember how those tough women strode in amongst us, staring at the rooms of the Castle which they had never seen, staring at the mutilated bodies, eviscerated, castrated, headless—at Lordsman Berhed, who had been nailed to the floor with "Lord Long" stuffed down his throat—at us, the rebels, the victors, with our bloody hands and defiant faces—at Kohadrat, whom we thrust forward as our leader, our spokesman.

He stood silent. He ate his tears.

The women drew closer to one another, clutching their guns, staring around. They were appalled, they thought us all insane. Their utter incomprehension drove one of us at last to speak—a young man, Tarsk, who wore the iron ring that had been forced onto his finger when it was red-hot. "They killed Ragaz," he said. "They were all mad. Look." He held out his crippled hand.

The chief of the troop, after a pause, said, "No one will leave here till this is looked into," and marched her women out of the Castle, out of the Park, locking the gate behind them, leaving us with our victory.

The hearings and judgments on the Rakedr Mutiny were all broadcast, of course, and the event has been studied and discussed ever since. My own part in it was the murder of the Lordsman Tatiddi. Three of us set on him and beat him to death with exercise clubs in the gymnasium where we had cornered him.

How we played was what we won.

We were not punished. Men were sent from several Castles to form a government over Rakedr Castle. They learned enough of Fassaw's behavior to see the cause of our rebellion, but the contempt of even the most liberal of them for us was absolute. They treated us not as men, but as irrational, irresponsible creatures, untamable cattle. If we spoke they did not answer.

I do not know how long we could have endured that cold regime of shame. It was only two months after the Mutiny that the World Council enacted the Open Gate Law. We told one another that that was our victory, we had made that happen. None of us believed it. We told one another we were free. For the first time in history, any man who wanted to leave his Castle could walk out the gate. We were free!

What happened to the free man outside the gate? Nobody had given it much thought.

I was one who walked out the gate, on the morning of the day the Law came into force. Eleven of us walked into town together.

Several of us, men not from Rakedr, went to one or another of the fuckeries, hoping to be allowed to stay there; they had nowhere else to go. Hotels and inns of course would not accept men. Those of us who had been children in the town went to our motherhouses.

What is it like to return from the dead? Not easy. Not for the one who returns, nor for his people. The place he occupied in their world has closed up, ceased to be, filled with accumulated change, habit, the doings and needs of others. He has been replaced. To return from the dead is to be a ghost: a person for whom there is no room.

Neither I nor my family understood that, at first. I came back to them at twenty-one as trustingly as if I were the eleven-year-old who had left them, and they opened their arms to their child. But he did not exist. Who was I?

For a long time, months, we refugees from the Castle hid in our motherhouses. The men from other towns all made their way home, usually by begging a ride with teams on tour. There were seven or eight of us in Rakedr, but we scarcely ever saw one another. Men had no place on the street; for hundreds of years a man seen alone on the street had been arrested immediately. If we went out, women ran from us, or reported us, or surrounded and threatened us—"Get back into your Castle where you belong! Get back to the fuckery where you belong! Get out of our city!" They called us drones, and in fact we had no work, no function at all in the community. The fuckeries would not accept us for service, because we had no guarantee of health and good behavior from a Castle.

This was our freedom: we were all ghosts, useless, frightened, frightening intruders, shadows in the corners of life. We watched life going on around us—work, love, childbearing, child-rearing, getting and spending, making and shaping, governing and adventuring—the women's world, the bright, full, real world—and there was no room in it for us. All we had ever learned to do was play games and destroy one another.

My mothers and sisters racked their brains, I know, to find some place and use for me in their lively, industrious household. Two old live-in cooks had run our kitchen since long before I was born, so cooking, the one practical art I had been taught in the Castle, was superfluous. They found household tasks for me, but they were all makework, and they and I knew it. I was perfectly willing to look after the babies, but one of the grandmothers was very jealous of that privilege, and also some of my sisters' wives were uneasy about a man touching their baby. My sister Pado broached the possibility of an apprenticeship in the clay-works, and I leaped at the chance; but the managers of the Pottery, after long discussion, were unable to agree to accept men as employees. Their hormones would make male workers unreliable, and female workers would be uncomfortable, and so on.

The holonews was full of such proposals and discussions, of course, and orations about the unforeseen consequences of the Open Gate Law, the proper place of men, male capacities and limitations, gender as destiny. Feeling against the Open Gate policy ran very strong, and it seemed that every time I watched the holo there was a woman talking grimly about the inherent violence and irresponsibility of the male, his biological unfitness to participate in social and political decision-making. Often it was a man saying the same things. Opposition to the new law had the fervent support of all the conservatives in the Castles, who pleaded eloquently for the gates to be closed and men to return to their proper station, pursuing the true, masculine glory of the games and the fuckeries.

Glory did not tempt me, after the years at Rakedr Castle; the word itself had come to mean degradation to me. I ranted against the games and competitions, puzzling most of my family, who loved to watch the Maingames and wrestling, and complained only that the level of excellence of most of the teams had declined since the gates were opened. And I ranted against the fuckeries, where, I said, men were used as cattle, stud bulls, not as human beings. I would never go there again.

"But my dear boy," my mother said at last, alone with me one evening, "will you live the rest of your life celibate?"

"I hope not," I said.

"Then . . . ?"

"I want to get married."

Her eyes widened. She brooded a bit, and finally ventured, "To a man."

"No. To a woman. I want a normal, ordinary marriage. I want to have a wife and be a wife."

Shocking as the idea was, she tried to absorb it. She pondered, frowning.

"All it means," I said, for I had had a long time with nothing to do but ponder, "is that we'd live together just like any married pair. We'd set up our own daughterhouse, and be faithful to each other, and if she had a child I'd be its lovemother along with her. There isn't any reason why it wouldn't work!"

"Well, I don't know—I don't know of any," said my mother, gentle and judicious, and never happy at saying no to me. "But you do have to find the woman, you know."

"I know," I said, glumly.

"It's such a problem for you to meet people," she said. "Perhaps if you went to the fuckery . . . ? I don't see why your own mother-house couldn't guarantee you just as well as a Castle. We could try—?"

But I passionately refused. Not being one of Fassaw's sycophants, I had seldom been allowed to go to the fuckery; and my few experiences there had been unfortunate. Young, inexperienced, and without recommendation, I had been selected by older women who wanted a plaything. Their practiced skill at arousing me had left me humiliated and enraged. They patted and tipped me as they left. That elaborate, mechanical excitation and their condescending coldness was vile to me, after the tenderness of my lover-protectors in the Castle. Yet women attracted me physically as men never had; the beautiful bodies of my sisters and their wives, all around me constantly now, clothed and naked, innocent and sensual, the wonderful heaviness and strength and softness of women's bodies, kept me continually aroused. Every night I masturbated, fantasizing my sisters in my arms. It was unendurable. Again I was a ghost, a raging, yearning impotence in the midst of untouchable reality.

I began to think I would have to go back to the Castle. I sank into a deep depression, an inertia, a chill darkness of the mind.

My family, anxious, affectionate, busy, had no idea what to do for me or with me. I think most of them thought in their hearts that it would be best if I went back through the gate.

One afternoon my sister Pado, with whom I had been closest as a child, came to my room—they had cleared out a dormer attic for me, so that I had room at least in the literal sense. She found me in my now constant lethargy, lying on the bed doing nothing at all. She breezed in, and with the indifference women often showed to moods and signals, plumped down on the foot of the bed and said, "Hey, what do you know about the man who's here from the Ekumen?"

I shrugged and shut my eyes. I had been having rape fantasies lately. I was afraid of her.

She talked on about the offworlder, who was apparently in Rakedr to study the Mutiny. "He wants to talk to the resistance," she said. "Men like you. The men who opened the gates. He says they won't come forward, as if they were ashamed of being heroes."

"Heroes!" I said. The word in my language is gendered female. It refers to the semidivine, semihistoric protagonists of the Epics.

"It's what you are," Pado said, intensity breaking through her assumed breeziness. "You took responsibility in a great act. Maybe you did it wrong. Sassume did it wrong in the *Founding of Emmo*, didn't she, she let Faradr get killed. But she was still a hero. She took the responsibility. So did you. You ought to go talk to this Alien. Tell him what happened. Nobody really knows what happened at the Castle. You owe us the story."

That was a powerful phrase, among my people. "The untold story mothers the lie," was the saying. The doer of any notable act was held literally *accountable* for it to the community.

"So why should I tell it to an Alien?" I said, defensive of my inertia.

"Because he'll listen," my sister said drily. "We're all too damned busy."

It was profoundly true. Pado had seen a gate for me and opened it; and I went through it, having just enough strength and sanity left to do so.

Mobile Noem was a man in his forties, born some centuries earlier on Terra, trained on Hain, widely travelled; a small, yellow-brown, quick-eyed person, very easy to talk to. He did not seem at all masculine to me, at first; I kept thinking he was a woman, because he acted like one. He got right to business, with none of the maneuvering to assert his authority or jockeying for position that men of my society felt obligatory in any relationship with another man. I was used to men being wary, indirect, and competitive. Noem, like a woman, was direct and receptive. He was also as subtle and powerful as any man or woman I had known, even Ragaz. His authority was in fact immense; but he never stood on it. He sat down on it, comfortably, and invited you to sit down with him.

I was the first of the Rakedr mutineers to come forward and tell our story to him. He recorded it, with my permission, to use in making his report to the Stabiles on the condition of our society, "the matter of Seggri," as he called it. My first description of the Mutiny took less than an hour. I thought I was done. I didn't know, then, the inexhaustible desire to learn, to understand, to hear *all* the story, that characterises the Mobiles of the Ekumen. Noem asked questions, I answered; he speculated and extrapolated, I corrected; he wanted details, I furnished them—telling the story of the Mutiny, of the years before it, of the men of the Castle, of the women of the Town, of my people, of my life—little by little, bit by bit, all in fragments, a muddle. I talked to Noem daily for a month. I learned that the story has no beginning, and no story has an end. That the story is all muddle, all middle. That the story is never true, but that the lie is indeed a child of silence.

By the end of the month I had come to love and trust Noem, and of course to depend on him. Talking to him had become my reason for being. I tried to face the fact that he would not stay in Rakedr much longer. I must learn to do without him. Do what? There were things for men to do, ways for men to live, he proved it by his mere existence; but could I find them?

He was keenly aware of my situation, and would not let me withdraw, as I began to do, into the lethargy of fear again; he would not let me be silent. He asked me impossible questions. "What would you be if you could be anything?" he asked me, a question children ask each other.

I answered at once, passionately—"A wife!"

I know now what the flicker that crossed his face was. His quick, kind eyes watched me, looked away, looked back.

"I want my own family," I said. "Not to live in my mothers' house, where I'm always a child. Work. A wife, wives—children—to be a mother. I want life, not games!"

"You can't bear a child," he said gently.

"No, but I can mother one!"

"We gender the word," he said. "I like it better your way . . . But tell me, Ardar, what are the chances of your marrying—meeting a woman willing to marry a man? It hasn't happened, here, has it?"

I had to say no, not to my knowledge.

"It will happen, certainly, I think," he said (his certainties were always uncertain). "But the personal cost, at first, is likely to be high. Relationships formed against the negative pressure of a society are under terrible strain; they tend to become defensive, overintense, unpeaceful. They have no room to grow."

"Room!" I said. And I tried to tell him my feeling of having no room in my world, no air to breathe.

He looked at me, scratching his nose; he laughed. "There's plenty of room in the galaxy, you know," he said.

"Do you mean . . . I could . . . That the Ekumen . . ." I didn't even know what the question I wanted to ask was. Noem did. He began to answer it thoughtfully and in detail. My education so far had been so limited, even as regards the culture of my own people, that I would have to attend a college for at least two or three years, in order to be ready to apply to an offworld institution such as the Ekumenical Schools on Hain. Of course, he went on, where I went and what kind of training I chose would depend on my interests, which I would go to a college to discover, since neither my schooling as a child nor my training at the Castle had really given me any idea of what there was to be interested in. The choices offered me had been unbelievably limited, addressing neither the needs of a normally intelligent person nor the needs of my society. And so the Open Gate Law instead of giving me freedom had left me "with no air to breathe but airless Space," said Noem, quoting some poet from some planet somewhere. My head was spinning, full of stars. "Hagka College is quite near Rakedr," Noem said, "did you never think of applying? If only to escape from your terrible Castle?"

I shook my head. "Lord Fassaw always destroyed the application forms when they were sent to his office. If any of us had tried to apply . . ."

"You would have been punished. Tortured, I suppose. Yes. Well, from the little I know of your colleges, I think your life there would be better than it is here, but not altogether pleasant. You will have work to do, a place to be; but you will be made to feel marginal, inferior. Even highly educated, enlightened women have difficulty accepting men as their intellectual equals. Believe me, I have experienced it myself! And because you were trained at the Castle to compete, to want to excel, you may find it hard to be among people who either believe you incapable of excellence, or to whom the concept of competition, of winning and defeating, is valueless. But just there, there is where you will find air to breathe."

Noem recommended me to women he knew on the faculty of Hagka College, and I was enrolled on probation. My family were delighted to pay my tuition. I was the first of us to go to college, and they were genuinely proud of me.

As Noem had predicted, it was not always easy, but there were enough other men there that I found friends and was not caught in the paralysing isolation of the motherhouse. And as I took courage, I made friends among the women students, finding many of them unprejudiced and companionable. In my third year, one of them and I managed, tentatively and warily, to fall in love. It did not work very well or last very long, yet it was a great liberation for both of us, our liberation from the belief that the only communication or commonalty possible between us was sexual, that an adult man and woman had nothing to join them but their genitals. Emadr loathed the professionalism of the fuckery as I did, and our lovemaking was always shy and brief. Its true significance was not as a consummation of desire, but as proof that we could trust each other. Where our real passion broke loose was when we lay together talking, telling each other what our lives had been, how we felt about men and women and each other and ourselves, what our nightmares were, what our dreams were. We talked endlessly, in a communion that I will cherish and honor all my life, two young souls finding their wings, flying together, not for long, but high. The first flight is the highest.

Emadr has been dead two hundred years; she stayed on Seggri, married into a motherhouse, bore two children, taught at Hagka, and died in her seventies. I went to Hain, to the Ekumenical Schools, and later to Werel and Yeowe as part of the Mobile's staff; my record is herewith enclosed. I have written this sketch of my life as part of my application to return to Seggri as a Mobile of the Ekumen. I want very much to live among my people, to learn who they are, now that I know with at least an uncertain certainty who I am.

An excerpt from *Moving Mars*

GREG BEAR

Greg Bear is a former president of the SFWA who has become one of the most important and accomplished writers of science fiction. He sold his first story at the age of fifteen, but began to win widespread acclaim for his work during the 1980s. His novels include *Hegira, Beyond Heaven's River, Eon, Eternity, The Forge of God, Queen of Angels,* and *Legacy.* His short fiction has been collected in *The Wind from a Burning Woman* and *Tangents.* Bear won two Nebulas in 1983 for his novella "Hardfought" and his novelette "Blood Music," which also won a Hugo; he won a third Nebula in 1986 for his short story "Tangents."

Moving Mars, a realistically and lovingly detailed look at a colonized Mars, won this year's Nebula Award for best novel. The following excerpt was published in an earlier version as a novella, and stands alone very well. About *Moving Mars,* Greg Bear has this to say:

"Like most of my novels, *Moving Mars* came together from a variety of sources and ideas, beginning with the timeline and history created in *Queen of Angels.* Following close on the heels of *Queen of Angels* was 'Heads,' a novella published as a book. 'Heads' reflected my time as a 'politician,' serving as president of SFWA for two years. The experience was worthwhile and enlightening—it taught me I never wanted to be a politician again. Not that I did a bad job—I didn't— but I certainly never had anything like the 'fire in the belly' necessary to really enjoy such work. Both 'Heads' and *Moving Mars* are about people who end up being chewed (some might say 'mauled') by politics.

"For years I have been pursuing an interesting approach to physics and looking at the universe, elucidated most clearly in *Blood Music* and *Anvil of Stars.* I refer to this as 'information mechanics' (apologies to Frederick Kantor) or 'my crackpot notions,' but some physicists have been kind enough to tell me the ideas are interesting. I took a few of these ideas from *Anvil of Stars* and elaborated upon them for *Moving Mars.* The biology of the ancient Martian life-forms derives in part from an early and otherwise unrelated short story, 'A Martian Ricorso,' as well as from some ideas developed for *Biosphere,* a motion picture collaboration with special effects master and longtime friend Phil Tippett. These ideas were developed for an early stage of the treatment and were not in the final product presented to Tristar Columbia executives, and rejected by them. (I've also detailed this biology for a forthcoming novel, *Legacy*, set in yet another universe!)

"Last, but certainly not least, I've always been partial to strong female main characters. I took on the challenge of writing the autobiography of a Martian woman with few trepidations and no 'gender-bending' goals, simply to write about a woman as a human being caught up in difficult times. Fortunately, the book seems to have met with some acceptance among women readers.

"Other sources . . .

"The first science fiction book I read was Robert A. Heinlein's *Red Planet*. I should point out that I'm married to one of the two women to whom Heinlein dedicated *Podkayne of Mars*. Other than writing about politics and science, I don't believe *Moving Mars* is otherwise a very Heinleinian novel—but the background is certainly there. I hope Mr. Heinlein would have approved.

"I dedicated the book to Ray Bradbury because he created a wonderful Mars completely different from mine, and because he and I have been friends for almost twenty-seven years. Ray is my literary poppa.

"People have asked why so many people have written books about Mars lately. I set my book on Mars because I've always loved the planet and the stories set there—from Edgar Rice Burroughs to Heinlein to Bradbury and now to Kim Stanley Robinson and so many others.

"Mars is simply a great place for the imagination. Always has been, always will be, even after we get there. And get there we will!"

A day on Mars is a little longer than a day on Earth: 24 hours and 40 minutes. A year on Mars is less than two Earth years: 686 Earth days, or 668 Martian days. Mars is 6,787 kilometers in diameter, compared to Earth's 12,756 kilometers. Its gravitational acceleration is 3.71 meters per second squared, or just over one-third of Earth's. The atmospheric pressure at the surface of Mars averages 5.6 millibars, about one-half of one percent of Earth's. The atmosphere is largely composed of carbon dioxide. Temperatures at the "datum" or reference surface level (there is no "sea level," as there are presently no seas) vary from −130° to +27° Celsius. An unprotected human on the surface of Mars would very likely freeze within minutes, but first would die of exposure to the near-vacuum. If this unfortunate human survived freezing and low pressure, and found a *supply of oxygen to breathe, she would still be endangered by high levels of radiation from the Sun and elsewhere.*

After Earth, Mars is the most hospitable planet in the Solar System.

The young may not remember Mars of old, under the yellow Sun, its cloud-streaked skies dusted pink, its soil rusty and fine, its inhabitants living in pressurized burrows and venturing Up only as a rite of passage or to do maintenance or tend the ropy crops spread like nests of intensely green snakes over the wind-scoured farms. That Mars, an old and tired Mars filled with young lives, is gone forever.

Now I am old and tired, and Mars is young again.

Our lives are not our own, but by God, we must behave as if they are. When I was young, what I did seemed too small to be of any consequence; but the shiver of dust, we are told, expands in time to the planet-sweeping storm . . .

2171, M.Y. 53

An age was coming to an end. I had studied the signs half-innocently in my classes, there had even been dire hints from a few perceptive professors, but I had never thought the situation would affect me personally . . . Until now.

I had been voided from the University of Mars, Sinai. Two hundred classmates and professors in the same predicament lined the brilliant white floor of the depot, faces crossed by shadows from sun shining through the webwork of beams and girders supporting the depot canopy. We were waiting for the Solis Dorsa train to come and swift us away to our planums, planitias, fossas, and valleys.

Diane Johara, my roommate, stood with her booted foot on one small bag, tapping the tip of the boot on the handle, lips pursed as if whistling but making no sound. She kept her face pointed toward the northern curtains, waiting for the train to nose through. Though we were good friends, Diane and I had never talked politics. That was basic etiquette on Mars.

"Assassination," she said.

"Impractical," I murmured. I had not known until a few days ago how strongly Diane felt. "Besides, who would you shoot?"

"The governor. The chancellor."

I shook my head.

Over eighty percent of the UMS students had been voided, a gross violation of contract. That struck me as very damned unfair, but my family had never been activist. Daughter of BM finance people, born to a long tradition of caution, I straddled the fence.

The political structure set up during settlement a century before still creaked along, but its days were numbered. The original settlers, arriving in groups of ten or more families, had dug warrens in water-rich lands all over Mars, from pole to pole, but mostly in the smooth lowland plains and the deep valleys. Following the Lunar model, the first families had formed syndicates called Binding Multiples or BMs. The Binding Multiples acted like economic superfamilies; indeed, "family" and "BM" were almost synonymous. Later settlers had a choice of joining established BMs or starting new ones; few families stayed independent.

Many BMs merged and in time agreed to divide Mars into areological districts and develop resources in cooperation. By and large, Binding Multiples regarded each other as partners in the midst of Martian bounty, not competitors.

"The train's late. Fascists are supposed to make them run on time," Diane said, still tapping her boot.

"They never did on Earth," I said.

"You mean it's a myth?"

I nodded.

"So fascists aren't good for anything?" Diane asked.

"Uniforms," I said.

"Ours don't even have good uniforms."

Elected by district ballot, the governors answered only to the inhabitants of their districts, regardless of BM affiliations. The governors licensed mining and settlement rights to the BMs and represented the districts in a joint Council of Binding Multiples. Syndics chosen within BMs by vote of senior advocates and managers represented the interests of the BMs themselves in the Council. Governors and syndics did not often see eye to eye. It was all very formal and polite—Martians are almost always polite—but many procedures were uncodified. Some said it was grossly inefficient, and attempts were being made to unify Mars under a central government, as had already happened on the Moon.

The governor of Syria-Sinai, Freechild Dauble, a tough, chisel-chinned administrator, had pushed hard for several years to get the BMs to agree to a Statist constitution and central government authority. She wanted them to give up their syndics in favor of representation by district. This meant the breakup of BM power, of course.

Dauble's name has since become synonymous with corruption, but at the time, she had been governor of Mars's largest district for eight Martian years and was at the peak of her long friendship with power. By cajoling, pressuring, and threatening, she had forged—some said forced—agreements between the largest BMs. Dauble had become the focus of Martian Unity and was on the sly spin for president of the planet.

Some said Dauble's own career was the best argument for change, but few dared contradict her.

A vote was due within days in the Council to make permanent the new Martian constitution. We had lived under the Dauble government's "trial run" for six months, and many grumbled loudly. The hard-won agreement was fragile. Dauble had rammed it down too many throats, with too much underhanded dealing.

Lawsuits were pending from at least five families opposed to unity, mostly smaller BMs afraid of being absorbed and nullified. They were called Gobacks by the Statists, who regarded them as a real threat. The Statists would not tolerate a return to what they saw as disorganized Binding Multiples rule.

"If assassination is so impractical," Diane said, "we could rough up a few of the favorites—"

"Shh," I said.

She shook her short, shagged hair and turned away, soundlessly whistling again. Diane did that when she was too angry to speak politely. Red rabbits who had lived for decades in close quarters placed a high value on politeness, and impressed that on their offspring.

The Statists feared incidents. Student protests were unacceptable to Dauble. Even if the students did not represent the Gobacks, they might make enough noise to bring down the agreement.

So Dauble sent word to Caroline Connor, an old friend she had appointed chancellor of the largest university, University of Mars Sinai. An authoritarian with too much energy and too little sense,

Connor obliged her crony by closing most of the campus and com-
piling a list of those who might be in sympathy with protesters.

I had majored in government and management. Though I had
signed no petitions and participated in no marches—unlike Diane,
who had taken to the movement vigorously—my name crept onto a
list of suspects. The Govmanagement Department was notoriously
independent; who could trust any of us?

We had paid our tuition but couldn't go to classes. Most of the
voided faculty and students had little choice but to go home. The
university generously gave us free tickets on state chartered trains.
Some, including Diane, declined the tickets and vowed to fight the
illegal voiding. That earned her—and, guilty by association, me, simply slow to pack my belongings—an escort of UMS security out of
the university warrens.

Diane walked stiffly, slowly, defiantly. The guards—most of them
new emigrants from Earth, large and strong—firmly gripped our elbows and hustled us down the tunnels. The rough treatment watered
my quick-growing seed of doubt; how could I give in to this injustice
without a cry? My family was cautious; it had never been known for
cowardice.

Surrounded by Connor's guards, packed in with the last remaining voided students, we were marched in quickstep past a cluster of
other students lounging in a garden atrium. They wore their family
grays and blues, scions of BMs with strong economic ties to Earth,
darlings of those most favoring Dauble's plans; all still in school. They
talked quietly and calmly among themselves and turned to watch us
go, faces blank. They offered no support, no encouragement; their
inaction built walls. Diane nudged me. "Pigs," she whispered.

I agreed. I thought them worse than traitors—they behaved as
if they were cynical and *old,* violators of the earnest ideals of youth.

We had been loaded into a single tunnel van and driven to the
depot, still escorted by campus guards.

The depot hummed.

A few students wandered down a side corridor, then came back
and passed the word. The loop train to the junction at Solis Dorsa
approached. Diane licked her lips and looked around nervously.

The last escorting guard, assured that we were on our way, gave
us a tip of his cap and stepped into a depot café, out of sight.

"Are you coming with us?" Diane asked.

I could not answer. My head buzzed with contradictions, anger at injustice fighting family expectations. My mother and father hated the turmoil caused by unification. They strongly believed that staying out of it was best. They had told me so, without laying down any laws.

Diane gave me a pitying look. She shook my hand and said, "Casseia, you *think* too much." She edged along the platform and turned a corner. In groups of five or less, students went to the lav, for coffee, to check the weather at their home depots . . . Ninety students in all sidled away from the main group.

I hesitated. Those who remained seemed studiously neutral. Sidewise glances met faces quickly turned away.

An eerie silence fell over the platform. One last student, a female first-form junior carrying three heavy duffels, did a little shimmy, short brown hair fanning around her neck. She let one duffel slip from her shoulder. The shimmy vibrated down to her leg and she kicked the bag two meters. She dropped her other bags and walked north on the platform and around the corner.

My whole body quivered. I looked at the solemn faces around me and wondered how they could be so *bovine*. How could they just stand there, waiting for the train to slow, and accept Dauble's punishment for political views they might not even support?

The train pushed a plug of air along the platform as it passed through the seals and curtains. Icons flashed above the platform— station ID, train designator, destinations—and a mature woman's voice told us, with all the politeness in the world and no discernible emotion, "Solis Dorsa to Bosporus, Nereidum, Argyre, Noachis, with transfers to Meridiani and Hellas, now arriving, gate four."

I muttered, "Shit *shit shit,*" under my breath. Before I knew what I had decided, before I could paralyze myself with more thought, my legs took me around the corner and up to a blank white service bay: dead end. The only exit was a low steel door covered with chipped white enamel. It had been left open just a crack. I bent down, opened the door wide, glanced behind me, and stepped through.

It took me several minutes of fast walking to catch up with Diane. I passed ten or fifteen students in a dark arbeiter service tunnel and found her. "Where are we going?" I asked in a whisper.

"Are you with us?"

"I am now."

She winked and shook my hand with a bold and happy swing. "Someone has a key and knows the way to the old pioneer domes."

Muffling laughter and clapping each other on the back, full of enthusiasm and impressed by our courage, we passed one by one through an ancient steel hatch and crept along narrow, stuffy old tunnels lined with crumbling foamed rock. As the last of us left the UMS environs, stepping over a dimly lighted boundary marker into a wider and even older tunnel, we clasped hands on shoulders and half-marched, half-danced in lockstep.

Someone at the end of the line harshly whispered for us to be quiet. We stopped, hardly daring to breathe. Seconds of silence, then from behind came low voices and the mechanical hum of service arbeiters, a heavy, solid clank and a painful twinge in our ears. Someone had sealed the tunnel hatch behind us.

"Do they know we're in here?" I asked Diane.

"I doubt it," she said. "That was a pressure crew."

They had closed the door and sealed it. No turning back.

The tunnels took us five kilometers beyond the university borders, through a decades-old maze unused since before my birth, threaded unerringly by whoever led the group.

"We're in old times now," Diane said, looking back at me. Forty orbits ago—over seventy-five Terrestrial years—these tunnels had connected several small pioneer stations. We filed past warrens once used by the earliest families, dark and bitterly cold, kept pressurized in reserve only for dire emergency . . .

Our few torches and tunnel service lamps illuminated scraps of old furniture, pieces of outdated electronics, stacked drums of emergency reserve rations and vacuum survival gear.

Hours before, we had eaten our last university meal and had a warm vapor shower in the dorms. That was all behind us. Up ahead, we faced Spartan conditions.

I felt wonderful. I was doing something significant, and without my family's approval.

I thought I was finally growing up.

The ninety students gathered in a dark hollow at the end of the tunnel, a pioneer trench dome. All sounds—nervous and excited laughter, questioning voices, scraping of feet on the cold floor, scattered outbreaks of song—blunted against the black poly interior. Diane broke Martian reserve and hugged me. Then a few voices rose above the dull murmurs. Several students started taking down names and BM affiliations. The mass began to take shape.

Two students from third-form engineering—a conservative and hard-dug department—stood before us and announced their names: Sean Dickinson, Gretyl Laughton. Within the day, after forming groups and appointing captains, we confirmed Sean and Gretyl as our leaders, expressed our solidarity and zeal, and learned we had something like a plan.

I found Sean Dickinson extremely handsome: of middle height, slight build, wispy brown hair above a prominent forehead, brows elegantly slim and animated. Though less attractive, Gretyl had been struck from the same mold: a slim young woman with large, accusing blue eyes and straw hair pulled into a tight bun.

Sean stood on an old crate and gazed down upon us, establishing us as real people with a real mission. "We all know why we're here," he said. Expression stern, eyes liquid and compassionate, he raised his hands, long and callused fingers reaching for the poly dome above, and said, "The old betray us. Experience breeds corruption. It's time to bring a moral balance to Mars, and show *them* what an individual stands for, and what our rights really mean. They've forgotten us, friends. They've forgotten their contractual obligations. True Martians don't forget such things, any more than they'd forget to breathe or plug a leak. So what are we going to do? What can we do? What *must* we do?"

"Remind them!" many of us shouted. Some said, *"Kill them,"* and I said, "Tell them what we—" But I was not given a chance to finish, my voice lost in the roar.

Sean laid out his plan. We listened avidly; he fed our anger and our indignation. I had never been so excited. We who had kept the freshness of youth, and would not stand for corruption, intended to storm UMS *overland* and assert our contractual rights. We were righteous, and our cause was just.

Sean ordered that we all be covered with skinseal, pumped from big plastic drums. We danced in the skinseal showers naked, laughing, pointing, shrieking at the sudden cold, embarrassed but greatly enjoying ourselves. We put our clothes back on over the flexible tight-fitting nanomer. Skinseal was designed for emergency pressure problems and not for comfort. Going to the bathroom became an elaborate ritual; in skinseal, a female took about four minutes to pee, a male two minutes, and shitting was particularly tricky.

We dusted our skinseal with red ochre to hide us should we decide to worm out during daylight. We all looked like cartoon devils.

By the end of the third day, we were tired and hungry and dirty and impatient. We huddled in the pressurized poly dome, ninety in a space meant for thirty, our rusty water tapped from an old well, having eaten little or no food, exercising to ward off the cold.

I brushed past a pale thoughtful fellow a few times on the way to the food line or the lav. Lean and hawk-nosed and dark-haired, with wide, puzzled eyes, a wry smile, and a hesitant, nervously joking manner, he seemed less angry and less sure than the rest of us. Just looking at him irritated me. I stalked him, watching his mannerisms, tracking his growing list of inadequacies. I was not in the best temper and needed to vent a little frustration. I took it upon myself to educate him.

At first, if he noticed my attention at all, he seemed to try to avoid me, moving through little groups of people under the gloomy old poly, making small talk. Everybody was testy; his attempts at conversation fizzled. Finally he stood in line near an antique electric wall heater, waiting his turn to bask in the currents of warm dry air.

I stood behind him. He glanced at me, smiled politely, and hunkered down with his back against the wall. I sat beside him. He clamped his hands on his knees, set his lips primly, and avoided eye contact; obviously, he had had enough of trying to make conversation and failing.

"Having second thoughts?" I asked after a decent interval.

"What?" he asked, confused.

"You look sour. Is your heart in this?"

He flashed the same irritating smile and lifted his hands, placating. "I'm here," he said.

"Then show a little enthusiasm, dammit."

Some other students shook their heads and shuffled away, too tired to get involved in a private fracas. Diane joined us at the rear of the line.

"I don't know your name," he said.

"She's Casseia Majumdar," said Diane.

"Oh," he said. I was angry that he recognized the name. Of all things, I didn't want to be known for my currently useless family connections.

"Her great uncle founded Majumdar BM," Diane continued. I shot her a look and she puckered her lips, eyes dancing. She was enjoying a little relief from the earnest preparations and boredom.

"You have to be with us in heart *and* mind," I lectured him.

"Sorry. I'm just tired. My name is Charles Franklin." He offered a hand.

I thought that was incredibly insensitive and gauche, considering the circumstance. We had made it to the heater, but I turned away as if I didn't care and walked toward the stacks of masks and cyclers being tested by our student leader.

Neither a Statist nor a Goback, Sean Dickinson seemed to me the epitome of what our impromptu organization stood for. Son of a track engineer, Sean had earned his scholarship by sheer brainwork. In the UMS engineering department, he had moved up quickly, only to be diverted into attempts to organize trans-BM unions. That had earned him the displeasure of Connor and Dauble.

Sean worked with an expression of complete concentration, hair disheveled, spidery, strong fingers pulling at mask poly. His mouth twitched with each newfound leak. He hardly knew I existed. Had he known, he probably would have shunned me for my name. That didn't stop me from being impressed.

Charles followed me and stood beside the growing pile of rejects. "Please don't misunderstand," he said. "I'm really behind all this."

"Glad to hear it," I said. I observed the preparations and shivered. Nobody likes the thought of vacuum rose. None of us had been trained in insurrection. We would be up against campus security, augmented by the governor's own thugs and maybe some of our former classmates, and I had no idea how far they—or the situation—would go.

We watched news vids intently on our slates. Sean had posted on the ex nets that students had gone on strike to protest Connor's illegal voiding. But he hadn't told about our dramatic plans, for obvious reasons. The citizens of the Triple—the linked economies of Earth, Mars, and Moon—hadn't turned toward us. Even the LitVids on Mars seemed uninterested.

"I thought I could help," Charles said, pointing to the masks and drums. "I've done this before . . ."

"Gone Up?" I asked.

"My hobby is hunting fossils. I asked to be on the equipment committee, but they said they didn't need me."

"Hobby?" I asked.

"Fossils. Outside. During the summer, of course."

Here was my chance to be helpful to Sean, and maybe apologize to Charles for showing my nerves. I squatted beside the pile and said, "Sean, Charles here says he's worked outside."

"Good," Sean said. He tossed a ripped mask to Gretyl. I wondered innocently if she and Sean were lovers. Gretyl scowled at the mask—a safety-box surplus antique—and dropped it on the reject pile, which threatened to spill out around our feet.

"I can fix those," Charles said. "There are tubes of quick poly in the safety boxes. It works."

"I won't send anybody outside in a ripped mask," Sean said. "Excuse me, but I have to *focus* here."

"Sorry," Charles said. He shrugged at me.

"We may not have enough masks," I said, looking at the diminishing stacks of good equipment.

Sean glared over his shoulder, pressed for time and very unhappy. "Your advice is not necessary," Gretyl told me sharply.

"It's nothing," Charles said, tugging my arm. "Let them work."

I shrugged his fingers loose and backed away, face flushed with embarrassment. Charles returned with me to the heater, but we had lost our places there.

The lights had been cut to half. The air became thicker and colder each day. I thought of my warren rooms at home, a thousand kilometers away, of how worried my folks might be, and of how they would take it if I died out in the thin air, or if some Statist thug pierced my young frame with a fléchette . . . God, what a scandal that would make! It seemed almost worth it.

I fantasized Dauble and Connor dragged away *under arrest*, glorious and magnificent disgrace, perhaps worth my death . . . but probably not.

"I'm a physics major," Charles said, joining me at the end of the line.

"Good for you," I said.

"You're in govmanagement?"

"That's why I'm here."

"I'm here because my parents voted against the Statists. That's all I can figure. They were in Klein BM. Klein's holding out to the last, you know."

I nodded without making eye contact, wanting him to go away.

"The Statists are suicidal," Charles said mildly. "They'll bring themselves down . . . Even if we don't accelerate the process."

"We can't afford to wait," I said. The skinseal wouldn't last much longer. The nakedness and embarrassment had bonded us. We *knew* each other; we thought we had no secrets. But we itched and stank and our indignation might soon give way to general disgruntlement. I felt sure Sean and the other leaders were aware of this.

"I was trying to get a scholarship for Earth study and a grant for thinker time," he said. "Now I'm off the list, I'm behind on my research—" He paused, eyes downcast, as if embarrassed at babbling. "You know," he said, "we've got to do something in the next twenty hours. The skinseal will rot."

"Right." I looked at him more closely. He was not homely. His voice was mellow and pleasant, and what I had first judged as lack of enthusiasm now looked more like *calm,* which I was certainly not.

Sean had finished weeding out the bad helmets. He stood and Gretyl called shrilly for our attention. "Listen," Sean said, shaking out his stiff arms and shoulders. "We've had a response from Connor's office. They refuse to meet with us, and they demand to know where we are. I think even Connor will figure out where we are in a few more days. So it's now or never. We have twenty-six good outfits and eight or ten problem pieces. I can salvage two from those. The rest are junk."

"I could fix some of them if he'd let me," Charles said under his breath.

"Gretyl and I will wear the problem pieces," Sean said. My heart pumped faster at his selfless courage. "But that means most of us will have to stay here. We'll draw sticks to see who crosses the plain."

"What if they're armed?" asked a nervous young woman.

Sean smiled. "Red rabbits down, cause up like a rocket," he said. That was clear enough. Martians shoot Martians, and glory to us all, the Statists would fall. He was right, of course. News would cross the Triple by day's end, probably even reach the planetoid communities.

Sean sounded as if he thought martyrdom might be useful. I looked at the young faces around me, eight, nine, or ten—my age—almost nineteen Terrestrial years—and then at Sean's face, seemingly old and experienced at twelve. Quietly, as a group, we raised our hands with fingers spread wide—the old Lunar Independence Symbol for the free expression of human abilities and ideas, tolerance against oppression, handshake instead of fist.

But as Sean brought his hand down, it closed reflexively into a fist. I realized then how earnest he was, and how serious this was, and what I was putting on the line.

We drew fibers from a frayed length of old optic cord an hour after the mask count. Twenty-six had been cut long. I drew a long, as did Charles. Diane was very disappointed to get a short. We were issued masks and set our personal slates to encrypt signals tied to Sean's and Gretyl's code numbers.

We had already gone over and over the plan. Twenty would cross the surface directly above the tunnels leading back to UMS. I was in this group.

There were aboveground university structures about five kilometers from our trench domes. The remaining students—two teams of four each, Charles among them, under Sean's command—would fan out to key points and wait for a signal from Gretyl, the leader of our team of twenty, that we had made it to the administration chambers.

If we met resistance and were not allowed to present demands to Connor personally, then Sean's teams would do their stuff. First, they would broadcast an illegal preemptive signal to the satcom at Marsynch, forcing on all bands the news that action in the name of contractual fulfillment was being taken by the voided students of

UMS. Contractual fulfillment meant a lot even under the Statist experiment; it was the foundation of every family's existence, a sacred kind of thing. Where Sean had gotten the expertise and equipment to send a preemptive signal, he would not say; I found his deepening mystery even more attractive.

Sean would personally take one team of four to the rail links at UMS junction. They would blow up a few custom-curved maglev rods; trains wouldn't be able to go to the UMS terminal until a repair car had manufactured new rods, which would take several hours. UMS would be isolated.

Simultaneously, the second team of four—to which Charles was assigned—would break seals and pump oxidant sizzle—a corrosive flopsand common in this region—into the university's net optic and satcom uplink facilities. That would break all the broad com between UMS and the rest of Mars. Private com would go through, but all broadband research and data links and library rentals would stop dead . . .

UMS might lose three or four million Triple dollars before the links could be repaired.

That of course would make them angry.

We waited in two lines spiraling from the center of the main trench dome. At the outside of the spiral lines, Sean and Gretyl stood silent, jaws clenched. Some students shook their red-sealed hands to get ready for the cold. Skinseal wasn't made to keep you cozy. It only protected against hypothermia and frostbite.

My own skinseal had come loose at the joints and sweat was pooling before being processed by the nanomer. I had to go to the bathroom, more out of nerves than necessity; my feet and legs had swollen, but only a little; I was not miserable but the petty discomforts distracted me from the focus I needed to keep from turning into a quivering heap.

"Listen," Sean said loudly, standing on a box to peer over our heads. "None of us knew what we'd be getting into when we started all this. We don't know what's going to happen in the next few hours. But we all share a common goal—freedom to pursue our education without political interference—freedom to stand clear of the sins of our parents and grandparents. That's what Mars is all about—

something new, a grand experiment. We'll be a part of that experiment now, or by God, we'll die trying."

I swallowed hard and looked for Charles, but he was too far away. I wondered if he still had his calm smile.

"May it not come to that," Gretyl said.

"Amen," said someone behind me.

Sean looked fully charged, face muscles sharply defined within a little oval of unsealed skin around his eyes, nose, and mouth. "Let's go," he said.

In groups of five, we removed our clothes, folding them neatly or just dropping them. The first to go entered the airlock, cycled through, and climbed the ladder. When my turn came, I crowded into the lock with five others, held my breath against the swirling red smear, and slipped on my mask and cycler. The old mask smelled doggy. Its edges adhered to the skinseal with the sound of a prim kiss. I heard the whine of pumps pulling back the air. The skinseal puffed as gas pressures equalized. Moving became more difficult.

My companions in the lock began climbing. My turn came and I took hold of the ladder rungs and poked through the hatch, above the rust-and-ochre tumble and smear. With a kick, I cleared the lip, clambered out onto the rocky surface of the plain, and stood under the early morning sky. The sun topped a ridge of hills lying east, surrounded by a dull pink glow. I blinked at the glare.

We'd have to hike over those hills to get to UMS. It had taken us half an hour simply to climb to the surface.

We stood a few meters east of the trench dome, waiting for Gretyl to join us. In just minutes, smear clung to us all; we'd have to destat for half an hour when all this was over.

Gretyl emerged from the hole. Her voice decoded in my right ear, slightly muffled. "Let's get together behind Sean's group," she said.

We could breathe, we could talk to each other. All was working well so far.

"We're off," Sean said, and his teams began to walk away from the trench. Some of them waved. I caught a glimpse of Charles from behind as his group marched in broken formation toward the hills, a little south of the track we would follow. I wondered why I was paying any attention to him at all. Skinseal hid little. He had a cute butt. Ever so slightly steatopygous.

I bit my lip to bring my thoughts together. *I'm a red rabbit,* I told myself. *I'm on the Up for the first time in two years, and there are no scout supervisors or trailmasters in charge, checking all our gear, making sure we get back to our mommies. Now focus, damn you!*

"Let's go," Gretyl said, and we began our trek.

It was a typical Martian morning, springtime balmy at minus-twenty Celsius. The wind had slowed to almost nothing. The air was clear for two hundred kilometers. Thousands of stars pricked through at zenith like tiny jewels. The horizon glimmered shell-pink.

All my thoughts aligned. Something magical about the moment. I felt I possessed a completely realistic awareness of our situation . . . and of our chances of surviving.

The surface of Mars was usually deadly cold. This close to the equator, however, the temps were relatively mild—seldom less than minus sixty. Normal storms could push winds up to four hundred kiphs, driving clouds of fine smear and flopsand high enough and wide enough to be seen from Earth. Rarely, a big surge of jet stream activity could send a high-pressure curl over several thousand kilometers, visible from orbit as a snaking dark line, and that could raise clouds that would quickly cover most of Mars. But the air on high Sinai Planum, at five millibars, was too thin to worry about most of the time. The usual winds were gentle puffs, barely felt.

My booted feet pounded over the crusted sand and tumble. Martian soil gets a thin crust after a few months of lying undisturbed; the grains fall into a kind of mechanical cement that feels a lot like hoarfrost. I could dimly hear the others crunching, sound traveling through the negligible atmosphere making them seem dozens of meters away.

"Let's not get too scattered," Gretyl said.

I passed an old glacier-rounded boulder bigger than the main trench dome. Ancient ice flows had sculpted the crustal basalt into a rounded gnome with its arms splayed across the ground, flat head resting on its arms in sleep . . . pretended sleep.

Somehow, red rabbits never became superstitious about the Up.

It was too orange and red and brown, too obviously dead, to appeal to our morbid instincts.

"If they're smart and somebody's anticipating us, there may be pickets out this far to keep track of the periphery of the university," Sean said over the radio.

"Or if somebody's tattled," Gretyl added. I was starting to like Gretyl. Despite having an unpleasant voice and an unaltered, shrew-like face, Gretyl seemed to have a balanced perspective. I wondered why she had kept that face. Maybe it was a family face, something to be proud of where she came from, like English royalty's unaltered features, mandated by law. The long nose of King Henry of England.

Damn.

Focus gone.

I decided it didn't matter. Maybe focusing on keeping a focus was a bad thing.

The Sun hung above the ridge now, torch-white with the merest pink tinge. Around it whirled the thinnest of opal hazes, high silicate and ice clouds laced against the brightening orange of day. The rock shadows started to fill in, making each step a little easier. Sometimes wind hollows hid behind boulders, waiting for unwary feet.

Gretyl's group had spread out. I walked near the front, a few steps to her right.

"Picket," said Garlin Smith on my right, raising his arm. He had been my classmate in mass psych, quiet and tall, what ignorant Earth folks thought a Martian should look like.

We all followed Garlin's pointing finger to the east and saw a lone figure standing on a rise about two hundred meters away. It carried a rifle.

"Armed," Gretyl said under her breath. "I don't believe it."

The figure wore a full pressure suit—a professional job, the type worn by areologists, farm inspectors, Statist police. It reached up to tap its helmet. It hadn't seen us yet, apparently, but it was picking up the jumbled buzz of our coded signals.

"Keep going," Gretyl said. "We haven't come this far to be scared off by a single picket."

"If it *is* a picket," Sean commented, listening to our chat. "Don't assume anything."

"It has to be a picket," Gretyl said.

"All right," Sean said with measured restraint.

The figure caught sight of us about four minutes after we first noticed it. We were separated by a hundred meters. It looked like a normal male physique from that distance.

My breath quickened. I tried to slow it.

"Report," Sean demanded.

"Armed male in full pressure suit. He sees us. Not reacting yet," Gretyl said.

We didn't deviate from our path. We would pass within fifty meters of the picket.

The helmeted head turned, watching us. He held up a hand. "Hey, what is this?" a masculine voice asked. "What in hell are you doing up here? Do you folks have ID?"

"We're from UMS," Gretyl said. We didn't slow our pace.

"What are you doing up here?" the picket repeated.

"Surveying, what's it look like?" Gretyl responded. We carried no instruments. "What are *you* doing up here?"

"Don't bunny with me," he said. "You know there's been trouble. Just tell me what department you're from and . . . have you been using code?"

"No," Gretyl said.

We had closed another twenty yards. He started to hike down the rise to inspect us.

"What in hell are you wearing?"

"Red suits," Gretyl answered.

"Shit, it's *skinseal*. It's against the law to wear that stuff except in emergencies. How many of you are there?"

"Forty-five," Gretyl lied.

"I've been told to keep intruders off university property," he said. "I'll need to see IDs. You should have UMS passes to even be up here."

"Is that a gun?" Gretyl asked, faking a lilt of surprise.

"Hey, get over here, all of you."

"Why do you need a *gun?*"

"Unauthorized intruders. Stop now."

"We're from the Areology Department, and we've only got a few hours up here . . . Didn't you get a waiver from Professor Sunder?"

"No, dammit, *stop right now.*"

"Listen, friend, who do you answer to?"

"UMS is secure property. You'd better give me your student ID numbers now."

"Fap off," Gretyl said.

The picket raised his rifle, a long-barreled, slender automatic fléchette. My anger and fear were almost indistinguishable. Dauble and Connor must have lost their minds. No student on Mars had ever been shot by police, not in fifty-three years of settlement. Hadn't they ever heard of Tiananmen or Kent State?

"Use it," Gretyl said. "You'll be all over the Triple for shooting areology students on a field trip. Great for your career. Really spin you in with our families, too. What kind of work you looking for, rabbit?"

Our receivers jabbered with the picket's own coded outgoing message. More jabber returned.

The man lowered his rifle and followed us. "Are you armed?" he asked.

"Where would students get guns?" Gretyl asked. "Who in hell is giving you orders to scare us?"

"Listen, this is serious. I need your IDs now."

"We've got his code," Sean said. "He's been told to block you however he can."

"Great," Gretyl said.

"Who are you talking to? Stop using code," the picket demanded.

"Maybe they're not clueing you, rabbit," Gretyl taunted.

Gretyl's bravado, her talent for delay and confusion, astonished me. Perhaps she and Sean and a few of the others had been training for this. I wished I knew more about *revolution*.

The word came to me like a small blow on my back. This was a kind of *revolution*. "Jesus," I said with my transmitter off.

"What's he doing?" Sean asked.

"He's following us," Gretyl said. "He doesn't seem to want to shoot."

"Not with *fléchettes*, sure enough," Sean said. "What a banner that would be!" I filled in the details involuntarily: *STUDENTS RIPPED BY BURROWING DARTS.*

More code whined in our ears like angry insects.

We marched over another rise, the guard following close behind.

and saw the low poke-ups of UMS. The UMS warrens extended to the northeast for perhaps a kilometer, half levels above, ten levels deep. The administration chambers were closest to the surface entrance and the nearby train depot. Train guides hovered on slender poles, arcing gently over another rise to link with the station.

Sean's teams were probably there now.

More guards emerged from the UMS buildings, armed and in full pressure suits.

"All right," came a gruff female voice. "State your business. Then get the hell out of here or you'll be arrested."

Gretyl stepped forward, a scrawny little red devil with a black masked head. "We want an audience with Chancellor Connor. We are students who have been illegally voided and whose contracts have been flagrantly broken. We demand—"

"Who in hell do you think you are? A bunch of fapping rodents?" The women's voice scared me. She sounded outraged, on the edge of something drastic. I couldn't tell which of the suited figures she was, or if she was outside at all. "You've crossed regional property. Goddamned Gobacks should know what that means."

"I'm not going to argue," Gretyl said. "We demand to speak with—"

"You're *talking* to her, you ignorant shithead! I'm right here." The foremost figure raised an arm and shook a gloved fist. "And I'm in no mood to negotiate with trespassers and Gobacks."

"We're here to deliver a petition." Gretyl removed a metal cylinder from her belt and extended it. One of the guards started forward, but Connor grabbed his elbow and shook it once, firmly. He backed away and folded his arms.

"Politics of confrontation," Connor said, voice harsh as old razors. "Agitprop and civil disobedience. You'd think you were on Earth. Politics doesn't work that way here. I have a mandate to protect this university and keep order."

"You refuse to meet with us and discuss our demands?"

"I'm meeting with you now. Nobody demands anything of lawful authority except through legal channels. Who's behind you?"

I looked over my shoulder, misunderstanding.

"There's no conspiracy," Gretyl said.

"Lies, my dear. Genuine lies."

"Under Martian contract law, we have the right to meet with you and discuss why we have been voided and our contracts broken."

"State law superseded BM law last month."

"Actually, it doesn't. If you want to check with your lawyers—" Gretyl began. I cringed. We were bickering and time was running out.

"You have one minute to turn around and go back to where you came from, or we'll arrest you," Connor said. "Let the legals sort it out. Do your families know where you are? How about your advocates? Do *they* know and approve?"

Gretyl's words bristled. "I can't believe you are being so stubborn. I'm asking for the last time—"

"Right. Arrest them, my authority, statute two-five-one, Syria-Sinai district books."

Some of the students began to talk, asking worried questions. "Quiet!" Gretyl shouted. She turned to Connor. "Is this your last answer?"

"You poor dumb rodents," Connor said. She swiveled to enter the open lock door. Connor behaved even more rudely than she had been portrayed to us in the briefings, supremely confident, intractable, and ready to provoke an incident. Guards moved forward. I turned and saw three guards behind us, also closing. We had to submit.

Gretyl stepped away from the first guard. Another flanked her on the right, coming between us, and she stepped back. There were twenty of us and ten guards.

"Let them take you," Gretyl said. "Let them arrest you." Then why was she resisting?

A guard took my arm and applied sticky rope to my skinsealed wrist. "You're lucky we're bringing you in," he said, grinning. "You wouldn't last another hour out here."

Two of the guards devoted themselves exclusively to Gretyl. They advanced with hands and sticky ropes held out. She backed away, held up her arm as if waving to them, and touched her mask.

Time got stiff.

Gretyl turned to look at the rest of us. Her eyes looked scared. My heart sank. *Don't do anything just to impress Sean,* I wanted to shout to her.

"Tell them what you saw here," Gretyl said. *"Freedom conquers!"*

Her fingers plucked at and then slipped beneath the seam of the mask. A guard grabbed at her arm but he wasn't quick enough.

Gretyl ripped away the mask and sprang to one side, sending it flying with a wide toss. Her long-nosed face flashed pale and narrow against the pink sky. She squeezed her eyes shut and clamped her mouth instinctively. Her arms reached out, fingers extended, as if she were a tightrope walker and might lose her balance.

Simultaneously, I heard small thumps and felt the ground vibrate.

Connor hadn't had time to enter the poke-up airlock. "Get her inside! Get her inside!" she screeched, pushing through her associates.

The guards stood still as statues for what seemed like minutes, then reached for Gretyl and dragged her as fast as they could to the airlock. She struggled in their arms. I saw her face pinking, blood vessels near the surface rupturing as the plasma boiled. Vacuum rose.

Gretyl opened her eyes and reached up with one hand to grab at her chin. She pulled her own jaw open. The air in her lungs rushed out, moisture freezing in a cloud in the still air.

"They've blown track," someone shouted.

"Get her INSIDE!"

Gretyl looked at the sky through rime-clouded eyes.

The guard in front of me jerked the sticky rope forward and I fell into the dirt. For an instant it seemed he might kick me. I looked up and saw narrow grim eyes behind the helmet visor, mouth open, face slack. He stopped and blinked, waiting for orders.

I twisted my head around to see how my companions were being treated. Several lay in the dirt. The guards systematically pushed us down and planted boots on our backs. When all nineteen lay flat, the guards stood back. The door to the lock opened again and someone stepped out, not Connor.

"They're under arrest," a man's voice said over the radio. "Get them inside. Strip that stuff off and put them in a dorm. Delouse them."

There have never been lice on Mars.

They separated us quickly. Three guards pulled five of us away from the airlock and marched us through chilly tunnels to the old dorms, seldom used now. The new dorms had been equipped with more modern conveniences, but these were maintained for an emergency or future overload of students.

"Can you get this off by yourself?" the tallest of the three asked, gesturing at our skinseal. She removed her helmet beneath the dimmed lights of the hall, lips downturned, eyes miserable.

"What did he mean, delouse?" another guard asked, a young, muscular male with West Indian features and accent.

The guards were all fresh Martians. That made sense. The new United Mars state would be their sponsor, their BM, and family.

"You can't just hold us here," I said. "What happened to Gretyl?" My four companions turned on the guards, pointing fingers and shouting. We all demanded our rights—communication, freedom, advocates.

It became an open rebellion until the third guard pulled a fléchette from his pack. He was the shortest, a slim man with plain, short-cut brown hair and perfect, saintly features. His eyes narrowed, very cold. I thought, *Here's a Statist sympathizer.* The others were merely hired hands.

"Blow it down, right now," he demanded.

"You injured Gretyl!" I shouted. "We need to know what happened to her!"

"Sabotage is treason. We could shoot you in self-defense."

He raised the pistol. All of us backed away, including the two other guards.

"That wouldn't be smart," I said.

"Not for you." The slim fellow gave us a cold thin smile and pushed us down the hall.

We entered a stripped-down double room, immediately sprawling on the bare cot and chairs, another small gesture of useless defiance.

"You're going to be here for a while, so get comfortable."

I didn't like him pushing his pistol and didn't want to provoke him any further. We peeled off our skinseal—it was a blessed relief to be free of it, actually. The West Indian tossed the shreds into dust bags. Enough smear floated loose to make us sneeze.

As if meeting for the first time, the five of us nodded and made introductions where necessary. We knew each other only slightly; one had been a classmate of mine, Felicia Overgard, about a year younger

nd two steps behind. I did not know Oliver Peskin well, a step
igher and an agro major, and I had only met Tom Callin and Chao
Ming Jung in the trench dome.

The slim fellow averted his eyes. Bizarre, waving a gun at us but
shamed of our bare flesh. He thrust the gun at the vapor sacks in
he washroom. "I don't know if you have lice, but you smell pretty
ank."

The vapor bags hadn't been refilled or filtered in some time and
ve didn't smell much better after the showers. Water was inadequate
o get rid of smear, and we carried itchy patches of red and orange
ll over. We'd have welts by tomorrow.

Three hours passed and we learned nothing. The guards stayed
1 their suits to avoid the dust. They had removed any identifiers and
would not tell us their names. The sympathizer grew more and more
rim as the hours crawled, and then ramped up to nervous, fidgeting
vith his gun. He whistled and pantomimed breaking it down and
eassembling it. Finally, his slate chimed and he answered.

After a couple of brief acknowledgements, he sent the female
uard out of the room. I wondered what they would do next, why
hey didn't want the woman there.

Surely they weren't *that* stupid.

Conversation with my companions became thin and quiet. Fear
ad worn off—we no longer thought we were going to be shot—but
he numbing sense of isolation that replaced it was no better. We
ettled into shivering silence.

The rooms were kept at minimum heat and we still didn't have
ny clothes. The three men suffered worse than Felicia and I.

"It's cold in here," I said to the sympathizer. He agreed but did
othing.

"It's cold enough to make us sick," said Oliver.

"All right," said the sympathizer.

"We should find them some clothes," said the West Indian.

"No," said the sympathizer.

"Why not?" Chao asked. Felicia had given up covering herself
vith her hands.

"You caused a hell of a lot of trouble. Why make it any easier
n you?"

"They're human, man," the West Indian said. He was not very

old, twelve or thirteen, and he had to be a recent immigrant. His West Indies accent was still obvious.

The sympathizer squinted and shook his head dubiously.

We've won, I thought. *With fools like this, the Statists don't have a chance.* I couldn't quite convince myself, however.

We spent ten hours in that dorm room, cold and naked, skin itching furiously.

I fell asleep and dreamed of trees too tall to fit into any dome, rooted unprotected in the red dirt of Mars: redwoods in red flopsand, lofting a hundred meters, tended by naked children. I had had the dream before and it left me for a moment with an intense feeling of well being. Then I remembered I was a prisoner.

The West Indian prodded my shoulder. I rolled on the thin carpeted floor. He averted his eyes from my nakedness and drew his lips tightly together. "I want you to know I am not all in this," he said. "My heart, I mean. I am truly a Martian, and this is my first work here, you know?"

I looked around. The sympathizer was out of the room. "Get us some clothes," I said.

"You blew up the train lines and these people, they are very angry. I just tell you, don't blame me when the shit sprays. People go up and down the halls—the tunnels. I look out, there is so much going on. They are afraid, I think."

What did they have to be afraid of? Had the LitVids grabbed Gretyl's injury or death and put our cause on the sly spin?

"Can you send a message to my parents?"

"The fellow Rick has gone," the West Indian said, shaking his head. "He meets with others, and he leaves me here."

"What happened to Gretyl?"

He shook his head again. "I hear nothing about her. What I saw it made me sick. Everybody is so crazy. Why did she do it?"

"To make a point," I said.

"Not worth losing your life," the West Indian said, frowning deeply. "This is small history, petty people. On Earth—"

My temper flared. "Look, we've only been here a hundred Earth years, and our history is small stuff by Earth standards, but you're Martian now, remember? This is corruption and dirty politics—and if you ask me, it's directly connected with Earth, and the hell with all of you!"

You really sound committed, I thought. Abuse could do wonders.

I awakened the others with my outburst. Felicia sat up. "He isn't armed," she observed. Oliver and Chao stood warily and brushed dust off their backsides, muscles tensed as if they were giving thought to jumping the man.

The West Indian looked, if possible, even more abjectly miserable. "Do not try something," he said, standing his ground with arms out, shaking his head.

The door opened and the sympathizer returned. He and the West Indian exchanged glances and the West Indian tilted and shook his head, saying, "Oh, *man.*" Behind the sympathizer came a fellow with short black hair. He wore a tight-fitting, expensive, and fashionable green longsuit.

"We're kept here against our will—" Oliver complained immediately.

"Under arrest," the man in the fashionable green suit said jovially.

"For more than a day, and we demand to be released," Oliver finished, folding his arms. The man in the suit smiled at this literally naked presumption.

"I'm Achmed Crown Niger," he said. His voice was high Mars, imitative of the flat English of Earth, an accent rarely heard in the regional BMs. I presumed he would be from Lal Qila or some other independent station, perhaps a Muslim. "I represent the state interests in the university. I'm going from room to room getting names. I'll need your family names, BM connections, and the names of people you'll want to talk to in the next hour."

"What happened to Gretyl?" I asked.

Achmed Crown Niger raised his eyebrows. "She's alive. She has acute facial rose and her eyes and lungs need to be rebuilt. But we have other things to talk about. Under district book laws, you are all charged with criminal trespass and sabotage—"

"What happened to the others?" I pursued.

He ignored me. "That's serious stuff. You're going to need advocates." He turned to the sympathizer and barked, "Damn it, get these people something to wear." He looked back at us and his ingratiating smile returned. "It's tough being legal in front of naked people."

Thirty armed men and women, as many LitVid agents, Chancellor Connor, and Governor Dauble herself stood in the dining hall, Connor and Dauble and their entourage well away from the offending students. We clustered in bathrobes near the serving gates, the twenty-six who had gone out with Sean and Gretyl, criminals caught in the act of sabotage. Those left behind in the trench domes had been collected as well. Dauble and Connor were about to celebrate their victory on LitVid across the Triple.

Medias and Pressians, my father called them: the hordes of LitVid reporters that seemed to rise out of the ground at the merest hint of a stink. On Mars reporters were a hardy breed; they learned early to get around the tight lips of BM families. Ten of the quickest and hardiest—several familiar to me—stood with arbeiter attendants near the Statist cluster, ear loops recording all they saw, images edited hot for transmission to the satcoms.

Diane stood in a group across the hall. She waved to me surreptitiously. I did not see Sean. Charles was five or six meters from me in our pack and did not appear injured. He saw me and nodded. Some from his group had sustained bruises and even broken bones. Blue boneknits graced three.

We said nothing, stood meek and pitiful. This was our time to be victims of the oppressive state.

Dauble came forward flanked by two advisers. A louder curled on her shoulder like a thin snake. "Folks, this has gone much too far. Chancellor Connor has been courteous enough to supply the families of these students—"

"Banned students!" Oliver Peskin shouted next to me. Others took up the cry, and another chorus followed on with, "Contract rights! Obligations!"

Dauble listened, face fixed in gentle disapproval. The cries died down.

"To supply all of their families with information on their whereabouts, and their status as arrested saboteurs," she finished.

"Where's Gretyl?" I shouted, hardly aware I'd opened my mouth.

"Where's Sean?" someone else called. "Where's Gretyl?"

"Family advocates are flying in now. The train service has been cut, thanks to these students, and our ability to uplink on broadband has been severely curtailed. These acts of sabotage—"

"Illegal voiding!" another student shouted.

"Constitute high felonies under the district book and United Martian codes—"

"Where's *SEAN?* Where's *GRETYL?*" Oliver shouted, hair awry, flinging up his hand, fingers splayed.

Guards moved in, shoving through us none too gently, and grabbed him. Connor stepped forward and raised her arm. Achmed Crown Niger ordered the guards to release him. Oliver shrugged their arms away and smiled back at us triumphantly.

Dauble seemed unaffected by the confusion. "These acts will be fully prosecuted."

"Where's *SEAN?* Where's *GRETYL?*" several students yelled again.

"Sean's *dead!* Gretyl's *dead!*" shouted one high, shrill voice. The effect was electric.

"Who says? Who knows?" others called. The students cried out and milled like sheep.

"Nobody has been killed," Dauble said, her composure suddenly less solid.

"Bring *SEAN!*"

Dauble conferred with her advisers, then turned back to us. "Sean Dickinson is in the university infirmary with self-inflicted wounds. Everything possible is being done to help him. Gretyl Laughton is in the infirmary as well, with injuries from self-exposure."

The reporters hadn't heard this yet; their interest was immediate, and all focused on Dauble.

"How were the students injured?" asked one reporter, her pickup pointed at Dauble.

"There have been several small injuries—"

"Inflicted by the guards?"

"No," Connor said.

"Is it true the guards have been armed all along? Even before the sabotage?" another reporter asked.

"We anticipated trouble from the beginning," Dauble said. "These students have proven us correct."

"But the guards aren't authorized police or regulars—how do you justify that under district charter?"

"Justify all of it!" Diane shouted.

"I don't understand your attitude," Dauble said to us after a few moments of careful consideration in the full gaze of hot LitVid. "You sabotage life-support equipment—"

"That's a lie!" a student shouted.

"Disrupt the lawful conduct of this university, and now you resort to attempted suicide. What kind of Martians are you? Do your parents approve of this treachery?"

Dauble screwed her face into an expression between parental exasperation and deep concern. "What in the hell is wrong with you? Who raised you—*thugs?*"

The meeting came to an abrupt end. Dauble and her entourage departed, followed by the reporters. When several reporters tried to talk to us, they were unceremoniously ejected from the dining hall.

How very, very stupid, I thought.

I felt a bit faint from hunger; we hadn't eaten in twenty hours. A few university staff, clearly uncomfortable, served us bowls of quick paste from trays. The nutritional nano was tasteless but still seemed heaven-sent. We had been provided with sleeping pads and blankets and were told winds were up and dust was blowing, grounding shuttles. No advocates or parents had yet come in to see us.

While being fed, we had been divided into groups of six, each assigned two guards. The guards actively discouraged talk between the groups, moving us farther and farther apart until we spread out through the hall. Oliver, considered a loudmouth activist, was prodded into a selected group of other loudmouths that included Diane. Charles sat with five others across the hall, about twenty meters away.

When we still tried to talk, the dining-hall sound system blared out loud pioneer music, old-fashioned, soul-stirring crap I had enjoyed as a kid, but found bitterly inappropriate now.

When I was free to speak with the Medias and Pressians, I thought, what a story I'd tell . . . I had seen and done things in the past few days that my entire life had not prepared me for, and I had felt emotions unknown to me: righteous anger, political confraternity and solidarity, deep fear.

I worried for Sean. All our information came through Achmed Crown Niger, who visited every few hours to hand out scraps of generally useless news. I took a real dislike to him: professional, collected, he was every gram the guvvie man. I focused on his pale, fine-featured face for a time, blaming him for all our troubles. He must have advised the chancellor and governor . . . *He* must have outlined their strategy, maybe even planned the banning and voiding of students . . .

I thought dreamily about a possible life with Sean, if he paid any attention to me after his recovery.

Nothing to do. Nothing to think. The lights in the dining hall went out. The music stopped.

I slept on the floor, nestled like a puppy against Felicia's back.

Someone touched my shoulder. I opened my eyes from a light doze. Charles leaned over me, his face thinner and older, but his smile the same: too calm, somehow, like a young Buddha. His cheeks had pinked as if smirched with poorly applied makeup: a mild case of vacuum rose. Most of the students around us still slept.

"Are you okay?" he asked.

I sat up and looked around. The lights were still dim, but it was obvious the guards had gone.

"Tired," I said. I swallowed hard. My throat was parched and I could feel the oxidant welts itching fiercely. "Where's our food and water?"

"I don't think we're going to get any unless we go for it ourselves."

I stood and stretched my arms. "Are you all right?" I asked, squinting at him, reaching up to his cheeks.

"My mask leaked. I'm fine. My eyes are okay. You look strong," Charles said.

"I feel shitty," I said. "Where are the guards?"

"Probably trying to get out of here any way they can."

"Why?"

He lifted his hands. "I don't know. They backed out about an hour ago."

Oliver Peskin and Diane walked over and we squatted on the floor in whispered confab. Felicia stirred and poked Chao in the ribs.

"What happened to Sean?" Diane asked Charles.

"He was planting a charge when it went off," Charles said. "They say he set it off on purpose."

"He wouldn't do that," Felicia said, face screwed up in disgust.

"Gretyl pulled her mask off," I said.

"Insane," Charles said.

"She had her reasons," Chao said.

"Anyway," Diane went on. "We need leaders."

"We're not going to be here much longer," Oliver said.

"Oliver's right. We're not guarded. Something's changed," Charles said.

"We have to stick together," Diane insisted.

"If something's changed, it has to have changed in *our* favor," Oliver said. "It couldn't get any worse."

"We still need leaders," I said. "We should wake people up now and see what the group thinks."

"What if we've won?" Felicia asked. "What do we do?"

"Find out how much we've won, and why," Charles said.

We explored the tunnels around the dining hall, venturing back to the old dorms, all quite empty now. We encountered a few arbeiters about their maintenance business, but no humans. After an hour, we began to worry—the situation was spooky.

Fanning out, we began a systematic exploration of the upper levels of the entire university, reporting to each other on local links. Charles volunteered to join me. We took the north tunnels, closest to emergency external shafts and farthest from the administration chambers. The tunnels were dark but warm; the air smelled stale, but it was breathable. Our feet made hollow scuffing echoes in the deserted halls. The university seemed to be in an emergency power-down.

Charles walked a step ahead. I watched him closely, wondering why he wanted to be so friendly when I had given him so little encouragement.

We didn't say much, simply stating the obvious, signaling to each other with whistles after splitting to try separate tunnels, nodding cordially when we rejoined and moved on. Gradually we moved south again, expecting to meet up with other students.

We explored a dark corridor connecting the old dorm branch with UMS's newer tunnels. A bright light flashed ahead. We stood our ground. A woman in an ill-fitting pressure suit shined her light directly into our faces.

"University staff?" she asked.

"Hell, no. Who are you?" Charles asked.

"I'm an advocate," the woman said. "Pardon the stolen suit. I flew in through the storm about half an hour ago. Landed during a dust lull and found a few of these abandoned near the locks. We were told there was no air in here."

"Who told you that?"

"The last man out, and he went in a hurry, too. Are you all right?"

"I'm fine," I said. "Where is everybody?"

The advocate lifted her face plate and sniffed noisily. "Sorry. My nose hates flopsand. The university was evacuated seven hours ago. Bomb threat. They said a bunch of Gobacks had dumped air and planted charges in the administration chambers. Everybody left in ground vehicles. They took them overland by tractor to an intact train line."

"You're brave to come this far," Charles said. "You don't think there *is* a bomb, do you?"

The woman removed her helmet and smiled wolfishly. "Probably not. They didn't tell us anybody was here. They must not like you. How many are here?"

"Ninety."

"They voided the reporters before they evacuated. I saw you on LitVid. Press conference didn't go well. So where are the rest of you?"

We led her to the dining hall. All the far-flung explorers were called in.

The advocate stood in the middle of the assembly, asking and answering questions. "I presume I'm the first advocate to get here. First off, my name is Maria Sanchez Ochoa. I'm an independent employed by Grigio BM from Tharsis."

Felicia stepped forward. "That's my family," she said. Two others came forward as well.

"Good to see you," Maria Sanchez Ochoa said. "The family's worried. I'd like to get your names and report that you're all safe."

"What's happened?" Diane asked. "I'm very confused." Others joined in.

"What happened to Sean and Gretyl?" I asked, interrupting the babble.

"University security handed them over to Sinai district police early yesterday morning. Both were injured, but I don't know to what extent. The university claimed they were injured by their own hands."

"They're alive?" I continued.

"I presume so. They're at Time's River Canyon Hospital." She started recording names, lifting her slate and letting each speak and be recognized in turn.

I looked to my right and saw Charles standing beside me. He smiled, and I returned his smile and put a hand on his shoulder.

"Will someone take this outside and shoot it up to a satcom? None of the cables or repeaters are working, thanks to you folks." Ochoa gave her slate to a student, who left the dining area to get to the glass roof of the administration upper levels.

"Now, some background, since I doubt you've heard much news recently."

"Nothing useful," Oliver said.

"Right. I hate to tell you this, but you didn't do a thing for your cause by acting like a bunch of Parisian Communards. The Statist government planted its own bombs months ago, political and legal, far away from UMS, and they exploded just two days ago. We have a bad situation here, folks, and that explains some of the delay in getting to you. The constitutional accord is off. The Statists have resigned, and the old BM Charter government has been called back into session."

The battle was over. But we were small potatoes.

Ochoa concluded by saying, "You folks have wrecked university property, you've violated laws in every Martian book I can think of, and you've put yourselves in a great deal of danger. What has it gotten you?

"Fortunately, it probably won't get you any time in jail. I've heard that former Statist politicos are shipping out by dozens—and that probably includes Connor and Dauble. Nobody in their right mind is going to charge you under Statist law."

"What did they do?" Charles asked.

"Nobody's sure about *all* that they've done, but it looks like the government invited Earth participation in Mars politics, sought kick-backs from Belter BMs to let them mine Hellas—"

Gasps from the assembly. We had thought *we* were radical.

"And planned to nationalize all BM holdings by year's end."

We met these pronouncements with stunned silence.

We stayed in the old dorms while security crews from Gorrie Mars BM checked out the entire university grounds. New rails were man-ufactured, trains came in, and most of us went home. I stayed, as did Oliver, Felicia, and Charles. I was beginning to think that Charles wanted to be near me.

I met my family in the station two days after our release, Father and Mother and my older brother, Stan. My parents looked pale and shaken by both fear and anger. My father told me, in no uncertain terms, that I had violated his most sacred principles in joining the radicals. I tried to explain my reasons, but didn't get through to him, and no wonder: they weren't entirely clear to me.

Stan, perpetually amused by the attitudes and actions of his younger sister, simply stood back with a calm smile. That smile re-minded me of Charles.

Charles, Oliver, Felicia, and I bought our tickets at the autobox and walked across the UMS depot platform. We all felt more than a little like outlaws, or at least pariahs.

It was late morning and a few dozen interim university admin-istrators had come in on the same train we would be taking out. Dressed in formal grays and browns, they stood under the glass sky-lights shuffling their feet, clutching their small bags, and waiting for their security escort, glancing at us suspiciously.

Rail staff didn't *know* we were part of the group responsible for breaking the UMS line, but they suspected. All credit to the railway that it honored charter and did not refuse service.

The four of us sat in the rearmost car, fastening ourselves into the narrow seats. The rest of the train was empty.

In 2171, five hundred thousand kilometers of maglev train tracks spread over Mars, thousands more being added by arbeiters each year. The trains were the best way to travel: sitting in comfort and silence as the silver millipedes flew centimeters above their thick black rails, rhythmically boosting every three or four hundred meters and reaching speeds of several hundred kiphs. I loved watching vast stretches of boulder-strewn flatlands rush by, seeing fans of dust topped by thin curling puffs as static blowers in the train's nose cleared the tracks ahead.

I did not much enjoy the train ride to Time's River Canyon Hospital, however.

We didn't have much to say. We had been elected by the scattered remnants of the protest group to visit Sean and Gretyl.

We accelerated out of the UMS station just before noon, pressed into our seats, absorbing the soothing rumble of the carriage. Within a few minutes, we were up to three hundred kiphs, and the great plain below our ports became an ocher blur. In a window seat, I stared at the land and asked myself where I really was, and who.

Charles had taken the seat beside me but, mercifully, said little. Since my father's stern lecture, I had felt empty or worse. The days of having nothing to do but sign releases and talk to temp security had worn me down to a negative.

Oliver tried to break the gloom by suggesting we play a word game. Felicia shook her head. Charles glanced at me, read my lack of interest, and said, "Maybe later." Oliver shrugged and held up his slate to spec the latest LitVid.

I dozed off for a few minutes. Charles pressed my shoulder gently. We were slowing. "You keep waking me up," I said.

"You keep napping off in the boring parts," he said.

"You are so fapping *pleasant*, you know?" I said.

"Sorry." His face fell.

"And why are you . . ." I was about to say *following me* but I could hardly support that accusation with much evidence. The train had slowed and was now sliding into Time's River Depot. Outside, the sky was deep brown, black at zenith. The Milky Way dropped between high canyon walls as if seeking to fill the ancient flood channel.

"I think you're interesting," Charles said, unharnessing and stepping into the aisle.

I shook my head and led the way to the forward lock. "We're stressed," I murmured.

"It's okay," Charles said.

Felicia looked at us with a bemused smile.

In the hospital waiting room, an earnest young public defender thrust a slateful of release forms at us. "Which government are you sending these to?" Oliver asked. The man's uniform had conspicuous outlines of thread where patches had been removed.

"Whoever," he answered. "You're from UMS, right? Friends and colleagues of the patients?"

"Fellow students," Felicia said.

"Right. Now listen. I have to say this, in case one of you is going to shoot off to a LitVid. 'The Time's River District neither condones nor condemns the actions taken by these patients. We follow historical Martian charter and treat any and all patients, regardless of legal circumstance or political belief. Any statements they make do not represent—' "

"Jesus," Felicia said.

" '—the policy or attitudes of this hospital, nor the policy of Time's River District.' End of sermon." The public defender stepped back and waved us through.

I was shocked by what we saw when we entered Sean's room. He had been tilted into a corner at forty-five degrees, wrapped in white surgical nano, and tied to a steel recovery board. Monitors guided his reconstruction through fluid and optic fibers. Only now did we realize how badly he had been injured.

As we entered his room, he turned his head and stared at us impassively through distant green-gray eyes. We made our awkward openings, and he responded with a casual, "How's the outside world?"

"In an uproar," Oliver said. Sean glanced at me as if I were only there in part, not a fully developed human being, but a ghost of mild interest. I specced the moments of passionate speech when he had riveted the crowded students and compared it to this lackluster shell and was immensely saddened.

"Good," Sean said, measuring the word with silent lips before repeating it aloud. He looked at a projected paleoscape of Mars on the wall opposite: soaring aqueduct bridges, long gleaming pipes suspended from treelike pedestals and fruited with clusters of green globes, some thirty or forty meters across . . . A convincing mural of our world before the planet sucked in its water, shed its atmosphere, and withered.

"The Council's taken over everything again," I said. "The syndics of all the BMs are meeting to patch things together."

Sean did not react.

"Nobody's told us how you were hurt," Felicia said. We looked at her, astonished at this untruth. Ochoa had checked into all the security reports, including those filed by university guards, and pieced together the story.

"The charges," Sean said, hesitating not a moment, and I thought, *Whatever Felicia is up to, he'll tell the truth . . . and why expect him not to?*

"The charges went off prematurely, before I had a chance to get out of the way. I set the charges alone. Of course."

"Of course," Oliver said.

Charles stayed in the rear, hands folded before him like a small boy at a funeral.

"Blew me out of my skinseal. I kept my helmet on, oddly enough. Exposed my guts. Everything boiled. I remember quite a lot, strangely. Watching my blood boil. Somebody had the presence of mind to throw a patch over me. It wrapped me up and slowed me down and they pulled me into the infirmary about an hour later. I don't remember much after that."

"Jesus," Felicia said, in exactly the same tone she had used for the public defender in the waiting room.

"We did it to them, didn't we? Got the ball rolling," Sean said.

"Actually—" Oliver began, but Felicia, with a tender expression, broke in.

"We did it," she said. Oliver raised his eyebrows.

"I'm going to be okay. About half of me will need replacing. I don't know who's paying for it. My family, I suppose. I've been thinking."

"Yeah?" Felicia said.

"I know what set the charge off," Sean said. "Somebody broke the timer before I planted it. I'd like one or all of you to find out who."

Nobody spoke for a moment. "You think somebody did it deliberately?" I asked.

Sean nodded. "We checked the equipment a hundred times and everything worked."

"Who would have done something like that?" Oliver asked, horrified.

"Somebody," Sean said. "Keep the students together. This isn't over yet." He turned to face me, suddenly focusing. "Take a message to Gretyl. Tell her she was a goddamned fool and I love her madly." He bit into the words *goddamned fool* as if they were a savory cake that gave him great satisfaction. I had never seen such a join of pain and bitter pride.

I nodded.

"Tell her she and I will take the reins again and guide this mess home *right*. Tell her just that."

"Guide the mess home *right*," I repeated, still under his spell.

"We have a larger purpose," Sean said. "We have to break this planet out of its goddamned business-as-usual, corrupt, bow-down-to-the-Triple, struggle-along mentality. We can do that. We can make our own party. It's a beginning." His eyes fixed on each of us in turn, as if to brand us. Felicia held out her splayed fingers and Sean lifted his free arm to awkwardly press his hand against hers. Oliver did the same. Charles stood back; too much for him. I was about to raise my hand and match Sean's. But Sean saw my hesitation, my change of expression when Charles stepped back, and he dropped his hand before I could decide.

"Heart and mind, heart and mind," Sean said softly. "You are . . . Casseia, right? Casseia Majumdar?"

"Yes."

"How did your family fare in all this?"

"I don't know," I said.

"They're fixed to prosper. The Gobacks will do well in the next government. It was funny, Connor thinking we were Gobacks. Are you a Goback, Casseia?"

I shook my head, throat tight. His tone was so stiff and distant, so *reproving*.

"Show it to me, Casseia. Heart and mind."

"I don't think you have any right to question my loyalty because of my family," I said.

Sean's gaze went cold. "If you're not dedicated, you could turn on us . . . just like whoever broke the timer."

"Gretyl handled the charge," Charles said. "Nobody else touched it. Certainly not Casseia."

"We all *slept,* didn't we?" Sean said. "But it's irrelevant, really. That part's over."

He closed his eyes and licked his lips. A cup came up from the wall-mount arbeiter and a stream of liquid poured into his mouth. He sucked it up with the expertise of days in the hospital.

"What do you mean?" Felicia asked in a little voice.

"I'll have to pick all over again. Most of you went home, didn't you?"

"Some did," Felicia said. "We stayed."

"We needed students to occupy and hold, to take the administration chambers and dictate terms. We could work from the university as a base, claim it as a forfeit for illegal voiding, claim it for damages . . . If I had been there, that's what we would have done."

I felt like crying. The injustice of Sean's veiled accusations, mixed with my very real infatuation and guilt at not serving the cause better, turned my stomach.

"Go talk to Gretyl. And you two . . ." He pointed to Charles and me. "Think it over. Who are you? Where do you want to be in ten years?"

Gretyl was less severely injured, but looked worse. Her head had been wrapped in a bulky breather, leaving only a gap for her eyes. She had been laid back at forty-five degrees on a steel recovery plate as well, and tubes ran from mazes of nano clumps on her chest and neck. An arbeiter had discreetly draped the rest of her with a white sheet for our visit. She watched us enter, and her silky artificial voice said, "How's Sean? You've been to see him?"

"He's fine," Oliver said. I was too unhappy to talk.

"We haven't been allowed to visit. This hospital shits protocol. What's being said outside? Did we get any attention?"

Felicia explained as gently as possible that we really hadn't accomplished much. She was ready to be a little harder with Gretyl than with Sean; perhaps she was infatuated with Sean as well. I had a sudden insight into people and revolutions, and did not like what I saw.

"Sean has a plan to change *that*," Gretyl said.

"I'm sure he does," Oliver said.

"What's on at UMS?"

"They're moving in a new administration. All the Statist appointees have resigned or been put on leave."

"Sounds like they're being punished."

"It's routine. All appointments are being reviewed," Oliver said.

Gretyl sighed—an artificial note of great beauty—and extended her hand. Felicia squeezed it. Charles and I remained in the background. "He thinks the charge that blew up was tampered with," Oliver said.

"It may have been," Gretyl said. "It must have been."

"But only you and he handled it," Charles said.

Gretyl sighed again. "It was just a standard Excavex two-kilo tube. We didn't pay a lot of money. The people who stole it for us may have tampered with it. They could have done something to make it go off. That's possible."

"We don't know that," Oliver said.

"Listen, friends, if we haven't attracted any attention yet, it's because—" She stopped and her eyes tracked the room zipzip, then narrowed.

"I have new eyes," she said. "Do you like the color? You'd better go now. We'll talk later, after I'm released."

On our way out of the hospital, in the tunnel connecting us to Time's River Station's main tube, a hungry-looking, poorly dressed, and very young male LitVid agent tried to interview us. He followed us for thirty meters, glancing at his slate between what he thought were pointed questions. We were too glum and too smart to give any answers, but despite our reticence, we ended up in a ten-second flash on a side channel for Mars Tharsis local.

Sean, on the other hand, was interviewed the next day for an hour by an agent for New Mars Committee Scan, and that was picked up and broadcast by General Solar to the Triple. He told our story to the planets, and by and large, what he told was not what I remembered.

Nobody else was interviewed.

My sadness grew; my fresh young idealism waned rapidly, replaced by no wisdom to speak of, nothing emotionally concrete.

I thought about Sean's words to us, his accusations, his pointed suspicion of me, his interview spreading distortions around the Triple. Now, I would say that he lied, but it's possible Sean Dickinson even then was too good a rabbler to respect the truth. And Gretyl, I think, was about to pass on some sound advice about political need dictating how we see—and use—history.

When we returned to our dorms at UMS, we found notices posted and doors locked. Diane met me and explained that UMS had been closed for the foreseeable future due to "curriculum revisions." Flashing icons beneath the ID plates told us we could enter our quarters once and remove our belongings. Train fare to our homes or any other destination would not be provided. Our slates received bulletins on when and where the public hearings would be held to determine the university's future course.

We were arguably worse off than we had been with Dauble and Connor.

Charles helped Diane and me pull our belongings from the room and stack them in the tunnel. There weren't many—I had sent most of my effects home after being voided. I helped Charles remove his goods, about ten kilos of equipment and research materials.

We ate a quick lunch in the train station. We didn't have much to say. Diane, Oliver, and Felicia departed on the northbound, and Charles saw me to the eastbound.

As I lugged my bag into the airlock, he held out his hand, and we shook firmly. "Will I see you again?" he asked.

"Why not?" I said. "When our lives are straightened out."

He held on to my hand a little longer and I gently removed it. "I'd like to see you before that," he said. "For me, at least, that might be a long way off."

"All right," I said, squeezing through the door. I didn't commit myself to when. I was in no mood to establish a relationship.

My father forgave me. Mother secretly admired all that I had done, I think—and they personally footed the bill for expensive autoclasses, to keep me up-to-date on my studies. They could have charged it to the BM education expenses, as part of the larger Goback revival. Father was a firm believer in BM rule, but too honorable to squeeze BM-appropriated guvvie funds, or take the victor's advantage.

When next I saw Connor, it was on General Solar LitVid. She was on the long dive to Earth, issuing pronouncements from the WHTCIPS (Western Hemisphere Transport Coalition Interplanetary Ship) *Barrier Reef*, returning, she was at pains to make Martians understand, to a kind of hero's welcome. Dauble was with her but said nothing, since day by day the awful truth of her failed Statist administration was coming out.

It so happened that there was a Majumdar BM advocate on that very ship, and he took it upon himself to represent all the BMs and other interests hoping to settle with Connor and Dauble. He served them papers, day after day after day, throughout the voyage . . .

By the time both of them got to Earth, ten months later, they would be poor as Jackson's Lode, born on Mars, exiled to Earth, doomed to dodging Triple suits for the rest of their days.

Appendixes

About the Nebula Awards

Throughout every calendar year, the members of the Science-fiction and Fantasy Writers of America read and recommend novels and stories for the annual Nebula Awards. The editor of the "Nebula Awards Report" collects the recommendations and publishes them in the *SFWA Forum*. Near the end of the year, the NAR editor tallies the endorsements, draws up the preliminary ballot, and sends it to all active SFWA members. Under the current rules, each novel and story enjoys a one-year eligibility period from its date of publication. If the work fails to make the preliminary ballot during that interval, it is dropped from further Nebula consideration.

The NAR editor processes the results of the preliminary ballot and then compiles a final ballot listing the five most popular novels, novellas, novelettes, and short stories. For purposes of the Nebula Award, a novel is 40,000 words or more; a novella is 17,500 to 39,999 words; a novelette is 7,500 to 17,499 words; and a short story is 7,499 words or fewer. At the present time, SFWA impanels both a novel jury and a short-fiction jury to oversee the voting process and, in cases where a presumably worthy title was neglected by the membership at large, to supplement the five nominees with a sixth choice. Thus, the appearance of extra finalists in any category bespeaks two distinct processes: jury discretion and ties.

Founded in 1965 by Damon Knight, the Science Fiction Writers of America began with a charter membership of seventy-eight authors. Today it boasts about a thousand members and an augmented name. Early in his tenure, Lloyd Biggle Jr., SFWA's first secretary-treasurer, proposed that the organization periodically select and publish the year's best stories. This notion quickly evolved into the elaborate balloting process, an annual awards banquet, and a series of Nebula anthologies. Judith Ann Lawrence designed the trophy from a sketch by Kate Wilhelm. It is a block of Lucite containing a rock crystal and a spiral nebula made of metallic glitter. The prize is handmade, and no two are exactly alike.

The Grand Master Nebula Award goes to a living author for a lifetime of achievement. In accordance with SFWA's bylaws, the president nominates a candidate, normally after consulting with previous presidents and the board of directors. This nomination then goes before the officers; if a majority approves, the candidate becomes a Grand Master. Past recipients include Robert A. Heinlein (1974), Jack Williamson (1975), Clifford D. Simak (1976), L. Sprague de Camp (1978), Fritz Leiber (1981), Andre Norton (1983), Arthur C. Clarke (1985), Isaac Asimov (1986), Alfred Bester (1987), Ray Bradbury (1988), Lester del Rey (1990), and Frederik Pohl (1992).

The thirtieth annual Nebula Awards banquet was held at the Grand Hyatt Hotel in New York City on April 22, 1995, where Nebula Awards were given in the categories of novel, novella, novelette, short story, and lifetime achievement (Grand Master). As part of a new program to honor older writers who are no longer writing and publishing, Emil Petaja was also honored as SFWA's first Author Emeritus.

Selected Titles from the 1994 Preliminary Nebula Ballot

The following lists provide an overview of those works, authors, and periodicals that particularly attracted SFWA's notice during 1994. Finalists and winners are excluded from this listing, as these are documented in the introduction.

Novels

Climbing Olympus by Kevin J. Anderson (Warner)
The Innkeeper's Song by Peter S. Beagle (Roc)
Brittle Innings by Michael Bishop (Bantam)

Mirror Dance by Lois McMaster Bujold (Baen)
Growing Up Weightless by John M. Ford (Bantam)
The Pure Cold Light by Gregory Frost (AvoNova)
Strange Devices of the Sun and Moon by Lisa Goldstein (Tor)
Ammonite by Nicola Griffith (Del Rey)
White Queen by Gwyneth Jones (Tor)
Wildlife by James Patrick Kelly (Tor)
Half the Day Is Night by Maureen F. McHugh (Tor)
Inferno by Mike Resnick (Tor)
End of an Era by Robert J. Sawyer (Ace)
Foreigner by Robert J. Sawyer (Ace)
The Porcelain Dove by Delia Sherman (Dutton)
Passion Play by Sean Stewart (Ace)
Lake of the Long Sun by Gene Wolfe (Tor)
Path of the Hero by Dave Wolverton (Bantam)

Novellas

"Remains of Adam" by A. A. Attanasio (*Asimov's Science Fiction*, January 1994)

"Almost Forever" by William Barton (*Tomorrow SF* #5, October 1993)

"The Last Plague" by Gregory Bennett (*Analog*, April 1994)

"Cri de Coeur" by Michael Bishop (*Asimov's Science Fiction*, September 1994)

"Symphony for Skyfall" by Rick Cook and Peter Manley (*Analog*, July 1994)

"Hard Target" by Charles D. Eckert (*Tomorrow SF* #7, February 1994)

"Melodies of the Heart" by Michael F. Flynn (*Analog*, January 1994)

"Kamehameha's Bones" by Kathleen Ann Goonan (*Asimov's Science Fiction*, September 1993)

"Les Fleurs du Mal" by Brian Stableford (*Asimov's Science Fiction*, October 1994)

Novelettes

"Cush" by Neal Barrett Jr. (*Asimov's Science Fiction*, November 1993)

"Yellow Matter" by William Barton (TAL Publications, November 1993)

"The Shining Dream Road Out" by M. Shayne Bell (*Tomorrow SF*, July 1993)

"Die, Lorelei" by Michael Coney (*The Magazine of Fantasy & Science Fiction*, May 1993)

"The Other Magpie" by R. Garcia y Robertson (*Asimov's Science Fiction*, April 1993)

"Ah! Bright Wings" by Howard V. Hendrix (*Full Spectrum 4*, Bantam)

"Fox Magic" by Kij Johnson (*Asimov's Science Fiction*, December 1993)

"Chemistry" by James Patrick Kelly (*Asimov's Science Fiction*, June 1993)

"Liberator" by Linda Nagata (*The Magazine of Fantasy & Science Fiction*, June 1993)

"Tin Angel" by G. David Nordley and H. G. Stratmann (*Analog*, July 1994)

"A Little Knowledge" by Mike Resnick (*Asimov's Science Fiction*, April 1994)

"Vox Domini" by Bruce Holland Rogers (*Full Spectrum 4*, Bantam)

"In the Distance, and Ahead in Time" by George Zebrowski (*Amazing Stories*, November 1993)

Short Stories

"Mrs. Lincoln's China" by M. Shayne Bell (*Asimov's Science Fiction*, July 1994)

"Thirteen Ways of Looking at a Dinosaur" by Gregory Feeley (*Dinosaur Fantastic*, DAW)

"In the Hole with the Boys with the Toys" by Geoffrey A. Landis (*Asimov's Science Fiction*, October 1993)

"Hugh Merrow" by Jonathan Lethem (*The Magazine of Fantasy & Science Fiction,* October/November 1993)

"Barnaby in Exile" by Mike Resnick (*Asimov's Science Fiction,* February 1994)

"The Light at the End of Day" by Carrie Richerson (*The Magazine of Fantasy & Science Fiction,* October/November 1993)

"Jukebox Gifts" by Dean Wesley Smith (*The Magazine of Fantasy & Science Fiction,* January 1994)

"Roadkill" by Sage Walker (*Asimov's Science Fiction,* April 1993)

"Bridging" by Rick Wilber (*Phobias,* Pocket)

Past Nebula Award Winners

1965

Best Novel: *Dune* by Frank Herbert

Best Novella: "The Saliva Tree" by Brian W. Aldiss
   "He Who Shapes" by Roger Zelazny (tie)

Best Novelette: "The Doors of His Face, the Lamps of His Mouth" by Roger Zelazny

Best Short Story: " 'Repent, Harlequin!' Said the Ticktockman" by Harlan Ellison

1966

Best Novel: *Flowers for Algernon* by Daniel Keyes
   Babel-17 by Samuel R. Delany (tie)

Best Novella: "The Last Castle" by Jack Vance

Best Novelette: "Call Him Lord" by Gordon R. Dickson

Best Short Story: "The Secret Place" by Richard McKenna

1967

Best Novel: *The Einstein Intersection* by Samuel R. Delany

Best Novella: "Behold the Man" by Michael Moorcock

Best Novelette: "Gonna Roll the Bones" by Fritz Leiber

Best Short Story: "Aye, and Gomorrah" by Samuel R. Delany

1968

Best Novel: *Rite of Passage* by Alexei Panshin
Best Novella: "Dragonrider" by Anne McCaffrey
Best Novelette: "Mother to the World" by Richard Wilson
Best Short Story: "The Planners" by Kate Wilhelm

1969

Best Novel: *The Left Hand of Darkness* by Ursula K. Le Guin
Best Novella: "A Boy and His Dog" by Harlan Ellison
Best Novelette: "Time Considered as a Helix of Semi-Precious Stones" by Samuel R. Delany
Best Short Story: "Passengers" by Robert Silverberg

1970

Best Novel: *Ringworld* by Larry Niven
Best Novella: "Ill Met in Lankhmar" by Fritz Leiber
Best Novelette: "Slow Sculpture" by Theodore Sturgeon
Best Short Story: no award

1971

Best Novel: *A Time of Changes* by Robert Silverberg
Best Novella: "The Missing Man" by Katherine MacLean
Best Novelette: "The Queen of Air and Darkness" by Poul Anderson
Best Short Story: "Good News from the Vatican" by Robert Silverberg

1972

Best Novel: *The Gods Themselves* by Isaac Asimov
Best Novella: "A Meeting with Medusa" by Arthur C. Clarke
Best Novelette: "Goat Song" by Poul Anderson
Best Short Story: "When It Changed" by Joanna Russ

1973

Best Novel: *Rendezvous with Rama* by Arthur C. Clarke
Best Novella: "The Death of Doctor Island" by Gene Wolfe
Best Novelette: "Of Mist, and Grass, and Sand" by Vonda N. McIntyre

Best Short Story: "Love Is the Plan, the Plan Is Death" by James
  Tiptree Jr.
Best Dramatic Presentation: *Soylent Green*
  Stanley R. Greenberg for Screenplay (based on the novel *Make
  Room! Make Room!*)
  Harry Harrison for *Make Room! Make Room!*

1974

Best Novel: *The Dispossessed* by Ursula K. Le Guin
Best Novella: "Born with the Dead" by Robert Silverberg
Best Novelette: "If the Stars Are Gods" by Gordon Eklund and
  Gregory Benford
Best Short Story: "The Day Before the Revolution" by Ursula K.
  Le Guin
Best Dramatic Presentation: *Sleeper* by Woody Allen
Grand Master: Robert A. Heinlein

1975

Best Novel: *The Forever War* by Joe Haldeman
Best Novella: "Home Is the Hangman" by Roger Zelazny
Best Novelette: "San Diego Lightfoot Sue" by Tom Reamy
Best Short Story: "Catch That Zeppelin!" by Fritz Leiber
Best Dramatic Writing: Mel Brooks and Gene Wilder for *Young
  Frankenstein*
Grand Master: Jack Williamson

1976

Best Novel: *Man Plus* by Frederik Pohl
Best Novella: "Houston, Houston, Do You Read?" by James
  Tiptree Jr.
Best Novelette: "The Bicentennial Man" by Isaac Asimov
Best Short Story: "A Crowd of Shadows" by Charles L. Grant
Grand Master: Clifford D. Simak

1977

Best Novel: *Gateway* by Frederik Pohl
Best Novella: "Stardance" by Spider and Jeanne Robinson
Best Novelette: "The Screwfly Solution" by Raccoona Sheldon

Best Short Story: "Jeffty Is Five" by Harlan Ellison
Special Award: *Star Wars*

1978

Best Novel: *Dreamsnake* by Vonda N. McIntyre
Best Novella: "The Persistence of Vision" by John Varley
Best Novelette: "A Glow of Candles, a Unicorn's Eye" by Charles L. Grant
Best Short Story: "Stone" by Edward Bryant
Grand Master: L. Sprague de Camp

1979

Best Novel: *The Fountains of Paradise* by Arthur C. Clarke
Best Novella: "Enemy Mine" by Barry Longyear
Best Novelette: "Sandkings" by George R. R. Martin
Best Short Story: "giANTS" by Edward Bryant

1980

Best Novel: *Timescape* by Gregory Benford
Best Novella: "The Unicorn Tapestry" by Suzy McKee Charnas
Best Novelette: "The Ugly Chickens" by Howard Waldrop
Best Short Story: "Grotto of the Dancing Deer" by Clifford D. Simak

1981

Best Novel: *The Claw of the Conciliator* by Gene Wolfe
Best Novella: "The Saturn Game" by Poul Anderson
Best Novelette: "The Quickening" by Michael Bishop
Best Short Story: "The Bone Flute" by Lisa Tuttle°
Grand Master: Fritz Leiber

1982

Best Novel: *No Enemy But Time* by Michael Bishop
Best Novella: "Another Orphan" by John Kessel
Best Novelette: "Fire Watch" by Connie Willis
Best Short Story: "A Letter from the Clearys" by Connie Willis

°This Nebula Award was declined by the author.

1983

Best Novel: *Startide Rising* by David Brin
Best Novella: "Hardfought" by Greg Bear
Best Novelette: "Blood Music" by Greg Bear
Best Short Story: "The Peacemaker" by Gardner Dozois
Grand Master: Andre Norton

1984

Best Novel: *Neuromancer* by William Gibson
Best Novella: "PRESS ENTER ■" by John Varley
Best Novelette: "Bloodchild" by Octavia E. Butler
Best Short Story: "Morning Child" by Gardner Dozois

1985

Best Novel: *Ender's Game* by Orson Scott Card
Best Novella: "Sailing to Byzantium" by Robert Silverberg
Best Novelette: "Portraits of His Children" by George R. R. Martin
Best Short Story: "Out of All Them Bright Stars" by Nancy Kress
Grand Master: Arthur C. Clarke

1986

Best Novel: *Speaker for the Dead* by Orson Scott Card
Best Novella: "R & R" by Lucius Shepard
Best Novelette: "The Girl Who Fell into the Sky" by Káte Wilhelm
Best Short Story: "Tangents" by Greg Bear
Grand Master: Isaac Asimov

1987

Best Novel: *The Falling Woman* by Pat Murphy
Best Novella: "The Blind Geometer" by Kim Stanley Robinson
Best Novelette: "Rachel in Love" by Pat Murphy
Best Short Story: "Forever Yours, Anna" by Kate Wilhelm
Grand Master: Alfred Bester

1988

Best Novel: *Falling Free* by Lois McMaster Bujold
Best Novella: "The Last of the Winnebagos" by Connie Willis

Best Novelette: "Schrödinger's Kitten" by George Alec Effinger
Best Short Story: "Bible Stories for Adults, No. 17: The Deluge" by
    James Morrow
Grand Master: Ray Bradbury

1989

Best Novel: *The Healer's War* by Elizabeth Ann Scarborough
Best Novella: "The Mountains of Mourning" by Lois McMaster
    Bujold
Best Novelette: "At the Rialto" by Connie Willis
Best Short Story: "Ripples in the Dirac Sea" by Geoffrey Landis

1990

Best Novel: *Tehanu: The Last Book of Earthsea* by Ursula K. Le
    Guin
Best Novella: "The Hemingway Hoax" by Joe Haldeman
Best Novelette: "Tower of Babylon" by Ted Chiang
Best Short Story: "Bears Discover Fire" by Terry Bisson
Grand Master: Lester del Rey

1991

Best Novel: *Stations of the Tide* by Michael Swanwick
Best Novella: "Beggars in Spain" by Nancy Kress
Best Novelette: "Guide Dog" by Mike Conner
Best Short Story: "Ma Qui" by Alan Brennert

1992

Best Novel: *Doomsday Book* by Connie Willis
Best Novella: "City of Truth" by James Morrow
Best Novelette: "Danny Goes to Mars" by Pamela Sargent
Best Short Story: "Even the Queen" by Connie Willis
Grand Master: Frederik Pohl

1993

Best Novel: *Red Mars* by Kim Stanley Robinson
Best Novella: "The Night We Buried Road Dog" by Jack Cady

Best Novelette: "Georgia on My Mind" by Charles Sheffield
Best Short Story: "Graves" by Joe Haldeman

Those who are interested in category-related awards should also consult *A History of the Hugo, Nebula, and International Fantasy Awards* by Donald Franson and Howard DeVore (Misfit Press, 1987). Periodically updated, the book is available from Howard DeVore, 4705 Weddel, Dearborn, Michigan 48125.

PERMISSIONS ACKNOWLEDGMENTS

"Seven Views of Olduvai Gorge" by Mike Resnick. Copyright © 1994 by Mike Resnick. First published in *The Magazine of Fantasy & Science Fiction* (October/November 1994). Reprinted by permission of the author.

"Inspiration" by Ben Bova. Copyright © 1994 by Mercury Press, Inc. First published in *The Magazine of Fantasy & Science Fiction* (April 1994). Reprinted by permission of the author.

"Virtual Love" by Maureen F. McHugh. Copyright © 1994 by Mercury Press, Inc. First published in *The Magazine of Fantasy & Science Fiction* (January 1994). Reprinted by permission of the author.

"None So Blind" by Joe Haldeman. Copyright © 1994 by Joe Haldeman. First published in *Asimov's Science Fiction* (November 1994). Reprinted by permission of the author.

"Fortyday" by Damon Knight. Copyright © 1994 by Damon Knight. First published in *Asimov's Science Fiction* (May 1994). Reprinted by permission of the author.

"In Memoriam: Robert Bloch" by Frank M. Robinson. Copyright © 1994 by Frank M. Robinson. First published in *Locus* (November 1994). Reprinted by permission of the author.

"The Martian Child" by David Gerrold. Copyright © 1994 by David Gerrold. First published in *The Magazine of Fantasy & Science Fiction* (September 1994). Reprinted by permission of the author.

"Basement Flats: Redefining the Burgess Shale" by W. Gregory Stewart and Robert Frazier. Copyright © 1994 Robert Frazier and W. Gregory Stewart. First published in *Air Fish* (Cupertino, CA: Omega Cat Press, 1994). Reprinted by permission of the authors.

"Flight Is for Those Who Have Not Yet Crossed Over" by Jeff VanderMeer. Copyright © 1993 by Jeff VanderMeer. First published in *The Silver Web* (Number 9, 1993). Reprinted by permission of the author.

"Spacer's Compass" by Bruce Boston. Copyright © Bruce Boston, 1993. First published in *Poems, 1968–1993* by Bruce Boston (Hoboken, NJ: Talisman, 1993). Reprinted by permission of the author.

"Understanding Entropy" by Barry N. Malzberg. Copyright © 1994 by Sovereign Media, Inc. First published in *Science Fiction Age* (August 1994). Reprinted by permission of the author.

"I Know What You're Thinking" by Kate Wilhelm. Copyright © Kate Wilhelm, 1994. First published in *Asimov's Science Fiction* (November 1994). Reprinted by permission of the author.

"A Defense of the Social Contracts" by Martha Soukup. Copyright © 1993 Martha Soukup. First published in *Science Fiction Age* (September 1993). Reprinted by permission of the author.

"The Matter of Seggri" by Ursula K. Le Guin. Copyright © 1994 by Ursula K. Le Guin. First published in *Crank!* (Spring 1994). Reprinted by permission of the author and the author's agent, Virginia Kidd.